Chronicles of the Imagination
STARANANA
Enhanced Classroom Edition

David Scott Fields II

Thrive
Christian Press

Anchorage, Alaska
www.thrivechristianpress.com

Thrive Christian Press
1120 Huffman Rd. Ste. 24-447
Anchorage, AK 99515

Published by Thrive Christian Press on 11/1/2016.

Standard Edition Paperback ISBN: 978-0-692-55350-3
Classroom Edition Paperback ISBN: 978-1-945995-00-2
Classroom Edition Hardcover ISBN: 978-0-9800600-9-6
Standard edition also available for Amazon Kindle and Barnes & Noble Nook.

Published in the United States of America.

To Mom and Dad,

~ Who have always loved me and encouraged my love of the written word. And, Mom, thanks for being the first family member to read my book, and most of all, thanks for liking it. May God eternally bless you both!

Table of Contents

Foreword

Thrive Christian Press is proud to present our flagship novel *Staranana* like you've never seen it before. This unique Christian-fantasy novel shares a classic theme of enduring faith in the face of overwhelming evil. Geared specifically toward students ages 11 to 14, it is our hope that this enhanced classroom edition will bring excitement, adventure, and hopefully deep discussion about the Christian faith to your home or Christian school classroom.

If you've ever read *Staranana* since the original edition was published in 2006, you just might notice a few exciting changes. In addition to a slight adjustment to the overall flow of the text, readers can expect to encounter new scenes and new insights into several key characters. Did repeated discussions of the traitor Kelcott in the original edition leave you with more questions than answers? Learn more about him in this stunning reworking of the original. Want to learn more about characters such as Speedway and Shortstop? You'll find those detail here. Don't miss a single, action-packed page. You won't be disappointed!

And there's more! As an English teacher himself, author David "Scott" Fields II recognizes the need for great Christian books for students. Thus, educators will find multiple bonuses including 38 pages of journal prompts and discussion questions, a multiple choice novel review test, a creative writing project, and 19 vocabulary activities utilizing terms from throughout the book. Teachers are encouraged to work through these activities with their students as they read the book. Many of the discussion questions prompt students to access the *Bible* and to answer deep questions about Christianity. It is our hope that this study will give you the chance to glorify Christ in your classroom and lead many of your students that much closer to a saving knowledge of Him.

Finally, there is one last bonus for the fans of *Staranana*. Since we are a Christian company, *Thrive Christian Press* is committed to seeing the Gospel of Jesus Christ taken to the ends of the globe. To that end, we provide the opportunity for our customers to request that a portion of their purchase price be donated to a Christian missionary or ministry of their choice. You will find details about this in the back of the book.

As our flagship novel here at *Thrive Christian Press*, *Staranana* will always remain one of our favorites. We hope you will feel the same, but ultimately our hope is that this book will help bring your students into a closer relationship with Jesus Christ and foster a passion for His Word. The Christian life truly is the most exciting life there is, and we hope all of our readers will live it to the full. God bless you and enjoy!

Before

He sat and watched.

The old woman bit her fingers. The frigid night had cut into them, leaving them little more than useless stumps, but it was not her fingers that were on her mind at the moment. How long had she and her people remained hidden? It could have been as many as fifty years, but that was over now. Today, death, delivered by some unknown hand of treachery, had come. Its first victim would be her granddaughter.

"Let her go, now!" the old woman demanded. She met the glowing red gaze of the creature before her as it wrapped its claws around the neck of the small girl. In her hands, she held a small club with a few rusted nails sticking out the end. It was a poor weapon, but she didn't care. She'd face the Devil himself with her bare hands if she had to. No one was going to hurt her granddaughter. There was only one problem. The creature was not alone.

Dozens upon dozens of tall, cloaked figures slipped from the shadows and moved toward the woman. None made a move to hurt her. One foolish, old woman feigning bravery was of little interest. Their targets were the cowering figures in the tiny village beyond her. They would be far more fun.

"Release her, or I will kill you!"

The creature's scaly lips split into a razor-toothed grin, and it squeezed its sharp claws deeper into the girl's throat. Tears rolled down the child's face, and she **whimpered**.

The creature hissed and took a step backward, closer to the edge of the cliff they were standing on. A hundred feet below, the Ice Sea spanned out endlessly toward the horizon. The creature extended the arm holding the girl outward so that she dangled above the frigid waters. "As you wish!" it hissed and dropped the girl.

He rubbed his red beard.

"NO!" screamed the old woman, but her sorrow was short-lived. Her back erupted in a fire of pain as the razor-edged blade of a dagger sliced into her. It tore through flesh and bone before finally piercing her heart. The creature only grinned as she slumped to her knees, fell forward into the snow, and died.

"Kill them all!" the creature commanded, and the troop moved forward. Among them were nearly two hundred hooded figures dressed in stained, brown robes and two **ebony** dragons, almost invisible in the black of night. The fifty ragtag rebels, with their sticks and stone weapons, didn't stand a chance.

He stood up.

The **horde** drew their swords and began the slaughter. Mothers screamed as their babies were ripped from them. Fathers did their best to protect their families, but to no avail. Before long, the pearl-white snow had become deep crimson. Life and hope had fled.

He drew his sword!

It took less than thirty minutes, and all fifty rebels were dead. Every man, woman, and child was gone. Flakes of snow were already starting to build on the bodies. It would be the only burial the victims would have. And to add insult to injury, the **horde** set the few pathetic shacks of the village ablaze.

It was time to kill!

In the distance, a mysterious figure sank a single, bare foot into the snow, and the cold fled from him. His sword glimmered in the starlight, and his glowing ***countenance*** burned with righteous anger. He had seen it all, and his very soul demanded justice. He knew it was well within his power to slaughter every last member of the ***horde***. They would not stand a chance.

He continued forward from his snowy perch, ready to cut them all down with one swift stroke, but something halted him. It was no great force, but the mere whisper of a still, small voice, **"Peace! Be still!"**

He knew the voice very well and sheathed his sword. As the ***horde*** vanished into the night, he sat down, rubbed his beard, and prayed. This was not over!

Chapter 1

The Moonbeams

"Sparkey! Sparkey, where are you?"

"Right here, Mama!"

The young cub turned his nose into the night and felt the frigid breeze lick it. He shuddered, but not from the cold. His bear-like, Starananian form was more than capable of dealing with the icy temperatures. The fact that his mother had a bubbling pot of soup inside helped to fend off the chill as well. What made him shudder was what he saw in the distance.

Far beyond the tree line, tiny lights dotted the sky. They were not stars, which seemed to flee from the skies of this godforsaken planet. No, these lights flickered from the most horrific structure on the planet, Cosmic Bubble Palace, or as many called it, the Palace of Death. It was a testament to the power of hatred and the overall dominance of evil.

Love, joy, peace - these were *relics* of a long forgotten era. For those few bears lucky enough to escape the Emperor's slave camps, there was only one word that concerned them now, *survival*.

"There you are, Sparkey. Come inside. I have some hot soup waiting."

"All right, Mama." Sparkey took his mother by the hand and followed her from the blackness of the night. He turned back momentarily to glance at the distant Palace one last time, and his mother saw him do it.

"Not tonight, honey bear. Not tonight," she whispered, and they went inside.

Gloria Moonbeam, Sparkey's mother, removed a shawl from about her head and dusted the snow from her shoulders as she and her son entered their home, a damp and poorly lit cave. Most free Starananians, if free was the right word, lived in caves. They were the best places to hide from the Emperor, but they certainly weren't built for comfort.

Gloria led her son to a rough and splintered, wooden table in the center of the cave. He sat down before a bowl of piping hot, vegetable soup and briefly glanced about his home. Against the far, rear wall of the cave, nudged in a corner, a fire crackled, and a kettle of soup hung over it. Above the fire, wires suspended a blinking device. Its function was to absorb the smoke and *eliminate* it. Four cots surrounded the fire, and each was covered in hides and furs. One was for Sparkey, another for his baby brother, Tommy, and two for his parents. His parents used to share a bed, but recently they had been having troubles.

Gloria turned her attention to the opposite corner of the far wall where figure stirred in the shadows. It was always stirring there. It was her husband. He had a workbench back there, and he always seemed to be *tinkering* with some gadget. Unfortunately, he often did it at the expense of showing love to his sons and his wife. But today, if only for today, that was going to stop.

"Spikey, your dinner is ready."

A worn voice huffed from the darkness, "I'll eat it later."

"The boys will be in bed later. They were looking forward to spending some time with you. Come and eat it now."

Spikey moved from the shadows and faced his wife. He was stocky. The fur on his face was *ruffled* and tinted red. He wore coveralls and an old, worn, plaid shirt. When he spoke, there was a hint of anger in his voice, "In case you had forgotten, we are in the middle of a war! I have work to do."

"War or no war, you need to eat, and the boys want to see

you. Now get over here!" Gloria commanded. She was the best doctor he had ever known. In the rebel hospital, she was firm and commanding. Her strength had helped many people to survive. Unfortunately, that same strength was often hard for him to resist. He shuffled across the room to the table and sat down.

Gloria sat next to Sparkey, bouncing Tommy on her knee. She asked, "So, Sparkey, what did you learn in your studies with Mr. Grass today?"

"Oh, lots, Mama! Mr. Grass taught me and the other kids about the Kodyax Moment. You know, when God created Emperor Iren."

Spikey had been staring into his soup up until this point, but finally, he said, "You'd do well to listen to your teacher, Sparkey, and to follow Emperor Iren's example. He was a fine leader, unlike his son!" Spikey felt the hatred bubbling in him. No one liked the current Emperor. He had plunged Staranana into an **eternal** winter and enslaved most of the **population**. Everyone had good cause not to like him, but Spikey especially hated him.

Gloria chimed in hoping to absolve the tension, "You know, I was talking to Dorothy Shortstop, General Shortstop's wife, the other day, and she…"

"No!" Spikey growled.

"No, what?"

"We're not leaving!"

Gloria was taken aback. She had been found out. Even so, she **feigned** ignorance. "Leaving?"

"I spoke to the General myself. He said that the transport ship the rebels have been building is complete. It should be able to escape the planet and head for Stararocka. There is enough room to **evacuate** all the rebels in the area. But we are not going!"

"Why not?" she demanded.

Spikey opened his mouth to rebuke her, but his eyes fell on his seven-year-old son. He calmed himself. "Sparkey, uh, why don't you take your brother, and go to bed."

"Why? I can hear you yell just as well over there as right here," the boy mumbled.

"That'll be enough, cub!" Spikey snapped.

Sparkey took his brother in his arms and walked away, and Spikey turned back to his wife. "I thought we had settled this. We're not leaving! We're not running like cowards!"

"We had settled it, but that was before the raid last week. Lizard Face and his goons killed over fifty rebels."

"That happened over two thousand kleps from here. There has never been a raid in our area."

"Our area? You're kidding, right? Ninety percent of the Nana Forest has fallen since Kelcott betrayed us. You know that. We're one of the last rebel cells left, and we're the closest to the Palace. We're a prime target, and I don't want to raise our sons in that kind of environment. We should leave. I've been to the ship. It's sturdy and well built. It has a good chance of making it."

"We can't leave. The Rebellion needs us."

"What Rebellion, Spikey? There are only a few hundred of us left. Emperor Seth has legions of dragons and goons at his command. We don't stand a chance."

"Gloria, if everyone decided to up and abandon this planet, what would happen to it? I'll tell you what! Without the Rebellion to slow him down, Seth will get even more powerful. In time, even Stararocka won't be safe for us."

"We're only four people, Spikey. It's not like we're holding the Rebellion together."

"The Rebellion needs good doctors and engineers."

"You're not an engineer, Spikey. You're an inventor."

"It's the next best thing!"

"And with the limited resources we have, there is not much more that I can do than provide first aid in our hospital. Besides, I think I know the real reason you don't want to go."

"Your point, Gloria?" Spikey *grimaced.* He was growing

tired of this conversation.

"I thought I had made that clear. If we leave Staranana, the boys can go to a real school. We can live in a real house and have real jobs. Our kids can have friends. We can grow crops and build a future for ourselves in peace."

"We can't just give up! If we turned our efforts toward fighting rather than running, we might be making a little more ground."

"Okay, say we do that. There is another matter. What about the **prophecies** of Iren? They say that no Staranananian will ever be able to overthrow the Emperor. Do you remember what happened the last time that some of our people tried to attack the Palace? One hundred of our best people were slaughtered."

"Gloria, I was there! And that only happened because we were betrayed by Kelcott, and it happened over fifteen years ago. Besides, if you're worried about **prophecies**, they do tell of a way that Seth can be overthrown."

"That's a long shot, Spikey."

"Not with my new invention. It will…"

"Enough!" Gloria silenced him. "The bottom line is that I'm not staying here. One way or another, I am going to be on that transport, and I am taking the boys with me."

Spikey stood and bore his teeth. "If you do that, then our marriage is over!"

"I can't put our marriage above the lives of our sons. Now, I'm going to bed. You can still come with us if you change your mind." She stood and retreated toward the fire and her bed.

Spikey remained at the table, speechless. He couldn't leave! This was his home, and he'd fight, even die, to protect it. But the loss of his family was a price he wasn't sure he was willing to pay. He got up from the table and went back to his workbench.

~

Sparkey kept quiet as his mother approached. He wanted her

to think he was asleep, but the truth was he didn't think he'd get much sleep this night. Usually, his mother kissed him on the forehead each night before she went to sleep. But she didn't tonight. Instead, she climbed straight into her own bed. Sparkey thought he could hear faint **whimpering** from his mother, and he knew she was crying. He began to cry too. His family was about to be broken apart. He rolled the words over in his head: war, loneliness, and death. That was all he knew, and if his family broke apart, that was all he would ever know. He pulled his fur blanket over his head and cried himself to sleep.

Chapter 2

The Meeting

General Henry Shortstop faced the multitude of Starananians in the community meeting cave. They were a rough looking bunch. Their clothes were *tattered*, their fur was *ruffled*, and there wasn't a smile to be found. Most of them had toddlers playing around their feet. Spikey and Gloria were there with their boys. Tommy was in his mother's arms against the rear wall of the meeting cave, while Spikey and Sparkey had wandered up front to hear what the General had to say.

Shortstop stood next to a stone wall with two lanterns shining upon its surface. The General held a piece of chalk in his hands. On the wall, he had made a rough sketch of a building. The artistry was poor, but everyone in the room recognized what it was.

He spoke, "Two days ago, we completed construction of our transport ship, the *New Life*. It can hold three hundred passengers. That is enough to *evacuate* all the rebels in the area. The ship is hidden deep inside the Nana Forest in an ice cave. We plan to launch in one week. Until that time, we want to slowly *evacuate* as many people to that area as possible. There is enough room in the cave to house all of us until launch time. However, we ask that you bring only items that are absolutely necessary: food, water, and blankets mostly. It should be a fairly easy and safe trip to the cave for you. According to our best intelligence, the Emperor doesn't even know that our rebel cell exists. The downside is there is a catch to all of this."

"What is that?" someone asked.

"Well, the ship has no power and no fuel. It only requires a few hundred pounds of liquid hydrogen to charge the ion thrusters. Once they're charged, we can link up the power cells, and have a virtually *inexhaustible* supply of energy."

"Where are we supposed to get that kind of fuel?" another asked.

General Shortstop gestured toward his drawing and explained, "This is a crude representation of Cosmic Bubble Palace. There is a launching *facility* on the roof. It should have the supplies we need. I plan to send in a team to capture them."

Spikey growled, "Are you crazy, General? The last time we tried to invade the Palace, dozens of our people were killed. Not the least of which was your father!"

Shortstop *winced* at the memory and then refuted, "With all due respect, Spikey, that was because we were betrayed by Kelcott. And to clarify, this is not an invasion we are planning. It's a covert operation. Our job is to get in and get out without being detected."

"How?" Spikey asked.

The General sketched something that looked like tunnels beneath his diagram of the Palace. He said, "These are the *aqueduct*s beneath the Palace. There are tunnels that lead directly to an entryway in the cellar floor. When Iren was the emperor, he built the secret entry and told no one but his most trusted friend, my *ancestor*, Ikkian Shortstop. That secret has since been passed down through the generations of my family. Iren used the passageway when he sneaked out of the Palace and into the Nana Forest to kill his firstborn son who had been *cursed* by Licen. I found out about it a few years after the betrayal of Kelcott, just before my mother died."

"Why didn't you tell any of us about this before?" Spikey asked.

"The **prophecies** of Iren say that no Starananian is capable of overthrowing Seth. I believe in the **prophecies**, or, at least, I do now after what happened with Kelcott. So I felt that the passageway would be useless to help us assassinate the emperor. Until now, it has been useless to us."

"If you're worried about **prophecies**, then I've got one for you," Spikey said. Then he quoted, "'*No bear by day, or bear by night shall **wield** any weapon that shall bring harm to the son of Iren. By serpent's fang and venom, he has been infected by unyielding evil. All who try to undo him shall be ashes before him. For this is the curse proclaimed by the Dreaded Judge of Heaven and Staranana, the Lord, for Iren's sin, the murder of his firstborn. And so evil has been established on his throne and shall remain there until the appointed time.*'"

"Exactly my point, Spikey. That's why…"

"I'm not finished," Spikey interjected. Then he continued, "'*At the appointed time, a door shall open to the land where life began. The son of Iren is of that land, and the Blood of the Land shall undo him. The Blood of the Land shall be washed and forgiven of his sins. The Lord shall know his name, and love him, and call him to our plight. Then the Blood of the Land shall come and **wield** the Dagger of Promise. With one thrust he shall undo the son of Iren and cast him into **eternal** fire. And the Blood of the Land shall rule with a just hand until the Lord comes.*'"

"Your point?"

"Well, we don't have to abandon our home. God promised us a deliverer. We just have to wait for him."

Gloria moved to the front of the crowd, enraged. He just never gave up, did he? She would put an end to this! "Spikey, enough is enough! We can't just wait around for some God that may or may not **deliver** us!"

"Don't any of you believe in the **prophecies**?" Spikey called out.

Shortstop replied, "Of course, we do, but there is nothing in them that says we all have to die. When this deliverer comes, we can come back, assuming he comes within our lifetimes. But right now, we should be worried about our own lives and the lives of our children."

"But there may be a way that it can happen within our lifetimes. Maybe even within the next few weeks, days even!"

"HA!" Gloria bellowed.

The General asked, "How, Spikey?"

"I've invented something."

"Always another invention," Gloria muttered.

Spikey ignored her and continued, "It's a device that can open a doorway through space. I've sent a few things through it, and I've even detected radio signals from the other side. All I need to do is test it on a real person."

"Even if this thing really works, how does it help us?" asked the General.

"The transmissions I picked up talked about a planet called Earth. According to the ancient texts, Iren was originally a spirit being. He sent a team of Starananians, who were also spirits at that time, to a planet called Earth to claim bodies for him and his people. The Starananians brought back genetic samples from the bodies of bears for themselves and a genetic sample from the body of a human man for Iren. From these samples, they created flesh and blood bodies for themselves. That means Earth is where Iren's blood came from, which means that is where Seth's blood came from, and that is where our salvation is," Spikey explained.

Colonel Speedway, the General's attaché, chuckled, "Oh, come on, Spikey, that's just a legend. There is no such place as Earth. You probably just picked up random transmissions from somewhere on Staranana. People tell their children those stories all the time. But we're adults, and it's our job to look past fairy tales."

"But we should at least try!"

Shortstop glared at Spikey, silencing him, and the inventor's shoulders slumped, and he turned and disappeared into the crowd. Shortstop turned back to his diagram and explained the rest of his plan. "We will proceed the day before the launch. We'll send in a team of five. Three of them will carry out one hundred pounds of liquid hydrogen each. The other two will carry out the power cells. Our team can reach the roof by a secret stairway, but the stairway is located on the tenth floor. They will have to sneak their way up there, which means they will need a diversion. A sixth team member will plant a bomb in the Palace courtyard. Once it explodes, the entire Palace defense force should be diverted to the courtyard. When they are, our team can make their way to the tenth floor. The secret passage is located behind a large, hand-carved, Nana Clock and can only be accessed by entering a combination code into the clock. Fortunately, the combination has been passed down through my family as well. After entering the combination, the clock's hands must be turned back to the correct time, or the door won't open. Once we get it open, we can proceed to the roof."

One Starananian, an **elderly** bear with graying fur, raised his hand to ask a question. "What if Seth has removed the clock and discovered the passage?"

Shortstop replied, "He can't. The clock is carved directly into the wall. And it is the central source that regulates all the clocks and the power in the Palace. If the clock is damaged, the Palace goes offline. That is why it is important to set the clock back to its proper time. If it is changed for more than thirty seconds, power will go down all over the Palace, an alarm will sound, and Seth's **minions** will know exactly where to look for us. So, we must work quickly."

Another rebel asked, "Begging your pardon, General, but isn't the Palace one hundred stories high? It could take hours to climb up ninety stories."

"It's the best we can do. At least we'll be hidden, and we won't have to make the trip back down."

"You won't?" the bear inquired.

"No. Each team member will carry a parachute with them. We will make this attempt by night, so no one will spot the team once we jump from the Palace. The air currents should carry us to the edge of the Nana Forest where we can proceed on foot."

"Who is going?" Gloria asked.

The General replied, "Colonel Speedway and I are going. Nicholas Grass has also volunteered. And two of our teens, the Nakan brothers, have also been recruited. That only leaves one other, the person who will carry in the bomb."

Shortstop paused, "I should warn you. The bomb carrier most likely won't survive. If they are not killed in the explosion, the Palace guards will likely kill them shortly thereafter. It's not the most coveted role, but it is a necessary position. Is there anyone, anyone at all, willing to play the part?"

There was a long, painful silence, and nobody so much as twitched. No one seemed willing to play the hero this time. Shortstop really didn't blame them. After all, how many people did he expect to volunteer to get blown to bits? He was the leader of this rebel cell. He would be needed in the weeks to come for the long journey to Stararocka, but if no one volunteered, it would be his responsibility to fill the role.

He waited a short while longer, but the silence was unbroken, so he **surrendered**, "All right then…"

"I'll do it," came a voice.

Shortstop scanned the crowd. The silence had been shattered, and everyone was murmuring, wondering who had just volunteered. Shortstop could not locate the voice's owner, but then a solitary Starananian stepped forward. He was short and stocky, dressed in coveralls and a plaid shirt. It was Spikey Moonbeam.

For the first time in months, Gloria actually expressed affection for her husband, albeit not with endearing words, when she exclaimed, "Are you crazy, Spikey?" As much as she disliked his methods, she still loved him, and she did not want him to die.

"Not at all. But if we can't use my plan, we might as well give this escape attempt a fighting chance. And besides, I'm the only one here who doesn't seem to want to go. I'm the logical choice. At least, I'll get to die fighting for my home."

Sparkey's ears perked up. He had wandered to the back and was playing with his brother. He had not paid much attention to the meeting. But when his father said he was going to die, his heart raced, and he rushed through the crowd and cried, "No, Dad, no!"

A tear came to Spikey's eye as he scooped his son into his arms. He spoke softly to him, "Sparkey, don't worry; I will be okay. But I need to do this to help all these good people. Pretty soon, you'll have a new home and a whole lot of places to play. Now, I'll do my best to survive. But just in case I don't, remember I'll be with the Lord, and He will always be watching over you."

The tiny cub was sobbing so hard, the fur on his face was completely drenched. He nodded once at his father, then threw his arms around his neck and hugged him tightly. Spikey began crying as well, but there was nothing they could do. This had to be done.

Shortstop broke in before Gloria could protest any further, "It's settled then. We go in six days. Until that time, my soldiers will coordinate the evacuation process. We'll move a few families at a time. Once we are all there, and the plan is complete, we'll launch. Traveling at ten thousand kleps per hour, it will take about three weeks to reach Stararocka. The journey won't be the easiest. There is limited room, and we'll have to live off of rations. But once we reach our destination, I think we'll all be a lot better off for it."

Spikey didn't believe that, but he kept his mouth shut. Shortstop asked, "Are there any more questions?" No one spoke, and finally, Shortstop said, "Okay, this meeting is over. Let's get to work."

Chapter 3

Farewells

A new snow littered the ground outside the Moonbeam cave. A family of three-eared, oboca rabbits scampered through the freshly-fallen powder. For once, the sun was shining. Its soft glow brought unusual warmth to the planet. However, neither its heat nor its light could penetrate the all-consuming darkness of the Moonbeam cave.

Inside, Gloria rolled up yet another blanket in silence. She had not spoken in nearly four days. Sparkey and Tommy had left with the evacuation team two days earlier. Nicholas Grass was caring for them now. That left Spikey and Gloria alone.

Spikey was filling an old burlap bag with roots he had grown in their family greenhouse. When the bag was full, he would then wrap the freshly salted fish he had caught earlier that morning. There were about five dozen of them, and they would provide his family with more than enough food to make the journey to Stararocka. The thing he worried about was the fact that wrapping the fish would only take about an hour. After that, he would have nothing left to do, and it would be time to speak to his wife, no matter how much he did not want to.

He never got his chance, because Gloria finally broke the silence. "You can't do it, Spikey! You just can't!"

"Don't think for a minute that I want to, but I'm the best person for the job."

"No, you're not! You're just the only person who volunteered, and you're the only one who doesn't want to leave. Let someone who doesn't have a family do it."

"You know there aren't that many people like that. And besides, this way we both get what we want. I get to die fighting for something I believe in, and you get to raise the boys in a better home. Just promise me two things. First, raise them to be good, God-fearing bears, and second, don't let them forget me."

Gloria's eyes swelled with tears, and she mumbled, "I will, and they won't."

Spikey took her in his arms and held her tightly. He had not done that in months, and in that moment, they became husband and wife again.

After kissing her gently on the cheek, he looked into her eyes and whispered, "No matter what happens, I'll do my best to survive. Promise me you'll do the same." She nodded, and they embraced once more.

~

Two days later, Spikey swept Sparkey into his arms. His son laughed hysterically as his father began to tickle him. He seemed to have forgotten the fact that he would be losing his father in only a few hours.

Spikey and Gloria had arrived in the ice cave deep within the forest just a day before liftoff. Later that night, the team would be dispatched to the Palace. There were still a few hours before that would happen. Until then, Shortstop had arranged a sort of *farewell* party. There were games and music, roasting fish and vegetables, and a cavern filled with people who for the first time in a long time seemed to be happy.

Spikey made his way about the cavern taking in his surroundings. A huge bonfire burned in the rear of the cave on top of some rocks. The cavern was primarily made of ice, so the fire had to be built in a place where the heat would **circulate**, but not melt the entire cavern.

In the center of the cavern sat an enormous spacecraft. The vessel was nearly one hundred feet long and three decks high. It was the shape of a missile, with a long pointed nose, several rows of circular windows, a black titanium hull, and five massive rocket boosters on its tail. It had no weapons, save a laser drill, which would be used to blast away the cavern roof in the event the launch doors failed.

The design of the ship was simple. Extravagant designs were not necessary. All that was necessary was for this ship, which they had christened the *New Life*, to take the rebels, and more importantly his family, to safety. Spikey hoped the ship would prove up to the task.

The rest of the cavern was filled with hundreds of cots. Many had people sleeping on them. Overhead there were huge, shimmering, razor-sharp icicles. They looked as if they would fall any second, but Shortstop had assured everyone they were quite safe.

"Spikey! Spikey, over here!"

Spikey turned. The voice was familiar, that of a friend. When he located the owner, he saw Nicholas Grass. "Nick! I haven't seen you in weeks. Why weren't you at the meeting?"

"Oh, you know, the same old excuses. This time it was my mother's birthday."

"That mother of yours! Is she still as cranky as ever?" Spikey chuckled at the thought of Mrs. Grass, his old teacher.

Nick laughed, "Worse even. She's like you, stubborn to the core. But I managed to convince her to come on board the transport."

There was a pause in their conversation; then Nick said, "So, I hear you volunteered to plant the bomb." There was really no polite way to bring up the subject, but Nick had to know.

Spikey nodded, "I get my briefing in half an hour, just before we head to the Palace."

"Well, I wish you luck. I know your boys will miss you, as

will I."

Spikey lowered his head, and then, always the optimist, he rose up tall and commanding. "There's a chance I'll live, Nick! Don't count me out yet."

"Okay, okay! Well, my briefing is right now. I'd better run. See you later?" Nick asked.

"Yeah, of course!" Spikey piped, watching his friend disappear into the crowd.

Spikey returned to the corner of the cavern where his family had set up camp. Gloria had built a small fire and had a kettle stewing over it. The aroma of fresh fish and vegetables caressed his nose as he drew closer. It would be good to enjoy one last meal with his family.

Gloria smiled as he approached and said, "The stew is almost ready."

"Good, I'm hungry!" Spikey rubbed his belly. There was nothing that could calm his nerves like a hot meal.

"I took the boys to see our seats onboard the transport. They aren't large, but they'll work," Gloria said.

"Good, but if I know those boys, they'll get into plenty of trouble along the way."

"You know, Spikey, there's still time for you to change your mind," Gloria said, gently touching his arm.

He knew she wasn't trying to **persuade** him. They had worked past their differences in the last few days. She knew he had to do this, as much as he knew she had to take their boys to safety. He did not speak, but simply shook his head, and she nodded at that.

"Okay, then let's eat our dinner."

Gloria called her two sons away from their friends, and Spikey gripped her hand and squeezed it. It was not long before Sparkey came waddling over, his baby brother in hand. Spikey took his son's hand, and they all bowed their heads in prayer.

Spikey prayed, "Dear Lord who made Staranana and all the stars of heaven, thank you for this meal. Thank you for this family, and please see them safely away. Your grace is forever. Amen." Then they sat down and ate.

~

A short time later, Spikey held the bomb *cautiously* in his hands as General Shortstop explained, "This is a high-yield, hydrogen explosive. Once activated, it can destroy everything within an area the size of the Palace courtyard. That's about one million square feet."

"What if I accidentally activate it?" Spikey asked.

"Impossible!" Shortstop exclaimed. He took the bomb in his hands. It was the shape of an egg with metal panels extending from both sides. The eggshell was clear but tinted greenish-yellow. Inside the shell, a *vast* amount of hydrogen had been sealed under pressure for the moment when it would surge forth and destroy completely everything caught in its blast.

Shortstop dropped the bomb.

"AHHH! Take cover!" Spikey screamed and dove for a nearby boulder.

Shortstop looked at him, trying his best to *restrain* a laugh. He picked up the bomb and said, "We added a compound that binds itself to the hydrogen molecules making them inert. The bomb can't explode."

"Then what use is it to us?" Spikey asked, rising to his feet.

Shortstop pulled a small vial from his pocket. "This substance will *neutralize* the compound. Not only that, but it will make the hydrogen even more volatile. You insert the vial into this panel on the right side, and then flip this switch on the left side of the bomb. After the switch is flipped and the hydrogen interacts with the compound, you will have ten seconds at most before the bomb goes off."

"Why not plant a time bomb? That way, I can make it out alive," Spikey asked.

"Security at the Palace is extremely tight. You'll most likely be detected, even before you plant the bomb. A time bomb can be disabled. This bomb can't. Once the fluids combine, there is no stopping them."

Spikey took the bomb in his hands. "Let's get this done, before I change my mind."

~

An hour later, the team members and their families convened at the entrance of the cavern. Outside a blizzard raged. Just making it to the Palace was going to be difficult. The rest of the rebels had already boarded the ship. There was no need to waste time once the supplies were *obtained*.

Nicholas hugged his mother one final time. The Nakan brothers, Toby and Cak, were also bidding their parents farewell. Shortstop was kissing his wife and daughter, and Speedway was tickling his only son. Only Spikey's farewells remained. His would be far more permanent than theirs.

Spikey knelt before Sparkey and said, "Now, listen to me, little cub. I want you to pay close attention to your mother. You'll be the bear of the house now. She'll be depending on you. Do you understand?"

"Yes, sir!" Sparkey piped.

"Good boy! Now, give your dad a hug!" The youngster laughed through sobs and threw his arms around his father again. Spikey held him tightly. He did not want to let go. He desperately did not want to let go! But, eventually, he eased his grip and lowered his son to the ground.

Tommy was asleep in Gloria's arms. Spikey kissed him gently, and then he faced his wife. "So, this is it," he said.

"I guess so," she replied.

There was a long moment of silence, and then Spikey asked, "Will you please smile?"

Gloria looked confused, and he explained, "I'd like to remember you that way. Please, smile."

She hesitated a moment. Then, struggling, she spread her mouth into a broad grin that eventually erupted into a smile. Spikey smiled too, and without another word, he turned from them and walked away. His team was already making its way outside. Most of them turned back to wave again, but Spikey did not. He had his memories, and he was not going to spoil them. A few seconds later, he disappeared into the snow swirled night.

In her heart, Gloria said, "And this is how I shall remember you, my husband, *alive.*"

Sparkey also spoke in his heart, and he said, "I'll save you, Dad. No matter what happens, or what it takes, I'll save you." Only, unlike most impossible, childish dreams, Sparkey was *intent* on carrying his out. And he would. He would!

Chapter 4

The Courtyard

The night was cold, bitterly cold as the team trudged through the Nana Forest. The swirling snow made it almost impossible to see, and it was not long before they were wading through it up to their waists. Even so, they pressed on through the night. By the time they reached the *aqueducts*, more than five hours had passed, and from there the journey was far from over. Recklor bats, cave gators, and viola crystals all stood in their way. When they had finally traversed the caverns, it was well past midnight, and they were all exhausted.

"Come help me with this, Spikey," Shortstop requested. He had his hands raised above his head touching the low ceiling of a stone chamber at the end of their path. A series of cracks formed a square in the stone.

"What is that?" Spikey asked.

"Our ticket inside!"

They were directly below the Palace's cellar. The Nakan twins had slumped to the ground and were removing water pouches from their packs. Nick was chewing on a salted fish he had brought along. Speedway was sitting on a rock with his eyes closed. Only Spikey and the General seemed to have any energy left. The problem was this night was far from over.

"On three, General!" Spikey said, and by the time he had finished his count, they had forced the age-worn panel open.

Had it not been for the centuries of dirt and rust that had built up in the cracks, the trapdoor might have opened quite easily. It was very light.

Shortstop crawled through the door first, followed by Spikey, then Nick, the Nakan brothers, and finally, Speedway. A single lantern, hanging on the stone wall of the cellar, illuminated the room. The cobblestone floor was damp underfoot, and the room had the *distinct* smell of wet hay. In the center of the room, a rusted and worn, iron staircase extended to the ceiling, leading to the next level of the Palace. Shortstop sat down at the base of the stairs and opened his pack.

Before he removed anything, he spoke, "Okay, bears, this is it! The fuel and the power cells are on the roof more than one hundred stories above us. It will take a while to reach them, and before we do, we'll lose at least one of our own."

Everyone's eyes fell on Spikey, and he felt himself flush at the attention. He knew they were all expecting a farewell speech. He just wasn't quite so sure he wanted to give one, but if it would improve their morale, and perhaps *inspire* them, he would muddle through.

He took a deep breath and began, "By daybreak, you'll all be on your way to a new life - a life filled with promise and hope. All my life I have said that I would fight for the good of my planet. I thought that meant that we all needed to stay here on Staranana and fight. But, in *recent* days, I have come to realize that maybe it isn't the planet that matters, but the people. You are all part of Staranana, and as long as you survive, this planet will survive. So I send you forth with all my prayers of blessing. Take your memories of this place to your new home. Remember the good times most of all. And wherever I am beyond all this on the Mountain of God, I will be praying for you. God be with you all."

Stories of Earth said that in some countries human men found it shameful to cry. Such things were not true on Staranana. All the bears were so moved by Spikey's words that each of them was sobbing. Each one took his turn to embrace Spikey, but eventually, Shortstop regained his composure and turned their attention back to the task at hand.

He removed the egg-shaped bomb from his pack and handed it to Spikey. "Activate this in twenty minutes. Once the guards are on their way to the courtyard, we'll make our way to the tenth floor."

Spikey took the bomb in his hands. This was it. He nodded at Shortstop, and without another word, he left. All that was left for the rest of them to do was wait.

~

Spikey Moonbeam stepped into the courtyard through a door on the side of the cellar. Above him, stars twinkled across a velvet-black sky. The storm had ended, but the courtyard remained *devoid* of activity. Even so, Spikey was amazed by what he saw there.

Environmental regulators had allowed lush, green bushes to grow. They had been arranged in rows extending along the walls surrounding the Palace. Two columns of uniquely shaped bushes formed a path leading to the front entry of the Palace, a massive, golden gate with two golden dragon idols sitting on either side of it.

The path to the gate was cobblestone, but precious gems had also been scattered among the stones. About halfway down the path, the walkway curved into two separate paths to make room for an enormous statue. The statue was not that of a bear, but of a man - a human. His body was young and carved so finely that the very veins of his lean muscles seemed to pop out. His eyes were made of diamonds, and the stone of his chest sported bronze armor. Spikey had never actually seen him in person, but he guessed it was a statue of Emperor Seth. It was *obviously* an *exaggerated* representation of the man's glory and the perfect reflection of his enormous *ego*.

By the time he had finished looking around the courtyard, ten minutes had passed. It was time to find a place to set up the bomb. A few of the bushes along the main path were cut into designs. A large bush just off the path had the image of a fat bear. Over that bush, another had been cut like a dragon poised to swallow its victim whole. Spikey guessed it was a symbolic representation of Seth's superiority over the bears. Whatever the intention, the design of the bear had left a large nook in its belly. It was a big enough space to hide in and plant the bomb.

~

High above him, a single light illuminated in the otherwise dark Palace. The shadow of a man appeared in the window. Spikey did not notice him, and from his height, the man did not notice Spikey either. He had other things on his mind.

Dressed in a long, black silk robe, he stood before the window staring out into the distance. To his right, a fire crackled in a hearth. Its light, shining off the window, reflected his face. He was clean-shaven with sandy-blond hair and piercing blue eyes. He was human, and his name was Seth.

Something had stirred him from his sleep. It was almost like an impending sense of doom. Something wasn't right. The last time he had had a sense like this, more than a hundred bears had invaded the courtyard, bent on his assassination. Had it not been for Kelcott, the bears might have been successful in their scheme. This feeling was not quite as intense as that one had been, but it was there nonetheless.

There came a rap at his chamber door. Who could be calling on him at this hour? *Cursed* servants! He approached the door and opened it. A figure stood shrouded in the shadows just beyond the door. It stepped forward into the glow of the firelight, and for a moment, Seth's heart skipped a beat at the creature's *hideous* form.

"Lizard Face, what are you doing here?" Seth demanded.

The creature before him stood five-and-a-half feet high. His body was speckled with green and white scales, except for the back of his neck, which bore a strip of black scales. Those scales extended down his back to the end of his tail, but that much was covered by his black jumpsuit. His head was similar to that of an iguana. Sharp spikes protruded through his skull, and a stubby snout extended forward from his face. He was every bit a freak of nature, and his name, though to the point, fit him well.

Lizard Face spoke, "Begging your pardon, Your Majesty. We have *sstarted* to move the cannons into place. They will be ready for firing in five minutes."

"Excellent, that will get my birthday celebration off to a good start. I have also thought of another gift I would like to give myself," Seth replied.

Lizard Face smirked, "What is that, Your Grace?"

"I want you to destroy the city of Katana!"

"But, *Ssire*, that is the *sspirit* city where all the members of your family choose their brides. Your mother was from that city."

"Yes, and two weeks ago, when I sought a bride there, I was rejected. It is time that they know the price of refusing my love!"

Lizard Face's scaly lips curved into a devilish smile. The task would be a pleasure. "As you wish, Your Majesty." Then, at Seth's direction, he turned and left the room.

~

"Five minutes left," Spikey Moonbeam whispered to himself. He had secured himself inside the bear bush. For the last few minutes, he had been praying, but now it was time to get the bomb ready.

He wedged the egg between two branches. Then he stuck his hand in his pocket. After fumbling about for a few seconds, he removed the tiny vial. He squeezed it tightly. There was no turning back now.

~

Lizard Face entered the courtyard and watched as the last cannon was moved into place. In another few minutes, they would launch a volley of fireballs over the Palace walls into the slave camps beyond. The fireballs would not cause much damage to the camps, though they would be annoying, and they would effectively announce that Seth's 5,018[th] birthday had arrived.

As he watched the troops working, Lizard Face thought he saw something rustling just down the walk. It was nothing, he convinced himself, and he turned his attention back to the cannons. But then, only a moment later, it happened again. One of the bushes, the one shaped like a large bear, was rustling. He moved down the front steps and onto the walk to investigate.

~

For the most part, Spikey was oblivious to what was taking place outside in the courtyard. He was too focused on what was about to happen to him. So focused in fact, that he didn't notice that he was trembling, and that trembling was causing the bush to vibrate. In addition, his palms were sweating, and his hands were shaking. He steadied himself to do what he knew he had to do.

Unfortunately, as he proceeded to slide the tiny vial into place, something terrible happened. The sweat on his palms had made his hands so slick that the vial slipped from them, and it tumbled from the bush.

A curse was halfway past his lips, before Spikey bit his tongue. It figured something like this would happen. Ah, well, he'd just have to reach out, grab the thing, and get this over with.

He extended his arm out of the bush. He could see the vial sitting there on the cobblestone path just out of reach. He stretched his arm and his fingers. The commotion in the courtyard was increasing. If someone saw him, he'd be dead sooner than expected. If he could only stretch his fingers another half-an-inch, he'd be able to reach the vial.

"Halt! Who goes there?"

Spikey attempted to jerk his hand back into the bush, but to no avail. A firm hand *seized* and nearly crushed his wrist. Spikey wheezed under the pain, and he soon felt the sting of branches cutting into him as that same hand dragged him from his hiding place. A moment later, he lie crumpled on the cold cobblestone path.

The branches had given him a few good scrapes. A gash above his left eye was oozing blood, turning his reddish-brown fur to deep crimson. In the dim light of the courtyard, he could not see the face of his attacker. Several torches burned on distant walls, but the shadows still concealed his captor like a veil.

"Who are you?" Spikey asked.

"I'll ask the questions, fool!" the figure snapped.

Spikey could not be sure, but he thought he heard the thing hiss. From the look of the creature's hands, he wouldn't doubt it. They were covered in green and white scales. Spikey knew that Seth used dragons in his defense force, but this creature was not much bigger than he was. That meant it could be only one person.

"You're Lizard Face, aren't you?"

The creature thrust a swift kick, sinking the claws of his foot deep into Spikey's side. Then he *seized* Spikey by the neck and dragged him to his feet. Spikey gasped for air. Was this how it was all going to end? He had failed his people, and now they would all die!

For the first time, the creature stepped into the light, revealing its *hideous*, reptilian features. There was no doubt in Spikey's mind now. This had to be Lizard Face.

The creature released its grip and asked, "What are you doing here?"

Spikey said nothing. By that time, two guards had joined

Lizard Face. Each had a projectile weapon, and they wore cloaks that concealed the majority of their features.

"*Ssearch* the bush!" Lizard Face demanded.

The guards set to work at their master's beckoning. It was not long before one had brought back a tiny vial, and the other an egg-shaped device.

"What are these?" Lizard Face raged. In the glow of the torchlight, his eyes shone with blood-red crests, and his nostrils flared. When he bared his teeth, Spikey feared he was about to be shredded limb from limb.

"What do you think they are?" Spikey snapped.

"How do they work?"

"You don't think I am going to be so stupid as to tell you that, do you?"

"Tell me, or I will kill you!"

"Go right ahead. I was going to die anyway when that bomb went off."

"It was a *ssuicide* mission?"

"That's right!"

"What did you have planned, an attack on the Palace? You will fail!"

Spikey's lips curved into a sharp-toothed, uncharacteristically wicked smile. "Don't be too sure! We have more than ten thousand bears ready to storm the gates. Even you won't be able to stand up against such odds!"

"That is a lie," Lizard Face smirked. "There aren't even that many bears left alive on this planet. I *sshould* know. I helped kill most of them."

"Well, I think you missed a few! Do you honestly think we tell you about all the children that are born to us? What kind of idiots do you think we are?"

"Enough!" Lizard Face snapped. He turned to his guards, "Take him inside and flog him. Try and get the real *sstory* out of him. If he won't talk, I'll deal with him personally." He chuckled as he turned back to Spikey, "I'd advise you to talk, bear. Trust me, a flogging would be like a walk in the *ssnow* compared to what I'd do to you."

Spikey's heart sank, but not because of what Lizard Face had just said. He had failed his friends. Now, they would never get off of Staranana. As the guards dragged him away, he did the only thing he could; he prayed.

~

With the intruder gone, Lizard Face turned his attention to the large clock over the main entry of the Palace. It was time for the twenty cannon salute to the Emperor. The salute had been a tradition held for centuries on Seth's birthday. The cannons would send fireballs flying into the slave camps. No one usually got killed, unless Seth was in a hyper mood and conducted a few executions just for the fun of it. But the fireballs always wreaked havoc in the slave camps. The ceremony was held at 3:19 in the morning on Seth's birthday, the exact time he was born.

Lizard Face took his place at the base of the steps in front of the main entry. All across the front of the Palace, stretching across hundreds of feet, cannons had been set up and readied to fire.

Lizard Face raised his right claw high into the air and commanded, "Gunners, take aim!" There was a click of metal against metal as the cannons were aimed over the courtyard's walls.

He commanded again, "Ready wicks!" Each officer coated his cannon's fuse in a wax-oil mixture and then removed a burning torch from the Palace's wall.

At last, the final command came, "Fire!"

Chapter 5

The Kitchen

Deep below the Palace, in a musty cellar, five bears waited in anticipation. The last twenty minutes had been an eternity, but now, finally, only another ten seconds and it would be time to get underway. Shortstop counted down, "Nine, eight, seven, six, five, four, three, two…" There was a pause, and Shortstop closed his eyes and plugged his ears before finally sounding, "One!"

The floor bucked beneath them, the lantern crashed to the floor, consuming the room in blackness, and a choking cloud of dust rose from the floor. The sonic boom sent everyone's hands shooting to their ears, an act that caused all to lose their grips and their footings. Cak smacked his head into the stone floor. Toby managed to land safely. Shortstop braced himself against the staircase and held his balance. The rest continued tumbling all over the cellar until the roaring thunder *subsided*.

When the blast ended, they all got to their feet. Toby lit a candle and said, "Well, it worked. Can we get going now?"

"Hold on a second!" ordered Shortstop. He didn't know what, but something wasn't right.

"But, General…" Toby started.

"Who's in charge of this mission, me or you? That explosion didn't have nearly the force it should have. Something isn't right here."

Speedway was confused. "Are you kidding, General? It

nearly brought the Palace down on us."

Shortstop nodded. That much was true, but he still had a bad feeling. "Okay, let's go. I have no idea where this staircase leads, so be ready for anything."

Shortstop led them up, but not without some additional hesitation. He couldn't shake the feeling that something had gone terribly wrong. When they finally reached the top, a heavy, wooden door barred their path.

"Great! How do we get past that?" Cak *cursed.*

"Take it easy!" Shortstop held up his hand to calm the teen. There was no need to be discouraged by such a simple obstacle. A long and rusty chain was attached where a door handle should have been. With their combined strength, he knew they would be able to pry it open.

"Okay, everyone take hold," he said. He grabbed the chain. Then they all latched onto each other, creating a chain of bears. "Pull!"

Speedway strained, Cak wheezed, and the rest grunted as if they were trying to drag the Palace itself off its foundations. For a long moment, the door wouldn't budge, but slowly it began to creak open. Eventually, they had opened it wide enough to pass through.

What they encountered on the other side was nothing remarkable. General Shortstop found himself reading labels, "Hmm. Bleached flour, honeysuckle apple cider, sugar, pepper, salt… Guys, I think we're in the Palace's pantry."

"Kinda small for such a big place," commented Cak. He was right. The room was no larger than a tiny storage closet.

"They must have a bigger one somewhere else. But we're not interested in their food. What we want is still a long way off. Let's keep moving."

"Speak for yourself, General. I…" Toby began.

"Hold it right there!"

Toby's heart leaped at the shrill voice, and he turned. But no sooner had he done so than a saucepan came crashing down on his head. The young bear slumped to the floor as Shortstop jumped on their attacker.

"You'll never get away with this! I'll stop you! I'll stop you!" The speaker was less than confident, and his strength was modest at best. Shortstop was having no trouble holding him down. However, his eyes widened at the individual.

"You're a Staranananian!" Shortstop exclaimed.

"Isn't everybody?" replied the figure, still struggling under the General's grip.

"No, I mean, you're a bear! What are you doing in the Palace?"

"*Cursed* ruffians! Don't I have enough trouble with all the Emperor's *minions* without you people always trying to steal from my kitchen?"

Shortstop released his grip and got off the bear. "We're not interested in anything in your kitchen. And we're not ruffians. We're members of the Rebellion. My name is General Henry Shortstop. What's yours?"

"General, what are you doing?" demanded Speedway.

Shortstop ignored his officer as their frightened attacker replied, "My name is Berry, Chef Timothy Berry. I am the head chef of the Palace. What are you doing here?"

Shortstop did not immediately answer him. The General was aware that Seth allowed the slaves to enter the Palace to complete various chores throughout the day. But, as far as he knew, they were all ejected back out onto the icy streets by nightfall. Any bear that actually lived inside the Palace was either an unknown *ace in the hole* or something very, very dangerous. The General accused, "You're a collaborator!"

"What! No, no! I come from Snowy Valley. My family grew crops there, and I just happened to learn to cook them quite well; that's all! The last head chef served Seth a bad meal and had his head chopped off. When Kelcott betrayed our village, I was taken prisoner. Seth learned of my skills and made me his new chef. That was fifteen years ago. My family was killed. I don't want to be here, but I do the best I can. After all, isn't that what a godly bear should do?"

Shortstop chuckled, "Boy, I imagine you and Spikey would have gotten along great!"

"Who?"

"Never mind. We're here on a mission. We need to get to the tenth floor. Can you help us?"

"The tenth floor? There's nothing of value on that floor."

"There is to us. Can you help us?"

"What's this all about?" Berry wasn't about to help them before he got more information, even if they were fellow bears.

Shortstop sighed deeply. He still didn't completely trust this bear, but he'd tell him just enough to get him to help them. "We are trying to leave this planet. There are supplies inside the Palace that will help us do it."

"Leave the planet?" Berry was shocked. "But you're the rebels. You're the last symbols of hope and freedom on this planet. Every slave has all of their hopes pinned on you. If you leave, what will they do?"

The General was growing worried. They had already spent too much time in this kitchen, and the guards were not going to stay in the courtyard forever. He apologized, "I'm sorry, but the rebels aren't strong enough to do any good anymore. We need to leave and get *reinforcements* from a nearby planet. Then we can come back and help everyone."

Shortstop wasn't exactly sure that was the truth. Most of the bears he knew were content with leaving Staranana behind and never, ever coming back. They were tired of war, and they were ready to live quiet, peaceful lives on Stararocka. But if his statement made Berry help them, he'd live with the lie on his conscience.

Berry seemed satisfied and said, "You can use the service elevator in the banquet room. It's just across the central chamber. But that's nearly a thousand feet away. The guards will stop you."

"Don't worry. We've arranged a little distraction for the guards. Thanks for your help," said Shortstop, stooping down to help Toby back to his feet. The young Nakan had a large lump swelling on the top of his head, but otherwise, he was none the worse for wear.

"Don't mention it," Berry replied. "I only ask one thing; take me with you!"

Shortstop was about to flat out **deny** the request, but he hesitated. Finally, he said, "All right, we'll take you with us." Then he asked, "Do you know the **aqueduct** system?"

"Are you kidding? I was practically raised in those tunnels!"

"Good, follow them to the edge of the Nana Forest. You'll find several caves there. Hide inside one of them until we come for you. And hurry; we won't be long!"

"How will you know which cave I'm in?" Berry asked.

Shortstop thought for a moment, but then his eyes fell on the silver chain he had around his neck. He removed it. It was in the shape of the Kodyax Turtle, an ancient **relic** said to possess great power according to Staranananian myth. "Hang this on a tree outside your cave. It should sparkle in dawn light. But don't hide too well. We don't have a lot of time!"

"Thanks!" Berry replied, and then, taking the necklace, he turned and disappeared into the pantry.

As the team continued across the spacious kitchen with its oak cabinets, gold-plated silverware, and potbelly stoves, Cak asked, "General, are you sure we can trust him?"

"If we can't, I'll deal with him myself. But don't worry. Remember the **prophecies**? They told us all about Kelcott's betrayal. We just didn't pay much attention to them back then. Well, except for Spikey. Even as a teenager, he wasn't fooled by Kelcott. Now people at least know the **prophecies**, even if they don't entirely believe them. One of them says, *'A bear of the night who gives flavor will find peace and rest from evil among friends who seek the skies.'* Now, Berry is a chef, and he gives flavor to things. And we, in a way, are seeking the skies. I think we can trust him.

Besides, there are no other ***prophecies*** about a bear betraying us, and with an event as important as this, you would think Iren might have at least mentioned it in his book."

Cak was satisfied by that assurance. By that time, they had reached the edge of the kitchen and were about to venture into the central chamber. Shortstop slowly drew back the heavy, purple curtain that separated the kitchen from the main chamber. He poked his head out to make sure the way was clear.

"Okay, there's no one out there. But let's make this fast, bears!" He opened the curtain and led the way out.

Chapter 6

Flames of Royalty

"Oh, my!" Shortstop's jaw dropped as he pulled back the curtain.

"What is it? I want to see," Cak pleaded.

When each of them finally stepped into the main chamber of the Palace, they all gasped at what they saw. It was like nothing they had ever seen before. The floor was wall-to-wall, white marble with swirls of blue and green. The outer rim of the room had a low ceiling supported by twenty pillars. The rest of the room had no ceiling. Instead, each story of the Palace had a balcony that circled the chamber and looked down on it. This continued all the way up to the Cosmic Bubble, a sphere of pink glass that spanned much of the one-million-square-foot roof.

In the middle of the chamber, there was a fountain. It was carved from transparent jade with flakes of gold and diamonds scattered throughout. Six naked angel babies - Shortstop remembered that they were called cherubs - also carved from jade, sat on the edge of the fountain spitting constant streams of water back into the pool. In the center of the pool, there was a beautifully carved column. On top of the column stood a huge, jade elephant, a creature long since extinct on Staranana. The *pachyderm* was balancing on its hind legs, and its muscular trunk stretched up toward the second story. A stream of water shot upward from its snout to about the fifth story and then dribbled back down over its large belly, causing its emerald surface to glisten that much more in the starlight. The sound of the fountain reminded Shortstop of tumbling rivers he would likely never see again.

The twenty pillars that circled the room and supported the balconies were carved into the shapes of dragons and **phoenixes**. No two of them were the same. Shortstop shuddered for a moment. He could have sworn the pillars were watching them, and perhaps they were. The way he was feeling right now, it would not have surprised him if one of those dragons opened its mouth and engulfed them all in flames.

"We're almost halfway there, bears," Shortstop whispered. They had been proceeding steadily across the chamber. So far, there were no guards in sight.

Cak pointed at the main entrance of the Palace and whispered back, "Yeah, we're prime targets for anyone who comes through that door!"

Shortstop growled at him. This was no time to be funny. They were almost to the fountain. After that, it would only be a few more minutes to the other side.

~

Two stories above them, Seth was pacing. On nights when he found it hard to sleep, he would pace the floors of the Palace. This night, he felt particularly restless, but he didn't know why. The cannon salute had gone well. The slaves in the camps just outside the Palace were no doubt scrambling to protect their meager belongings from the growing flames. In a few short hours, he'd go with his dragon guards to Katana and watch as they burned the ancient city to ashes. This was going to be the best birthday he had had in centuries. Still, he couldn't shake the sense that something bad was about to happen.

Just ahead was the second story balcony. He would look down on the fountain for a few minutes. Somehow, that always seemed to relax him. He drew near and slumped against the railing. The drips of crystal-clear water went pitter-patter against the sparkling, green stones. There was something hypnotic about it. Centuries earlier, when he had been a boy, the fountain had entertained him for hours on end. Somehow now, as he watched the water splash, he was transported back to those more innocent days.

As he sat *mesmerized*, something caught the corner of his eye. A shadow? No, it was several shadows creeping along the floor of the main chamber. He watched for a moment. Was it some of his off-duty guards trying to sneak a midnight snack? If it was, they were heading in the opposite direction of the kitchen. He couldn't be sure who it was since it was so dark, but there *was* a way to shed a little light on the situation.

At night, the only source of light in the central chamber was starlight magnified through the Cosmic Bubble, but an ancient trap had been set for just such an instance. If the creeping shadows were goons, they'd soon be dead, but that meant nothing to Seth. If the shadows were someone or something else, his feelings would be *confirmed*.

~

Oblivious to the fact that they were being watched, the team continued toward their destination. "What would Dad think if he could see this?" Cak asked.

"Are you kidding? He'd have a heart attack! I was surprised he even let us come!" Toby replied.

"Would you two be quiet! We have to…" Shortstop didn't get the chance to finish his sentence because Hell exploded around them. The room had been engulfed in a raging inferno.

The bears fell to the floor, horrified. Each of the dragon columns was spewing a flame that raged across the room. The fire was so intense that they could not budge from the floor, lest they be consumed. Even the floor was becoming *intolerable* as

41

the marble heated below them. But it was not the blistering flames that scared them the most. It was who was looking down on them.

~

Seth clenched his fists, and his nostrils flared. The rebels! He should have known! His voice was as intense as the fires roaring beneath him as he cried out, "Guards! Guards! Intruders! Kill them! Kill them now!" His eyes, cold spheres of death, reflected the terror of his victims. His feeling had been right, and as it had been with Kelcott, all these bears would die!

~

Outside, Lizard Face heard his Master's call. "Guards to arms! Everybody get back inside!" The twenty goons in the courtyard raced into the central chamber and felt the blistering heat of the inferno. The flames hindered any further approach, and Seth seemed unwilling to subdue them.

In fact, the bears half expected the Emperor to open his mouth and consume them with a flame of his own. Shortstop managed to put out the flames on his clothing, but that wouldn't matter. The fire was growing hotter. He had to get his team out of there, now!

He screamed above the roar, "Get to the fountain! Drench yourselves, and then run for the *phoenix* columns. I don't think they can hurt us."

Everyone did as they were told without a word. Each in turn rolled onto their bellies, feeling blisters swelling on their backs, and crawled to the fountain. Cak and Toby were the first ones in, followed by Nick, Speedway, and finally, the General. They *lingered* in the waters for a moment, granting their flesh a much-needed moment of relief. Then they leaped from the fountain and made a flying dash toward the nearest *phoenix* column.

"Stop them!" Seth **cursed** from above, but it was too late. The bears had escaped the flames. Now, all they had to do was make it into the banquet room, which wouldn't be easy. Lizard Face's **minions** were on the opposite side of the room. Even if the team ran along the outer wall, they'd meet their foes in the middle just outside the banquet room. Unfortunately, it was the only choice they had.

"RUN!" Shortstop shouted.

He hoped they wouldn't have to engage the goons in battle, but there was no way he would let this mission fail. He'd take down all the goons by hand if he had to. The only safe place left for them was the secret stairway, but that was still a long way off.

Lizard Face and his goons took off toward the banquet room doors. Faster and faster each side came, like two mighty armies rushing into battle. Sweat dripped from pores, drenching both flesh and fur. Each side was equally determined to make it there first, but in the end, the bears prevailed.

It almost seemed that they were home free, but then Shortstop lost his footing and went flying toward the goons. Had it all come down to this? Would his team be slaughtered, and would the *New Life* be stranded all because he had tripped over his own big feet? NO! He would not let that happen. As he flew past the doors toward the **horde**, he reached back with his hand and caught the golden door handle in his grip. His team hurried through as he did a kick off one of the goons, an act that sent several of the goon's fellows tumbling. Shortstop whirled his legs in midair and vaulted into the room. He came sliding to a stop on his rear end, and Toby and Cak pulled the door shut and snapped the lock in place.

The General jumped to his feet as the pounding on the door began. "Come on!" he ordered. "We haven't got much time."

They rushed across the darkened room to the service elevator, which stood open on the far side. All they could make out in the expansive hall was a marble table in its center that must have been at least twenty feet long.

When they reached the elevator, Cak **cursed**, "Ugh! Out of order! That idiot Berry tricked us!"

"Either that or he just didn't know about it. Anyway, we don't have time to worry about it. Everybody up the shaft!" Shortstop commanded.

"What?" Cak questioned.

"It's either that or stay here and die!"

"On my way!" Cak exclaimed. After popping a panel from the ceiling, he led the way up the shaft. Shortstop was the last one through, and he put the panel back into place. He hoped that would at least confuse the guards for a few minutes. However, the danger was not over. By now, every guard in the Palace would know about them. Only by the grace of God would they survive this night.

~

"Again!" Lizard Face demanded, and all twenty goons slammed their bodies into the door. With the final heave, the hinges ripped loose, and the heavy wooden doors crashed to the floor.

"*Ssearch* the room!"

One of the goons waved a lantern across the banquet hall. "It's no use, Master. They're gone."

Chapter 7

The Clock

"Only four floors to go, guys! Keep moving!" Shortstop encouraged. He thought they were making excellent time, but judging from the wheezing of his troops, he didn't figure they shared the same enthusiasm. His team was panting so hard that by the time they had climbed to the tenth floor, he feared they would all pass out. To make matters worse, once they entered the secret door, they'd still have another ninety stories to climb. At least then, though, they would be fairly safe.

Five minutes later, they arrived on the tenth floor. Everyone, except Shortstop and Speedway, found a spot on the ledge of the shaft and sat down. The two officers dug their fingers into the door and pried it apart. "All right, we're in!" Shortstop whispered. "Let's go!"

Cak rolled his eyes and extended his hand to his brother, who was already standing. They all emerged into the hallway and found it, unexpectedly, picturesque. The walls were a soft green, trimmed by edges of hickory wood on both the floor and the ceiling. The floors were covered in a green carpet, and small, crystal chandeliers hung from the ceiling down the entire length of the hall.

"Where's the clock?" Speedway asked.

"I don't know," Shortstop replied.

"What?" Toby shrieked.

"All I know is that it is somewhere on this floor."

"We should spread out. We can cover more ground that way," Cak suggested.

Shortstop countered, "No! We're not splitting up. We can figure this out by using our brains."

Nick, the teacher of the bunch, spoke first, "Okay, we're looking for a concealed staircase. So, we can rule out the central balcony and the outer edges of the building. A staircase would have been found there. So, what's left?"

Shortstop shook his head. "It would have to be at the dead end of a hallway. Because if it were along a wall, it would go into one of these rooms, and again it would have been found."

"But, sir, these halls run around in circles. There aren't any dead ends," Toby pointed out.

"That does present us with a challenge, doesn't it? Where can that clock be?" the General wondered.

Cak wandered a few feet down the hall. He was only fifteen, and this was all still a bit overwhelming. He had never had an adventure like this before. Once, his father had taken him along to *liberate* a slave camp. He and Toby had sat safely in the trees as their parents helped *evacuate* the slaves right under the noses of their goon taskmasters. That had been about the extent of the excitement in his life. Now, he was putting his life on the line for something they all believed in. He wanted to do a good job. He wanted to impress everyone, and when he heard the faintest ticking coming from just down the hall, he knew he'd get his wish.

"Hey, General, you should take a look at this!"

Shortstop rushed to his side. Cak was standing in front of two wooden doors. Shortstop poked his head inside. It was dark, but he could tell the room was barely four feet deep, and it had the powerful stench of ammonia. There were also several brooms and a moldy, old, mop bucket.

The General was annoyed, "Cak, it's just a broom closet."

Cak, perhaps a bit more aggressively than he should have,

pushed the General back inside and said, "Just listen, sir!"

Shortstop narrowed his brow and cocked his ears. For a moment, there was nothing, but then, there it was, clear and constant. *Tick-tock-tick-tock.*

Shortstop squeezed Cak's shoulder, "Well done, son! Well done!" He gestured for the rest of them to follow him into the closet, and they set to work.

The room was almost twenty feet long despite being barely four feet wide. They had to climb over several boxes and slip in-between shelves that had been set up in very *precarious* positions. The clock was located at the far end of the room, along with a light and an off/on chain hanging from the ceiling. Shortstop pulled the chain, and when the light came on, he smiled at the clock.

It looked just like a grandfather clock of Earth, though that wasn't what it was called on Staranana. Its hands were pure gold arrows. Its body was wide with a long golden *pendulum* swinging behind a glass door. The numbers were in Starananian script and had been handcrafted from diamonds. The clock was remarkably handsome and well maintained for being over ten thousand years old and hidden in the back of a broom closet.

"Why do you think Emperor Iren put the clock in a broom closet?" Nick whispered.

"This was probably Seth's idea. The clock was a matter of pride for Iren. Seth no doubt wanted to shame every good thing his father had created. I'm surprised it's in as good a condition as it is," Shortstop said, pulling a piece of paper out of his pack.

"What was that combination again?" asked Speedway.

"Don't worry," Shortstop assured, "I've got it right here." A glass door guarded the face of the clock, but it did not have a lock. Shortstop pulled the door open and set to work.

"First, both hands to twelve," he said, moving the golden arrows to the correct position.

"Okay!" they all replied in *unison*.

"Right past two twice, landing on it the third time!" he

continued.

"Okay! Okay!" Their voices tensed.

"And last, left past seven once, landing on it the second time."

The team exhaled in **unison** as the General said, "Now, I have to set it back to the correct time. What time is it?"

Speedway pulled an old, golden, pocket watch from his uniform and said, "It's 4:30."

"Is that **synchronized** with the Palace clocks?"

"Yes, yes! Go, General!"

Shortstop moved both the hands gently back to their correct positions, and they waited for the secret door to open. Unfortunately, nothing happened.

"Did we put in the wrong combination?" Toby wondered.

"No, it was correct. Maybe…" the General started.

His surmise was interrupted as the clock began to click. Within it, back behind the swinging **pendulum**, a tiny panel slid open. They all looked at it in wonder, but also with a bit of disappointment.

"That's it? We won't fit through that in a million years," Cak balked.

"We'll have to," Shortstop began, but a noise in the **corridor** sent a finger to his lips, silencing his team. Someone was out there.

One voice hissed, "*Ssearch* every room!"

Though he was whispering, there was panic in Cak's voice when he said, "They found us!"

"Come on. Let's move!" Shortstop commanded. He gestured for the two teens to climb through first. It took a little effort and the repositioning of some flub, but both managed to squeeze through. Next came Nick and Speedway. They were both slim and slid through the passage with little effort. Finally, it was Shortstop's turn. He pushed his legs through the tiny panel first and then tried to move on from there. When he came to his belly, he was stopped dead. His flub would not let him pass.

"Dang it!" he *cursed*. That settled it, when he got to Stararocka, he was going on a diet! That was if he lived that long. There was only one thing he could do. He breathed in deeply allowing his chest to rise and his belly to slim. As his flub popped through the panel, he exhaled, shrinking his chest, allowing the rest of him to squeeze through the panel. Just then, the *corridor* door flew open, and Shortstop swung the panel door shut. They were safe, at least for the moment.

The rest of the team had found seats on the base of the stairs. The steps were wooden and well-aged. It would be a miracle if they held up under the weight that they were about to be forced to endure. They climbed skyward in a spiral, a very narrow spiral. It made Shortstop dizzy just looking at them. But for the good of the mission, he'd make do.

There was no light to illuminate the stairs, but Speedway found an old, unlit torch on the wall and used a match to light it. He set it on the wall, and they all, with the exception of Shortstop, slumped to the floor.

"Let's go, guys! We haven't got all night!" Shortstop hurried.

"Ah, come on, General. We've trudged through blizzards, journeyed through caverns, been attacked by a chef, almost been roasted by stone dragons, climbed through elevator shafts, and squeezed through secret passageways. We need a break!" Toby complained.

Shortstop hated to admit it, but Toby was right. He nodded, and they all started searching through their packs. Before long, each one was gnawing on roots or fish, or slurping down water. Shortstop wasn't very hungry. His *adrenaline* levels were racing, and he was *anxious* to get underway again.

His mouth still full of fish, Cak asked, "So what now, General?"

Shortstop sat down against the stone wall, allowing himself to relax just a bit. "It should take about an hour to reach the roof if we climb fast. Once there, we'll find the power cells and the fuel, and then we'll dive off the Palace and paraglide to safety.

We need to be back at the cave by 7:00. Seth sends his dragons on patrol every morning at 8:00. If we hurry, we can be in space by 7:45. If we are, they'll never catch us. Dragons can't fly in space."

"I'll bet the equipment is pretty heavily guarded by now. How will we get past the guards?" Speedway asked.

"This stairway ends just below a ventilation shaft on the roof. We can climb into the shaft and observe the roof safely from there. Without more information, that's the best I can do. We'll just have to figure something out once we get there."

They all nodded and set back to eating. Shortstop **surrendered** and pulled a piece of oboca meat from his pack and started to chew. This night had shown them many perilous dangers, and it was far from over.

Chapter 8

The Roof

Shortstop huffed as he made the last few steps to the roof. It had taken them less than an hour to climb the stairs, which was better than he had expected. At the top was a secret door that led into the hundredth story. However, that was not their course. Their objective was the roof. Directly above them was a panel that would take them into the ventilation system and then out onto the roof.

"Everybody ready? Have you all got your parachutes, your fuel containers, and your portable radios?" Shortstop asked. They all checked their packs and responded positively. "Good, let's get into the shaft. Once the mission is carried out, we'll stay in contact by radio. Do your best to land near the caves at the edge of the Nana Forest. Everybody understand?" They all nodded, and he led the way into the ventilation shaft.

~

"Whoa, that's killer!" Toby piped.

"Be quiet!" Shortstop scolded in a loud whisper. They were hiding inside of a large vent. From the vent, they could make out most of the things in their area. The Cosmic Bubble took up a great deal of the space, but there was still a lot of space left. A ring of torches had been set up along the *perimeter* and lit the entire area. Three huge tanks were lying near the Cosmic Bubble across the middle of the roof. No doubt they contained the fuel. Five aircraft, similar to helicopters, were sitting on slabs on the far side of the roof, which looked out over the Ice Sea far below. Only a single spacecraft was present. It was a tiny, two-person orbiter, and it sat on a launch pad about twenty feet from the vent.

The vent was in the northwestern corner of their section of the roof, and in the opposite corner in the southeastern part stood several storage lockers. Shortstop had a *hunch* that was where the power cells were. The only trouble in getting to them would be rounding the gigantic glass bubble. Not to mention the countless guards that were wandering across the rooftop.

"Now, this could be a problem," Speedway muttered.

"Take it easy. Any ideas?" the General asked.

Cak looked around a moment. "Hey!" he finally whispered. "The fuel tanks are only a few feet away. We could probably get close enough to fill our packs without being noticed."

"Yeah, but what about the power cells?" Nick asked.

Shortstop wondered that as well. There was no way they could fight their way to the storage lockers. Then his eyes landed on something he hadn't noticed before.

"What are those?" he asked. He was pointing at several long cords that were wound up the poles of the torches.

"They look like power cords, sir. It would be my guess that they supply the electrical power which ignites the torches," Speedway replied.

"I thought they were old fashioned, hand-lit torches," Cak commented, confused.

"Are you kidding?" Speedway asked. "Palace technology has remained pretty much the same since the place was built, but you can't expect them to stay too far behind the times. I mean, they have to have electricity. How else could they power all the computers that help them run this planet?"

"That's right," Shortstop mumbled, half to himself. There

had to be a way they could use that to their advantage.

"Okay, let's get the fuel. Then, I have an idea. We'll go one at a time. Cak, you go first, then Toby, and then I'll go. Speedway and Nick, wait here."

Cak hopped quietly out of the vent and quickly took to the shadows. He crept along with the *stealth* of a thief in the night, right past two goons, before he reached the closest tank. He connected his pack to a tiny faucet and turned a knob. His pack filled within seconds. Then, as swiftly as he came, he returned to the vent. Toby was next and returned equally as fast. Shortstop put both the Nakan boys to shame, returning in half the time they had.

Shortstop asked Speedway and Nick, "How well can you make your way in the dark?"

"What?"

"I'm going to put those torches out of commission."

"How?" Nick asked.

"The clock, remember? If the time on its face isn't correct, it'll disrupt power all over the Palace."

"General, we don't have time. It's almost 5:45. Even if we run, and the weather is good, it will take more than an hour to reach the cave once we land at the edge of the Nana Forest. It took us almost an hour to climb the stairs. How are you going to get down any faster?" Speedway asked.

"We'll be pressed for time, but don't worry. I'll cut the power; you get the cells. I'll jump from the tenth story and meet you by the caves. Be ready to move in ten minutes," Shortstop commanded, and then he disappeared down the shaft.

~

When he had been a cub, Shortstop and his brother had often had races through the Nana Forest. They would start at one end of their village and see who could make it to the other end the fastest. Usually, it was his brother, Tabak Shortstop, since he was over ten years older. He had been killed, when the General was only ten, in a goon *ambush* on a supply convoy. Shortstop missed his brother, but their races had prepared him for vaulting down these stairs now. Even if he was out of condition, he knew exactly how to breathe and when to let gravity do the work for him. In the past three minutes, he had passed over thirty stories. In a few more minutes, he'd reach the bottom.

When that moment finally came, Shortstop squeezed through the secret entrance again and entered the clock room. Thankfully, all the guards had left.

He wasted no time. He yanked open the door over the face and grabbed the hands of the clock. He spun them in chaotic directions and prayed. There was a brief pause, and then the room and all the surrounding hallways went black.

Shortstop felt his heart leap. He crept to the *corridor* door and poked his head out. In the darkness, he couldn't see or hear anyone. That was a good sign. The guards must have moved on. He was safe for the moment, and the nearest window was only a few feet away. Now, it was all up to his team.

He slipped into the *corridor* and slowly tiptoed to the window. Once there, he unhooked the tiny brass lock, pushed it up, and set his feet through.

"Bring the prisoner over this way!" a voice commanded.

Shortstop paused. *Prisoner?* The voice had come from a neighboring *corridor* and seemed to be moving away from him. He was safe, but seeing who the prisoner might be was worth the risk of being spotted. He could be back to the window and gone before they had any chance of catching him.

As he sneaked down the hallway, he heard the voice say, *"Power has been disrupted everywhere in the Palace. So much for the attack on Katana! It'll take days to get everything up and running again."*

Another voice, one Shortstop recognized very well, replied with contempt, *"Good! That'll show you idiots you can't mess with us! Our attack is probably already underway. In another few minutes, you'll all be dead!"*

Shortstop arrived at the corner just in time to see two shadowy figures throw their fists into the **silhouette** of a bear. The General's eyes grew wide, and he **cursed** under his breath, "Spikey!"

Part of him was overjoyed that his friend was still alive, but another part was horrified. He wanted to save his friend, but judging from the shadows, there were at least ten guards in the hall, and if he and the contents of his pack were lost, the transport ship might never get off the ground. He had no choice. He had to go, and he had to go now. He returned to the window, looked back one last time, and jumped.

~

"Let's go!" Speedway whispered. The rooftop was now pitch black, and all the guards were shouting in confusion. It was utter **chaos**. But hey, Speedway thought, now and then, a little **chaos** isn't such a bad thing.

In the blackness, no one could tell a bear from a goon. The Colonel led the team across the roof to their destination. All the goons were still crying out in alarm. All the better, for they had no clue that four bears were moving among them, trying so hard to reach the place they had fought to reach all night long.

With Shortstop gone, and Toby and Cak already toting packs, only Speedway and Nick could carry the power cells. That had been the plan from the start. Still, the cells were far heavier than the fuel. They'd each be carrying over a hundred and fifty pounds on their backs. Their ancestral bear strength could handle that, but it was pushing the limits.

When they reached the lockers, Speedway commanded, "Okay, get these things open!"

Toby removed a tiny kit of metal tools from his pack and set to work on the locks. He had picked many a lock in his day, both for good and evil. Although, that was something he would never admit to his parents. These simple padlocks wouldn't be a problem. Still, in the darkness, it was hard to tell what he was doing. Eventually, however, one by one, the locks began to fall away.

Shortstop had been right. Inside the lockers, there were dozens of power cells sitting on shelves. Speedway and Nick filled their packs quickly. When the job was finished, Speedway wheezed at the new weight upon his back.

"Come on, we have to go!" he commanded.

Toby and Speedway ascended the ledge, and Cak was about to until something smacked him to the ground. "Sorry!" a raspy voice said. Cak looked up. It was still dark, but the tiniest amount of starlight revealed the *silhouette* of a goon. Its hand was extended to help him up.

Cak realized the goon had no idea who he had run into. He *altered* his voice to make it as raspy as the goon's and replied, "That's all right." He stood without the goon's help and asked, "Do you know what's going on?"

"No. I'm trying to find my way back inside the Palace."

"Good thinking! I'll stay here and try to help." Cak heard the goon move away, and he joined his friends on the ledge.

The roof was still dark, and the goons were still shouting chaotically. Cak took the initiative and dove from the Palace first. Shortly thereafter, his brother joined him. For a moment's time in the darkness, Speedway lost sight of them. Then, two massive shapes took form in the brilliance of the starlight. Their chutes had opened, and they were safely on course for the Nana Forest. Only he and Nick remained.

"Go!" Nick demanded.

"No, you first! I'm in charge here."

"I think I can get a few more cells into my pack, but there is no need for both of us to wait," Nick said.

"Are you sure?"

"Yes, now go!"

Speedway wasn't that crazy about the idea, but after only a

few more seconds of hesitation, he jumped.

Nick hopped down from the ledge and made his way back to the lockers. They had already captured more than enough cells to get them off the planet, but his pack was a bit larger than the rest of theirs. He knew extra supplies would come in handy somewhere along the way. When he finished stowing the new cells, he climbed back onto the ledge.

"Halt!" demanded a voice, and a flash of light washed across his body. One of the goons had lit a torch, and the light shone directly onto Nick.

Nick felt his heart leap into his throat as he heard the click of the goon's pistol. Nick turned his eyes to the stars, appreciating them one last time. Then he closed his eyes and jumped.

He hung in midair for what seemed like an eternity. He had not yet opened his chute, but it was as if he were hanging effortlessly among the stars themselves on the tiniest breath of wind. Then a single bullet ripped through his body and brought him screaming back to reality.

Nick wailed in agony, and his body began to plummet to the ground a hundred stories below. He had to reach his rip cord. He just had to! The bullet had ripped through his shoulder, rendering his left arm useless. It had also caught the corner of his heart and left his body through his chest. He was going to die; there was no question about that. If he could only reach the ripcord with his working hand, the winds would carry his lifeless body to the Nana Forest.

The cord flapped in the wind, and Nick made several grabs for it, but to no avail. As his vision hazed and as his soul seemed to be hanging on by a single tenuous thread, he lunged his hand forward one last time and *seized* the cord. His chute exploded from his pack, and the winds bore him upward. He would never again touch the ground, alive.

~

General Shortstop and Chef Berry stood together at the edge of the forest. The General could see Cak and Toby landing a few hundred yards off, and they were already racing to his position. He had been in contact with Speedway who was still airborne, but was nearly ready to land. Only Nick remained to be heard from.

"Nick...Nicolas Grass! Are you there? Please answer!" Shortstop called over his tiny radio.

For a moment, there was a crackle of static, but no response. Then a weak voice replied, *"I'm...here...General."*

"Nick! How long till you land?"

"I'd guess...two minutes...but, sir...I'm not going to make it. I've been shot. Can't breathe. Can't see. Sir, take...my supplies, and get our people to saf..." The voice cut off there. The night winds wailed with an agony of their own, and Shortstop joined them. Somewhere, a friend had just died.

Speedway scolded himself, "I should never have let him turn back for those supplies!"

Shortstop said nothing. When the body of their friend finally crashed through the trees, he went to it, removed the pack, and gave it to Berry. He said in a hoarse whisper, "Let's go. We're almost out of time." Then he turned and ran into the forest as his team followed. A single tear fell from his eye, and it froze before it hit the ground. It was time to leave this godforsaken planet!

Chapter 9

The Escape

Gloria Moonbeam grabbed General Shortstop by the collar and demanded, "What do you mean Spikey is alive?"

The General squirmed in her grasp. They had arrived back at the cave shortly after 7:00, and Shortstop had told Nick's mother of his death. She had taken it better than he expected. She knew her son had died a hero, and that was something to be proud of. However, he had neglected to tell Gloria that her husband was still alive until just this moment, which was nearing 7:45. They now stood alongside Gloria's family's seats in the *New Life*.

Shortstop replied meekly, "Well…um…at least he was alive the last time I saw him. Some of Seth's goons were taking him to a holding cell, I think. I saw him on the tenth floor just before I had to leave."

"Why didn't you help him?" she demanded, finally releasing her grip.

"That would have been suicide for both of us. There was nothing I could do against all those guards."

She sighed. In a weird and twisted way, she almost wished Spikey had been killed. It would have been better than knowing he was alive, but probably being tortured by Seth's *minions*. But she had to ask, "General, why isn't he dead?"

"I don't know." Shortstop was puzzled about that himself.

He had heard the bomb go off. He had suspected something was not right when that happened, but he had let the feeling slide. Something had to have happened, though. Something…oh, no!

"The courtyard!"

"What?"

"When I jumped from the Palace, I caught a glimpse of the courtyard. It was still perfectly *intact*. With the *adrenaline* rush of the moment, I didn't even think about it. I forgot about it altogether once Nick was killed. But if the courtyard was still *intact* that means the bomb never went off."

"But you said you heard and felt an explosion. What happened?"

"I don't know, but one thing is certain; we have to get out of here now. For all we know, they could be torturing Spikey for information about us. They might very well be on their way here right now. We have to go!"

"Not on your life!" she halted him. "We have to go back and help Spikey!"

"No we don't!" he growled.

"But, General!"

"But nothing! I'm not going to risk three hundred lives for one bear. We're leaving, and we're leaving now!" He didn't give her the chance to protest further, but instead he quickly moved past her to the flight deck of the *New Life*.

Gloria slumped into her seat. Tears were forming in her eyes, and she struggled to *restrain* them. But she had to. She had to be strong for the sake of her sons. Little did she know what one of them, young Sparkey, was already plotting.

Sparkey sat alongside his mother in the center seat of their three-seat row. His eyes were shut, and he was snoring softly. She believed him to be asleep, but the truth was he had heard the entire exchange with the General. And he knew *now* was the time to keep his promise.

He stirred and mumbled, "Mama? Mama, what's going on?"

"We're about to lift off, honey bear. Go back to sleep."

"But, Mama, I have to go to the bathroom!"

Gloria sighed, "Oh, all right. Go quickly. If we start to launch before you get back, sit with Mrs. Grass. She has a seat right by there, and I think she could use the company. I'll look for you there once we get into space."

"Yes, Mama!" Sparkey piped more excitedly than he should have for just wanting to go to the bathroom. Of course, he had no intention of going anywhere near the *lavatory.*

"Secure all hatches and airlocks!" sounded a voice over the intercom.

Gloria secured her safety belt across her lap as Sparkey wandered away. Once he was out of her sight, Sparkey approached a hatch on the side of the ship. It was still open, but an officer was moving to secure it. He had to do something, but what? He thought quickly, and then, with all the cleverness that young children are often famous for, he tugged on the bear's shirt. "Mister, mister!"

"Cub, what are you doing here?" scolded the officer. "Where are your parents?"

"My mama is back there in her seat. Mister, I really gotta go to the bathroom, but I can't find it."

"Well, it's just down that way. Now, get going, quickly, and then find a seat," the young attendant commanded.

"I looked down there. I didn't see nothing."

"Are you blind, kid? It's just down the passageway as plain as day. Now, get going! I have to secure this hatch."

The attendant pulled the hatch shut. Then he removed a large, silver key ring from his waist. Sparkey counted at least ten keys on the ring, all of which were silver, except for a single brass key. The attendant twisted that key in the lock of the hatch.

"Maybe you'd better show me the way," Sparkey smiled.

"Oh, all right, but we'll have to hurry. We're about to take off."

The officer took the cub by the hand and guided him down the passageway. When they arrived at the *lavatory,* he said,

"Okay, we're here. Get to it! I've got to get back to work."

Sparkey said nothing, but he smiled coyly at the attendant. As he turned away, Sparkey reached for the attendant's waist and then quickly moved his hand behind his back. The attendant turned around abruptly, **suspicious**. The only response he got from the child was a broad, sharp-toothed grin as he opened the *lavatory* door. The cub stepped inside, and, shrugging, the attendant moved away.

"Yes!" Sparkey squeaked. He could hardly contain his excitement as he removed his hand from behind his back. In his palm, he held a large, silver key ring.

He returned to the hatch only seconds later, but there were too many people around to risk opening it. One officer shouted, *"Nibs, how does the fuel flow look?"*

Another piped, *"Oxygen levels are stable."*

One, an old woman, even asked, *"Has anyone seen my quilt? My granddaughter is cold."*

In all the hustle and bustle, no one seemed to notice the small cub. Of course, when he opened the hatch, someone was sure to notice that. A voice called over the intercom, *"This is General Henry Shortstop. This vessel is secured for launch. Please take your seats. We will be lifting off in one minute."*

Within seconds, the entire **corridor** had been vacated. It was time to move! Sparkey took the brass key in his hand and slid it into the lock. It clicked twice, and then it made a grinding noise, almost as if the key had become jammed. Then, finally, with the scrape of metal on metal, the lock slid open. Sparkey grabbed the twist valve that sealed the airlock, turned it several times, and with a hiss of air, the hatch flew open.

"Alert! Alert! Airlock **compromise** *in Section 7!"* sounded the onboard computer.

Sparkey's chest heaved. His heart was pounding. Down the **corridor**, he could hear a group of attendants heading his way. Through the hatch, he could see the cave, and a gust of cold air **ruffled** his fur. It was dark out there now, so likely no one would see him if he hid quickly. There would be no turning back now. He took a deep breath and jumped.

The ground was nearly fifteen feet below, a fact Sparkey had not considered before he leaped into flight. It was too late to worry about that now, though. He fell through the frosty air and soon came to a sudden stop as he smacked into the cold, stone floor. He felt his breath leave him, and for a moment, he lay crippled. The engines of the *New Life* began to spark into life, and he filled his lungs again just in time to scramble behind a boulder. Within seconds, two bears were in the hatchway. They held lanterns and spanned the light out across the cavern. One of the beams went right over the top of Sparkey's head, but they **obviously** didn't see him. After only a few seconds of scanning the cavern, they turned back inside and sealed the hatch. Sparkey was safe and alone.

~

On the flight deck of the *New Life,* Speedway reported, "Everything is ready. Initiating engine firing sequence. One minute and counting!"

There was a momentary hush as Shortstop, in the pilot's seat, adjusted a few controls, and then Hell invaded the cavern! A **spew** of purple and blue flames consumed the viewport before them, and the cavern shook, sending rocks and ice slamming into the hull.

"Great Iren! Colonel, what is going on?"

"I don't know, sir! We're still 30 seconds from liftoff!"

They stared through the viewport into the flames and felt the heat lick at their furry flesh even in the cockpit, but they saw nothing. A few more seconds passed, and then a pair of cold, black eyes broke through the inferno. They were followed by two rows of yellow, razor-sharp fangs, and finally, the blackish-green scales of a dragon came into full view.

The creature was enormous. Its neck and head alone filled

the entry of the cavern, dwarfing the *New Life*. It spoke with a voice like thunder that shook the cavern again, *"Rebels, I am Captain Perdi Torinth of the Dragon Guard. Prepare to be destroyed!"*

"How did they find us?" Speedway exclaimed.

"Who knows? They may have known about this cave for weeks. Or maybe someone followed us from the Palace. Or maybe Spikey gave us up. But we don't have time to worry about that! We're getting out of here! Ignite the engines, and fire the laser drill through the cavern ceiling!" Shortstop commanded.

"That'll bring the whole place down on us!"

Shortstop ignored him and initiated the controls. He knew it was probably suicide, but they had to try. If nothing else, they could take this dragon out with them. They had lost the option of using the launch doors. This was the only way.

Fumes puffed beneath the *New Life*, and then, fueled by the dragon's fire itself, those fumes ignited into flames and propelled the vessel upward. Speedway manned the laser drills. They had been added for just such an emergency. They were not meant to be weapons, but with the **dire circumstances** facing them, they might just have to be.

~

In the cavern below, Sparkey had slid into a nook under a pile of boulders. The stones were protecting him from the full force of the heat, but just barely. They also gave him shelter against the falling ceiling. As he looked on, he saw the *New Life* moving slowly upward. She soon passed beyond the ceiling of the cavern. At least she had made it that far and was now soaring into the new morning sky. However, she was being pursued by not one, not two, but three dragons. Sparkey prayed for their success, and he believed they would succeed, despite all the odds against them. Even so, he knew he could do nothing for them. With the dragons now gone, he emerged from his hiding place, left the cavern, and headed into the woods.

~

On the flight deck of the *New Life*, Shortstop struggled with his controls. "Blast it! The hull is critically damaged. We can't take much more of this!"

"We only have to make it to 60,000 feet in altitude. Beyond that, we will be too high for the dragons."

"We still have twenty thousand feet to go. They'll take us down well before that!"

"Can we increase our speed?"

"No, we're at maximum!"

Speedway narrowed his brow. The flames of the attacking dragons continued to pound against them. The vessel was small enough to evade the dragons' grips, but not their flames. *Their flames? Of Course!*

"Dump the fuel, General!"

"Are you crazy?"

"No, sir! That fuel we stole from the Palace is enriched hydrogen, very similar the fuel in our bomb. That's why it only took a few hundred pounds to charge our ion thrusters. If we dump it all at once, the resulting explosion will be catastrophic, but it should push us beyond the range of the dragons instantly!"

"And how the blazes are we going to travel through space without fuel? The ion thrusters aren't fully charged yet. We'll lose them completely if we dump the fuel. Besides, could this explosion get us into orbit? If it can't, we'll fall back to the surface and be destroyed."

"I believe the explosion will get us out of the atmosphere. As for space travel, we have enough compressed oxygen to service the ship's atmosphere for five years. We don't need anywhere near that much air, so if we can vent the airlocks in a controlled manner that should give us the thrust we need to fly the ship. The trip will take a little longer, but at least we'll be safe and alive!"

Shortstop did not allow himself to think about it any longer. He flipped the intercom switch and sounded, "Attention all hands, brace for impact! We are dumping the fuel tanks!" And he did just that. He flicked yet another switch, the rocket boosters died, and the tiny vessel began its free fall toward the surface. Speedway pulled a lever, and the flush of fuel could be heard throughout the ship. If Speedway was wrong, they would all be dead within seconds.

The dragons didn't even see it coming, but in the hell of their own mouths, they met their demise. The fuel ignited in a fireball that would have dwarfed a supernova. The blast was far more than the bears expected. Its fierce heat pressed against their already damaged hull, ripping pieces from it. All the while it pushed them higher and higher. On the flight deck, the two officers felt sweat dripping from their brows and the tips of their snouts. The ship was being destroyed. It had been a valiant effort, but the battle was over. Shortstop did not fight death. He closed his eyes and let the blackness consume him.

~

"General? General, are you all right?" came a gentle, female voice.

Shortstop thought the voice was that of an angel. He managed to open his eyes, but his sight was hazing. He blinked a few times, and finally, his vision cleared. He was not dead, he realized, but he was lying on the floor of the flight deck with Gloria and Speedway over him.

"What happened?" he asked.

"We're in space, sir," Speedway reported. "But the ship is badly damaged. I have teams working on repairs. We should have the ship back to semi-operational status within a week, and then we can be on our way. For the moment, we're dead in the water. I already have them modifying the airlocks to use as thrusters."

Shortstop pushed himself to his feet and said, "Good, then

let's all get to work."

Gloria broke in, "There is another problem, sir. Sparkey is missing. He is nowhere on the ship. We've searched everywhere. He must have gotten off before we launched. We have to go back for him." She knew how insane the suggestion was, but sometimes being a mother meant being a little insane.

Shortstop hated being the bad guy, but Gloria was getting on his last nerve. She had lost two members of her family, true, but from his perspective, that was a small loss compared to saving over three hundred lives.

"We press on!" he said, and she did not argue further. He turned to Speedway and ordered, "Try to get a few bursts from the airlocks and get us moving. We'll make repairs on the fly. We need to get as far away from Staranana as we can."

Speedway nodded, and the two officers left Gloria alone, staring through the viewport at the cold, war-torn planet they had left behind. Ahead of them was freedom and life, but even then she knew in her heart she would be back!

Chapter 10

The Door

Sparkey stumbled into the Moonbeam family cave, exhausted. Sneaking through snowdrifts and wading through half-frozen ponds to avoid the Emperor's guards had taken its toll. His heart sank at the sight of his home. Once filled with the noises of the crackling fire, bubbling pots, and the mechanical whines of any invention his father happened to be working on, it was now dead silent, and cold, terribly cold. You could hardly tell the difference in temperature as you walked inside.

The walls, which were once covered with pictures, were now bare, and harsh stone had replaced the soft, fur rug that once stretched across the floor. A single, dirty fur rug remained near the empty fire pit. This place was no longer a home. It was just a sorry reminder of the small amount of happiness he had once known.

Despite the emptiness, there was still one thing that was of great interest to him. In the far corner of the cave, in the shadows, where his father had so often hidden, sat Spikey's workbench. Most of his tools had been removed, but a few broken inventions still littered the tabletop. One, in particular, drew Sparkey's attention.

The *Door,* as his father had so appropriately christened his latest invention, sat next to the table. It stood six feet high (few Starananian bears were taller than that) and was little more than a long, metal doorframe extending from a heavy base filled with computer circuitry. Along the frame were bulbs. They looked almost like light bulbs, but they were blue in color and seemed to be made of some precious gem. The device was impressive from Sparkey's seven-year-old perspective. Whether or not it could help him fulfill his plans remained to be seen.

Sparkey was young, but he was not stupid. He knew he had no hope of rescuing his father on his own. However, with the rebels now gone, the only people left in the area were the slaves outside the Palace walls. It would take more than a day walking to reach them, and by that time, he was likely to freeze to death or be captured by Seth's guards. Plus, the fact that all the slaves had been weakened by starvation and beatings did not make the likelihood of them helping him very good. So, as far as he saw things, he had only one hope.

Ever since Sparkey had been very young, he had heard stories from the *Text of Iren*, the most sacred book on Staranana. The most recurring stories dealt with the *Blood of the Land*, the only person who could overthrow Seth. This person was said to come from the mythical planet Earth, the world of humans. Seth was the only human on Staranana, and **prophecy** foretold that only another human could defeat him. The trouble was, after 5,000 years of torment under Seth's rule, most had lost faith in the promise of the *Blood of the Land*. Spikey was not one of those, and he had instilled his faith in his son. Now it would be on Sparkey's faith that the hope of all Staranana would rest.

The device seemed simple enough to Sparkey's eyes. He figured all he had to do was step through the doorway, and he'd be on Earth. He **cautiously** stepped through the metal frame, but to his regret nothing happened. He scratched his head a moment. The base of the door was covered with dozens of switches, each of which was labeled in code. Sparkey had no idea what they did.

One particular switch, a long and heavy iron lever attached to the side of the base, was the most likely candidate to turn the thing on. Sparkey grasped it in his small hands. He tugged and pulled, but it would not move. He then went around to the other side and pushed, but to no avail. The lever would not budge.

After returning to the other side of the apparatus, he decided to give it one last pull before he tried something else. He wrapped his furry fingers about the cold iron one by one. Then he braced one foot against the base (unaware of the switches he was compromising), and finally, he pulled with all his might.

For a moment, he wheezed under the strain, but he never let go, and slowly the lever started to move. He continued pulling until a sharp, nasal-pitched voice sounded, *"IDENTIFY YOURSELF! Oh, it's you, young Mr. Moonbeam. I do apologize. How may I be of service?"*

"Ah!" Sparkey released the lever and fell backward in alarm. He looked around the cave. No one was there, but the *Door* had come to life, lights flickering and a motor humming. It was odd too because he had barely budged the lever.

"Who said that? Who's there?"

"Why, it is I, young friend, the Door!" replied the voice.

Sparkey was quite confused by now. "The *Door?* I didn't know you could talk."

The device giggled, or at least Sparkey thought it was a giggle. *"Neither did your father until I surprised him one afternoon while he was fiddling with me. Oh, well, that's what you get when you mess with alien technology."*

"Okay, okay, hold it! Back up. What in the great name of Iren are you talking about?"

*"Well, you see, it all started about four hundred years ago in a laboratory on the planet Takillia. The scientists there (all **artificial** intelligences I might add) decided to create a series of devices to help them explore the galaxy. I was one of those devices, Takillian Bionic Intelligence, or just plain TB for short. I wandered the galaxy for centuries collecting data for my people. Then, I was captured by Lord Nimbus about 50 years ago, and…"*

"Who? Oh, wait, forget I asked. I'm sorry, Mr. TB, or whatever your name is, but I don't have time to listen to your whole life story. My dad is in trouble, and I need to use the *Door* to help him."

"Spikey is in trouble! Well, why didn't you say so sooner? What happened?" asked TB.

Sparkey found it more than a little odd that he was speaking to someone with neither mouth nor body. He had never encountered an **artificial** intelligence before. He certainly never expected to find one in his own home. The thought occurred to him that this might be a trap, but Seth had no reason to suspect that anyone would return to this cave. Plus, the fact was that it was unlikely that he would even know where it was or care if he did. Spikey was known as something of a quack and an **extremist**. Thus, his family did not sit too highly in the bear social order. So, until proven otherwise, Sparkey decided to trust TB.

"Well, I don't know exactly. He was supposed to get killed by a bomb, but…"

"A bomb!" exclaimed TB.

"Yeah, it was a suicide mission, but somehow he got captured. Now, I have to save him."

"Good luck, little one. You don't stand much of a chance against Seth's people."

"That's why I need your help. My dad said that you could open a doorway to Earth. Can you?"

"Can I? Well, yes. But I don't recommend it."

"So Earth is a real place?"

"Well, real in the loosest sense of the term. People there are barbaric and warlike. Here bears don't hurt one another. There have only been rare exceptions to this. On Earth, people lie, cheat, steal, and hurt each other, all for personal gain. It's a fallen and sinful place."

"If it's such a terrible place, why is it called the *Land of Promise*, the *Garden of God*, and the *Foundation of Eternity* in the *Text of Iren*?"

"Well, because, it is all those things. Humans were intended to be perfect, but as the Text of Iren tells us, the first humans, Adam and Eve,

sinned against God and lost their perfection. Seth came from that bloodline. God promised a redeemer, one who would buy back humanity from sin. That redeemer was a man named Jesus Christ, the Son of God, but that's another story entirely. In any case, humans must fulfill all the promises given to bears by God. Only a human can overthrow Seth."

"How do you know all this stuff?"

"Takillia is close to Earth; they call our sun Proxima Centauri. I spent some time on Earth two hundred years ago. Plus, your father has told me a great deal as well."

"That's all well and good, but tell me, are you going to help me or not?"

"It is too risky, young Mr. Moonbeam!"

"Ugh, come on, dang it! My dad is in trouble, and I am going to save him with or without you. You already said it was suicide for me to try this on my own. Now, I'll give you two options. The first is you open a *Door* to Earth, and let me find the *Blood of the Land*. Then, I'll come back and save my dad. The second is I go to the Palace by myself and probably get killed. Sooner or later my dad will get killed too, and then you'll be responsible for two deaths. How do you like that, Mr. TB?" Sparkey crossed his arms and glared at the machine.

TB was silent for a long moment. The device clearly had feelings of a sort. Finally, it replied, *"All right, I'll open a Door for you. But you must remember a few things."*

"Okay, what are they?"

"First, you must return within one day of leaving. Spikey did not leave my system with much power. I have enough to open the Door, and then I will remain active for the next day. At the end of that time, I will open a second Door for you to come home. If you don't pass through the Door at that time, you will be stranded on Earth forever."

"How big is the planet? Will it be easy for me to find the *Blood of the Land?*"

"Earth is pretty big. By now, based on my calculations, there are six or so billion people."

Sparkey felt his heart sink in his chest. "Six billion people!

Are you crazy? I'll never be able to search through all of them in time."

"No one said it would be easy, but you can remember this. The Text of Iren is not specific about who the Blood of the Land will be, just a human. It does say that they must be cleansed and forgiven of their sins. Which is another thing you should remember; humans have many different opinions on what is right. It will not be easy to find someone who truly believes God is Lord over all. If you find a person like that, you are likely to have found the Blood of the Land."

"Okay, anything else?"

"One thing, when you get to Earth, most people won't be able to see you."

"Why not?"

"I'm not exactly sure why. When I was there two hundred years ago, I tried to get the attention of people, but it never worked. Either humans are the biggest stuck up snobs in the universe, or they just plain can't see people from other worlds. Maybe God wants to keep them closed off from His other creations until His plan of salvation is complete. Your best bet is to become friends with a human child. They were the only ones who were ever able to see me, and then, it was only the shyer ones. Those you might call dreamers."

"Why?"

"I don't know. Maybe you'll be better able to find out when you're there."

"Yeah, maybe, but I am more worried about my dad. Is there anything else?"

"No, that's it. Just be careful, young Mr. Moonbeam. I have no idea where you will end up. I can keep you out of the oceans, but other than that, it is up to you to find people. Do you have any questions?"

Sparkey shook his head, and TB said, *"Okay, here we go."*

The chilled air was still for a moment, but then a slight buzz broke the calm. It grew louder and louder until it became a sharp whistle. As the noise was becoming almost deafening, the eight bulbs along the edges of the *Door* sparkled into life. Sparks began to jump between them as the bulbs grew brighter. Soon, the entire area between the bulbs was alive with electrical current.

After a few moments, the dancing energy coalesced into a swirling, blue vortex.

TB sounded over the noise, *"Okay, it's ready! Go for it!"*

Sparkey hesitated. He didn't have much experience with electricity, but he knew that it could hurt. The way those currents were jumping all over the place looked like they would hurt a lot. But this was for his dad, and he could not let him down. He squared his shoulders and stepped through the *Door.*

Chapter 11

Scotty

The ringing sounds of laughter echoed against the walls of the small elementary school. It was a typical morning recess. Tom Hostetter, the most charming fourth grader on the playground, was trying once again to impress Sara Hickle, the most popular girl on the playground. Luke Marcus was kicking a soccer ball around, as usual, with some of his friends. Paul Baxter was making his way to the front door, nursing a bloody nose he had gotten after falling from the jungle gym. Yes, it was a typical morning on the fourth-grade playground of Lone Oak Elementary School. The air was chilly, the mood was great, and the sun was bright.

In the far corner of the playground, beyond the asphalt, the swings, and the jungle gym, beneath the shadow of what had been *deemed* the *Elephant Tree,* sat a small, blond-haired boy. He was possibly the most imaginative boy on the playground, but he was also one of the shyest. Even so, in his mind's eye, the playground was constantly being transformed into new lands of adventure. His friends were repeatedly swept away by his imaginary adventures, finding themselves transformed into daring knights, bold astronauts, or countless other heroes the boy wanted to meet that week. For the other children, the games were just make-believe, to be forgotten as soon as the school bell rang. Little did they realize how precious those adventures were to him. He truly longed for a real adventure far beyond the confines of fourth-grade life.

To Sparkey Moonbeam, however, this young boy was just another face in the crowd. The cub had stepped through the swirling blue **vortex** moments before and found himself standing in the warmest place he had ever been. There were plants growing on the ground that were strikingly green and alive. The sky overhead was light blue, as opposed to Staranana's **consistently** gray sky, and a bright, yellow sun shone down its warmth on his furry face. In fact, it was a little bit too warm for Sparkey's tastes.

The most amazing sight of all had to be the people. They were very odd. They had no fur, except for a small patch on the top of their heads. Their faces were pink, and their noses were slender and small. No doubt they had a very **diminished** sense of smell. Most of them stood about four feet tall. They were children, which made Sparkey's job a little easier.

"Okay...kids...that's good," Sparkey thought to himself. *"Now to find the right one."* He began to move through the playground. One boy sat very close to the red brick building. A group of children had gathered around him, and they were all talking quite loudly about something. Sparkey didn't know for certain, but he figured the *Blood of the Land* would be a person that would draw people's attention, so he headed over.

TB had been right about at least one thing. So far, no one had noticed him. But with the way the boys were chasing the girls or kicking balls or playing any number of games, it was a wonder they noticed anything at all. Sparkey listened as he approached the ever-growing crowd.

"You dumb jerk...ugh...you moron! Look what you did, you idiot!" screamed the boy sitting next to the wall. For the first time, Sparkey noticed the smaller, redheaded boy standing next to the screaming child. He held a curious looking thing in his hands. It was in the shape of a human man with strange, green clothing that clung skintight to his body, revealing an array of **obviously exaggerated** muscles. It was a *chima* in Starananian, or as Sparkey soon learned, a *toy* in the human language, and a broken one at that.

"You ripped his arm off, Justin. Now what am I going to do?"

"I'm sorry, Steve! I really didn't mean to."

"Yeah right!" screamed Steve. The boy's cheeks reddened, and he stood up. He faced Justin and then raised his fist and struck the smaller boy. Sparkey gasped! Justin was crying, and Steve's lips curled in satisfaction. The whole scene seemed unimaginable to Sparkey. On Staranana, bears did not hurt one another. There were often disagreements, but his people had learned long ago that if they did not stick together, they would all die together under Seth's cruel hand. Sparkey now understood what TB meant when he called these people barbaric.

Sparkey called out, "Hey! Leave him alone!" Then he darted to the boy's side. He reached out to grab the stronger boy, but something **bizarre** happened. His hand passed right through the prepubescent's arm. Once more, no one seemed to notice him at all. It was as if he didn't even exist.

Sparkey shrugged and withdrew from the crowd. He was beginning to believe this whole mission was pointless. How could he possibly find one godly person among billions of barbarians? He began to pace back and forth across the large playground, hoping, even praying someone would notice him, but no one ever did.

~

On the other side of the playground, the blond-haired boy sat beneath the *Elephant Tree* and laughed. His name was Scotty Fields, and the source of his laughter was a tiny bird struggling with a somewhat larger bird over a very plump worm. Neither creature seemed willing to **surrender** it, and finally, the worm was pulled apart not quite evenly, and both of the fowl departed with their breakfast.

Scotty immediately whipped out his journal and *jotted* down a few notes. None of the other children seemed particularly interested in an adventure that morning, and when that was the case, Scotty would spend his time writing. He loved to make observations, like with the two birds, but his true passion was writing and telling stories.

"You'll be a famous author one day, Scotty!" he remembered his third-grade teacher, Mrs. Muffle, saying last year. That had been shortly after he had read one of his stories to his class to rave reviews. Truth be known, Scotty's journal was a far greater friend to him than any of the other children. He had yet to realize that friends more real and wonderful than anything he could possibly imagine were about to enter his life.

~

Sparkey's heart leaped in his chest at the sudden whining of an alarm. He was confused for a moment, but then the *hordes* of children began to pour into the building. Sparkey did not know what the building was, but he made his way to follow them. He had almost reached the entryway when he felt something grab his shoulder.

"Who are you?" asked a small voice.

Sparkey turned to see a small, blond-haired boy staring directly at him. By this time, all the other children were gone, and the two of them were left alone.

"You mean you can see me?" replied Sparkey, startled, but also hopeful.

"Yeah, of course. You're strange looking. Are you an alien?" asked the boy.

Sparkey found it amazing that the child could see him and was not afraid of him. He figured walking, talking bears might set these people a bit on edge. The human boy also thought it was amazing that he felt a strange sense of confidence flowing through himself. He often doubted himself around the other children, but with this creature, it was as if he knew exactly what to do.

"Ah, I don't think I'm an alien. I've never heard that word before. But I know what you are; you're a human."

"No kidding! Isn't everybody?"

"No, I'm a Starananian. My name is Sparkey Moonbeam, and I am looking for a human."

"My name is Scotty Fields."

"Glad to know you. Do you think you could help me?" asked Sparkey. The fact that this boy could see him pointed to the possibility that he could be the *Blood of the Land*. Sparkey was not about to lose this opportunity.

"Yeah, sure!" Scotty smiled. "But I have to go to school right now. Why don't you come with me?" Sparkey nodded, and they headed inside.

The school was like nothing Sparkey had ever experienced before. He had had tutors, like Nicholas Grass, come to his home and tell him stories and teach him to read from the *Text of Iren*. They also had him do mathematics problems with chalk on the rough stone walls of his home, but it was nothing like this.

In this place, there were long hallways lined with rooms. The floors of the halls were covered in smooth tile, as opposed to sand and stone. The sound of laughter was everywhere. It was amazing! Sparkey had never heard so much laughter in one day.

Scotty stopped at the room numbered 23, and his teacher, Mr. Finch, greeted him. The man was tall with curly, black hair and a boyish expression. The room had five rows of desks made of both wood and metal. There were about twenty children sitting in the desks, leaving the entire back row empty. There was also a long whiteboard with blue writing on it in the front of the classroom.

Sparkey asked, "What is all this?"

Scotty was a little confused. "It's my classroom. I'm in the fourth grade. Don't you have a school where you come from?"

"Not like this. It's so clean and bright! It looks like so much fun."

Scotty did not quite agree with that statement. His schooling, being one of the shyer boys, had not been all that fun, but he did not comment. Instead, he said, "Class is about to start. Why don't you find a seat, and we'll talk after school."

Sparkey sat down in the back row. For the next few hours, he sat enraptured by what he was hearing. There was a lesson about growing flowers immediately following recess. Sparkey observed while Scotty got his hands covered in dirt planting a tiny seed.

Later, Mr. Finch read a story from an actual book. On Staranana, other than the *Text of Iren*, there were few books, and none were for entertainment purposes. Mr. Finch's book was filled with colors, pictures, and the most amazing words.

The day ended with a mathematics quiz. The problems challenged even Sparkey, who looked over Scotty's shoulder as he took the quiz. The human school was one of the most amazing things Sparkey had ever encountered. You didn't have to keep quiet for fear passing patrols might hear you. You were free to learn as much and whatever you wanted. Were it not for his planet's **dire** situation, Sparkey would have been content to stay there forever.

The school day ended far too soon, as far as Sparkey was concerned. Even so, it was time to get down to business. He approached his new friend and asked, "Okay, what now?"

"We'll take the bus home and figure out how I can help you."

Sparkey wondered what a bus was, but he did not express it verbally. It was only another moment before he was filing into the crowded hallway with the rest of the children, who could still not see, hear, or touch him. In fact, it was quite an odd sensation whenever one of them passed through his body.

They arrived outside before a row of long, yellow vehicles moments later. Sparkey wiped a bit of perspiration from his forehead and panted in the incredible heat. Actually, it was only about sixty-five degrees. They boarded a bus, and a few minutes later, they were moving down the road.

The bus was so crowded that there were no extra seats by the time everyone boarded. Sparkey was already seated when a very chubby boy squished in next to Scotty, pressing the human boy against the window and trapping Sparkey under the fat boy's flub. Before long, the bus turned down a country road and arrived at Scotty's house.

Sparkey was relieved to be out from under the fat boy, and he quickly forgot the experience when he saw Scotty's house. It was small and gray, with flowers hanging from a covered porch. There were several smaller vehicles (Scotty called them bicycles) lying at the end of a gravel driveway near the house, as well as several large and bushy trees growing up about the house. And, confined behind a chain-link fence, there were two spotted creatures that Scotty called Dalmatians. (Sparkey swore one of the animals actually looked directly at him and barked.) It was a modest house in human terms, but as far as Sparkey was concerned, it might as well have been a palace.

Scotty climbed from the bus and led his new friend inside. "It's all right. No one is home," he said as they walked through the door. The inside was equally impressive. Sparkey immediately walked over and felt the smooth, polished woodgrain of a table in the dining room. Right next to the dining room was a sunken living room. It had a large device called a television, a long couch with flower designs on it, and wall-to-wall white carpet. There was also an oak coffee table, littered with magazines, and a tall glass cabinet filled with porcelain elephants.

"Those are my mom's," Scotty commented, seeing Sparkey looking into the cabinet. Then he pointed at a small, jade elephant and said, "I made up a character called Green Elephant. That statue actually *inspired* me. It was given to my mom by her grandmother before she died. She always loved to tell stories too. I like to write, so I thought it would be cool to write one about her elephant."

"What is this word *cool* you keep saying? It is not very cool in here at all!"

Scotty shook his head, "Never mind." Then he led Sparkey over to the couch and continued, "So, tell me about, well, about everything. Who are you, and what is this Staranana?"

Sparkey realized it would be hard for Scotty to understand unless he heard the whole story. "It all begins long ago, back to the beginning of even your world. God created two people, Adam and Eve."

"Yeah, I know. The *Bible* talks all about how He created the world," Scotty commented. He was amazed that this strange creature was talking to him about God.

"Well, what you call the *Bible* says God created the *heavens* and the Earth. As I understand it, the creation of the Earth is detailed, but the creation of space is not. That is where Staranana comes in. On the first night after creation was complete, Adam and Eve sat together in the Garden of Eden. In the perfection of that moment, they gazed up at the stars. Curiosity got the best of them, and they began to imagine all that God might have put up there by those distant specks of light. God knew their thoughts, and He chose to honor them. From that spark of imagination within their hearts, He created a new planet far from Earth. He called it Staranana, which means, *Star of the First Born*," Sparkey explained.

"What happened next?" Scotty asked.

"God created people for Staranana. Only, they were not beings of flesh and blood like you and me. They were spirit beings. Every last person was a spirit, like what you would call an angel, only a little different. Over all those beings, God placed an emperor named Iren. Iren was both gentle and wise. Even after Adam and Eve sinned, Iren remained sinless. It is rumored in legend that God and Iren once walked through the gardens of Cosmic Bubble Palace together and spoke face to face. Angels visited Staranana from Heaven in those days, and they often brought word of Earth. Their stories intrigued Iren, and he had them take him there once. When he returned, he had fallen in love with the place, and he issued a decree that his people should take on physical form. God had not forbidden this, but neither had He desired it. Just as He does not desire sin, even though He allows it to happen.

"Iren sent a crew of his best people to Earth. He told them to gather blood samples from animals for the people of Staranana. You see, the spirit beings had the ability to temporarily mimic any form they wanted. I think you would have called them shape-shifters. In order for their transformation to become permanent, they needed samples of DNA. Iren thought that by choosing animals for his people they would be kept safe from the curse of sin. It didn't quite work out that way.

"He also commanded that they bring back a human blood sample for him. Iren thought he could resist sin, which he did for many centuries. He also wanted to take on the image of God that the Lord (we call Him the Hidden King) gave to all humans.

"The crew left and returned with blood samples from bears of all sorts and a single blood sample from one of Adam's many sons. It is said that the moment Iren opened his new human eyes for the first time, more power shone forth than is possible for us to imagine. It is called the Kodyax Moment, the moment of new life.

"All but a few hundred spirits took the form of the bear. The ones that didn't live in the city of Katana to this day. The bears soon began to marry, and our *population* began to grow. After about five hundred years, Iren himself took a wife from the city of Katana so that his bloodline might remain pure. In a short time, a baby was born to them, and they threw a huge party. Unfortunately, they had an unexpected guest."

"Who?" Scotty interjected.

"We call him Licen, but I believe your word for him is *Satan* or the Devil! Iren had never seen him before and welcomed him, but when the individual called for the crowd to be quiet that he might raise a toast to the infant, Iren grew concerned.

"Satan said, *'All who dwell on the Earth are mine. Man has chosen my ways, and I am their king. The men here cannot escape this.'* Then Satan bent over the infant and said, *'**Cursed** be your life! All your days, evil shall flow through your veins! You shall be mine from the womb and shall not know God!'*

"These words horrified Iren, and he believed them, despite the fact that Satan is the father of lies and has no power to fulfill such a curse. Two angels, named Michael and Gabriel, were at the party, and they dragged Satan from the room. The party did not continue after that. From that day forward, Iren did not see God's face again."

Sparkey paused briefly. "Well, what happened after that?" Scotty begged. He was a little kid for sure and just had to hear the end of the story.

"Well, Iren prayed and wept for the next several weeks, and then, finally, he made up his mind. He would commit his first sin. Under the cloak of night, he stole away into the Nana Forest with the infant. Once he had reached a place that still no one knows, he gave the baby a gentle poison, and it died. When he returned the next morning, he said nothing to his wife. She was a spirit woman, quick to forgive, though she feared what he had done. They were separated for over 900,000 years after that."

"900,000 years! People don't live that long! In fact, even the Earth isn't that old!" Scotty exclaimed.

"Humans do where I come from. As for how Staranana is now older than Earth, even though it was created second, it has something to do with temporal mechanics. At least, that is what my dad says. I have no idea what it means," Sparkey explained. Then he continued the story, "When Iren was almost 1,000,000 years old, he and his wife reconciled, and soon, they had another child. Satan did not show up at this one's party. The boy was named Seth, and he grew up to be the most holy man in all of Staranana. He loved God with a passion, despite the fact that he had never seen Him. However, everything changed on the morning of his eighteenth birthday, when he had a most disturbing dream.

"He found himself standing on a cliff, looking out over a river of molten lava. The air stank with sulfur, and his lungs burned in the heat. He was very confused, but then something appeared on a cliff on the other side of the river of fire. It was a shadowy figure dressed in a black cloak. Its face was hidden beneath the cloak. Seth had no clue what it was, but no sooner had it appeared than it vanished again.

"Seth thought it was gone for good, but then he felt hot breathing on the back of his neck. He turned to see the figure again. He was face to face with it for only a moment before it started to transform. It became a *hideous*, red cobra. The snake was taller than Seth and quickly coiled itself around his body.

"Finally, it spoke, *'Renounce God, or die!'* Seth, of course, held fast and said, *'No!'* The snake did not accept this and sank its poisonous fangs into Seth's naked chest. Again it made its demand, and again Seth refused, and with each refusal, the snake bit harder. Finally, he could not bear it anymore. It was the type of pain that would not kill him, only leave him alive to suffer endlessly. So, Seth gave in and said, *'I renounce God!'*

"The snake let him go immediately, and he sat bolt upright in bed. He told his father the dream, and though Seth was repentant, Iren **banished** him forever from the Palace. Unfortunately, on the eve of Iren's 1,000,000th birthday, Seth returned in disguise and got his father drunk. Then he stabbed the Emperor and threw him from the highest window of the Palace. Needless to say, Iren died that day.

"Since that time, 5,000 years ago, Seth has ruled Staranana with a cruel hand. He blew up our moon, altering the orbit of our planet so that it is always winter. Angels don't visit us anymore. Many have resisted and died for it. My mama and little brother escaped on a ship into space, but my dad was captured. I came here to find you, so we can rescue him and save my people."

"How could I possibly help?" Scotty was beginning to

wonder whether this was all some sort of wild dream. His new friend, who walked and talked but looked like a bear, was enough to deal with. Now, this fantastic story was over the top!

"The *Text of Iren* says that only a human can overthrow Seth. This human is called the *Blood of the Land*. He must be cleansed of his sins and serve the Hidden King. Most of the stories I've heard describe him as being a child or at least having child-like faith. So far, that describes you. Besides that, so far you're the only person who can see me."

Scotty thought for a long moment, and then he said, "Well, I am a Christian, and that means I am cleansed of my sins by Christ, and **obviously**, I believe in God. Okay, I'll help you. What do we do?"

"Tomorrow, a doorway will open to Staranana at your school. We need to be there when it opens. If we're not, I'll be stuck here forever."

Scotty shook his head in dismay, "That's a problem. Tomorrow is Saturday. There is no school!"

"Well, can't we take one of those things with wheels outside?" Sparkey asked.

"Uh, you mean the bikes? No, the school is much too far away!" Scotty was beginning to see a problem forming. If he didn't figure out a way to get them back to the school, an entire world might be destroyed, to say nothing of Sparkey's dad.

"Well, what can we do?" asked Sparkey.

Scotty was a little kid, but all the imaginary adventures he had embarked on had more than prepared him for an adventure like this. He rubbed his chin as if stroking whiskers that would not grow there for years. Finally, he spoke, "I'll tell my mom that my friend Bobby invited me over to his house to spend the night. He lives right next to the school. My mom can drop us off, and then we can run over to the playground. It will also buy us some time. No one will miss me when I go to your world."

"Should we lie to your mom?" Sparkey asked.

"I guess you're not supposed to, but I don't think my mom

will understand. Maybe one day we can tell her what is really going to happen. For now, we should keep it between us."

"Okay, so what do we do next?" Sparkey asked.

"We wait for my mom to get home. She should be here any minute." Sparkey nodded at that, and Scotty set to showing the young bear around his home. It was a small, country house with three bedrooms, one bathroom, and a modest living room. The backyard was huge, with two enormous trees, a swing set, and, of course, the Dalmatians. It was all a bit much to take in for the Starananian who had spent his entire life living in a cave, with no pets or yards to run around in. For him, the act of playing was as strange as his new friend.

"Scotty, I'm home!" the sweet voice of the boy's mother called through the house.

"Mom, Mom!" Scotty yelled, running over and kissing his mom on the cheek.

"Well, that was quite the greeting. Where are your brother and sister?"

"Samantha is at choir practice you know, and Noah is at soccer practice," he replied.

"That's right, I have to pick Noah up in about an hour, and then Sam is going over to Sarah's to spend the night," Mrs. Fields said to herself.

"Yeah, and, Mom, Bobby invited me over to spend the night at his house."

"Really! Well, I guess I'm in for a quiet evening. Noah has a date. Anyway, I'll just call Mrs. Thompson and let her know you'll be right over."

Scotty felt his neck tense, "NO!"

"What?"

"Ah, I mean, well, their phone is broken. You can't call. Bobby just told me to come on over."

"Oh, really?" she eyed him suspiciously. "Young man, are you lying to me?"

Scotty's face flushed. What was it about moms? They could

always tell when you were lying. Scotty didn't dare tell her the truth, though. She'd think he was crazy. He had to think of something, but what? Fortunately, his salvation came; the phone rang. Mrs. Fields went to answer it, and Scotty turned back to Sparkey.

"My gosh…you're a terrible liar!" Sparkey insulted.

"What do you want from me? I'm no good at lying. Besides, it's bad."

"I'm sorry. Well, don't worry. We'll think of something."

A moment later, Scotty's mom returned. "Hey, guess who that was?"

"Who?" Scotty replied.

"Mrs. Thompson!"

"Uh-oh!" the boy gulped, and Sparkey grew equally tense.

"It seems Bobby wants you to come over and spend the night."

"What?"

"Yes, he just asked his mom. But, Scotty, why did you lie about the phone not working? I would have let you go anyway."

"I'm sorry, Mom. It was wrong," he apologized, but what he was really thinking was, *"Thank you, Lord!"*

Mrs. Fields nodded and said, "I'll take you over when we go to pick up Noah. Be sure you're ready." Then she left the room.

Scotty let out a deep sigh of relief, and he turned back to the bear, "What luck, huh? Now we can go save your dad!"

"Yeah, except for one problem!" Sparkey exclaimed.

"Oh, what?"

"Now you really do have to spend the night at Bobby's!"

"Oh, yeah, that is a problem." Scotty rubbed his chin again. Then, after only a moment, he slapped his forehead as if he felt stupid he hadn't seen the answer sooner. "You said the doorway wouldn't open till tomorrow, right?"

"Yeah, tomorrow morning."

"When did you get here? I mean what time?" Scotty asked.

"I don't know. You and the other kids were all outside

playing."

"So that would have been morning recess between 9:00 and 9:15 a.m. All we have to do then is sneak out of Bobby's house around that time."

"Won't he notice?"

"Are you kidding? Bobby never gets up before noon on a Saturday. Boy, that guy loves to sleep! I think he has a condition."

"Okay, what about his mom?"

"We'll have to sneak past her, but I think we can manage that."

"All right, then let's do it."

An hour later, Scotty was dropped off at Bobby's house along with Sparkey, who had had a rather uncomfortable ride, once Noah had gotten in and sat his sweaty body right on top of him. The night that followed was typical. Bobby and Scotty played battle for the empire, a make-believe game with imaginary characters. The game pleased Sparkey because he actually got to play. Scotty just had to tell Bobby everything the cub was doing. Bobby never suspected that Sparkey was real. After that, they played a game called chess, had a snack, and then they went to bed. Bobby was out like a light fast, but Scotty lay quietly talking to Sparkey.

"What should I expect when we get to Staranana?"

"Well, for one thing, it is a lot colder there than it is here. But I think we have some old furs you can wear. We'll have to find some way of getting to the Palace, and that won't be easy. My dad got in through the *aqueducts* beneath the Palace, but those are very dangerous."

"Ha! I laugh in the face of danger!" piped the boy.

"What?"

"Never mind. It's a human expression. Anyway, we had better get some rest." Sparkey agreed, and they were both soon sound asleep.

Chapter 12

Breakfast and New Worlds

Scotty scratched his head, yawned, and placed a warm hand on his chest. He had slept more soundly that night than he had in a long time. The previous day's events were a blur, and he actually allowed himself to believe that it had all been a dream. Then he rolled over, and there, as clear as day, was the young bear sleeping on the floor next to him.

Scotty looked at the clock. It was 8:10 a.m. and time to get going. He pulled on a fresh shirt and some pants, and then he tapped Sparkey and whispered, "Sparkey, come on. We don't have much time."

Sparkey stood without a word. He had also had a very comfortable night's sleep. In fact, it had been so warm, by Starananian standards, that he didn't even need a blanket. Now it was time to go home. If all went well, he would be seeing his dad again before the day was out.

Scotty moved to the doorway and peeked through.

"What do you see?" Sparkey asked.

"Dang it! Mrs. Thompson is out in the kitchen frying bacon and eggs," Scotty replied.

"What's that?"

"Food!"

"You mean like fish?"

"Yuck! I hate fish! But I love bacon. Maybe we should eat

before we go."

"Wait a minute, Scotty! You can't let her see you. We need to get out of here now. We don't have time to waste."

"But I'm hungry! One slice of bacon won't hurt."

"Scotty!" Sparkey exclaimed, but it was too late. His human companion was out the door. By that time, Mrs. Thompson had piled a large stack of bacon on a plate on the counter. The eggs were still sizzling in the pan, but she had left momentarily to change the laundry.

The nine-year-old crept toward the counter. He could already taste the *savory* flavor of nice, crispy bacon in his mouth. The eggs were tempting too, but he knew that would be pushing it. He reached for the stack and selected a large piece, and then he went for a second, for Sparkey, of course! Unfortunately, the second piece stuck to the plate, and when he tried to pull it free, the entire dish crashed to the floor.

"Bobby, is that you?" called Mrs. Thompson from the laundry room.

Back in Bobby's bedroom, Sparkey watched in horror as Scotty stood paralyzed. What could he do? He had to do something, but he couldn't think of a thing! Thankfully, they were saved again. The eggs in the pan were beginning to burn, and a device on the ceiling started to wail. Simultaneously, a large tabby cat waddled into the room and started chewing on the bacon. Scotty raced from the kitchen before Mrs. Thompson could see him.

"You stupid cat! Outside with you!" Mrs. Thompson scolded, tossing the tabby out the back door. Then she set to work cleaning up the mess. So much for breakfast!

"Ya happy now?" Sparkey growled.

"I'm sorry, but here, I saved you a slice."

Sparkey eyed the shriveled piece of meat. "What is it?"

"Bacon, you know, it comes from pigs."

"What's a pig?"

"Oh, never mind! Just try it. It's so good!"

Sparkey hesitated a moment longer, and then he gave in. Scotty was right; it was good, and he almost found himself wanting more, but he knew it was time to focus. "So, how do we get out of here?"

"We climb out the window," Scotty said matter-of-factly.

"The window! Then why were you looking out the door in the first place? We could have been gone already."

"It's rude to climb out of other people's windows!"

"Said the bacon thief!"

Scotty **grimaced**, "Oh, come on! Let's get going." Then he walked over to the window, slid it open, and climbed out. Sparkey followed, all the while wondering if Scotty really was the *Blood of the Land*. All he seemed to be so far was a very sneaky, very clumsy kid. As for Bobby, the poor boy never heard a thing.

~

Sparkey and Scotty arrived on the playground a few minutes later. Once so full of activity and life, it was now completely empty, which was understandable since it was Saturday. Scotty asked, "Okay, where did you first arrive?"

Sparkey pointed to a tall, wire fence at the far end of the playground. It was a baseball backstop, grown thick with weeds from **disuse**. "The doorway should open there. How much time do we have?"

Scotty glanced at the golden watch on his wrist. He had *accidentally* borrowed it from Noah's sports bag. "It's five minutes till 9:00."

"Good, let's get over there!"

When they arrived, Sparkey pointed to a patch of burned grass on the ground. "See, here is where the *Door* opened up. When it opens again, it will look like lightning. Some of the bolts may even hit you, but don't be afraid. It won't hurt. The wind will also start rushing, and there will be a loud noise. When you see the *Door* opening, wait for my signal. If it is not open all the way, it could collapse when we enter it, and who knows where we would end up? Probably dead!"

Scotty was about to make a comment when another voice broke in, *"Mas…Mast…Master Sparkey, are you there?"*

"What was that?" Scotty exclaimed.

Sparkey recognized the voice, though it was **garbled** with static. "That's TB. He's the computer that runs the *Door*." Then he replied to the voice, "Yes, TB, can you hear me?"

"Yes, Master! Oh, thank the Lord!"

"TB, how can you talk to me? I don't have a radio."

*"I opened a **microscopic** doorway. It is just big enough to let sound through. It isn't even big enough to see. I was thinking that while you were gone, I could save power by testing to see if you had come back this way. Then you would have had a better chance of getting back. I am glad to see my plans were unnecessary."*

"It wasn't easy getting back, but I managed."

"Did you find the Blood of the Land?" TB asked.

"Well, he's not exactly Mister Holy, but I think he'll do."

"Hey, wait a minute!" Scotty interjected.

TB cut him off, *"Good, I'm opening a Door now. Standby."*

Sparkey turned to his friend, "Look, I just want to thank you. This means so much to me, and I know it will mean a lot to my dad. He is about the only one left who still believes in you. You're going to change the future of my entire world."

Scotty felt his shoulders heave with some unseen weight. On Earth, he was just a kid, and not a very popular one. Now, he was going to rescue an entire world. It was not an easy load to carry, but he squared his shoulders, smiled, and said, "I'll do what I can."

The air around them lit up. Bolts of lightning surged through their bodies. Wind gushed and whined so piercingly that they both had to cover their ears. When the sound, the wind, and the lightning finally leveled off, Sparkey took Scotty's hand, and they stepped through the *Door*, together.

Chapter 13

Return to Staranana

"Oh, my gosh! Oh, my gosh!" Scotty screamed as he fell to the floor. He began rubbing his arms over his body, and the color quickly drained from his face. He then curled into a ball and disappeared inside his sweatshirt.

"What's wrong?" Sparkey asked. He and Scotty had just stepped from the playground into the dimly lit Moonbeam cave.

"It's cold!" Scotty screamed.

TB intervened, *"My goodness, yes! By human standards, it's twenty degrees below zero Celsius. Quick, Sparkey, wrap him in that fur rug by the fire pit. Then get some wood and build a fire."*

Sparkey wrapped Scotty tightly in the dirty fur rug, and then he raced to build the fire. Thankfully, his parents had left some firewood behind. TB also set to work. Through remote control, he activated a series of gadgets on Spikey's workbench. One device poured water into a kettle. Then a heating unit under the kettle glowed into life. Finally, a thick liquid that looked like applesauce slid down a chute into the kettle.

"What are you doing?" Sparkey asked TB.

"Your father left his micro-oven, kettle, water, and a supply of honeysuckle apple juice behind. I've activated them. When I'm finished, I believe we will have something called apple cider. It's an Earth **delicacy.** *It will warm him up."*

"Good thinking!"

Within minutes, they had a roaring fire. They also cut holes in the fur rug so Scotty could wear it like a parka, and they gave him the apple cider. Soon their guest was quite comfortable again. Sparkey even killed a wild oboca rabbit and chopped it up to throw into a stew with some carrots and celery that had been left behind. It didn't take long before they had both eaten their fill.

"Thank you. I feel much better and much warmer now," Scotty said.

"How is he going to manage the cold outside? It's a lot worse out there," Sparkey asked TB.

"If I may, sir, your father left behind another invention you may find of use. Go to that wooden chest by the far wall."

"You mean this old and rotten one?" Sparkey asked.

"Yes, that's the one."

"I never could understand why my dad kept this thing around. What could it possibly have in it that could help us?"

The old chest was a sorry sight. The wood was moldy and rotten. The hinges were broken off, and the lid had nearly fallen apart. It was trash, but when Sparkey opened it up, he learned why it was so valuable.

Inside was a book with a worn, yellow cover and yellow pages. There was writing on every page, but it was in another language that Sparkey didn't understand. Underneath the book was what looked like a child-size, black jumpsuit, with a head mask and a plastic visor.

TB explained, *"That suit should protect the boy from the cold."*

"And what about this book? The letters are in Starananian script, but the words aren't. Other than the *Blood Language*, our world only has one language. Where did this book come from?"

"It is a coded language long since forgotten by the Starananian people. But it is the secondary language of the Stararockans, next to the Blood Language, of course," TB explained.

"How did my dad get it?"

TB hesitated, *"Look, Master Sparkey, I know many things about your father that even you don't know. He should be the one to tell you those things. Sufficed to say, when he was a cub, he couldn't handle the cold here either. That suit was his first invention. It is a thermal suit. It should fit your friend, and it will keep him warm in temperatures down to 200 below."*

Scotty spoke up, "Ah, my name is Scotty, since we haven't been formally introduced. But who are you? I can't even see you. Sparkey said you're a computer."

*"Yes, I am. My name is Takillian Bionic Intelligence or TB for short. I'm over four hundred years old, and I have visited many different worlds. One of those was Earth, about two hundred years ago, I might add. A decade ago, the last ship I was on was destroyed. My **components** were set adrift with the debris, but they remained **intact**. Sometime later they fell down onto this planet. Spikey found me and repaired me. Later, he integrated me into his Door. I can also control any of his other inventions."*

"Yeah, well, nice to know you! My name is Scotty Fields. I'm nine years old, and I live in Prineville, Oregon. I've never been to another planet, except in my imagination, and I want to know exactly what it is I am supposed to do here."

"A few questions first," TB insisted.

"Fine."

"What race are you?"

"Human."

"Who created your world?"

"God!"

"Which god?"

"What do you mean, which God? There is only one!"

"Have you washed?"

"Well, I took a bath yesterday."

"No, I mean, have your sins been washed away?"

"I don't quite know what you're getting at, but where I come from, we are taught about a Man named Jesus. He is God's only Son. He was crucified and died to pay the price for the sins of the human race. Three days after He was buried, God brought Him back to life. And by that very act, He **conquered** sin and death and opened the door to Heaven. Anyone that believes in

Him, repents of their sins, and trusts Him with their life will get to live in Heaven when they die.

"My Sunday school teacher also told me that one day, when Christ returns in glory to Earth, all believers who have died will be **resurrected** and will rule with Him victoriously. Being a believer doesn't mean that you never do anything wrong again. You just have someone to help you get back on track when you do. Believe me, I've messed up a lot, but I know God forgives me."

"You are only nine. How do you know all these things?"

"I pray, and I read my *Bible*, and I go to church. But as much as I love God, I still don't know why you're asking me all this."

"Sparkey told you the story about Seth, didn't he, and how God was involved?"

"Yes."

Sparkey broke in, "Well, you see, only one who is on God's side can help us. God created man, man has **cursed** our world, and now, only a man can free us."

"I'm just a boy!"

"You'll be a man soon enough," TB interjected.

"Fine, what do I need to do?"

"You must go to Cosmic Bubble Palace and kill Seth!" TB continued.

"What? No one said anything about killing anyone! I didn't come here to be a murderer!" Scotty protested.

"If you don't, thousands of people are going to die, including young Sparkey's father!"

"But I'm just a kid. I don't think I could do it, even if I wanted to."

Sparkey interrupted, "Look, let's not worry about it. Let's make our goal right now to rescue my dad. Then maybe he can figure out what to do about Seth."

"Right, that sounds good to me. So what do we do first?" Scotty asked.

*"The two of you should go to the entrance of the **aqueducts** and follow*

the tunnels to the Palace. Spikey drew up several maps that chart the way. He took most of them, but there is still one left. It is on a shelf over there. Do either of you know how to read a map?"

Scotty shrugged, but Sparkey said, "Yeah, my dad taught me."

"Good! Now, other than getting there, I am not sure what your next step should be," TB said.

"I am," Sparkey interjected. "When I was on the *New Life,* I heard General Shortstop say that my dad was taken to a holding cell on the tenth floor. All we have to do is figure out a way to get up there without being noticed."

"How?" Scotty asked.

"I don't know, but I'll think of something."

"Very well then," TB said. *"You should not go unarmed."*

"What can we use as weapons?" Scotty asked.

A light on the base of the *Door* lit up. It was large and bright, and its beam began to move about the room. After a brief time, it rested on a pile of logs near the entrance of the cave. They were long and slender, like baseball bats. They would be easily manageable for two children.

TB said, *"Those should do for now."*

"All right then," Sparkey began. "I'll pack some of this leftover rabbit meat and go catch a few fish. Sorry, Scotty, you'll have to make do. Go ahead and put your thermal suit on. Then get some water. You'll find several empty bottles under my dad's workbench. Go outside, get some snow, and fill the bottles. We'll also need a first aid kit."

"I believe your mother took them all," TB put in.

"Uh-huh, that's what you think." Sparkey walked over to his bed, which was nothing more than a poorly crafted wooden cot, with one ratty sheet remaining on it. He put his hands beneath the sheet and moved them about a bit. When they reemerged, he held a tiny, rabbit skin bag.

"I always used to like to play doctor when I was very little. It's bad I know, but I stole a bunch of my mom's medical supplies, and I put them in this bag. I guess it's a good thing now. Anyway, there should be enough here to help us."

Scotty nodded, and TB would have if he had had a head, and they all set to work. Spikey's thermal suit fit Scotty like a glove, and it covered every **exposed** piece of his skin. He filled the water bottles, and Sparkey returned with some fish. They placed their belongings in wolf skin backpacks and made slings for their bats. They were ready to go within an hour.

"Uh, I don't want to seem dumb," Scotty started, "but has anyone considered the possibility that Mr. TB could open a *Door* straight to your dad and make this a whole lot easier?"

"I am sorry, young one. Unfortunately, I no longer have the power to open a Door to anywhere. Besides, I have never opened a Door to a place on this world, only to other worlds. I am not even sure it would work."

"Good thinking, though," Sparkey said. "I think we're ready to go then."

"Tell your father I said hello."

Sparkey smiled, and he and Scotty started to head outside. Then the human paused. He turned back to TB and asked, "Mr. TB, ah, being a machine and all, can you pray?"

"God can hear anyone who calls on Him, Scotty."

"Then will you pray for us, sir?"

"I certainly will, Scotty. I certainly will."

Chapter 14

Aqueducts: The Gators

"Wow! This place is beautiful!" Scotty shouted.

"Shh! You have to be quiet here. Seth has ears everywhere," Sparkey scolded.

Scotty hushed to a whisper, "Oh, sorry, but this place is amazing. I mean, look at those trees. How tall are they?"

"Some get as high as two-hundred-fifty feet."

"Look at this snow! It's like pearl-white and so powdery."

"Don't you have snow where you come from?"

"Well, sure, during the winter time, but never this much. And never this beautiful."

"Huh, well, it snows here every day. Well, except during the Marsh Season, but that is only one month a year."

Scotty was about to ask about the Marsh Season, but then a softly glowing, white ball high in the sky caught his attention.

"Is that your sun?"

"Yes."

"It's so small and white."

"It's a white dwarf star."

"And it keeps your planet warm enough?"

"Not hardly! It's a good thing my *ancestors* chose the bodies of bears for themselves. If they had chosen human bodies, well, without thermal suits, we would all be long dead.

Our planet used to be much closer to the sun, and we had a moon. The weather was quite comfortable and warm, but then Seth became emperor. Because Licen...um, *Satan*...controls him, he wanted to make life as ***miserable*** for us as possible. Somehow, he created a bomb and used it to destroy the moon. It was an act of God that none of the lunar debris hit the planet, but the explosion ***altered*** the orbit of our planet, casting us into a bitter and ***eternal*** winter."

"I'm sorry."

"So am I."

They continued walking through the forest, and each additional sight amazed Scotty even more. Tiny creatures were scurrying about on the ground. Many even ran over the boys' feet. Some looked like rabbits, others like squirrels, and there were many more that did not look like anything Scotty had ever seen before. If the rest of the planet proved true to form, this was going to be the adventure of a lifetime.

"So what do you call this forest?" Scotty asked.

"This is the Nana Forest. All the free bears near the Palace lived here before they left," Sparkey replied.

"*Nana?* What does that word mean? It kind of sounds like *Staranana.*"

"You're right; it does. *Nana* means firstborn. Staranana means *star of the firstborn.*"

"But you said Earth was created first. How is this place the *star of the firstborn?* It's not even a star! It's a planet."

"Firstborn refers to Adam and Eve, and to their first spark of imagination from which God created this world. One of the first things Adam and Eve ever imagined was what it would be like to have children. Iren was ***conceived*** of those thoughts and created as a spirit being here. As for the planet being a star, well, it looks like a star from Earth, or it did. After man fell, humans could no longer see our world. As for the forest, Iren's first son was named Nana. After Iren killed him, he was buried somewhere in these woods. No one knows exactly where, and the forest was named after him."

"So, how far is it to these aqua thingamabobs?" Scotty asked.

"***Aqueducts*** – about a twenty-minute walk. Once we're inside, we'll have to be careful. There are lots of dangerous creatures. When my mom was little, a cave gator ate her older brother. There are also giant bats and many other strange creatures."

"Sounds like fun!" Scotty could not hide his sarcasm. Only a day ago, he was a shy, little kid on a playground. Now, he was putting his life on the line for a people he hardly knew. He had no regrets. This adventure would no doubt change his entire life from this point on.

Sparkey noticed the edge of the tree line and said, "In a minute, we'll get to a clearing. The entrance is on the other side of it, but you must be careful. Seth has dragons flying over the forest all the time. If you spot one, fall on the ground, and curl into a ball. You should look like a rock. I'll do the same. Once we reach the entrance, we should be safe from the dragons. Then we'll only have to deal with the wild animals."

When they reached the clearing, Scotty found himself hesitating. He looked back at Sparkey who gestured him forward. He set one foot beyond the protective shadows of the trees, and then another and another, until, finally, he was well into the clearing. The rest of the trip across passed without incident. There were no dragons on patrol, which, in a way, was disappointing. Scotty would have loved to see one, despite the danger. That would have to wait, however. Before long, they were at the entrance of the ***aqueducts***, ready to face all the danger within.

"Follow me," Sparkey said. He led the way through a tiny crevice between two rocks into the ***aqueducts***. There was nothing but blackness beyond.

Scotty turned back to the forest and quipped, "It was nice knowing you!" Then he followed Sparkey into the ground.

The instant Scotty stepped inside, he noticed something

different. It was the temperature. It was significantly warmer. Also, a stream of fresh, warm water was running over their feet. Scotty's feet were remaining quite dry thanks to his thermal suit, but Sparkey enjoyed the sensation of the warm water flowing over his furry toes.

"I guess I won't need this anymore," Scotty said, removing his mask.

"No, but keep it close, just in case we have to go back outside."

"It's dark in here. How are we going to see?" Scotty asked.

"Don't worry. I packed two lanterns in my bag and enough candles for several days." Sparkey set down his bag, removed the lanterns, and lit them. Then he handed one to Scotty.

"All right, let's go, but be quiet. I'd like to rescue my dad without getting eaten by gators or whatever else might live down here."

"Okay, but can I at least whisper? I still have a lot of questions."

"Sure, go ahead."

"Well, for starters, how is it that you speak my language? I mean, I have people in my own town who don't, and you live on another planet."

"That's easy. Most of our legends and stories are from Earth or about Earth. When the angels used to visit us, they always told us stories. Some of them even wrote them down for us in the strange languages of the humans. There was a special language called the *Blood Language*. That is what the *Text of Iren* is written in. Iren wrote it in the language that he knew the *Blood of the Land* would speak. Every Staranian, whether they believe in the *Blood of the Land* or not, learns that language."

"So, you're saying you all speak *English* because of me?"

"Looks that way."

"Cool!" Scotty was starting to like this place more and more all the time.

"Okay, then here's another question," Scotty began.

"Wait, quiet, listen!" Sparkey said. For a moment, all Scotty heard was the rush of the stream. Then, in the distance, he heard something new. It was splashing. Not the type of **consistent** splashing a waterfall might produce, or even a rockslide. Rather, he heard huge random splashes. Almost like some troop of little boys was doing cannonballs into a pool.

"What is that?" Scotty asked.

"I don't know, but I don't think walking in the stream is safe anymore. We need to find another way."

Their journey had taken them deep underground by that point. High above them, razor sharp rocks hung menacingly. The walls beside them had a series of tunnels cut into them, no doubt leading everywhere imaginable in the region of the Palace.

Sparkey pulled out his map, and, after a second of reading, asked, "How are you at climbing?"

"What?"

Sparkey pointed to the map. "See, here is where we are, and just around this bend is where that splashing noise is coming from." He pointed to another spot higher on the map. "This tunnel leads to an overhang that looks over the spot where the splashing is coming from. Then from there it has a path that leads back to this level. The trouble is, it is the highest tunnel on the wall, so we will have to climb to get to it."

"All this for just some splashing. Can't we just take our chances?" Scotty pleaded.

"Sure, but if it is gators, you won't like it one bit. First, they jump on you and break your neck, but you don't die. Then they eat one arm, then the next, then one leg, and then the next. Then they chew on your head or midsection a while, but they don't touch your heart or crack your skull. Oh, no, you quite literally get to see yourself being eaten alive. Sometimes, they don't even kill you. They just leave your half-dead carcass to rot in their caves; or they carry you back to their nests for dozens of baby gators to feed on. But if that sounds all right to you, be my guest."

"On second thought, I've always wanted to learn how to climb," Scotty confessed and quickly embraced the rock.

"Hold on; you'll need this," Sparkey stopped him. He handed him one end of a long coil of rope that he had in his bag. "Tie this around your waist and let me go first." Scotty obeyed, and soon they were on their way.

There were only a few slips and stumbles on Scotty's part, but nothing serious. Within an hour, they had climbed to the top. As they stepped into the entrance of the tunnel, Scotty fell flat on his face.

"You all right?" Sparkey asked.

"I...I...need some, some water!" Scotty panted.

Sparkey opened the boy's pack for him and withdrew a bottle of water. After giving it to him, he sat down next to him. "Do all humans get tired so easily?" he asked.

"What do you want? Noah is the athlete in my family, and besides, I'm just a little kid!" Scotty protested. The water was helping, though. He could already feel his strength returning. In fact, the water was sweeter and fresher than anything he had ever tasted. It made Earth water seem oily by comparison.

"I'm sorry," Sparkey apologized. "It's just, my people have to run all the time. Usually, we are running away from people who want to kill us. It is rare to find one of us who isn't at least somewhat physically fit."

"I guess I'm going to have to start working out if I want to stay on your planet, huh?"

Sparkey chuckled and said, "Let's get going."

The tunnel before them was nothing but bare rock. It had been carved by the rebels centuries earlier, and it had maintained a stable structure. Long ago, the bears had learned the value of using the **aqueducts**, their version of a sewage system, to help them in their battle against Seth. Dragons were too big to maneuver through the tunnels, and it would be beneath the Emperor to tramp around in filth. That left only the goons, which the bears could handle. So, they had carved thousands of tunnels leading all over the planet, and to that day Seth had never *compromised* them.

"There, look!" Sparkey pointed. They stepped out onto an overhang, and their lanterns shone down on an *immense* reservoir far below. In the water, there were tiny things bobbing, moving left and right and every which way. Every once in a while, the water was disturbed by the snap of what looked like a scaly snout.

"Are those your gators?" Scotty asked.

"Yeah, but I don't get it. That lake is not on the map. If we had kept walking, we would not only have been eaten, but most likely drowned."

"Well, maybe it came from the snow," Scotty speculated.

"Maybe. In any case, we need to get around it."

"Well, like you said, we just…Oh, no!" Scotty stopped and pointed his lantern down the path leading to the cavern floor.

"It's flooded!" Sparkey shrieked.

"Yeah, now what are we going to do?"

"We need a boat."

"A boat? Where do you think we're gonna get a boat, Sparkey?"

"I don't know! Maybe we can go back outside and drag one of my dad's fishing boats in here."

Scotty frowned at that. He did not like the idea of starting this journey over again, but what else could they do? He was about to give in to the idea when something caught his eye. "Hey, what's that?"

"What?"

"That, over there?"

"You mean that huge slab of stone? I hate to break it to you, Scotty, but on this planet, stones sink."

"They do on Earth too, but that's not the point."

"Well, then what is?"

"Last year, when I was in third grade, I watched a science video about rocks. Some of the rocks they showed on it could float. That slab kind of looks like one of them. It is long enough to make a comfortable boat, and I am guessing it is tall enough so the gators can't jump on board."

"Good idea, but how do we get it to the water?"

"Hey, that's your job. I thought up the boat."

Sparkey began to rub his chin. He had noticed Scotty doing it, and he found it actually worked when you were trying to concentrate. He thought for a long moment, and then the answer came to him.

"I've got it!" he shouted.

"What! What!"

"You're not going to like it."

"Never mind that! Just tell me."

"Well, gators are pretty strong. If we could find a way to get them to drag the slab, it would be a piece of cake."

"How do we do that without getting eaten ourselves?"

"Well, it's gonna cost us some of our food. See, we find a way to tie the two ends of the rope to the slab. That will make a big loop. Then we bait the loop with pieces of oboca and fish. After that, we make a lot of noise to get the gators' attention. They'll start walking up the path. When they do, they'll smell our food and start eating it. Then we yank on the rope hard, and it will get caught in the gators' mouths. Whenever a gator thinks he's in trouble, he heads back for water. It's a well-known fact. When they do, they'll drag the slab, and we can set sail."

"Nice work, Einstein!"

"Who?"

"Never mind. There is just one flaw with your plan," Scotty established.

"Oh, what?"

"What if the gators attack us?"

"Are you kidding? Gators may be dangerous, but they're also lazy. If they can get a free meal without having to work for it, they will. That is what our food will give them," Sparkey assured.

"All right then, let's get this over with," Scotty *surrendered.*

God was with them as they carried out Sparkey's plan. There were two interconnecting holes in the surface of the slab. They allowed the rope to be sent through, tied, and secured. The meat also fit securely on the rope. All that was left was to call the gators to dinner.

"So, how do we do this?" Scotty questioned.

"Get some rocks, and we'll start throwing them into the water," Sparkey instructed. Scotty did so. After a few minutes, he had a small pile of flat stones.

"Peg them on the head, but don't hit their eyes. Gators go crazy if you hit them in their eyes. Start yelling too."

"I got it!" Scotty assured, and he let the first stone fly.

~

Far below them, a pair of plump gators sat floating. The echoes of screeching recklor bats caused them to perk up for a moment, but only for a moment. Not much had happened to disturb their quiet floating for some time. A few days ago, several bears had wandered by. But after ten gators had been killed, and the underground dam had been breached, they had left them alone. Now, they filled their bellies on fish from the reservoir. Everything was quiet and peaceful.

Splash! The unexpected surge of spraying water was not the last. Another and another came until the entire lake was erupting. Stones! Stones from the sky were falling, turning the once calm surface of the water into a frightful rage of tumbling currents. The worst thing of all was the noise, the terrible noise coming from above.

~

"Hey, you stupid things, get up here!"
"Dumb crocs, want a bite to eat!"
"Hey, pea-brains, you can't catch us!"

"I've seen scarier houseflies, you stupid things!"

Scotty and Sparkey were not sure exactly who was throwing out which insult, but it didn't matter. The important thing was it was working. Three gators had left the water and were heading up the slope.

"You had better be right about this, Sparkey!"

"Yeah, well, you better be right about that rock being able to float! I've never heard such a foolish idea before."

"Don't worry!" Scotty assured. "Try having a little more faith." Then he drew his bat. "Here they come!"

In the twinkling of the lantern light, the gators were a horror to behold. Rugged black and green scales, covered in seaweed and marsh, sent forth a stench of rotting flesh. Rows of razor-sharp, yellow teeth oozed spittle from bloodied gums. And the eyes, the horrible eyes, yellow split by a black diamond and intensified by pure, cold, mindless hatred, glowed in the blackness.

"They're taking the bait!" Sparkey squealed. Two of the gators had found the meat and were sinking their teeth into it. The last gator had his eyes on two different pieces of meat.

"Yeah, but their big brother is still coming after us!" Scotty screamed.

"What'll we do?" Sparkey screeched.

"Looks like we'll get to see if those stories you told me are true. AHHHH!"

"Scotty, what are you doing?" Sparkey screamed, but it was too late. The young human charged forth with his bat, screaming, and yelling curses, and jumping about like a wild thing. He landed several good blows square on the gator's head, and the creature could not touch him. It was time for Sparkey to do his part.

The cub leaped onto the stone slab and yanked back on the ropes. There was a roar of pure rage and fear from the gators. Not to mention pain, for Sparkey had hidden ten fishing hooks in the meat. They had now secured themselves into the creatures' flesh. Panic-stricken, the gators began to waddle back toward the lake, all the while dragging the slab behind them.

"Scotty, jump on!" Sparkey shouted to his friend, but the boy had been backed into a corner.

Scotty smacked the creature again and shouted back, "You go, Sparkey! Save your dad!"

"It's pointless without you!" Sparkey knew that without Scotty, his dad, and most likely his world, would die. Despite the weight of the stone, the gators were moving quickly. He did not have much time, but he had to save his friend.

He leaped from the rock and charged toward the gator. Before he could think twice, he was on the beast's back. With one hand, he held on as tightly as he could as the creature wailed and pitched and bucked, trying to throw him off. With the other hand, he beat the thing's head with his bat.

Scotty managed to get around to the tail, and with one solid whack, he succeeded in breaking it. That would cripple the creature in the water, but it was still more than a match for them on dry land. Things seemed to be going their way, but then Sparkey made a *crucial* mistake. He landed a blow squarely on one of the gator's eyes and crushed it. The pain and the shock of being half-blind sent the creature into a panic.

"Sparkey, get off now!" Scotty shouted, but it wasn't soon enough. The creature bucked and sent the tiny bear flying into the rock. He fell to the ground, unconscious.

Scotty ran to his friend as the gator closed in, one eye gleaming and fangs dripping. They had barely started their journey. Was this how it was going to end? Scotty looked up, ready to pray his last, and then he saw the razor sharp rocks hanging from the ceiling. There was one directly over the creature. He only had time to try this once. He felt around for a stone and met the creature's gaze.

"Go back to the frozen Hell you came from!" the boy screamed. Then he stood and chucked the stone with all the force he could muster. It shot toward the ceiling as Scotty felt the gator's hot, putrid breath on his neck. The rock made contact and ricocheted into the blackness. Nothing happened!

Scotty closed his eyes, ready for death, trying to imagine what Heaven would be like, but he felt something hit his head. Rocks and dirt were falling from above. Keeping a single eye on the creature, he looked up. The stalactite was breaking free. It crumbled and cracked, and an instant later the razor-sharp tip of the projection was plummeting from the cavern ceiling.

The gator was about to sink its teeth into Sparkey's leg, but the rock came first. It *pierced* the beast's backside. The point cut through gnarled scales and bone, and finally, spilled a belly filled with half-digested fish.

By that time, the other gators were near the water's edge. There would be no waking Sparkey, so Scotty did the only thing he could. He picked up the small bear and ran after the gators. Ordinarily, the cub might have been too much for him to carry, but his body was surging with *adrenaline*, and he shot down the path at speeds that would have impressed even the athletic Noah. By the time the gators reached the water, both Sparkey and Scotty were back onboard their stone ship.

The gators dragged the slab out into the deep, and as Scotty had guessed, it floated. He laid Sparkey down and cut the rope free. They had done it! They had their boat, and all that remained was to face the hellish dark of the *aqueducts*.

Chapter 15

Everyone Else

"All dead!"

"Yes, Master *Sseth*, all three dragons were burned to death in their own flames. The rebel vessel escaped. I am *ssorry*, *Ssire*," Lizard Face hissed.

The Emperor drew near the captain of his Dragon Guard, **lingered** a moment, enough to make the creature cringe, and then **seized** him by the throat! Lizard Face grasped at his master's hands, but 5,000 years of war had made Seth far too strong. Seth held him just long enough to watch the life start to fade from his eyes. Then he threw him against the wall of his royal chambers.

Lizard Face gasped, "I'm...I'm *ssorry*, Your Majesty! We'll *sstop* them!"

"They are deep into space by now. How could we possibly stop them?" Seth scoffed.

"*Ssire*, please, you have a grand *sspace* fleet. We will pursue them!"

"Fleet, what fleet? That yard of rusting wreckage in the White Desert? Let it be **cursed**! It remains a monument to my only failure in 5,000 years."

"Yes, *Ssire*, I remember, the battle against Lord Nimbus, it was a tragedy to be *ssure*."

"As I recall, it was your idea, five hundred years ago, to attack the worlds of Lord Nimbus! Now my fleet is nothing but a pile of rusted metal and twisted bulkheads."

"My recommendation to attack was a mistake, *Ssire*! I feared the **prophecies** of the *Blood of the Land*, and I feared that Lord Nimbus was he. No one could have guessed how *sstrong* his people would be."

"That's true, and such people they were! Who could ever forget the stench of those **miserable** gorillas? And to this day, centuries later, I have no words to describe the *Shifters*. Lord Nimbus may have exiled me to one of those jungle choked worlds for over fifty years, but he *never* defeated me...and I certainly didn't come away empty-handed."

"The goons, *Ssire*?"

"Yes. Licen's curse transformed the beautiful Kodi in my **hideous** goon army, but my escape was still a bloody one. It was only by mere chance that I was able to steal one of their ships and return home, being shot at all the way! By the time I returned to Staranana, half of my new troops had been slaughtered."

"Yes, Master, a tragedy to be *ssure*, but what a glorious day when you returned!"

"And what did I find when I returned? My empire had been overrun with bears, and some fool named Splash Moonbeam had been made their emperor! That's what I get for taking your advice!"

"But, *Ssire*, you won that victory. You turned *Ssplash's* city and all those in it to *sstone* by the power of Licen, and you *ssank* it beneath the surface."

Seth smirked, "I did, didn't I?"

"Yes, and no one has claimed a victory over you in centuries."

"That's true, too! But how are we going to find one tiny ship in the vastness of space, and is it truly worth it? A few hundred bears pose no threat to my empire. It would be a waste of time and resources."

Lizard Face hissed, "Perhaps it would, but consider this.

They would not have left this planet unless they had *ssomewhere* to go. Their vessel is not big enough to *ssustain* them forever. All we have to do is find out where they are going and attack that location."

"Yes, but where is that?"

"I do not know, but there are rumors of another world, a free world, in this *ssolar ssystem*."

"Impossible! The only other planets are chunks of barren rock."

"Yes, Your Highness, but no one has ever explored the rings of the *ssun*. There are asteroids there as large as small planetoids."

"They'd be too hot to be livable."

"The bears are very **resourceful**, *Ssire*." Lizard Face had his own agenda for seeking out the rebels. He wanted this new world for himself, but he would use Seth in every way he could to accomplish that.

"Very well, send word to the captain of my goons. Tell him to go to the White Desert and prepare a ship. When it is ready, you will lead an assault team. In the meantime, go *interrogate* that bear we are holding. See if you can find out where this world is."

Lizard Face's mouth split into a sharp-toothed grin, and he headed from his master's chambers. Before long, he'd be the new master, and then that maggot of an emperor would be licking his scales.

"Oh, Lizard Face, one more thing," Seth halted him.

"Yes."

"When you find this planet, destroy it. If you fail this time, I will kill you. Have a good evening now." Seth waved him away, and the reptile stepped into the hall and shut the chamber doors behind him.

He sneered, "When I find that planet, I will kill all who resist me and turn the rest into *sslaves*. Then I will take whatever power they have and come back here and lay this planet to waste. Then I, Your Majesty, will be the emperor, and I will most definitely kill you!"

~

"Total count of the wounded, seventy-three, but nothing serious, General," reported Gloria Moonbeam. Though she was originally only supposed to be a passenger on the *New Life*, in the last two days, she had more or less taken over all the medical duties of the ship.

Shortstop replied, "That's good." Then he turned to his first officer and asked, "How are the repairs coming?"

"The hull damage will take another couple of days. However, we have completely overhauled the airlock system. Our makeshift thrusters are online. They can give us enough speed to make it to Stararocka in four weeks. And we'll have enough fuel to make the trip twice more without refueling if we want," reported Colonel Speedway.

Gloria's eyes lit up, but Shortstop shot her a cold glance. "We don't want to! Our job is to make it to Stararocka, and get on with our lives."

Gloria clenched her fist. She felt like socking the General in his already rosy-red snout, but she restrained herself and changed the subject. "Sir, once we arrive, we will not be able to **disembark** right away. Stararocka is within the purple ring of our white dwarf sun. It passes within 400,000 kleps of the photosphere. On a cold day, temperatures fall as low as 95 degrees, but the average temperature is 150 degrees."

"How do the Stararockans survive?" Speedway asked.

Gloria replied, "Most of the people live in air conditioned biospheres. However, the planet has thick vegetation and many jungles. The trees filter a great deal of the heat. You can survive there. That's where the first Staranians who discovered the planet settled at first. Most of their crew suffered heat sickness before they got the first biosphere built, though."

"What do you suggest to protect our people?" Shortstop

asked.

She pulled a syringe filled with a dark blue liquid from her pocket. "For lack of a better term, this is *ice blood*. I created it last week using small engine coolant and samples of my own blood."

"You created it in your cave?" Speedway questioned.

"No, we have lab equipment aboard the *New Life*. I used it before we launched. The genetic engineering I did makes this substance capable of self-replication. We can grow as much as we want."

"Is it dangerous?" Shortstop asked.

"No, not at all. The engine coolant is nothing more than water filled with temperature sensitive enzymes. When the area around them heats up, the enzymes react and cool the engines down. Now that it is bonded with blood, it will do the same for a bear's body. My blood is the universal donor *Type R*, so it should work for everyone."

"Great! Get enough ready for everyone," Shortstop commanded.

"There is just one problem," Gloria continued.

"What?"

"None of our bears can go inside a biosphere for at least three weeks after we arrive. Their bodies need to adapt to the new environment. The *ice blood* will help that go faster. However, if they enter a biosphere before their bodies have adapted to the natural environment, they may become dependent on the **artificial** environment. Even just stepping outside would kill them."

"Well, they'll have been living on a spaceship for a month. Won't it be the same?" Speedway asked.

"Not if we start altering the ship's atmosphere and temperature gradually. Starananians prefer an average temperature of twenty degrees. The ship's temperature is set to that. For the next month, if we raise the temperature three-and-a-half degrees every day and give everyone a shot of *ice blood*, by the time we reach Stararocka, the ship will be…"

"The ship will be on fire; that's what it will be!" Speedway interrupted.

"Not quite. It'll be one-hundred-twenty-five degrees. At which point, I suggest we land in the Rocka Jungle. It is the thickest jungle. The average temperature is eighty-five degrees. And it is only five kleps from the largest biosphere, so we can make contact with the locals," Gloria reported.

"How do you know so much about Stararocka?" Shortstop found it odd that Gloria seemed to have the inside scoop. To the best of his knowledge, she had not been briefed on any of the intelligence reports the rebels had, and even those had mainly been rumors. There had been no word from the planet since the first colonists escaped Staranana and settled there. That message had simply been, *"We're safe and free!"* But there had been nothing more, no detailed reports. It had been rumored that the massive ion storm that had shifted Staranana's orbit twenty-two years past, and for one month every year melted the ice and turned the planet into a swamp, had been caused by some technology on Stararocka. However, they had no proof.

Gloria's only reply was, "Sorry, that's a Moonbeam family secret. Now, we need to get to work."

Shortstop nodded, and she and his first officer left. He rubbed the shaggy fur on his face and turned back to the viewport of the **cockpit**. Outside, a tiny white star twinkled, banded by three rings: one purple, one green, and one red. Somewhere within the jagged asteroids and raging solar flares of the purple ring, a tiny planet spun. They had to find it. They just had to.

~

"*SSPEAK* NOW!" Lizard Face demanded as his forked tongue hurled streams of spittle into Spikey's face. "Where are your people going?"

"What the heck are you talking about?" Spikey had spent the

past two days being tortured under the whips of the goons. The fur on his back had been stripped to the skin in places. Blood poured from lashes on his legs, and it was all he could do to see through two puffed up eyes.

Lizard Face sank his claws into the bear's stomach and twisted. "If you don't tell me what I want to know, then you are of no use to me. I can have you killed. You already lied about the invasion, and you never told us about the device you were carrying. Remember, the egg *sshaped* thing and the vial?"

Spikey wheezed under the stress on his stomach, but finally gasped, "Put them together! Find out what they do!"

Lizard Face's scaly eyes narrowed. He turned to a goon standing close by and said, "This is getting us nowhere. We'll execute him at dawn." Then he turned to the bear and said, "Make whatever peace you have to with your God, fool. This is the last day you *sshall ssee*." Then he turned and left the room.

~

Moments later, Lizard Face returned to Seth. "I could not get anything out of the bear, but the captain of your goons is already at the White Desert. One heavily armed vessel will be ready within a week. Her engines will reach nearly 100,000 kleps per hour – far more speed than the rebels could possibly attain. Long before it ever reaches its destination, we'll have laid that world to waste. Then we can bring the *Sstarananians* back here to face execution. We'll teach them the price of defying *Sseth*." Then he thought to himself, *"And we'll add another to the number being executed - a certain human I know sso well."*

Seth did not face him but continued staring out his chamber window. From its height, in the afternoon light, he could see the slave camps stretching out as far as the eye could see. Beyond that, fires burned, forests and cities consumed in the flames of his hatred. "Very good, Lizard Face. Inform me when the ship is ready."

"There is another matter, *Ssire*."

"What?"

"The city of Katana - You were going to destroy it for your birthday. Are you *sstill* going to?"

"After the present crisis is complete, yes. Now, leave me. I need to think."

Lizard Face smirked as he closed the doors behind him, and he whispered, "You're not going to live beyond the present crisis."

Chapter 16

Aqueducts:
Bats and Crystals

"Ah! What's going on?" Sparkey screamed.

"Oh, good, you're awake." Scotty sat cross-legged next to his friend on their floating stone vessel. The glow of their lanterns cast some illumination on the murky waters, but not much. A few gators floated lazily nearby, and every once in a while they would take a snap at the stony barge. If things weren't bad enough, the cavern ceiling had disappeared into an *ominous* blackness. There was no way of telling what dangers hung above them.

Sparkey, who had been sprawled unconscious on the stone slab for quite some time, asked, "What happened?"

"You got knocked out in the fight with the gator. I killed him, and then I carried you to the slab," Scotty replied.

"You killed him?" Sparkey furrowed his brow.

"That's right! And I've conked more than a dozen that have tried to attack the boat. But they've left us alone for a while now."

"How long have I been out?"

"Let's see, according to Noah's watch, oh wait! That's right, I lost it! Gator took it right off of my wrist. Noah's going to kill me! That is if I ever see him again. Anyway, I don't know, at least a couple of hours. I hope you meant for us to go in the same direction as when we started because that's where the current is taking us. Slowly, I might add, and we don't have any oars."

"That'll work," Sparkey replied. "You know, it is hard to imagine these caverns flooded so much in only the last few days. I wonder what really happened."

"Who knows? What can we expect from the rest of the **aqueducts**?" Scotty asked.

Sparkey felt around for his bag. Luckily, it had not fallen off his back in the fight. Scotty had set it near the center of the slab while he was unconscious. He reached inside and pulled out the map. He then drew one of the lanterns close as he unfolded it. He placed his finger on a point that seemed to indicate a steep incline.

"No matter how much the tunnel has flooded, it would never flood beyond this point. When we run aground, we'll have to follow this incline to the upper levels. Once we're there, we'll pass through this chamber here, and after that, we'll have to walk along these extremely narrow ridges around Black Eye Canyon. If we make it around, the next chamber is under the Palace."

"Good, then let's hope we hit shore soon."

"By the way, thank you," Sparkey said in a hushed voice.

"For what?"

"For saving my life. I guess my plan wasn't exactly the best in the world, and you were right about the rock, and you did kill that gator. Not many bears can make such a claim."

"I'm glad I could help. I'm sure I'll have many other chances."

"I'm sure you will too," Sparkey smirked.

"Yeah, in the meantime, I'm kind of sleepy. I think I'm gonna take a nap. You mind watching the boat?"

"Not a problem," Sparkey assured.

Scotty stretched out. After placing his bag under his head for a pillow, he thought, *"You know it's tough business rescuing a whole planet, but somehow I have to. No matter what it takes, I know I have to."*

Then he stared into the blackness, and after a few more minutes, he fell asleep.

~

"Uh, Scotty!" Sparkey shook his friend.

"Leave me alone. I want to sleep!"

"Um, I can't do that!"

"Leave me alone!"

"Fine, but I think that waterfall might change your mind!"

Scotty was awake instantly. To the right of their boat, they could hear the thundering sound of countless tons of water pounding against even more water and stone. The currents were also getting swifter, dragging their boat in the wrong direction.

Sparkey explained, "We need to go straight ahead, but the water is dragging us to starboard. I think we're almost to shore. We'll have to abandon the ship and swim the rest of the way."

"What about the gators?" Scotty panicked.

"No gator is going to swim anywhere near a waterfall, especially if he has a chance of going over it."

"Well, there is one other problem," Scotty said.

"What?" Sparkey was growing **anxious**.

"I can't swim!"

"Ugh! Well, it looks like I get to save your life this time. Just hold onto me. We can't be far from shore. I should be strong enough to fight the currents."

"What about our stuff?"

"It'll get a little wet, but I think it will be okay. Except that we'll have to put the lanterns out. I'll just have to pick a direction and go and hope we make it. Now, grab your stuff, and then grab onto me."

Scotty puffed out the two lanterns. Then he loaded both packs onto his back. Finally, he wrapped his arms around Sparkey's neck. Sparkey asked, "Ready?" Scotty nodded, and Sparkey jumped.

They hung in the air for a timeless instant, and Scotty recalled the time when he took swimming lessons when he was six. After jumping from the side of the pool, he sank straight to the bottom. It was not until his instructor pulled him back up that he returned to the surface. Since then, he hadn't even gone near the water.

The instant ended with a splash! Both human and bear were soaked to the brim, and they were swiftly being drawn toward the waterfall. "Hang on!" Sparkey commanded and began to stroke his arms and kick his feet. A few times, Scotty's feet got in the way. To which Sparkey said, "Hey, knucklehead, knock it off." But, eventually, he gained strength over the current, and soon they were on land again.

Scotty staggered onto the shore and collapsed in a heap. He panted, "The next…next time we save anybody, let's stay…stay on dry land."

Sparkey smirked, though Scotty couldn't tell from the blackness. In the distance, the cub heard the **distinct** sound of rocks smashing against one another. "That was our boat!"

"It was a good ship."

"Yes, it was," Sparkey replied. "We can't go any further until the lanterns dry out. I wish I knew what time it was."

"Time to go save your dad," Scotty began. Then he stopped. They had come ashore at the base of the steep path Sparkey had spoken of. It extended upward a good hundred feet until it leveled off at the entrance to another chamber. From that passage, high above them, something was glowing, something bright and green.

"What's that?" Scotty asked, but before Sparkey could answer, the nine-year-old had run off toward the light.

"Scotty, wait!" Sparkey screamed. He was beginning to learn that human boys were very curious creatures. Scotty was possibly the first human boy ever to visit an alien world, so there was plenty for him to be curious about.

Scotty reached the entrance to the chamber, and his jaw

dropped. From cavern floor to cavern ceiling, the chamber glowed with every color imaginable. From the ground and the walls, formations of rock extended upward and outward. At the **pinnacle** of each formation, a gem pulsed with light. Each jewel radiated with a fire more dazzling than that of a thousand diamonds. Those on the walls were mostly blue. Red hung overhead from the ceiling. Purple sprouted from the center of the stone room, and gems of almost every other color were spread out in no particular **concentration**. The green gems were the most populous, and they were concentrated near the chamber entrance. Green had been Scotty's favorite color since early childhood, and the effect these gems had on him was almost hypnotic. He simply had to touch one. He reached his hand forward.

"NO!" he heard Sparkey shout, and an instant later, a furry hand had wrapped around his wrist, and he was being thrown to the ground.

"Sparkey! What are you doing?"

"Are you crazy? Don't ever touch those!"

Judging from the bear's exasperated expression, Scotty thought he had almost violated some secret treasure or religious icon. He had no idea the real reason Sparkey had stopped him. "Why?"

"Because they're poisonous! One touch would kill you instantly!"

Scotty looked up at the glowing green gem and swallowed hard. "Kill me?"

"Dead as you can get, pal! They're called viola crystals. Viola means poison."

"Oh, well, thanks then. But how are we going to get past them?"

"There is a path through them, but we'll have to be careful. At least this way, we don't have to stop. The jewels will light our way, and by the time we reach the other side, the lanterns should be dried out."

"Good, then I'll have time to ask you more questions."

"Do all human boys ask so many questions?"

"Sure, it's how we learn the best. Now, tell me about your dad. Who is this great bear we're going to rescue?"

Sparkey sighed and began to lead the way through the deadly crystals. "My dad, what can I say about him? Well, he's an inventor. He's been making things since he was a kid. He was adopted, but I don't think even he knows where his real parents are. He's never mentioned them. He's probably the most faithful bear on this planet. He was the only one who wanted to stay behind and fight. He believes very much in God and the **prophecies** of Iren."

"Is he a good dad?" Scotty asked.

For a moment, Sparkey didn't quite know how to answer the question. Most of his childhood, his father had been busy with the war. He was always **tinkering** with a new invention; he never had much time for his children. Sparkey answered, "You know, I never really got to spend much time with him because of the war. There were times, though, times when a new snow had fallen, or he had just finished a new invention, that he would wake me up in the middle of the night. We'd both bundle up and go out to the river by my cave and fish all night. And under the stars, or even under the falling snow, we would talk until dawn. Usually, Mama would have to come wake us up in the morning. But no matter how tired I was, after nights like that, I always seemed to have good days."

"Wow, that's pretty cool!"

"What about your family?" Sparkey asked.

"Oh, well, my mom's a teacher, and my dad's a fireman."

"They any good?"

"Are you kidding? You never did see a better teacher than my mom. And my dad, well, he saves people's lives all the time. He's a hero. I think he's probably a lot like your dad. He's funny too. You should see him on Christmas morning. He…"

"Wait!" Sparkey interrupted him. They had nearly traversed

the entire path of the crystal chamber.

"What is it?" Scotty asked.

"Listen."

"Boy, you bears have good ears!"

"Never mind that! Just listen!" Sparkey hushed him. In the distance, something big and horrible was shrieking, like a **banshee** straight from the **abyss**. Its cry was so horrid that it sent shivers down the human boy's spine as it echoed through the gigantic chamber just beyond them.

"What is that?" Scotty asked half hoping the answer would be a good one.

"A recklor bat!"

"A what?"

"Don't you have bats where you come from?"

"Yeah, somewhere on Earth. Not around me, I don't think, though. But I could be wrong."

"Well, anyway, recklors are giant bats. They live in Black Eye Canyon, and they are very, very dangerous."

"Why do they call it Black Eye Canyon?" Scotty asked.

"See for yourself," Sparkey replied. He knelt, lit the lanterns, and they stepped out of the crystal chamber onto a ledge. Beyond them was an expanse of black **encompassing** a hole that appeared to have no bottom at all. In what looked to be the center of the expanse, barely visible in the dim, lantern light, was a tall, jagged pillar of stone with a flat top. The entire area was shaped like an eye, and the pillar marked its pupil.

"Oh, wow!"

"You think that's impressive? Look up there." Sparkey pointed to the ceiling.

Scotty felt his breath leave him. High above him, swirling in rings and screeching, or hanging from the cavern ceiling, were hundreds upon hundreds of thousands of tiny, black bats. They hung like a swarm of insects and covered every inch of the gray stone in furry black.

"I thought you said the bats were gigantic?" Scotty

questioned.

"They will be," Sparkey assured. "These are their nesting grounds. One adult recklor watches the young ones. When they are about half grown, they'll leave and span out in *aqueducts* all over the planet. Some will even take to the surface and attack forest dwellers."

"So where is the parent?"

Sparkey stepped dangerously close to the edge and extended his arm out with the lantern in his hand. The light was directed at the pupil of the canyon. "Do you see that black thing that looks like a rock on top of the pillar?"

Scotty stepped closer, "Yes."

"Watch it closely."

Scotty extended his lantern as well, and in the combined light, he could see that the rock was moving. For it was no rock at all. It was heaving as if breathing heavily, and it was wrapped in a ball and furry. It was the mother recklor bat.

"We'll have to be careful," Sparkey warned. "The babies pose no threat, but the adults have fangs of poison and an appetite for flesh and blood."

"How will we get across?"

Sparkey pointed to a narrow path that began next to them and led around the southern rim of the canyon. "We have to follow that path around. According to the map, it is dangerous and narrow. We also need to be quiet. If we draw the attention of the recklor, we won't get out of here alive."

"To think I could have spent the day watching cartoons, but, oh, no! Here I am about to die! Well, I guess we all have to go sometime," Scotty laughed.

"Wait here," Sparkey commanded, and he retreated into the crystal chamber.

"Where are you going?"

"To get something!"

"What?" There was no reply.

After several minutes, the young bear returned and asked,

"You ready to go?"

"What were you doing?"

"Getting something that will help us."

"What?"

"I'll show you later. Now, let's get moving. Here take this." Sparkey withdrew another rope from his pack and handed one end to Scotty. He tied the other end to his waist and gestured for Scotty to do the same. "Now if one of us falls, the other can grab hold of something and save him."

"Or both of us can plummet to our deaths!"

"Are all humans so pessimistic?"

"I don't even know what that word means, but come on. Let's get moving." For the first time, Scotty led the way. The path was barely wider than their bodies. The two had to practically hug the wall to keep from falling. They inched along step by step. Once or twice, a few pebbles slipped from beneath them and fell into the eerie darkness below. They never heard them hit bottom.

"Ya know, I sure can't complain about being bored. This has probably been the most exciting day of my whole life!" Scotty whispered.

"You don't do things like this on Earth?" Sparkey asked.

"Heck, no! Most I could hope for is to see something like this on TV!"

"What's TV?"

"It's like a box with pictures, and it talks, kind of like Mr. TB. Lots of people watch it to entertain themselves."

"Oh, we don't have anything like that. It kind of sounds boring anyway. Why would you want to just watch a story, when there is so much outside you can do?"

Scotty shrugged. To be honest, he was guilty of watching a little bit too much TV himself. He had to admit, though, with places like Staranana to visit, he might just give up TV altogether.

"So what is Earth like anyway? The *Text of Iren* talks about it a little bit, but not much. And I only got to see a small ***portion*** of it."

"Earth, how can I describe it? Well, as far as looks go, it is one of the most beautiful places you'll ever see. Snow covered mountain peaks, fields of flowing grain, valleys of endless green grass, and crystal clear streams are about the best things, but there is so much more too. There are also thousands of cities. Some are all right, but the ones I've seen are all junky and dirty. Mostly people get along where I live, but there are also lots of wars and bad things."

"We bears don't have time to fight with each other. We have to stick together, or it would be much easier for Seth to defeat us. In fact, only one bear in our whole history ever went bad. His name was Kelcott, or as some call him, Killcott. He betrayed a group of bears that were attacking the Palace. In the end, Kelcott and all but two of the bears were killed. My dad actually rescued the two that survived. He was only fifteen at the time."

"I wish human people stuck together as well as Starananians do. Unfortunately…" Scotty began.

"EAKKK EAKKK REEEEEK!" The shriek tore through the night infested cavern like thunder. The two children turned their attention in the direction of the sound and the pupil of the eye. Sparkey extended his lantern over the edge. On the rock formation, two furry wings extend from a bulk of flesh. Just above that, only slightly visible in the lantern light, Sparkey thought he caught a glimpse of two fiery, red eyes.

"She's awake!" was all Sparkey had time to get out before the cavern ceiling erupted with the screeches and squeals of a million bloodthirsty bats. By dozens, then hundreds, they began to drop from their rocky perches. Soon, they had filled the cavern chamber with a swarm of thick fur and fangs. And their cries, their horrible, piercing cries, sent the young boys' hands shooting to their ears.

Scotty yelled over the *chaos*, "What do we do now?" The swarm had completely encircled them. They had only barely managed to maintain their footing on the ledge.

Sparkey called back, "Nothing! We should wait it out! I think it's feeding time!"

"One mother to feed millions of babies? How does that work?"

"She'll only feed a few hundred today. Those will be the strongest ones. The weak ones will die and the really ambitious ones will leave and find another giant recklor. The rest will wait," Sparkey replied.

By that time, the noise had died down considerably. Though the boys could not see it, more than three hundred bats had attached themselves to an equal number of nipples on the giant recklor. The rest were settling back to their places, save a few thousand that were darting down other passages and a few hundred who were descending into the black pit. No doubt, they were the ones that would soon die.

By the time all the bats had cleared, Scotty could feel his heart thumping like a hammer inside his chest. "I don't know about you, Sparkey, but I'm ready to get out of here."

"Agreed! We're not far now." Sparkey took the lead and continued along the path. "You know, we're lucky it was just feeding time. I've heard of recklors doing far worse. In fact…uh, uh, NO!" Sparkey bellowed in agony, but it was too late. The ledge he was standing on crumbled from beneath him, and he plummeted into the pit. Scotty scrambled to grab hold of something, but his attempt was in vain, and he was also consumed by the void. A moment later, there was nothing left of them but the echo of their last dying cries.

Chapter 17

More with Everybody Else

Spikey Moonbeam held his breath as the last slivers of the white sun sank beneath the horizon. His tiny cell had a single, circular window, which allowed him to see the sky and the sun. Using the sun, he had tracked the course of the day. If it was night that meant he only had a few hours left before they were going to execute him.

He slumped down onto the pile of wet and moldy straw they had given him to sleep on. Two days earlier, he had held his wife in his arms and kissed his boys. He took some comfort in the fact that they were safe. However, it was still painful to think that he would never see them again. Perhaps if the bomb had killed him, things would have been easier. He was totally focused then, but now, all he had were his thoughts - thoughts of wasted years with his family when he could have been happy. Even in the worst of times, if you have a family, you can still be happy.

He had **squandered** his own chance for happiness in the **relentless pursuit** of victory. A lot of good that had done him as his fellow rebels had opted to turn tail and run, completely **forsaking** the **prophecies**. If only he could somehow get back to his cave and use the *Door*. Then he could make a difference. Oh, well, no sense dreaming now. Death was all that awaited him - death and a broken promise.

~

On the *New Life*, Gloria held a tiny vial of the dark blue *ice blood* up against the light - another perfect dose. Aided by Jesse Nova, a bear in his mid-twenties that had helped out often at the rebel hospital, she had now completed over one hundred doses. That left only two hundred to go.

"How's it going?" asked a familiar voice. It was General Shortstop.

Gloria did not look at him but began to prepare another vial. She replied, "Not bad at all. By tomorrow, we should be ready to start injecting people."

"Good! That's very good news. One step closer to our new life."

"Ah, General, there is one more thing." She turned to him. "Yes?"

"When we get to Stararocka, um, I would like to request permission to take one of the maintenance pods back to Staranana." As the words came out of her mouth, she knew how crazy they sounded. A maintenance pod was a tiny craft that could fit no more than one person. They were used to repair hull damage outside the ship. Each was cramped, with no room for provisions, and they could not exceed a speed of one hundred kleps per hour. At that rate, it would take years to return to Staranana, and the pilot would starve and suffocate well before that.

Shortstop gave her a *'you have to be kidding'* look and said, "Gloria, we need you. You're the best doctor we have. You also seem to have inside information about our new home that will help us survive there. I can't let you go. Besides, you would never make it in a maintenance pod."

"I can't just leave my family!" she said, teeth clenched and a tear forming in her eye.

Shortstop stepped closer to her and whispered, "But you

would abandon your baby son to save them?" That seemed to get to her. He placed a gentle hand on her shoulder and said, "If you love Spikey, trust him, trust the **prophecies**, and pray that God will help him and Sparkey, because, right now, He is the only one who can."

In her heart, Gloria knew he was right. She nodded and turned back to her work. This was going to be a very long trip.

Chapter 18

Aqueducts:
Escape from Black Eye Canyon

Scotty felt the trickle of blood from his nose, but he couldn't see it. He couldn't see anything because he was surrounded by an **impenetrable** blackness. He dared not move. He had no idea where he was, but chances were he was only inches away from continuing his fall to certain death.

Despite the blackness, his ears still worked. The bats had settled down and were not making any noise, but something still caught his attention. A muffled whine, almost like...No, it couldn't be. Wait, wait, yes, it could! It sounded like a young boy crying, and Scotty knew exactly who the boy was.

"Sparkey, is that you?"

The sobbing stopped, and after a brief pause, a quivering voice replied, "Scotty, is...is that you?"

"Yes, Sparkey. Why are you crying?"

"I thought you were dead. I brought you all this way from your home, only to get you killed. I've been sitting here for almost half an hour."

"Yeah, I think I got knocked out by the fall. I just woke up. My nose is bleeding, but otherwise, I think I'm fine. Are you all right?"

"Just a few scrapes. I'm so glad you're alive, though."

"Where are we?"

"Far down into the canyon, I imagine. This ledge must have broken our fall. Do you still have your pack?"

Scotty felt around in the darkness. It was not long before his hands met with the fur of his wolf skin pack. "Yes, I have it," he replied.

"Good, I've got mine too, but I lost my lantern. Do you have yours?"

Scotty again searched the darkness with his hands, nothing. "No, it's gone, but here's my club."

"A lot of good those will do us! I have mine too, but without light, I don't see how we're going to get out of here."

It was a problem to be sure, and Scotty despaired momentarily, but then it struck him! "Hey, didn't you put extra candles in my pack, and matches too?"

"No."

"Oh, well, it must have been me then. I saw them sitting on a shelf in your cave. I didn't think it would hurt anything to take them. I hope you don't mind."

"Are you kidding? You're a lifesaver! Quick, light one up!"

Scotty complied, and after some fumbling in the dark, he had a single candle burning. There was not much light, but it was enough to see his friend. Sparkey was only a few feet away on an *adjacent* ledge. There was a small gap in-between their two ledges. He could easily jump it, but if he had tried to walk across it in the dark, he would have plummeted to his doom. Scotty's ledge extended out at least another ten feet. There was plenty of room to move around. However, Sparkey's ledge was very narrow. It ended only a few inches from where the young bear sat.

Sparkey stood and jumped across the gap to join his friend. Scotty lit a second candle and handed it to him. The pair stood there for a moment gazing into the void. "So, how do we get out of here?" Scotty asked.

"The only way," Sparkey said. "We climb!"

"You have to be kidding! I've never climbed a rock wall before!" Scotty protested.

"That fall must have given you amnesia. We climbed a rock wall when we first entered the *aqueducts*."

"Oh, I was hoping you had forgotten about that. Besides, that was nothing compared to this."

"We have no choice, Scotty!"

Scotty stared upward toward the invisible cavern ceiling and gulped, but Sparkey stepped immediately to the rock face. It took him a moment to find his footing, but, soon enough, he was slowly moving up the stone wall. Somehow, in the fall, the rope that had connected them had been lost. Now they couldn't depend on each other's strength to get them up the wall, which was perhaps for the best. If one fell, the other didn't have to join him.

Scotty sighed. This day was getting more interesting all the time. Taking hold of the rock, he followed his friend.

~

Two hours passed, and Scotty was quite proud of what they had accomplished in that time. A series of ledges along the way up had given the duo places to rest, and they were making excellent time. Scotty estimated the top of the canyon was only fifty more feet above them.

The human laughed, "Ya know, maybe when I get home, I'll have my mom sign me up for rock climbing class. This is kind of fun and a good workout too."

"If you want to go home, that is."

"What do you mean by that?"

"Well, the human who defeats Seth will be made emperor in his place. That could be you. You could be our new ruler!"

"Wait a minute, buddy! I promised to help rescue your dad, and if I can, stop this crazy Emperor of yours. But I'm just a kid. I can't rule! Besides, my parents would be worried sick. They might eventually think I died."

"I only know what the *Text* says. Maybe you can bring your parents here."

"Unlikely! Remember, I was the only human who could see you. I doubt they could even be **persuaded** to believe this place exists, let alone be brought here."

"Well, we can worry about that later. Right now, we have a wall to climb."

"Yeah, and…"

"EAAK AKK EAAK!"

"Oh, no! Not again!" Scotty shrieked.

The pair turned their heads, hands still gripped tightly to the rock wall. Two big, glowing, red eyes met theirs, along with a putrid smell that could only be recklor breath. A set of sharp fangs then materialized in the light of the candles they had secured at their sides.

"Great! Now *she's* hungry!" Sparkey screamed. He was right. The giant recklor flapped her massive wings only a few feet from the two boys, her fangs dripping saliva and her nostrils enticed with the smell of fresh meat.

Scotty released the wall with his right hand, holding all the tighter with his other three limbs, and removed his club. He swung it wildly in the air, hoping to hit the creature.

That seemed to **detour** her for a moment, but then Sparkey called out, "Wait! Let her catch you!"

Scotty kept swinging as he yelled back, "Are you crazy?"

"No! She won't kill us until she is ready to eat us. And she won't eat us until she is back on her perch!"

"Oh, that's encouraging! We still die if we let her get us!"

"No, I have an idea. She can get us to the other side of the canyon a lot faster. Scotty, you have to trust me. Get out the matches, and be ready to pass them to me once she grabs us in her claws, and whatever you do, keep your arms free; you'll need them."

Scotty **grimaced** and let his club drop. It clattered against a ledge, before disappearing into the void. With his free hand, he maneuvered his pack until he could reach inside and grab the matches. Seconds after he had them, the recklor took him in her claws. Sparkey soon followed.

Scotty stared into the ***foreboding*** black pit as the bat's wings beat heavily, carrying them back to her nest. His heart was pounding so hard, he was scared it would break through his chest. He was also having trouble breathing. It was all he could do to keep from blacking out.

Sparkey, however, still had his wits about him. "Give me the matches!"

"What?"

"The matches, now!" Sparkey exclaimed.

Scotty hesitated only a moment before passing the matches to his companion. Sparkey set to work instantly. He began by ripping the sleeves off his shirt. He then wrapped the cloth around the end of his club. With his pack still loose, he delicately maneuvered it to remove one of the extra candles Scotty had given him. He broke it and smeared chunks of wax over the cloth. He then removed a fish from his pack, ripped its belly open with his teeth and let its guts spill on the cloth. When this was done, he struck a match and lit the cloth. It burst into flames.

"Fish guts are the best source of fuel for fire here," he said. Then, with his free hand, he clutched the fur of the recklors belly and swung the fiery stick with all his might into the leg holding him. The recklor shrieked, and the sound nearly deafened Scotty. She also released her grip on Sparkey, who was now held up by only a few hairs he had managed to get a hold of. He swung until his feet latched into her underside. Then he placed the torch in his mouth, careful to keep the flame away from himself and the beast, and crawled up onto her back. When he was safe, he leaned over and gripped Scotty's arm. He then hit her other leg with the torch. When she released her grip, Sparkey pulled Scotty up onto her back.

Scotty was breathing easier and was in his right mind just a few minutes later, but the creature continued flying toward her home, unaware her food still rested on her back. Scotty asked, "So, what exactly did that accomplish?"

"Watch this," Sparkey said. He carefully crawled out onto the creature's head and extended his torch as far he could out the left side of her head. The bat huffed for a moment and then turned in the direction of the light. Sparkey moved to her right side and held the torch out again. She then moved in that direction.

"Recklors are attracted to light," he explained. "All we have to do is hold this in the direction we want to go, and she'll take us all the way there. She probably found us in the first place seeing the light from our candles."

Scotty smiled, but then asked, "So, how do we shake her, once we get off?"

"Simple, I'll just throw my torch into the canyon. Recklors are more enticed by light than they are by fresh meat. She'll leave us alone, and we will be at the entrance of the Palace."

Sparkey moved the light in the direction they wanted to go, and the recklor followed. Scotty snuggled down into her fur to rest for a little while. It would be good to get out of these stinking caves and out into the open air again. He just hoped what they had been through so far hadn't been the easy part of this adventure. If it had, they were in big trouble!

Chapter 19

The Goons

An hour passed before Sparkey and Scotty finally *ditched* their recklor escort. When they got close to the far ledge that led to the Palace, Sparkey flung the torch onto the ledge, and the creature landed as expected. He and Scotty then jumped off, and Sparkey kicked the torch back into the canyon. The recklor dove into the *abyss* after it, just like a moth to the flame.

Sparkey and Scotty walked into a small chamber of stone. Their path through the *aqueducts* ended there, and Scotty sank to the ground. First to his knees, and then he fell forward and lay on his belly, breathing heavily.

Sparkey knelt next to him. "You all right?"

"Yeah, this is just all so much. Talking bears, interplanetary *Doors,* evil emperors, ancient *prophecies*, wild gators, and giant bats - it's all just impossible!"

"Welcome to the world of the impossible, my friend! And might I say, you haven't seen anything yet."

Scotty sighed deeply and pushed himself to his knees. He felt his stomach rumble. Neither he nor Sparkey had eaten anything since early that morning. Now the day, and he imagined a good *portion* of the night was well spent. "Hey, I'm hungry!"

Sparkey's mouth split into a sharp-toothed grin, and he said, "Sorry, buddy, but the only thing still eatable after all we went through is the fish."

"Are you serious? Ugh, I hate fish!"

"You've never tried Starananian fish. You might like them."

"Don't bet on it!"

"Would you rather starve?"

Scotty scowled, and he reluctantly took a fish from Sparkey. He held it in front of himself, staring at it. For a dead, stinky fish, it was very pretty to look at. The scales were comprised of a rainbow of colors. The eyes were large and blue, and they had dotted black pupils. The fins were larger than any other river fish he had ever seen, and the mouth sported several rows of sharp teeth. Scotty asked, "Can we at least cook it?"

"No time. Eat up!" Sparkey directed. He was nearly finished with his own fish and had a second at the ready.

Scotty held his nose and moved the fish to his mouth. Reluctantly, he bit a piece out of the back and began to chew. It was, as he had expected, the vilest taste in the world, and he could feel the bile rising in his throat. So much for liking Starananian fish! He forced himself to take another bite and another. Eventually, he began to ignore the taste and became satisfied with the fact that his stomach was being filled. After what seemed like an eternity, he finally finished the fish.

"Want another?" Sparkey asked, flopping another fish in the human's face. He himself had already finished two fish.

"No, thanks," Scotty said, and he pushed the fish away. "So what's next?"

"We go inside and find my dad."

"And exactly how are we going to do that? We're at a dead end here."

"That's what you think. Look up there." Sparkey pointed to the stone ceiling. It was barely five feet high - perfect for two little kids. For the most part, the ceiling was smooth stone. However, near the center, four cracks formed a square barely two feet wide.

"That? What is it?" Scotty asked.

"That, my friend, is a trapdoor that leads into the cellar of the Palace. It is a secret that has been kept for thousands of years. Not even Emperor Seth knows about it."

"Cool, give me a leg up," Scotty said.

"A what?"

"You know, a boost. Lift me up, so I can open the door."

"Hey, buddy, as I recall, you are two years older than me. So it only stands to reason that you would be stronger and should lift me up first."

"Oh, well, is that a fact? It seems to me, you were the one who carried me on your back and swam me to shore in the lake back there. You also pulled me up onto the recklor's back. I think you're the stronger one. Besides, you see stuff like this all the time, and I don't. Let me go first."

"You honestly believe I have ever been in the Palace before?"

"Sparkey!"

"Oh, all right! Here, give me your leg."

The young bear *hoisted* the human boy until Scotty sat squarely on his shoulders. Then using both hands, expecting the stone to be heavy, Scotty pushed the trapdoor open. It was lighter than he expected. He opened it just high enough to see through and gazed about the cellar.

"What do you see?"

"Not much - stone floors and walls, piles of hay, and a rusted metal staircase in the center of the room leading to the ceiling."

"Nothing else?"

"No, I think it is safe; come on." Scotty began to push the door open wider, but then he stopped. Something above, somewhere, was making noise. It was the *distinct* noise of something very heavy being dragged over stone and then what was clearly the sound of footsteps on the staircase. This was *confirmed* when the rust-encrusted structure began to rattle. Scotty lowered the trapdoor, leaving it open barely a crack, and two tall figures came into view.

"What do you see?" Sparkey whispered.

"Let me down."

Sparkey complied, and he again asked, "What did you see?"

"I don't know what they were. They were tall, and they were wearing these long, stained brown robes, with lots of holes in them. They also had hoods on. I didn't see their faces."

Sparkey's heart jumped into his throat. "Praise God you didn't!"

"What do you mean?"

"They were goons! Seth has two armies at his command, the Dragon Guard and the goons. Legend has it that they were once one of the most handsome groups of people in the universe. In many ways, they looked like humans, though they have no ancestry or heritage on Earth. They were also very proud and arrogant. Seth found their home centuries ago when my **ancestor**, Splash, briefly overthrew his empire. Using the power of Satan, Seth **cursed** them to become so hideously ugly that anyone that looked at their faces would go insane and then transform into a goon. With his new army, he returned to Staranana. The goons killed thousands of bears, and tens of thousands more joined their ranks."

"Great! So, how exactly are we going to get past them?"

Sparkey seemed to mull that over, but then a light sparkled in his eyes. He began to dig through his pack. Continuing to dig, he said, "I knew this would come in handy!" He pulled a small, glass jar from his pack. In the jar was a small chunk of glowing crystal.

"Sparkey, are you crazy?" Scotty exclaimed, recognizing what Sparkey had. "How did you get that?"

"Remember when I turned back into the crystal chamber for a few minutes? Well, I broke this off with my club and scooped it into this jar."

"You're lucky you didn't get killed! What are we supposed to do with that?"

Sparkey only stared at him, and Scotty realized what he wanted him to do and was filled with horror. "Oh, no! I'm not going to kill anyone! I don't care how bad they are."

"Ah! It's my dad, not yours! I thought you were supposed to be this great *savior*, but I'm doing all the work. Why don't you just go home? I'll save my dad by myself!"

Scotty stared at Sparkey *dumbstruck*. It was the first time he had heard the cub lose his temper. He placed a hand gently on the bear's shoulder and said, "First off, there is only one *Savior*, and His name is Jesus Christ. Second, I'm not going to leave you, my friend, but we need to find another way."

Sparkey huffed, his flash of anger beginning to *subside* and a single tear moving down his furry face. "How?"

Scotty didn't know, but he wasn't about to give up. He stared at the crystal in the jar, and then it hit him. "Jesus Christ!"

"Scotty, watch your mouth!" Sparkey screeched.

"No, you don't understand. Jesus Christ - He's the answer. Look, didn't you say that the goons were made ugly by the power of Satan?"

"Yeah, so?"

"I remember this one story from *Vacation Bible School*. It was about when Satan tempted Jesus in the wilderness. When he was there, he quoted Scripture to try and *persuade* Jesus. Of course, Jesus slapped Scripture right back in his face, but what that tells me is that Satan knows the *Bible*."

"So?"

"So, if he knows the *Bible*, maybe he knows the *Text of Iren*, and I bet these guys do too. I wonder what they would do if a human suddenly popped into the room? It would probably scare the tar out of them."

"But they'd turn you insane in seconds!"

Scotty looked to the ground, and he located a small pile of stones. "How good a shot are you?"

"Pretty good I guess. I killed that oboca we ate for breakfast at fifty feet with a stone."

"Good, I saw a lantern in there with them. You throw a stone and take out the light. Then I pop up with this," he took hold of the crystal jar, "and say a few words to scare the heck out of them. While I have them distracted, you sneak around in the dark and peg those guys in the head and knock them out. Then we head up into the Palace."

"I like it."

"Good, but I have one question to ask first."

"What?"

"When we lost our lanterns back in the canyon, why the heck didn't you pull this thing out to give us some light?"

"Oops!"

~

"Cellar duty! What's the point? Nothing exciting happens down here," one of the goons complained.

"Quiet! I'm not gonna complain about getting a little shuteye," his companion said and leaned against a wall. "Besides, since those bears broke in here, and our chef disappeared, His Lordship wants the entire Palace searched for secret entrances."

"Ah, this is stupid! There are no secret entrances down here!"

The second goon was about to retort, but then a void of black consumed the room with the crash of glass against stone.

"What the..."

*"Be silent, ye who have been **cursed** by the enemy of the Most High!"*

"Who goes there?"

A shining maroon light hovered in the darkness, and it moved to reveal the *silhouette* of a human face.

"What are you?" one of them screeched.

*"I am **prophecy** fulfilled! I am the servant of the Most High God! I am the Blood of the Land!"*

"You can't be!"

"Seth's evil reign is over. I come with fire and death to return this world to the One True God."

"We'll see about that!" The two goons drew their swords and

began to move toward the glowing face. Had there been more light, they might have already removed their hoods to drive their victim mad. Unfortunately for them, they had barely walked two steps before, *thwack, thwack,* and they hit the ground.

Sparkey lit a candle and joined Scotty. "Great shot!" Scotty congratulated.

"Yeah, you were right. We didn't have to kill them."

"Let's hope we stay that fortunate."

Sparkey knelt down and picked up one the goons' swords. "Could we use these?" Despite the size of the goons, the swords were small and light, no more than oversized daggers to the monsters that wielded them. Perhaps they thought their most deadly weapons would be their faces.

"Yeah, we lost our clubs. We might as well replace them." Sparkey handed him a sword, and Scotty asked, "What now?"

"Up we go," Sparkey said, and he pointed to the stairs.

Scotty nodded and moved to the twisted metal staircase. He hesitated only a moment at the first step, staring upward. Then with his pack secure, sword at his side, candles in hand, and eyes flashing with determination, he mounted the stairs with his friend close behind. There was no doubt that many dangers still lie ahead. Neither one could say for certain what those dangers would be, or even if Sparkey's father was still alive. However, one thing was certain. They had finally arrived at Cosmic Bubble Palace!

Chapter 20

Back to the Kitchen

"Real food, oh, yes!" Scotty squealed. They had passed from the cellar, up the stairs, past a heavy-looking, ajar door that they would never have been able to open on their own, and they now stood in a tiny pantry just outside the kitchen. A bag of large, silver apples had caught Scotty's eye, and he wasted no time digging into it.

"Oh, wow, these are amazing! There is like honey mixed in with them, and they're so cold and crisp! Here you want one?" Scotty asked.

Sparkey shook his head. "They're honeysuckle apples. The apple cider you drank this morning was made from them."

Scotty nodded his head and sank his teeth in for another delicious bite. Sparkey growled at him, "Scotty, honestly, put that bag away! We don't want anyone to know we're here."

"Everyone will know we're here once those goons wake up."

"They may be out for hours. I gave them quite a smack. Either way, we have to go get my dad and get out of here as fast as we possibly can. We have to find a way to get to the tenth floor."

Scotty frowned and hefted the bag back up onto the shelf, but not before dropping a few more apples into his pack. He then tossed his apple core back down into the cellar and gestured that Sparkey should lead the way.

The large kitchen was vacant to their relief. A few copper pots still bubbled and simmered atop a long line of potbelly stoves, but there was not a person to be found. Everything was neat and clean. A large stack of glass plates, bowls, and cups rested at the end of a counter. It appeared that they had just been washed after a great feast, but no one had gotten around to putting them away. An old-fashioned mechanical clock, resting near a pile of folded aprons, indicated the time.

"Ten o'clock! Oh, my goodness, I had no idea we were down there that long. I hope my dad is even still alive." Sparkey rushed to the exit of the kitchen, which was nothing more than a heavy, purple curtain draped across a wooden doorframe. He peeked outside.

The room beyond the curtain was enormous. Marble floors extended hundreds and hundreds of feet in all directions. A jade fountain spouted streams of sparkling water, and several stone pillars, carved in the shapes of *phoenixes* and dragons, supported the stories above. There were also many tables set up. A grand banquet must have taken place. In the far corner, near the enormous outer doors, a pile of ashes sat on the floor. Sparkey could not tell exactly from his distance, but it also appeared that a long stream of blood extended from the ashes across the *threshold* of the outer doors.

"Oh, no!"

"What is it?" Scotty begged, tugging at the bear's shirt.

Sparkey only waved his hand away and kept watching. Several bears in *tattered* rags were cleaning up. They were *obviously* Palace slaves. The two goons that were supervising them held large, menacing energy rifles. One wrong move and those bears would be vaporized. It was a great *incentive* to work quickly and accurately. Thankfully, the goons' heads were hooded, and their *hideous* faces were covered with black cloth masks.

The two creatures spoke with each other, and Sparkey could

just barely hear them. "Well, I think that went well, don't you?" said the first.

"Yeah, the Emperor's birthday party is always fun. We all get bonuses. Did you know I got to turn three bears into goons? I love seeing them writhe in agony when they see my face. The sheer sense of panic on their faces when they realize they are being transformed is even better."

"No joking! I got a new energy rifle. Lizard Face let me use it on any bear that I wanted. I used it on an old slave woman. You should have heard her family scream when I killed her. It was great!"

"Ha...ha! And those public executions, what a treat! I can still hear the screaming of that first bear when they lit him on fire, but nothing compares to the wailing of his family when we cut their throats."

"Who were the victims, by the way?"

"Just some random family that was dragged off the streets."

"Nice!"

"Of course, the Emperor wasn't too happy about having to postpone his party until today. His birthday was yesterday, but after that bear raid and the power going out, he was lucky we could even do it today."

"Yeah, what happened to that bear they captured?'

"Lizard Face tortured him for information, but he never got anything. He is scheduled to be executed at dawn."

"Now that will be something to see!"

Sparkey had to hold back the hatred bubbling inside of him. *"Hee shea cek te mea!"* he **cursed** and then slapped a hand over his mouth. He was lucky his mother wasn't there.

"What does that mean?" Scotty whispered.

Sparkey pulled back inside the curtain and turned to Scotty. "Let's just say, they are the Staranian **equivalent** of some very dirty words. I'd get killed if my parents heard me. But I couldn't think of anything more **appropriate** for those murderers. Seth is the worst of them. He's gonna kill my dad at dawn. We have to find him and get out of here fast!"

"Okay, what do we do?"

Sparkey shook his head. "Well, we can't go out there. We'd be dead in a heartbeat. I guess we'll just have to wait until everyone leaves. I hope they don't take too long."

Scotty sighed and glanced around the room. His eyes landed on a pair of wicker, cupboard doors. "Maybe we don't have to wait!" he said and headed toward the doors.

"What?"

Scotty pulled open the doors to reveal a large compartment with a golden chain down the middle. "It's a ***dumbwaiter!***"

"A what?"

"I read about them in a book in school once. They're like little elevators rich people have in their kitchens that can take food to an upper floor. With Seth being an emperor and all, it figures he'd have a big one. Look, we can both fit inside, and then we pull this chain and ***hoist*** ourselves all the way to the tenth floor."

"What if we get tired?"

Scotty looked at the base of the ***dumbwaiter*** and fingered a small, metal latch. "Simple, we just flip this latch, and it locks in place wherever we are."

Sparkey smiled, "That's great! Come on!"

"After you, sir!" Scotty beckoned him with a wave of his hand, and Sparkey climbed inside. Scotty joined him, and they began pulling the chain together, moving upward to the tenth floor. This was too easy!

Chapter 21

Lizard Secrets

"I can't take it anymore!" Sparkey squealed. "We have to stop! You're too fat!"

"Fat! I'm the skinniest boy in my class. You're the one that needs to take off a few pounds, Tubby."

"Where are we?" Sparkey asked.

Scotty flipped the latch and looked out through the wicker doors of the *dumbwaiter* into the room beyond. "I'd say we're at about the sixth or seventh floor. We can wait here for a few minutes. There is no one in that room."

"Good! We're only three floors from finding my dad."

"Any ideas how we can bust him out once we find him?"

"None. Nobody knows much about the Palace. I'm not even exactly sure how we'll get out of here once we do find him."

"Well, God got us this far. He'll take us the rest of the way. Maybe we can…"

"Shh!" Sparkey hissed. "Someone is coming in!"

"Let's get out of here!" Scotty went to release the latch, but Sparkey grabbed his hand.

"No, it will make too much noise! Just wait; no one will see us."

Through the small holes in the wicker doors, the boys could see the chamber doors opening and two figures stepping into the room. One walked over to a lantern and lit it, revealing their features. The first was a goon. The other was medium height with a stubby snout and speckled green and white scales. A long strip of black scales ran down the creature's spine, but they were mostly covered by a black jumpsuit. Its scaly lips split into a grin, revealing a mouth filled with razor-sharp teeth. He was a lizard.

~

"Are you *ssure* everything is in place?" the reptile asked.

"Yes, sir. We are repairing the *Space Shark*. It was once one of our most destructive warships, and it will be again. We are equipping it with energy weapons, ion torpedoes, and plasma mines. It will also have engines faster than any other."

"Excellent! And the crew?"

"Comprised of goons *loyal* to you, sir. Their opinions of Seth are less than glowing."

"Very good. Nearly three-fourths of the goons are with us. We'll carry out the mission to find the rebel *sship* as planned. When we find the planet they're heading to, we'll lay down ground troops and *sstart* turning whatever **population** there is into goons. Then, we'll bring the rebels back here, but instead of delivering them to the Emperor, we'll crash their *sship* into the Palace. In the **chaos**, I'll order the rest of the goons to rise up, and then I will personally *sslit Sseth's* throat," Lizard Face hissed.

"Achoo!" The sound came from across the room.

"What was that?" the goon asked.

~

"Oh, great, now you did it!" Sparkey scolded.

"I think it's time that we got out of here!" Scotty started to release the latch, but it was too late.

"Well, what do we have here?" The **dumbwaiter** doors swung open, and Lizard Face **seized** both boys by their throats. He yanked them out and slammed them down onto the floor.

"A *Sstarananian* cub, and a..." The lizard felt his throat constrict. "What...what are you?" he asked, pointing at Scotty.

Scotty leaped to his feet, and with all the courage he could muster he shouted, "I'm the *Blood of the Land*, bucko! So I suggest you back off!" He drew his sword and helped Sparkey to his feet.

"You're a human!"

"That's right! My name is Scotty Fields! If you have a problem, lizard lips, I suggest you keep it to yourself, or we'll blab all over what you are planning to do."

"The name is *Lizard Face*, and don't threaten me!" He pointed at Sparkey, "Who are you?"

"Sparkey Moonbeam."

"Our prisoner's name is Moonbeam."

"He's my dad!"

"Yeah, and if you know what's good for you, you'll let him go!" Scotty bellowed.

Sparkey shook his head. Scotty was going way too far. It was Lizard Face who spoke, though, "*Sshut* up!" he hissed and then backhanded Scotty. The human boy fell, and his sword clattered away across the floor.

Lizard Face turned to the goon, "Take them and put them with the other bear. I'll go inform the Emperor." Then he looked at Scotty and chuckled, "If you're what God had in mind to defeat *Sseth*, then He's an even bigger idiot than the Emperor thinks."

"Watch your mouth! God will not be **mocked**!"

"I'm *sshaking* in my *sscales*!"

Sparkey felt the pain of a strong set of fingers digging into his shoulder as the goon took hold of him. After he had Scotty in his grip, he pulled them both from the room. This wasn't exactly what they had planned, but at least, Sparkey thought, at least he would be seeing his father again very soon.

Chapter 22

Reunion

"Hey, Fuzz Face, wake up! Ya got company!"

Spikey stirred at the sound of the raspy voice. "What? What are you talking about? What time is it?"

"11:15 p.m." came the reply. Spikey heard the grind of metal against metal as a key turned in the lock of the heavy, wooden door of his cell. The door creaked open, and three silhouettes stood in the shadows. One was clearly a goon, but the other two were much smaller.

The goon pushed one of them forward so hard he fell on his face. The figure, now distinctly a Starananian cub, began to **whimper**, and Spikey **cursed**, "What the..." But then **recognition** set in.

"Sparkey?"

"It's me, Dad."

"Sparkey, what are you doing here? You're supposed to be on your way to..." He caught himself. "Well, you're supposed to be gone."

"I had to save you, Dad! General Shortstop told Mama that you weren't killed. She wanted to come back, but they wouldn't let her, so I sneaked off the ship. And I brought help!"

"Help? Who?"

The goon pushed Scotty forward. He fell against the stone

floor so hard that he cut a gash in the side of his face. Spikey helped him up and stared at him in amazement as the door slammed shut and locked again.

"Who? What? How?" was all Spikey could manage.

"You forgot - when, where, and why," the boy said.

"Dad, allow me to introduce Scotty Fields, the *Blood of the Land*, I guess."

"The *Blood of the Land!*" Spikey squealed in delight.

"I went back to the cave and tried to use the *Door*. I met TB, and he sent me to Earth. I found Scotty and brought him back."

"He's really the *Blood of the Land?*"

"He meets all the **qualifications** I know. He's a servant of God, and he's helped me a lot."

Scotty spoke up, "I'm only sorry I got us caught by sneezing and acting dumb. We were coming to rescue you, sir. I guess that isn't going to happen now."

"First off, you can call me Spikey, Scotty, and I wouldn't be giving up so quickly. This **prophecy** hasn't played all the way out yet."

"What do you mean, Dad?"

Spikey quoted the *Text of Iren*, "*Stone and bar shall hold him not, nor prison be his home. By light he shall be brought to freedom and escape the enemy's every scheme.*"

"What does that mean?" Sparkey asked.

"I don't know exactly, but if Scotty is the *Blood of the Land*, this cell won't hold him for long."

Sparkey wrapped his arms around his dad and squeezed hard. "I'm glad we found you, Dad!"

Spikey returned his embrace. "Me too, son. Me too."

Chapter 23

The Humans

"What?"

"Yes, *Ssire!* He is a human boy, and he's no older than ten. He was with the *sson* of the prisoner."

"Where did he come from?"

"I do not know, Your Majesty. We have not yet had the chance to **interrogate** him. He claims to be the *Blood of the Land*."

"If that is true, he could only be from one place - Earth!"

"I thought that planet was a myth."

"Idiot! My father may have been a fool, but he wasn't a liar. His **prophecies** have proven true over the millennia; that means Earth is real. My throne is in **jeopardy**."

Lizard Face snickered under his breath, *"More than you know!"*

"What!"

"Nothing, Emperor *Sseth*. It's just, how can a *ssimple* boy defeat the most powerful man on the planet?"

"I don't know, but if a human is going to stop me, I can promise you, it won't be him. I plan to continue ruling this rotting carcass of a planet for a few thousand more years. I want to find out how he got here and destroy whatever gateway bridges our two worlds. Then I will make an example of him. Once he's dead, I'll have his body carted to every city on the planet. When they see their precious *Blood of the Land* slain, they'll abandon the **prophecies**. If no one believes the **prophecies**,

God has no reason to honor them."

"I'll begin interrogating him at once, *Ssire!*"

"No!"

"Your Majesty?"

"Bring him here. I'll do it myself!"

~

Spikey smiled and ripped a fish in half with his teeth. "I can't believe they let you keep your packs."

"They took our swords, though," Sparkey said.

"Even so, these fish are delicious! I haven't had a bite in almost two days."

"I'm glad you like them. Scotty hates fish."

"That's too bad!"

"Hey, but would you like an apple, Mr. Moon. . . I mean, Spikey?" asked Scotty, digging through his pack. "Hey, wait a minute!" he squealed and pulled from his pack the glass jar with the chunk of glowing crystal in it.

"What are you doing with that?" Spikey scolded. "You could have been killed!"

"It was Sparkey who got it!"

"Sparkey!"

The young cub seemed at a loss for words, but Scotty quickly interjected, "Never mind the *lecture*! Maybe this can help us."

"How?" the bears asked.

"Well, it glows! I mean it gives off light. Maybe this is what the *prophecy* meant about light leading me to freedom." He had no sooner said the words than the tiny glowing crystal began to flicker, then dim, and finally went dark. All that was left was a colorless chunk of stone.

"What the. . ." Scotty *cursed*. The gem was worthless now.

"Oh, I'm sorry, Scotty," Spikey said. "Those gems glow because they are connected to the thermal energy of the planet. They can only stay lit for a few hours after they have been broken free from the formation they grew from. Our light of freedom will just have to come from another source."

"But where?"

Spikey was thinking of an answer when a key began to turn in the lock. When the door opened, Lizard Face stepped into the cell, "Emperor *Sseth* wishes to *sspeak* with the human."

"Tough!" Scotty bellowed.

"It is not an option!" Lizard Face retorted, placing a hand on the **hilt** of a dagger at his side.

"Scotty, go!" Spikey urged, though it came off as more of a command.

"Adults, what do they know?" Scotty thought, but Sparkey made a motion that Scotty should **comply**, so he **surrendered**. He marched up to Lizard Face and said, "Well? I haven't got all night!"

Lizard Face led the way, and two goons fell into step behind Scotty. Once they were gone, another guard shut the door and locked it, leaving the two bears alone.

~

Despite the situation, Scotty could not help but be impressed with the Palace. The halls were filled with the most marvelous pieces of art. There were statues of bears, and dragons, and **phoenixes,** all carved from the purest marble. The door handles were all either gold or diamonds, and emeralds hung from chandeliers, casting a soft green light throughout the halls.

The most remarkable things were the elevators, if they could be called that. Though they had clearly passed what had to be typical elevators, with typical elevator cars, the device that brought them to the 99th story, and the Emperor's chambers, required a different name. It was a long, glass tube extending all the way from the first floor to the 100th floor. There was neither a car, nor were there any visible mechanics, just an empty, glass tube. When Lizard Face pushed him toward it, Scotty tried to dig his feet into the carpet. Were they going to execute him? His question and his resistance did not last long because Lizard Face grabbed him by the arms and walked into the tube with him.

What followed was not a ten-story drop to death. Rather, the instant they stepped into the tube, an invisible energy field formed beneath their feet and shot them skyward. Scotty was no great fan of roller coasters, and speeding past dozens of stories in seconds, this tube could have put the best of them to shame. Somehow, though, they were able to remain standing, and Scotty didn't get that queasy feeling in his stomach. It seemed no sooner had they stepped inside the tube than they arrived at the 99th story.

Lizard Face pushed Scotty out of the tube. "We're here," he said and stepped toward the large pair of double doors just outside the tube. Scotty shuddered, and he felt his stomach churn as he looked at them. Two wooden statues with huge wings stood along the sides of the passage as if guarding Seth's chamber. They had the bodies of men, with thickly muscled torsos, arms, and chests. It would have been easy to believe that the statues were angels if you didn't bother to look at their faces. Once you did, there was no doubting they were demons straight from Hell.

One had the face of a pig, with a knife protruding from its left eye. The mouth of the wooden pig was drooling a red liquid into a drain on the floor. Scotty hoped it wasn't real blood. The second *angel* had the head of a snake with pearly-white fangs stained red at the tips, and it was also dripping the red liquid.

The doors themselves were wooden and heavy. Jewels of every type and color were embedded throughout the wood, and the door handles were made of gold. At the center, where the two doors came together, from the top to the bottom, was carved a huge number six.

Lizard Face pulled the doors open and announced, "Your Royal Majesty, may I present *Sscotty* Fields of the planet Earth, *sservant* of the Living God."

Scotty stepped into the enormous room, and the doors snapped shut behind him. Lizard Face was gone, and with the doors closed, the only light in the room came from the fire of a huge hearth carved out of marble into more demonic designs. Scotty could just barely make out a large, overstuffed bed on the other side of the room, a good hundred feet away. In front of him, at the far end of the room was a bay window that extended the entire length of the outer wall. Outside, fires billowed in the distance, *obviously* destroying hundreds of trees and hundreds of lives.

"Have a seat, please," came a soft voice.

Scotty turned his attention back to the fire, near which sat two large, leather chairs. A man sat in one of them. Scotty approached until he could clearly see the man's features. He was young. He looked no older than 20, but his eyes betrayed the coldness of thousands of years of hate. He was clean-shaven. In fact, the skin on his face was so smooth that it looked like not so much as a single whisker had ever grown there. The rest of his skin was as equally baby smooth with not a spot or *blemish*. At least, none that Scotty could see, as the Emperor was fully clothed in a long, purple silk robe. His hair was sandy blond, and there was a featureless, golden crown resting on his head.

"I am Emperor Seth. Please sit down."

Scotty sat as Seth continued, "I'd like to welcome you to my world."

The firelight glistened in his eyes as Scotty *mocked*, "Lovely."

"I take it you have never been off your home world before?"

"No."

"Pity, space travel is delightful."

"At least for those who aren't oppressed!" Scotty scowled.

Seth stood and stepped to a small table next to the fire. It had a pitcher of a purple fluid on it. Next to the pitcher were two glasses. Seth poured the liquid into the glasses and offered one to Scotty. Scotty shook his head. He didn't believe Seth would poison him, at least not yet. But there was no way that he was going to accept the hospitality of a murderer.

"Suit yourself," Seth said. "This is a **delicacy** here. It is called plume-berry juice. It is extremely rare and quite delicious. You should not **deny** yourself the pleasure."

Scotty remained silent, and Seth continued, "I don't know what you've heard, but I am really not such a bad guy."

Scotty gazed past him to the fire and destruction beyond the windows. "Yes, I can see that!"

Suddenly, Seth pounced on him, and the human boy jumped in his seat. The Emperor wrapped his hands around the arms of Scotty's chair and moved his face inches from the boy's. "All right, enough pretense! Who are you, and how did you get here?"

"You know who I am! As for how I got here, I'll never tell!"

"You can't possibly expect me to believe you are the *Blood of the Land*, a foolish child!"

"Maybe I'm not, but one thing I am is a servant of God. Any enemy of His is an enemy of mine!"

"God is an idiot! You are a fool to follow Him!"

"BEFORE THE MORNING DAWNS, YOU'LL KNOW HOW WRONG YOU ARE!" The words were out of Scotty's mouth before he knew he had said them. Where had they come from? He definitely hadn't thought them. Oh, well, too late to take them back now.

"What do you mean by that?"

"I don't know! But, well, uh, you'd better listen!"

"You listen to me!" Seth screamed and spat into Scotty's face. "I am not going to have my empire overthrown by a child!"

"YOUR EMPIRE SHALL BE PLUCKED FROM YOU BY THE MOST HIGH GOD, AND YOU SHALL BE LAID LOW!" There it was again! It was as if his mouth was speaking without him telling it to. Oh, well, as long it got Seth's goat.

Seth pushed himself away from Scotty's chair and went to a large chest of drawers near the hearth. He removed a tarnished dagger with a jagged blade. He returned and pressed it against Scotty's throat just enough to draw blood. "Do you want to know what I am going to do to you?" he asked.

Scotty shook his head **cautiously**.

"I am going to take you outside the Palace tomorrow morning after you watch your friends die. I will call all the slaves to me and show them that I have another human with me. They will think their deliverance is at hand, and then, in front of their eyes, I will cut your throat with this dagger. You know, I used this dagger to kill my own father 5,000 years ago. I never even cleaned his blood off, and soon yours will wet the blade. Then, after you are dead, I will cart your body across the entire planet, showing each and every bear that their precious *Blood of the Land* was no match for the Great Seth. They will abandon the *Text of Iren* and God, and this world will be mine forever."

Seth stepped away, and Scotty said, this time clearly under his own power, "Some of the greatest men in history have been destroyed because they dared to oppose God. I don't know what God has planned for this world, but on Earth, you don't mess with His plans. If He wants it to happen, it will happen."

Seth had turned his back on Scotty, but now he spun around, his eyes flaring. He raised the dagger over his head as if he planned to thrust it into the boy, but at the last second, he seemed to change his mind. He put the dagger back in the chest of drawers.

"God abandoned me when I needed Him the most. I was His greatest saint, until the snake!"

Sparkey had told Scotty the story of how the once godly Seth had been tortured by a snake in a dream until he agreed to serve Satan. The result was Seth falling into the evil life he now led.

Scotty sneered, "How ironic! You weren't the first human to be seduced by that particular snake, and I doubt you'll be the last. In any case, I doubt you were totally on the up and up with God. The whole holier-than-thou thing was probably just for show. No true servant of God could come to this. Besides, the *Bible* says all of our righteous acts are as filthy rags before God. It is only through the saving blood of Christ that we *obtain* any favor before Him."

Seth was beyond outrage. He wanted to kill, but somehow, all he managed to do was scream, "Lizard Face!"

When the lizard entered, Seth commanded, "Take the boy back to his cell. They all die at dawn!" Lizard Face led Scotty out, but as they left, Scotty caught a glimpse of Seth picking up the pitcher of plume-berry juice and smashing it against the floor. The *Blood of the Land* and his Lord would not be so easily defeated.

Chapter 24

The Light

By the time Scotty returned to the cell, it was past 1:00 a.m. Never in all his days had he stayed up so late before, but he had a feeling he would be up even later still. He told the two bears what had happened, and they took it as well as could be expected. They were astonished to hear that someone, or something, had been speaking through Scotty and that whatever it was had made Seth extremely angry. Spikey seemed confident in the *prophecies*. He and his son curled up next to each other and were quickly asleep, *obviously* exhausted. Scotty, however, found a pile of hay and stretched out, thinking.

Only the night before, he had been playing battle for the empire with Bobby. Who would have known that just over twenty-four hours later, he would be battling to save a real empire? He just wasn't too sure he could save this one. Spikey seemed to think so, though. That bear had some incredible faith. It was unlike the faith of anyone he had ever known.

"Do not underestimate your own faith, young one."

Scotty sat up with a start. He had not been speaking. He had only been thinking. But the voice, whoever's it was, clearly knew what he was thinking. He looked around his dingy and smelly cell. Spikey and Sparkey were sleeping soundly; much more soundly than they should have been, given the *circumstances*. Scotty could not figure out where the voice had come from, and he was beginning to believe he had just imagined it.

As he lay back down, his eyes fell on the tiny window. A chill breeze was blowing through it. He was glad he still had his thermal suit on. Though, he had to admit, this cell was much warmer than the Moonbeam cave.

Outside the window, three stars twinkled. One of them was unusually bright. Scotty found himself staring at that star. It somehow caused him to feel at peace. It hung there, bright and beautiful, but then it moved ever so slightly.

"No!" Scotty couldn't believe it, but then it moved again. At first, he thought he had merely mistaken some form of aircraft for a star, but then it did something quite odd. It moved straight up from its previous position leaving a band of burning red light behind it. Then the star broke free from the band, moved out a little ways, and passed over the first band with a second shorter band, also burning red. It was unmistakably a cross.

With the flaming cross still burning in the sky, the star began to move again. This time, it was moving directly toward the window, growing bigger and brighter as it drew closer and closer. The nearer it got the greater the overwhelming sense of peace became. Of course, at the same time, there was a deep sense of dread growing in Scotty. This was no aircraft! Within moments, the star, now blindingly bright, passed through the window.

"Fear not, young one!"

Scotty stared **dumbstruck** at what was before him. It was a man in a long, flowing, white robe. About his chest was a golden band. The hair on his head was red, and he had a neatly trimmed, red beard. His skin was flawless, and his mouth broke into a broad grin, revealing two rows of pearly white teeth. All about him was the piercing, peaceful, and yet dreadful light.

"Who…what are you?" Scotty managed to mutter.

The figure knelt next to him. *"You know what I am, young servant of the Most High God. As for who I am, my name is Joshua. I am a servant of the Lord Jesus Christ and the Father God, companion to the Archangel Gabriel, witness* to the fall of Lucifer, and the guardian angel of all Staranana."

"You're an angel?"

"Yes."

Scotty felt the dread ebbing, but only slightly. "What are you doing here?" he asked.

The angel quoted, *"Stone and bar shall hold him not, nor prison be his home. By light he shall be brought to freedom and escape the enemy's every scheme."*

"You're the light?"

"Yes."

"So, have you come to free us?" Scotty asked eagerly.

Joshua looked at the two bears, still sound asleep, and his smile faded, a tear forming in his eye. *"Not yet,"* he said, turning back to Scotty. *"But before the light of dawn, the Lord's words will come to pass."*

"What do you mean?"

"Did not the Lord say that by dawn Seth would know how wrong he was?"

"So, it was God talking through me! I couldn't figure out why my mouth kept talking when I wasn't controlling it."

"The Lord your God has spoken."

"So, if you're not going to free us now, why have you come?" Scotty asked.

"To give you a lesson."

"A lesson?"

"That's right!" Joshua stood again, and the brightness of his *countenance* increased tenfold. When he spoke, it was with a volume so incredible, Scotty was surprised the bears still did not wake up.

"Hear the words of the Most High God, young one. There is one God and one Mediator between God and men, the Man Christ Jesus. His Gospel is the power of God unto salvation as written in the pages of the Bible. Any who proclaims another god or any other way is already

appointed his place with the devil and his angels in Hell."

"I have done neither of these things!" Scotty protested, growing more **petrified** every instant.

Joshua's tone eased, *"Fear not, young one. I do not come with accusing lips, only with a message. In ages past, God spoke through Emperor Iren, and He instructed him to write down certain messages to the people of this world. Iren honored God, but when he killed his son instead of trusting in God, God decided that he must be punished. For the eighteen years Seth was growing up, God described to Iren what He wanted to be written in his text. He also described the dream Seth would have. Only, He did not say it would be Seth. He only said that Iren would be able to know the one who would kill him, because that one would describe such a dream to him. Iren was horrified when he learned it was his own son."*

"What does all this have to do with me?" Scotty asked.

"God promised the bears that one day He would free them from Seth."

"By the *Blood of the Land*, right?"

"Yes."

"Am I the *Blood of the Land*?" Scotty asked **tentatively**.

"Yes, and no."

"What do you mean?"

"Listen, and by that gain wisdom and understanding. The Text of Iren says of the Blood of the Land in one place, 'They blot out the blemishes and bathe in the blood of the Lamb,' *and in another place, it says,* 'He shall **wield** the Dagger of Promise, and by it, lay the emperor low.' *The Blood of the Land is both a they and a he."*

"What does that mean?"

"Young one, this world belongs to God, as do all the worlds, but Christ died only for the children of men. He did not die for bears, nor did he even die for angels. Even so, '...the creation itself will be liberated from its bondage to decay and brought

into the freedom and glory of the children of God.' **Staranana and the whole universe are part of that creation, and so this world and all the servants of whom they call the Hidden King will be liberated. The** *they* **the** Text *of Iren* **refers to is all Christians everywhere who serve Christ with all their hearts. Any of them could have become the** Blood *of the* Land **and freed these people from Seth were they here. But the** *he* **is God's chosen one,** *you.* **But He did not send you here because you are greater than the others, but because you are the least of them. Many proud men have tried to claim a piece of the divine, claiming to know the thoughts of God, only to do wickedness. When they died, they found themselves bound to Hell for all eternity. My message to you, young one, is to not be as they were. You are the Lord's servant, and when you die, you will be with Him for eternity, but even Christians can fall victim to their on pride. If you do, God will rip this world from your hands."**

"Then I am to rule?"

"That is not for me to say, but you will have access to this place until the appointed time."

"And when is that?"

The angel did not reply, and Scotty asked, "Can I be permitted to ask one more question?"

Joshua nodded and Scotty asked, "What exactly is this place? I mean, I'm not just dreaming am I?"

"This place," Joshua began, **"is a whisper, a hope, a promise. God created this world to honor the imaginations of men. Men lost such pure imagination when they fell into sin, and this place has suffered for it. But in the great and terrible Day of the Lord, for those who have done well, such pure imagination will be restored to them. As for if it is real, to you, it will be very real. For God did not send you here because of what you could do for them, but what they could do for you. Your greatest adventures are still ahead with the people of Earth, and that will always be your home."**

Scotty was about to say something more, but Joshua's light was beginning to *diminish*, and his body was becoming transparent. As he faded, he said, *"When fang and scale make clear your way, go to the end of this hall and cross over the way to the barrier. At the edge, you will find all you need to escape. Go quickly, young one."*

With those words, he was gone.

Chapter 25

Escape from
Cosmic Bubble Palace

"Sparkey! Spikey! Wake up now!" Scotty screamed, shaking his two fellow *inmates*.

Spikey rubbed the sleep from his eyes and asked, "What is it?"

Scotty moved a finger to his lips, now regretting having screamed, and tiptoed over to the door. Through the door, he heard the sound of heavy snoring - a sound he *loathed* because he had spent many a sleepless night listening to Noah snore. It did tell him one thing, though. The guard was asleep. Yes!

Scotty whispered, "Guys, I don't know if you're gonna believe me, but I just got visited by an angel. He said his name was Joshua. He also said he was the light that would free us."

Spikey's eyes twinkled with the recollection of a fifteen-year-old memory and his own encounter with the angel Joshua just before the betrayal of Kelcott. He began to grin, but then he remembered that he had been sworn to secrecy about that visitation. He collected himself and asked, "Why wouldn't we believe that?"

"Well, not many humans would."

"Listen, Scotty, the *Text of Iren* says that when the *Blood of the Land* comes angels will dwell with us again for a short time. In the days of Iren, before he killed his firstborn son, angels were as common as bears along our streets. I do have one question, though," Spikey said.

"What?"

"If he came to free us, what are we still doing in here?"

"He said that tonight's visit was just to teach me a few things, but we are supposed to be delivered just before the sun rises."

"How?" Sparkey asked.

"He said something about going to the end of the hall and crossing over to the barrier. He said that the one with fangs and scales would make our way clear and that we would find everything we needed at the barrier."

"What barrier? What scales? What fangs? What does it all mean, Dad?" Sparkey asked.

Spikey didn't hesitate for a moment, "It's **obvious**. The outer wall that surrounds the Palace courtyard is ten stories high. There must be some sort of bridge that leads from this floor to the top of the wall. Joshua must want us to use that to escape. Pity we didn't know about it before. It would have made breaking in here much easier. As for the fangs and scales, I can think of only one person that could be."

"Lizard Face?" Scotty questioned.

"Lizard Face!" Spikey returned. Then he said, "It has to be pushing 3:00 a.m., and dawn is just after 6:30. We're going to need all the rest we can get. Come on, let's get back to sleep. I'll wake you both up before there is even a hint of the sun in the sky."

Scotty curled up next to the two bears, sharing in their warmth, but he wasn't sure he would sleep. This had been one wild day. He laid his head down, content to spend the next few hours thinking and praying. However, his head had no sooner touched down on his pillow of hay than he was out like a light.

~

"Boys...Boys, wake up, come on," Spikey urged.

"No, Mom! It's too early. Come back later," Scotty

mumbled.

"I am not your mom!" a deep voice growled.

Scotty bolted up. He was still in the prison cell. He couldn't have gotten more than three hours of sleep, but he felt completely rested. Sparkey was just stirring. Outside, the sky was still pitch black, and Scotty asked, "Spikey, how do you know it is time to get up?"

"Look at the sky," he said. Scotty did. It was pitch black, but just barely visible through the tiny window was a band of deep purple just along the horizon. Spikey continued, "This is the time of the morning I go fishing every day. I know the look of the sky well. Dawn is about twenty minutes away."

"But what woke you?"

"Listen," he said. Outside, some sort of bird made a shrill cry. It was almost painful to the ears, but then the cry broke into the most beautiful song.

"What is it?" Scotty asked.

"We call them snow *phoenixes*. They sing only for the dawn. In fact, no one has actually ever seen one, but no other bird on Staranana makes such a cry. Legend has it that if you catch one, it will take you to a secret city that is safe from Seth's evil. Of course, it's just a legend. We don't even know what the snow *phoenixes* look like, but I have trained myself to wake to their song every morning."

By that time, Sparkey was fully awake. They passed apples all the way around, and Spikey and Sparkey shared a fish, the last one. When they finished, they all sat silent for a moment until Scotty said, "You know, today is Sunday, which means I would usually be going to church. Guess that won't happen today."

"Well, is there any law against having church in a stinking dungeon?" Spikey asked.

"Church is anywhere believers are, so I guess not."

"Well, go on then."

"Me?"

"Why not? Tell us something from the *Bible*, and then we'll pray."

Scotty thought about it for a moment and then said, "In Sunday school, we get to memorize verses. My favorite one is *Joshua 1:9*. In the passage, the Israelites were just about to enter the *Promised Land.* There were many dangers ahead, but God gave them these words of encouragement, *'Have I not commanded you? Be strong and courageous. Do not be terrified; do not be discouraged, for the Lord your God will be with you wherever you go.'* This promise was originally given to the Israelites, but I have to believe it holds true today. If we trust in God, He will see us through."

Scotty held out his hands, and the two bears clasped them, also taking each other's hands. They then bowed their heads in prayer. Scotty prayed, "Dear God, we're in a bit of a bind here. But You promised to **deliver** us, and I thank you for that. Thank You also for my new friends, and may I help them with whatever strength You give me. You alone will save them. Please give us power over the evil one, and may Seth be defeated swiftly. We thank You in Jesus's name, amen."

~

It was fifteen minutes until dawn, and Lizard Face stood in Seth's chambers. Seth sat upright in his bed, bare-chested and hair **tousled.** As he pulled on his silk robe, he stood before Lizard Face.

The lizard said, "It is nearly dawn, Majesty. I assumed you would want to *ssee* it."

"Oh, yes!" Seth smiled. "I want the little bear to go first. We'll do it in my throne room. We'll torture him in front of his father and the boy. The more they beg for **mercy**, the more we'll make the cub suffer. In the end, we'll shoot him to put him out of our misery.

"Then I want a doctor present for the older one's execution. We'll pump him full of neural stimulants so he can endure extreme levels of pain without passing out. Then we'll have a field day! No form of torture is restricted. Get creative. **Mutilate** him. But don't kill him until the precise moment I say. Just before that moment, I'll bring a goon in and expose his face. As the bear is writhing in agony, just before he turns into a goon himself, we'll slit his throat. We'll add both their hides to the carpeting on the sixteenth floor. I'll kill the human boy later this morning in front of all the slaves."

"That is *sso* cruel, Majesty! I love it!" Lizard Face hissed. "After the executions, I must be on my way to the White Desert to take command of the *Sspace Sshark*."

Lizard Face turned to leave, but Seth halted him, "Not so fast."

"*Ssire?*"

"Lizard Face, you are my most dependable servant, my most capable captain, and second only to me in this empire," Seth said.

"By your grace alone, Majesty."

"Yes, well, I have heard some disturbing things of late, rumors of an uprising among my own people."

Lizard Face felt a lump jump into his throat, but he recovered quickly, "Rumors are not to be trusted, Majesty. I am *ssure* everything will be all right."

Seth eyed him suspiciously and said, "You may be right. Nevertheless, I would like you to remain around the Palace. Put one of your top goons in command of the *Space Shark*. I would feel so much better knowing you were here to protect me."

Lizard Face knew the only reason Seth wanted him around was to keep an eye on him. Someone must have tipped Seth off to his plans. In any case, he had to maintain appearances for now. He bowed slightly at the waist and said, "As you wish, Majesty. The prisoners will be waiting in your throne room within minutes."

~

Ten minutes before dawn, Spikey, Sparkey, and Scotty sat waiting in their cell. The prayers had ended, their bellies were full, and now, all that was left was to wait. Seconds later, the waiting was over. A key turned in the lock of the door, and with a horrid creak, it swung open.

Lizard Face stepped into the room. Two goons stood behind him in the shadows, swords drawn. The lizard said, "It's time to…" But a third goon, racing toward him, cut him off.

"Lizard Face! Lizard Face!" the goon screamed.

"What is it?" he hissed.

The goon approached, panting, and replied, "Sir, there is an angel in the courtyard!"

"A what?"

"It's true! He's bright as the sun, maybe brighter. He has a red beard and hair and white clothes. He is ripping down the outer gates, and the slaves are storming in!"

Lizard Face commanded all the goons in the area, "All of you, let's go! We'll have to deal with these three later." One of them pushed the door shut, and they all headed away. Lizard Face paused behind them, thinking he had forgotten something. He couldn't remember what, so he hurried after them.

"What luck!" Sparkey squealed.

"Luck had nothing to do with it," Scotty said. "That goon described Joshua perfectly."

"So what! We're still trapped in here!" Spikey said.

Scotty wasn't so sure. He walked over to the door and put his fingers along the edge. It took a few seconds to get a good grip, but then he did. He pulled as hard as he could, and the door opened.

Spikey laughed, "They forgot to lock the door. Oh, my goodness, this is great!"

"No time for that now, Dad. We have to go!"

"You're right, son. Come on boys, let's get out of here!" Spikey commanded, and he led the way out into the hall.

The run to the bridge that led to the wall was not long, and thankfully none of Seth's *minions* were present. Just as Joshua had promised, they found everything they needed at the top of the wall. It was mostly climbing equipment that would allow them to rappel down the wall and run back into the forest. However, there was also one unusual device, at least to Sparkey and Scotty it was unusual. To Spikey, on the other hand, the device was quite familiar.

He held the egg-shaped object in his hands and exclaimed, "The bomb! This is great! Your angel friend gave us back our bomb."

"Good, we may need it!" Sparkey said.

Spikey put the egg-bomb in Sparkey's pack and the vial to activate it in Scotty's. He wanted to keep them separate, just in case. He then set up the climbing equipment, and moments later, they were rappelling down the Palace wall. Within no more than twenty minutes time, they would be back inside the Nana Forest, and hopefully, somewhat safe.

~

Two minutes before dawn, Lizard Face met Seth in the throne room. "What!" Seth screamed.

"I'm *ssorry*; it is true, Majesty! There was no angel. The goon had only dreamed it, but he *ssaid* it *sseemed* absolutely real. I have already had him killed."

"And what about the prisoners?"

"Escaped, I'm afraid. In all the **chaos**, one of the guards forgot to lock their cell. I had all the guards who were with me killed as well, *Ssire!*"

Seth looked down on the lizard, hatred and fire burning in his eyes. "I should have you killed too, but for now, just get out!" Lizard Face hesitated, and Seth screamed, "GET OUT!"

As the reptile retreated, Seth went over to the bay window and leaned against the glass, his head hung low. On the horizon, a tiny strip of light crept into view. He lifted his head and met the golden band with his fiery gaze. In his mind, he heard the words, **"BEFORE THE MORNING DAWNS, YOU'LL KNOW HOW WRONG YOU ARE!"**

Chapter 26

Return to the Moonbeam Cave

"We have to hurry!" Spikey urged as he raced into his family cave, two exhausted boys right behind him. The climb down the Palace wall had been fast. Faster than proper safety *precautions* would have allowed. Once their feet had touched the snow, it had been a dead sprint into the forest. Four hours later, they returned to the Moonbeam cave.

"What's the rush?" Scotty asked, panting.

"Do you honestly think Seth is just going to let his archenemy go? These woods will soon be crawling with goons."

"Where can we go?" Sparkey asked.

"Only one place," Spikey said. He walked over to the rotting trunk near his workbench. He lifted the lid and then turned back to Scotty.

"That thermal suit looks good on you, by the way," he smiled.

Scotty blushed and nodded, and Spikey pulled out the thick, dusty, dog-eared book Sparkey had found before. Spikey blew away the dust and opened it to a particular page. He said, "We have to go to Stony City."

"Stony City!" Sparkey shrieked. "It was destroyed over 500 years ago."

"I know! I know! Seth turned the city and everyone in it to stone, and it sank beneath the ice, but we have to go there."

"How can you read that, Dad?" Sparkey asked. "It isn't even in our language."

Spikey huffed and hesitated. Sparkey was waiting for an answer, but Scotty could tell there was more to that old book than Spikey was ready to share. He interjected, "Why do we have to go to Stony City?"

"Because the *Text of Iren* says that when the *Blood of the Land* defeats Seth, he will use the *Dagger of Promise*. Our **ancestor**, Splash Moonbeam, was the last one known to have the dagger. He tried to use it to defeat Seth when the Emperor returned from the Nimbus solar system. Unfortunately, the dagger wouldn't work for a bear, and his city was destroyed because of it."

"But if the city sank beneath the ice, how are we going to find it?" Sparkey asked.

"I know the general area it's in. Once we get there, we'll have to get below the surface. Some of the buildings should still be **intact**, so we can enter the city through one of their roofs. Then, assuming the city isn't a solid block of ice, we'll search for the dagger."

"What are the chances of that?" Scotty asked.

Sparkey answered, "Pretty good. Remember how warm the **aqueducts** were?"

"Yeah."

"Most of the underground is like that. Only the surface is frozen. Plants that grow in the wild have very strong, very deep roots that go into the warm soil to bring them **nutrients**. The city may have been a solid block of ice at one point, but by now it is entirely possible that the thermal energy of the planet has melted most of the ice."

"Well, with all that settled, let's start packing," Spikey said.

"Wait!" Scotty hesitated.

"What is it?" Sparkey asked.

"Well, I don't think I can go."

"What? Why not?" Spikey demanded.

"I've already been gone for almost two days. My parents are going to be worried sick, and I don't even want to think about how much trouble I'll be in."

"Do not worry about that, Mr. Fields," said a high-pitched voice. It was TB. No one had remembered him when they reentered the cave, but he had overheard their conversation.

"TB, my friend!" Spikey exclaimed. "I'm glad to see the *Door* worked so well."

"I'm glad to see the mission was successful, and I am very pleased that you are still alive, Spikey."

"It took an act of God to get me out of there, but here I am."

TB turned his attention back to Scotty, *"As I was saying, you don't need to worry about your parents. After you left, I took the liberty of opening a small Door back to your world. It was just like the one I used to communicate with you and Sparkey, just before bringing you here. Anyway, I managed to tap into a power line. My power was almost at zero, but I was able to draw enough from the power line through the Door to recharge my entire system. After that, I tapped into a phone line. I learned your phone number and the phone number of your friend. I also opened small doors into your home and the home of your friend and took recordings of your mother's voice and the voice of your friend's mother. I then called your mother using Mrs. Thompson's voice. I asked if you could stay another night. Your mother said yes. Then I called Mrs. Thompson using your mother's voice and said that I wanted you to meet me at a local restaurant and that you should walk there. Mrs. Thompson said she had to run an errand, so she just called out to you through the bedroom door. I used your voice and said okay, and she left. All that should have bought you at least one more day."*

"I had no idea you could do all that!" Scotty exclaimed.

Spikey beamed with pride, but TB said, *"Well, I am technology beyond anything any of you have ever imagined."*

"Don't bet on it!" Spikey growled.

"Sorry, Spikey," TB apologized.

"Anyway, I don't like deceiving my parents like that, and I can't stay away forever."

"Maybe you won't have to," Spikey said and walked over to

his workbench. Beneath it sat a tiny metal box. Spikey lifted it to the tabletop. Then he fished around in a drawer until he found a key. He placed it in the lock on the box and opened it. From inside, he pulled what looked like a necklace. At the end of it was a green gem encased in mechanical *components*. He walked over to Scotty.

"Put this on. Make sure this gem is touching your skin," Spikey said, handing the necklace to Scotty.

Scotty held it in his hands and eyed it for a moment. "What is it?"

"An invention I've never had the pleasure of using. I created it specifically for the *Blood of the Land*. You see, one thing that the *prophecies* made clear was that the *Blood of the Land* would be a human with a life and people who loved him on Earth. Taking him from there unexpectedly might cause serious problems. I created this to solve that possible problem."

"What does it do?"

"Simple, when it touches your skin, it scans your entire mental system, from memory, mannerisms, likes and dislikes, and attitudes. It then transmits that data to the *Door*. I have equipped the *Door* with a device that can create a particle duplicate of you."

"That doesn't sound simple to me, and what is a particle duplicate anyway?"

"Think of it as a field of energy that looks exactly like you. To the touch, it will even feel like flesh and blood, and it will duplicate everything about you from scars to warts if you have any."

"I don't have any warts!" Scotty protested.

"It will also think and act exactly like you. It will do this mainly because it will have access to your brain. In a sense, your one brain will actually be controlling two bodies. Of course, the duplicate will be controlled only on a subconscious level, and there will be some side effects."

"Such as?"

"Well, since a ***microscopic*** *Door* must follow the duplicate wherever it goes, there will be large concentrations of static electricity all around it. The duplicate must release this energy often through a conductive source, or it may start to interfere with its matrix. Simply touching a door handle or something made of metal would work. This should be done every two hours or so. Also, the duplicate will not know that it is a duplicate, so these energy discharges must be preprogrammed. Finally, the duplicate will not be able to maintain any memory of Staranana. If it could, it might become jealous and wish it were the one here saving the day and not you. Those negative emotions could be ***transmitted*** back to you and cause you severe problems."

"Can all these side effects be dealt with?" Scotty asked.

"Absolutely, I already took care of it. All you have to do is put the necklace on, and the rest will take care of itself."

"Well, it all sounds good, but I still don't like the idea of being away so long."

"That's the best part of it. The instant you take the necklace off, the duplicate will be deactivated, and all its memories will be ***transmitted*** back to you. You will be able to remember anything that happened while you were gone. And if you don't like the way your duplicate is handling things, you simply put the necklace back on and set your mind to do things a different way. It will be just like you never left, even to you."

"Wow, okay, I guess we can give this a try. Are you sure it will work?"

"I don't build things that don't work!" Spikey piped.

"You know, everything on this planet seems so primitive, and yet there are so many amazing pieces of technology. Where did it all come from?" Scotty asked.

"The Starananian people have always been able to balance the primitive and the sophisticated. It is just the way we live. As for where all my technology came from, well, that is a secret I'm going to have to keep for now."

"Suit yourself," Scotty said and slipped the necklace on and

David Scott Fields II

placed it under his thermal suit. The instant it touched the skin on his chest, the gem began to pulse and glow. Simultaneously, a control on the *Door* activated, and the passage began to swirl with colored energy. From the midst of the chaotic light, a form took shape, and soon, a human body stepped forward.

Scotty stared in utter amazement at a perfect replica of himself. It even had the scratch on his cheek from when he had collided with the floor in the dungeon, and the crusted blood on his neck from when Seth had cut him slightly with his dagger. The duplicate also wore the same thermal suit Scotty did.

Spikey stepped to the *Door's* controls and said, "I'll just make a few modifications." He flipped a switch, and the scratches and blood were gone. Its clothes also morphed into a light blue T-shirt and a pair of blue jeans. The duplicate did not speak. It just stared ahead blankly.

Scotty said, "I hope it will be a little more lively on Earth."

"Don't worry! It is programmed not to **interact** with anyone on Staranana, except the computer in the *Door*. As soon as it gets to Earth, it will act just like you."

"But, Spikey, no one could see Sparkey when he was on Earth. Will they be able to see this thing?"

"If a Starananian wore the necklace, no, but since you are from Earth, it should work," Spikey replied. Then he said to TB, "TB, do your stuff!"

The *Door* began to hum and a pinprick of light appeared at its center. Slowly the duplicate began to dissolve, and one by one the particles that comprised its body were sucked through the tiny opening in space.

"There, it's done," Spikey said. "The duplicate will appear at your house in a few minutes, and everything will be fine."

"It's still kind of early for me to have come back from Bobby's house, but I guess I can't have everything perfect."

"Oh, there is one more thing I forgot to tell you about. There is an uncertain temporal differential between Earth and Staranana."

182

"What in the world does that mean?"

"Well, think of it this way, Earth is older than Staranana because it was created first. However, we have lived through 1,005,018 years of history. Earth is nowhere near that old. How can that be? The only thing that I can figure is that time passes more quickly here at times, and at other times it passes more slowly. It is like when there is a storm; sometimes the wind blows fast, and at other times, it blows slowly. When you get back to Earth, you may find that only a few hours have passed."

Scotty just stared at Spikey blankly. These science types were really weird. Sparkey had tried to explain the same concept earlier, but he still didn't quite get it. He would just have to trust that Spikey was right. Spikey shook his head and said, "Never mind; let's get ready. We've already taken way too much time."

Everyone began to shove new supplies into their packs. Scotty had Sparkey take him outside, and they killed several three-eared oboca rabbits. After they were skinned and cleaned, they were wrapped and put in the packs. The bears also caught a large supply of fish and put them in their packs. Scotty broke down and added two fish to his own pack. They also put candles, matches, and lanterns in their packs, and a few other odds and ends. Spikey also packed a tent and several blankets.

"Exactly how long is this trip going to take?" Scotty asked.

"One week. We have to cross the White Desert."

"The White Desert! Dad, that's great!" Sparkey piped. "We can stop that ship that is going to attack Stararocka and the *New Life!*"

"Don't worry," Spikey said. "The Stararockans can take care of themselves."

"How do you know?"

"Trust me, I just do."

"All right," Sparkey said, certain his father was hiding something. "But what about the *New Life?*"

Spikey **cursed** under his breath, then said, "All right, if we run into them, we'll do what we can. But we are not going out of our way. Our first priority is to save Staranana, and I am not putting Scotty in danger for a bunch of people who have no faith in God!" If Spikey had been a human, his face would have been bright red with anger. Scotty felt a little embarrassed that his safety was the cause of this argument.

"Dad, what's wrong?" Sparkey demanded.

Spikey did not answer him, but moved over to the *Door*. "TB, make sure the duplicate keeps working. If you can open a second *Door* to a power line, like you did before, you should have a limitless supply of energy. It may be a long time before we are back, so hold down the fort. If any goons enter this cave, use the *Door's* defensive systems, and zap them. This village is fairly well hidden, so I don't think they will find you. But if they do, you are to protect the *Door* at all costs. Do it even if it means you have to collapse the cave entrance."

"You can count on me, Spikey!" TB assured.

Spikey nodded, and then gathered his things. He made one last pass through the cave, making sure he had everything. Then he said, "Let's go!" And without another word, he led the way out into the snow.

Chapter 27

The Transmission

Six Days Later

"You have to be kidding!"

"No, seriously, General, you have to listen to this." Speedway twisted a knob on the control panel of the *New Life*, and the radio clicked into life.

Speedway tuned the radio until an extremely *garbled* sound came over the *cockpit's* speakers, *"Sh...put...identify...course...speed...Stararocka!"* The same *garbled* message repeated several times before Speedway turned the radio off.

"Where did that come from?" Shortstop asked.

"I don't know exactly. Somewhere inside an asteroid field about eighty thousand kleps off our course to Stararocka. The most likely possibility is that it came from a ship. Look at this." Speedway pointed to a computer screen that had a map grid displayed on it. Three tiny red dots marked points in space. "We received transmissions from each of these areas on the same *frequency* and carrier wave."

"Can you reply to the message?"

"I can send a general signal. I don't know if they will receive it, and chances are it will be even more *garbled* than theirs was once it reaches them."

"Do what you can. In the meantime, how are the repairs coming?"

"Complete, General. However, we have nearly exhausted our extra supplies as far as metal and wiring go. I have asked the passengers to donate anything they might have that is made of metal or could be used as wiring. We still have three weeks to go, and we may need them."

"Hey, guys, how's it going?" The two bears turned as Gloria Moonbeam stepped into the *cockpit*. "I've been hearing rumors of a transmission."

Speedway played the transmission for her and said, "We're trying to send a response."

"Are you sure that's wise?" she asked. "We don't know who sent this message. It could be one of Seth's ships."

"Not likely! Most of Seth's ships are rusting away in the White Desert. Besides, the transmission mentioned Stararocka. The best intelligence we have says that Seth doesn't even know that Stararocka exists," Speedway countered.

"Still, it's risky!"

Shortstop changed the subject, "Uh, Gloria, how are the passengers and crew doing?"

She sighed, "Good, I suppose. Everyone has been injected with *ice blood*, and the temperature is being raised. They should be ready to *disembark* once we arrive. Food supplies are at a comfortable level. We have no room for binge eating, but no one will starve. Oh, and there is one more thing."

"How many times do we have to go over this? You can't go back to Staranana!" Speedway snapped.

"That was not what I was going to say, Colonel!" Her eyes flared at him, and it was all she could do to keep from smacking him.

"Sorry, Gloria. What is it?" Shortstop asked.

"Some of the people have been talking about starting a study of the *Text of Iren*. They want to know more about the *prophecies* and to decide for themselves whether or not it is right to go back and fight."

"This was your doing, wasn't it? Gloria, when will you accept that we are free now? Iren wrote those **prophecies** for Staranana, not Stararocka. Besides, if there is a God, what is taking Him so long to save us? As for me, I am starting a new life and forgetting everything about Staranana," Speedway **cursed**.

"That's enough, Colonel!" Shortstop growled.

"Lo, you have abandoned Me and turned from My teachings. Therefore I have cast you far from Me, even to the stars. In the Day of Deliverance, I will bring you back, and you will bow before Me, the One True God. In that Day, I will forgive your faithlessness and restore you, and you will know that I am God!" Gloria paused briefly in her **recitation** of the *Text of Iren*. Then she said, "Tell me that does not concern us!" She then stormed from the **cockpit**.

Shortstop said only, "Keep trying to make contact." Then he left as well.

Speedway adjusted a few controls, then raised his head to the window and gazed out into the blackness. "God, where are you?" he whispered between clenched teeth, and a single, frustrated tear fell from his eye. He wiped it away and went back to his work.

Chapter 28

The White Desert

It had been six of the hardest days of Scotty's life. They had walked nearly thirty miles a day through snowdrifts, blizzards, and half-frozen ponds. Had it not been for his thermal suit, he never would have made it. He couldn't imagine how the bears could stand it with only their fur and a suit of *tattered* clothing on their backs, but, somehow, they managed.

Thankfully, the nights had been somewhat more comfortable. Spikey had planned his route so that they would end each day's journey near a cave. Once inside, they would build a fire and disrobe, allowing their clothes to dry over the fire. Scotty did this as little as possible. His thermal suit did not require it, but Spikey said drying it out would help it function more efficiently. However, sitting half-naked, even in the shelter of the cave, could have easily killed Scotty. In the few instances when he was forced to disrobe, he wrapped himself in the hides of some deer Spikey had killed along the way and sat very close to the fire.

Along the journey, Scotty had killed and eaten more oboca rabbits than he cared to remember. Even the fish were beginning to taste good, but he convinced himself it was just the cold getting to him. On this, the sixth night of their journey, they sat in a tiny cave, beside a roaring fire, all still fully clothed to Scotty's relief. They were only one day away from Stony City.

Spikey's mood had improved slightly since they had left. He had come to the realization that he did not want all those people to suffer aboard the *New Life* if he could prevent it. The fact that his wife and one of his sons were aboard furthered to ebb his mood.

Sparkey had worked particularly hard that day and had already fallen asleep near the fire. Spikey and Scotty sat chatting quietly. "So, what's the game plan for tomorrow?" Scotty asked.

"Well, we have two choices. If we head west from here, we'll reach Stony City by tomorrow night. Or we can head east, and in half a day, we'll reach the shipyard. I have never been there, but I understand it's the only one. If Seth is going to send a ship after the *New Life,* it will launch from there."

"So what are we going to do?"

Spikey looked at the young human boy. His blond hair was now black with dirt, and his face was smudged as well, but to Spikey, he looked more beautiful than anything he had ever seen. "I think I'll leave that decision to the future emperor of Staranana."

Scotty blushed and said, "I wish you guys would stop treating me like I was made of cake or something. I'm just a kid!"

"Yeah, but look how far you've come already. Can you honestly tell me that two weeks ago you would have believed that you would shortly travel to another planet, break into an evil palace, tell off an emperor over 5,000 years older than you, have a chat with an angel, and rescue an alien bear?"

"No, I don't suppose I would have believed it."

"You have also demonstrated a profound faith in God, which I am sure is not typical for boys your age."

"Well, I do have a lot of time to read the *Bible,* and I do ask a lot of questions. But anything that has happened here is all to the glory of God. I can't do anything without Him. No one can! It is Jesus Christ who deserves the credit. If I had my way, I'd place Him on the throne of Staranana."

"The Lord sits on the throne of the universe. To Him, Seth's throne is like a baby's highchair, or worse yet, a toilet's seat. I welcome the day when all life sees Him and bows before Him. But He did promise to restore goodness to the throne of Seth through the *Blood of the Land.* As far as I can tell, that's you," Spikey smiled.

"Well, maybe, but I…" Scotty began.

"Hey, are you guys ever gonna go to sleep?" Sparkey had been stirred and now sat up from under his thermal blanket.

"Sorry, son. We'll go to bed as soon as Scotty makes a decision," Spikey said. Then he simply looked at Scotty.

Being a leader was something Scotty never imagined himself capable of. On Earth, he had never led anything, nor had he ever demonstrated any natural leadership potential. Here it was an entirely different story. The future of an entire world rested on his shoulders, and now, three hundred runaways had been added to that. He hesitated a moment and then said, "We will go to the shipyard tomorrow. Then we'll go on to Stony City the next day."

"It's settled then," Spikey said.

"Good, now everyone go to sleep!" Sparkey bellowed.

Spikey and Scotty snuggled down under their covers. The next day they would face their enemies once again. Spikey was confident they would succeed. Scotty wasn't so sure. However, like all times like this, he did the only thing he could; he prayed.

~

Fifteen kleps away, the snow fell softly in the night. Amidst the shadows, a cloaked figure moved swiftly toward the *fuselage* of a derelict spacecraft. When it reached the craft, it raised a single scaly hand and rapped on a tiny, airlock *portal.* Another cloaked figure opened the *portal* from within, and the first figure stepped through. Once inside, it removed its hood, revealing its scaly features. It was Lizard Face.

The goon that had opened the door led his master into a

small compartment. It was empty except for a cot with a blanket on it and a tool kit. Lizard Face sat on the cot and said, "Report, Captain Gonish!"

"All is well, sir. The *Space Shark* will be ready for launch late tomorrow afternoon. Within two days, we will overtake the rebel vessel. We can do as you wish with it, sir. We have enough firepower to lay down a major assault on whatever planet the rebels are going to and still blow that sorry excuse for a ship to ashes. It is your command. You can make the decision on how we will proceed."

"There is a problem, Captain," Lizard Face began.

"What is that, sir?" Gonish asked.

"I'm not going. I think *Sseth* is growing *ssuspicious* of me. He definitely knows there is *ssome* plot against him. He *ssaid* he wanted to keep me close for extra *ssecurity*, but I believe he really just wants to keep a close eye on me. One of the dragons *loyal* to me brought me here tonight. I was only able to come and *ssee* you because *Sseth* is out with one of his patrols personally *ssearching* for the human boy."

"I heard about him. What do you make of it? Do you think the *prophecies* could be true?"

"Iren was a *lunatic*, and the God he *sserved* hasn't *sshown* his face on this world for millennia. Besides, what harm can a *ssmall* boy really do?" Lizard Face balked.

"Quite right, sir!"

Lizard Face hesitated, "But, then again, this boy did manage to get *Sseth* extremely angry, and he did escape from the Palace. We can't underestimate him. He is the first new human on *Sstaranana* in five thousand years. He could pose a real threat to our plans to overthrow *Sseth*."

"The *prophecies* say *he* will overthrow Seth."

"True, and if that happens, we'll all likely be hunted down and killed."

"What should we do, sir?" Gonish asked.

"How many troops do we have here?"

191

"Nearly five hundred, sir."

"How many does the *Sspace Sshark* need?"

"Three hundred, sir."

"All right, here is what we will do. Take no more than one hundred-fifty crewmembers aboard the *Sspace Sshark*. Figure out a way to make it work. The two hundred workmen who were not assigned to the crew will return to the Palace, *sso Sseth* will not be *ssuspicious*. The one hundred-fifty that are left behind will *sstart* repairing another *sship*. It *sshould* be fast and able to handle, at least, a few hundred goons. I don't care if we have to pack them in with no room to move. If the worst happens, and this boy overthrows *Sseth*, this will be our escape plan. I'll bring as many goons as I can, and we'll head into *sspace*. I don't know where we will go, but one day, we'll come back and reclaim what is ours. In the meantime, we'll continue as planned. I'll go back to the Palace and head up the goon rebellion there. You carry out the mission. When you return, contact me, and I'll rally the troops. *Ssave* enough firepower to attack the Palace. We'll be waiting to take advantage of the **chaos**."

"Excellent plan, sir!"

Lizard Face's mouth split into a wicked grin. He nodded, then put his hood back on, and headed for the airlock. If all went well, in a few days, he would be the new emperor of Staranana.

~

"Look at all of them!" Sparkey whispered, frantically. He, his father, and Scotty lay on a bluff overlooking a valley in the White Desert. Spikey had brought along his portable telescope, and they were using it to observe the valley. Below them, countless, lifeless fuselages littered the ground. Hundreds of goons also milled about. Most of them were around a single vessel that seemed to be **intact**. That had to be the *Space Shark*.

"How are we going to take on all of them?" Scotty asked. For him particularly, it had been a rough morning. They had headed out at what must have been four in the morning. There had been no time for breakfast. Scotty had chewed on a piece of oboca meat to satisfy himself, but it had been less than filling. That, combined with having to wade through a lake that challenged the limits of his thermal suit's capabilities, had taken its toll. They reached the shipyard by high noon.

Spikey removed his pack and reached inside. His hands came out with the yellow-green egg they knew so well. "We'll stop them with this," Spikey said.

"Good idea, Dad!" Sparkey began. Then he paused and said, "Wait, how are we going to do that? The whole reason you went on a suicide mission in the first place was because the bomb would go off too quickly for you to escape its blast. Wouldn't the same thing happen here?"

"Oh, yeah, I forgot about that," Spikey said. "I'm all for dying for the cause, but I can't leave you kids out here alone."

"Yeah, and I'd hate to think of all we went through to rescue you, only to have you die now," Sparkey said.

"So what are we going to do?" Scotty asked. The bears shook their heads. The bomb was their best chance, but now, no one was *expendable*. They all had to get out of there alive.

Scotty laughed and made a joking suggestion, "It's too bad you can't just stick an icicle in the hole the vial goes in and let it slowly melt into place."

Scotty knew how stupid it sounded, but he was shocked at Spikey's response. "That's a great idea!"

"It is?"

"Yes, it should work. The questions are how do we get the ice to melt, and where do we put the bomb? With all these goons around, I highly doubt we'll be able to get aboard the ship," Spikey said.

Sparkey peeked over the bluff again and asked, "Hey, Dad, what is that?"

Spikey followed his son's pointing finger to the floor of the valley, and he adjusted his telescope to see. Most of the ground was covered with powdery snow, but patches here and there glimmered in the morning sunlight.

"Ice!" Spikey gasped.

"What?" Scotty asked.

Spikey explained, "At least part of that shipyard is sitting on a frozen lake. If we can get the bomb beneath the surface, when it explodes, it will sink the ship."

"Yeah, but an icy lake doesn't seem like the best way to melt the icicle," Scotty said.

Spikey nodded. It was true, but there had to be a way to get it done. He looked back into the valley and smiled. "Look at that, boys," he said. The youngsters followed his gaze to the vessel they had **deemed** the most likely candidate for the *Space Shark*. Out the side of the ship, a large pipe extended, bent like an elbow, and then bore down into the ice. On the upper part of the pipe, near the joint, was a compression valve that appeared to be connected to a miniature airlock.

"What is it?" Scotty asked.

Spikey chuckled, "A sewage pipe! That's where we'll put the bomb!"

"In a sewage pipe!" Scotty exclaimed, then he covered his mouth, realizing he had spoken a little too loudly.

"Yes, goon sewage is like acid. It will melt the icicle quickly. The pipe will also take the bomb under the surface," Spikey replied.

"Great idea, Dad! Let's go!" Sparkey said.

"Wait a minute, son! Only one of us should go. We won't have the cover of night, so it will be easier if just one goes. And that one will be me. I know how the bomb works, and I can overcome any other technical problem. Now, find an icicle," Spikey commanded.

It wasn't hard to find an icicle. Sparkey returned with a small one, and Spikey jabbed it into the hole. He put the vial in his pocket. There was no reason to take chances by putting it into the hole early. He then turned to the boys and ordered, "Wait here. I'll be back as fast as I can. Be ready to run if there's trouble." The boys nodded, and Spikey headed into the valley.

~

"We're ready to go, Captain," came a knock on the door. *"A vehicle is ready to take us to the Space Shark."*

"All right!" Gonish replied and stood from the toilet where he had been sitting. He pushed the flush lever. The quartering ship was the only one with plumbing. A pipe network regulated water from the lake throughout the ship, and then it dumped the sewage back into the lake. The *Space Shark* had a portable system, but it had not yet been brought online. As such, Gonish took it upon himself to make sure he had fully relieved himself before they set out on the twenty-klep drive to the *Space Shark*. It beat going out in the frigid desert all the way around.

~

Spikey emerged from yet another snowbank. They dotted the ground throughout the valley, and thankfully, proved to be the perfect places to hide. Each time he came close to being seen, he would dive into a bank and remain still until the goons were gone. Moving through the valley this way had taken more than an hour-and-a-half, but, at least, it had kept him alive. He was now within a few feet of the ship and the pipe.

All things considered, this had been far too easy. As he stepped up to the pipe, he caught the stench of goon waste and had to brace himself against the **fuselage** to keep from keeling over. This wasn't going to be pleasant.

He removed the bomb from his pack and the vial from his pocket. The icicle had melted slightly, and he poured the excess water from the hole. He took a deep breath and slid the vial into place. It barely fit given the ice, and he prayed it wouldn't fall out before the ice melted. However, there wasn't time to worry about that now. Taking the valve of the tiny airlock in his hands, he twisted until, with the hiss of escaping air, the hatch came open.

The stench of the goon waste increased a hundredfold, and Spikey felt like he was going to vomit. He had to get this over with fast. He lifted the bomb to the hole, flipped the activation switch, and dropped it inside the pipe. It vanished beneath a surge of brown liquid.

Spikey went to reseal the hatch, but an alarm sounded! His teeth clenched, and his heart pounded as a voice over a loudspeaker bellowed, *"Alert! The plumbing system on the quartering ship has been* **compromised.** *Will the party responsible please enter the* **appropriate** *access code at the nearest computer terminal? Security teams report to the area, and return with a full report."*

"Quartering ship? Oh, no!" Spikey **cursed.** That was why so many goons were around this ship. It was where they slept. It wasn't the *Space Shark.* The bomb was going to destroy the wrong ship!

"Hold it right there!" a raspy voice screamed. Spikey whirled, and his eyes met with the stained robes of a goon, about fifty feet away. The mangled creature's rifle was pointing directly at him. Spikey took a deep breath and then sprinted away from the ship.

A rain of energy bolts began to rip through the ice next to Spikey's feet as he continued to fly across the snow. The first goon screamed after him, and two others barred his path. Spikey did not slow down. Instead, he lowered his head, stuck out his elbow, and slammed into them. They went flying, and he continued running. He had to make it to the edge of the lake before the bomb went off, and that could be mere seconds away.

The nearest goons were a hundred yards behind him now. Though they were running after him, they had no chance of catching him in time. But just as he neared the bank, he felt his feet slipping from under him. *Ugh! Not now!* He adjusted the movement of his body and directed his fall so that it sent him flying toward the shore. When he crashed into the snowbank beyond, he lay there panting.

The *horde* of goons was still racing toward him. Spikey got up to move again, and then...BOOM! The entire lake erupted in a fireball that towered into the sky and even threatened his position. Shortstop had *obviously* underestimated the power of his bomb. Had it gone off when it was originally supposed to, it could have easily blown away half the front of the Palace.

Spikey looked in the direction of the quartering ship. The water beneath it was boiling, and the vessel had fallen into the bubbling brew. Spikey caught one last glimpse of the *fuselage* before it disappeared into the deep. It wasn't the only ship either. Every derelict vessel that had rested on the lake's frozen surface was now submerged. Dozens of vessels were gone. A few goons still swam about in the boiling water, screaming, their bodies on fire. But soon, even they disappeared. Spikey scrambled from the bank and headed back to the boys. It was time to go.

When he returned to the bluff, he grabbed Sparkey and Scotty by the arms and began pulling them away. Scotty asked, "What's wrong?"

"We hit the wrong ship! It was nothing more than a dormitory. That's why there were so many goons around it. The *Space Shark* is probably nowhere near here. We should never have come! Now Seth will know exactly where to look for you!" Spikey *cursed.*

Scotty lowered his head. It had been his choice to come, and they had failed. Some *Blood of the Land* he was making. He said nothing as they headed into the desert. Two hours later, the *Space Shark* launched.

Chapter 29

Stony City

Thirty-six hours later, Scotty felt his knees buckle under him. His eyes were heavy, but sleep had not been an option. Spikey had pressed them onward, with little more than ten-minute breaks, for almost two days. At one point, he had collapsed in exhaustion, so Spikey had carried him for about an hour. That was all the sleep he had gotten, and now, he couldn't go another step.

"We'll rest here for a while," Spikey said. They had arrived at a small bundle of trees, all alone in the desert. It was well past midnight, and the icy winds were howling. Spikey gathered a few sticks and lit a fire.

"How much further do we have left?" Scotty whined. He had propped himself up against the trunk of a tree and was doing his best to stay awake, but he was losing the battle.

"About a klep…a mile is your terms," Spikey said casually.

Scotty felt a jolt of **adrenaline** shoot through him, and he demanded, "What? That close? Why did we stop?"

"You're the one who stopped," Spikey said.

"Oh, yeah."

"Hey, Dad, I recognize these trees. Look at the fruit," Sparkey said.

Spikey reached a hand up and plucked a large, silver apple. Scotty squinted at it in the firelight and said, "A honeysuckle apple! I remember those too."

Spikey tossed both boys an apple and said, "Eat those. They will restore your strength, and they'll let you go a few more hours without sleep."

"Really? They can do all that?" Scotty questioned.

"Yes, if your body really needs the strength. Otherwise, they just make you hyper and jittery," Spikey said.

"How do you know we're only a mile from the city, Dad?" Sparkey asked.

"The trees," Spikey said.

Both boys looked at him, puzzled, and he explained, "Let me give you both a little agricultural lesson, boys. Honeysuckle apple trees are some of the most *resilient* trees on this planet. They can thrive in even the harshest winter conditions. Their roots can bore through, and take *nutrients* from, solid ice. Their seeds are also able to grow through solid ice for years before they ever break through the surface and see the sun. These trees here are probably at least four hundred years old."

Sparkey was impressed, but still confused. "So what?" he said.

"Well, before it was destroyed, Stony City was a leading producer of honeysuckle apples. They had orchards all over the area. The largest orchard was located in the heart of the city. When the city was destroyed so was the crop, but the seeds survived. It took many years, but eventually, the seedlings broke through the surface and grew new trees. After five hundred years, this entire area has become an apple tree forest. When we find the largest *concentration* of trees, we'll have found the city's center. It shouldn't be hard to find a building and enter the city through its roof."

Scotty was worried. "Uh, that's great, Spikey, but I have a question," he said.

"Certainly, Scotty. What is it?" Spikey replied.

"Well, when I was with Seth, I got the sense that he knows the *prophecies* very well. He may want to fight them, but he still knows them. And if that is true, he knows about the *Dagger of Promise*, right?"

"I'm sure he does."

"Then, if he was the one that destroyed this city, he knows the dagger is here. What makes you think he hasn't already come and taken it, or worse, what if he has a troop lying in wait for us?"

Spikey wasn't fazed. "Seth wouldn't risk touching the dagger. You see, its blade is made out of something called brillium amber. It is a very rare, very valuable amber. The amber also has powers. Some people, mainly goons and dragons, believe it is magical power. But the bears tend to believe that it is **endowed** with holy power from God. The blade is incredibly sharp. Even a slight graze could chop off a finger. Still, it can't hurt servants of God. However, if an evil person, like Seth, were to be even nicked by the dagger, a **vortex** would open and suck him alive into the *Black Lava Pits*, which, I believe, is the Staranian version of what you call Hell."

"If it's so dangerous to Seth, why didn't it stop him when Splash tried to use it?"

"That's another long story, but, in brief, it doesn't work for bears. When Seth first became emperor, he had all the amber he could find destroyed. However, Iren had had a dagger of the amber made before Seth was born. His intention was to attack the Devil with it if he showed up to Seth's birth celebration, but the Devil never showed up. When God told Iren to begin writing his text, He also sent an angel to take the dagger. The angel blessed it saying, *'By this weapon, evil shall be undone. Flesh like your flesh and blood like your blood will wield it unto victory.'* The angel hid the dagger in the city of Katana far from the Palace. Thousands of years later, Splash found it. He had already overrun the dragons and Lizard Face; and Seth was stranded in the Nimbus solar system. He put the dagger on display in his city to give his people a sense of security. Their mistake was that they ignored what the angel had said. When

Seth returned, the dagger didn't work, and he destroyed the city. Seth can't risk touching the dagger, because he is human, and he could fulfill the angel's **prophecy** and defeat himself. As for anything else evil, the dagger would destroy them simply for what they were. Seth left the dagger where it was, hoping no one would ever find it. But a few bears were out of the city at the time it was destroyed. They knew where the dagger was and passed the secret on through the centuries. No one wanted to risk using it again. At least, not until now."

"Okay, so what if Seth is waiting to **ambush** us?" Scotty asked.

"We'll just have to take our chances," Spikey shrugged. "So, what do you say, Scotty? Do we keep going or set up camp?"

"Wait a minute! The last time I made a decision, we almost got killed, and we still might get killed because of it. I don't want to make the decision this time."

"We have a better chance of dying out here than in the city. There are no caves here, and a patrol could easily spot our fire, but we couldn't survive the night without it. The city is large, and no doubt the buildings have supplies. We could sleep in one until dawn. If there are goons there, we most likely won't run into any. Unless, by chance, they just so happened to choose the same building as us," Spikey said.

Scotty sighed, "Oh, all right, let's go!"

Sparkey put out the fire, and they got underway again. As they were walking, Scotty asked, "So, when we get the dagger, how are we going to get back to the Palace?"

"Well, there's only one way," Sparkey said.

"Oh, no! You mean..."

"Yup, the **aqueducts**!" Sparkey giggled.

"Great!" Scotty **grimaced**. "Why didn't we just take that way in the first place?"

"We were in a rush to get here. It is a faster trip over land. Once you have the dagger, we'll be a little safer. It will take ten days to get back through the **aqueducts**, but it will be a much calmer journey," Spikey explained.

"Oh, sure! We'll just have to fight off gators, recklors, viola crystals, and who knows what else!"

Sparkey and Spikey laughed. Scotty wasn't exactly the most courageous boy in the universe. Of one thing they were sure, though. He was the fulfillment of a promise, and he had the makings of a great emperor.

~

"Mom!" Scotty wailed and sat up from under his thermal blanket. He had been dreaming of home. In the last week, what with living on the edge of death every second, he hadn't had much time to think about home. But the dream had been so real, and now, he longed to be back in the arms of his family. Staranana was amazing, but he wanted to go home.

They had set up camp on the top floor of a skyscraper in Stony City. It had been the only one they could find with an entrance on the roof. The windows were encrusted with ice, so there was no way to see down into the city. The furniture, mostly wooden, was either rotten or had been turned to stone and was broken. They had also seen several stone bears throughout the floor. It gave Scotty an eerie feeling to think that the statues had once been alive.

Spikey and Sparkey were still asleep, and the longing for home was so intense that Scotty decided to throw caution to the wind. He reached down and removed the necklace. That would deactivate his duplicate and allow all its memories to flood back to him. If anyone happened to be looking at the duplicate at that moment, they were in for a shock.

It was an odd sensation to have a week's worth of memories flash through his mind in only a few seconds. To Scotty, it was just exactly as if he had lived the eight days he had been gone back on Earth. Sunday, he had returned home to a verbal lashing from Noah, whose watch was missing, and Scotty was the chief suspect. The sixteen-year-old, all-star athlete had put his little brother into a headlock until he confessed he had lost the watch. Though, he did not say where. The real Scotty knew he had lost it in the **aqueducts**. That had gotten him grounded. On Monday, he and Bobby had gotten into a fight, because he had never bothered to say goodbye. Now, he and Bobby weren't speaking. However, the duplicate had made friends with two new boys, Sammy and Christopher. Apparently, the duplicate did not share Scotty's **intimidation** of other human children, or, more likely, Scotty's confidence with the bears was bleeding over to his copy. On Tuesday, Scotty's mom was so glad that he was making some good friends that she canceled his grounding and invited the boys over for dinner. She also bought Noah a new watch. On Wednesday, Bobby and the duplicate made up, and Bobby joined the new band of friends. The rest of the week had been filled with more laughter and fun. However this adventure turned out, when he got home, things were going to be okay. No more imaginary adventures would be needed. He slipped the necklace back on and lay down. He had other friends to help now.

~

"Boys, come on. We need to get going." To Scotty, it seemed he had been sleeping only about half an hour when Spikey woke him up again. *Time for another bright day on Staranana!* Or, in this case, another dark day in a dank and smelly cave.

The boys began to pack up their sleeping supplies, and Spikey removed some rabbit meat, fish, and honeysuckle apples. The food was cold, but satisfying, as they sank their teeth into it. Soon their bellies were full, and it was time to begin exploring the city.

Spikey lit their lanterns and said, "History doesn't exactly tell us where Splash was when he tried to use the dagger. No one who was in the city survived Seth's attack. If it weren't for those who had been away from the city, we might not even have known the dagger was here. Though, Seth did boast in his report that he defeated the dagger that was supposed to slay him. If I were to guess, I would say we should look for the dagger in the central market. It would have been in the center of the apple tree orchard there, and it would have been the perfect place for a confrontation with Seth."

"Okay, how do we get out of here?" Sparkey asked.

"There is a staircase at the end of this hall, but it's about twenty stories down to the ground," Spikey said.

"Nothing we can't handle," Scotty piped.

"Then let's go!" Spikey said, leading the way out.

A short time later, they stepped from the skyscraper out into the city. Scotty looked upward and gasped. Hundreds of feet above, a sheet of sheer ice replaced the skyline. Thousands of icicles dangled overhead as well, and through them, the white sun shone down, sending tiny rainbows throughout the sunken city. Most amazing were the hundreds of thousands of roots that extended from the ice, halfway down the tallest buildings. They came from the honeysuckle apple trees growing on the surface.

The city itself was a little less appealing. Many of the buildings had collapsed, the streets were broken apart, and the city was filled with thousands of lifeless statues. Many of the statues had been shattered. Heads were smashed. Arms were broken away, and bodies were crumbled. Very few of the statues were left *intact*. The worst of it was to think that only a few centuries past, these cold, lifeless hunks of stone were living, breathing bears.

"Where do we go first?" Scotty asked.

"This way," Spikey said. "The center of the city isn't far. Just around this corner, and...Oh, dear Lord!"

"What is it, Dad? We...oh, no!"

"What are you guys...uh!" Scotty felt his knees begin to shake. In the past nine days, he had seen many new creatures, both strange and wonderful. There was one creature, however, that he still longed to see. The bears had spoken of them. They had told him of their unyielding evil, their flaming breath, and their powerful jaws. The very description brought terror to the weak-hearted, but Scotty still had to see one. He got his chance. As he stepped around the corner, he came face to face with his first dragon.

"Get back!" Spikey barked and pushed the boys behind a building. The massive creature was curled into a ball and lie in the central market, breathing softly. Its scales were a mix of blue and green. A long strip of spikes protruded through its back down the entire length of its spine to the tip of its tail. The feet were massive, no doubt powerful, and each had four razor-sharp, *ebony* claws. From the long snout, a goatee of whiskers grew that must have been at least ten feet long. The creature's eyes were shut. It was sleeping.

"How did he get in here?" Scotty asked. "I thought you said dragons couldn't fit down into these caves, Sparkey?"

Sparkey shook his head, and Spikey said, "It doesn't matter how he got here. The question is how do we get past him?"

"He's asleep. Maybe we can tiptoe past?" Sparkey suggested.

"I don't see any other way. Okay, put out your lanterns, and be very, very quiet. Our goal should be that tiny building across the way. Once we're all safely there, we'll continue looking for the dagger," Spikey said.

The dragon continued to breathe softly as they crept from the shadows. Scotty sneaked past its massive snout first. Spikey thought he could see beads of sweat dripping from the youngster's forehead. Scotty made it past, and next it was the two bears. Spikey tiptoed safely by. However, just as Sparkey was nearly safe, his darkened lantern slipped from the loop of clothing it was hanging on and crashed to the ground.

Sparkey froze. Scotty and Spikey held their breath, but the dragon did not move. Sparkey sighed deeply. He was safe. He continued toward his father and Scotty.

"NOT SO FAST!" bellowed a thundering voice that shook

every building in the dead city.

The dragon was awake and had uncoiled its massive body in an instant. It filled the entire area. As Spikey and Scotty dove for cover, the beast opened its mouth and enveloped the tiny bear. Only, it was not fire that spewed forth from the creature's scaly lips. Instead, a stream of water shot forth, followed by an icy puff of air. Sparkey was drenched in the flood, and the frigid breath locked him in a solid block of ice.

"No! Sparkey!" Spikey screamed and charged toward his frozen son. The elder bear's fate was the same.

Scotty did the only thing he could. He ran, tripping and stumbling all the way, as the massive dragon maneuvered to claim him as well. Scotty made it to the building they were trying to reach. He knew the dragon could easily lay it to waste, but it didn't. Instead, it curled into a ball and went back to sleep. Its two frozen victims were still very near its snout. Scotty was safe for the time being - safe and *alone*!

Chapter 30

The Dragon and the Dagger

"Okay, take a deep breath! Everything is going to be okay. I'm alone, in a frozen city, and there is a huge dragon right outside. Nothing to worry about." Scotty slapped his forehead. Who was he kidding?

He had taken shelter inside a half-collapsed, three-story building. His friends were still *imprisoned* in ice, and he had no idea if a Starananian could survive something like that. All he did know was that somehow, all by himself, he had to rescue them. The dragon seemed to be resting comfortably, but Scotty wasn't about to risk sneaking past him again.

He quietly made his way up a case of crumbling stairs to the roof. Maybe from up there he could come up with an idea. Even though the building was small, Scotty figured it must have been important at one point, judging by what he found. There were dozens of stone bears throughout the halls, all of which were still *intact*. Many of them wore what looked like military uniforms. Scotty stumbled across a plaque on one of the doors that read *Military Headquarters 1*.

The roof was littered with debris. Chunks of stone, broken bear statues, and even pieces of tree roots were everywhere. However, in the center of the roof, a single bear statue remained *intact*. Scotty couldn't exactly tell from his distance, but it appeared the statue was holding onto something orange.

When he reached the statue, he discovered it was in less pristine condition than it had appeared from across the roof. The face was worn away and covered with frost. One of the ears had also been broken off. In the right hand, though, as pure and as shining as if it were brand new, was a gleaming dagger with a translucent, orange blade. The weapon was held tightly in the bear's hand. It could not be removed. Scotty rubbed a bit of frost away from what appeared to be a nametag on the statue's chest. It read *General Splash Moonbeam*.

Scotty tried to work the dagger free as he said, "Look, General, I've got some relatives of yours to save, so I'd **appreciate** it if you could just loosen your grip on the dagger. Come on now! Oh...Come on!" The dagger would not budge.

"You might try saying please!"

"Thanks, but I…AHHHH!" Scotty screamed. The voice that had spoken was deep and husky. For a moment, he thought it was Splash. That, of course, was impossible, which left only one other possibility.

Scotty ducked into the shadows, and the voice spoke again, "Oh, it's no use; I can still smell you, even if I can't see you. Come out, now."

Scotty did not **comply**, but called out, "Who are you?"

"My name is Hydro, and I am a water dragon. The only one of my kind, I might add. I was sent here by Emperor Seth to find you."

"Well, I am…"

"I know very well who you are. You are the *Blood of the Land*, chosen of God to overthrow Seth and restore peace to this world. It is a difficult task to be sure."

"Not impossible?"

"I do not concern myself with the politics of Seth. I only do what I am told. You may yet succeed, but one thing I am sure of, you will never see your friends again."

Scotty wasn't about to settle for that. **Prophecies** or no **prophecies**, he needed the Moonbeams to help him. There had to be a way, but what? He asked, "You been here long, Hydro?"

"A few days. Seth didn't know if you knew about this place, but he wanted to play it safe, so he sent me. I can transform into water and fit into the caves. I was the only dragon that could get inside the sunken city."

"Why didn't Seth come himself with a squad of goons?"

"Are you kidding? Seth wouldn't lower himself to tramp around in these caverns like a commoner."

"Sounds like you don't have a very high opinion of His Majesty?" Scotty continued to talk with the dragon, but he had another objective in mind. Next to Splash's statue, there was a long chunk of stone, almost like a club. This was going to cost the ancient Moonbeam his arm, but there was no other choice. Scotty would break the dagger free if he could.

"Seth killed my brothers. He turned them into stone because they dared to guard this city. They were the only rebellious dragons in the history of Seth's rule. He sent their statues into space so that they could never be found again."

"Yet you still serve him?"

"I was only a *hatchling* then, and my parents were devout servants of Seth. They taught me his lies, and I believed them. My parents were killed in the attack on the rebel vessel."

"That wasn't even two weeks ago."

"Indeed! Since that time, Seth has seemed very *suspicious* of me. I am an elemental dragon – the only type of dragon ever to oppose him. I have been *loyal* all these centuries, but recently I have had my doubts about him. Perhaps it is only fear that keeps me in line. What do you think of that, human? Human?"

Scotty had had enough of this monster's sob story. It was time to act! Heart pounding in his chest, he charged forward and scooped the stone club into his hands. It was light, but it felt strong. He shattered Splash's arm with a single swing, and the dagger clattered away across the rooftop. It came to rest at the very edge of the roof.

"What are you doing, human?" Hydro bellowed, and the

blackened city filled with light and began to shake. The **immense** form of the bluish-green dragon rose above the rooftop. His eyes glowed, his fangs dripped icy spray, and his massive wings filled the cavern. His body was a mesh of liquid and flesh, and from the water radiated a beautiful, blue light. The light was so bright that it blinded Scotty. There was only one way this was going to work.

Scotty prayed, "Oh, dear God, be with me, please!" Then he sprinted full force into the blinding, blue light. It was clear from his poise that Hydro was ready to kill him. The dagger was his only shot of survival. The trouble was he couldn't see, so it was a guessing game to figure out where the dagger was. He lowered his hand as he continued to run, a spray of icy liquid forming around him all the while. Even if the bears could survive being locked in a solid block of ice, he could not. Just as it seemed the ice from Hydro's breath would ensnare him, his hand met with the **hilt** of the dagger, and the ice stopped.

Now what? He had come to a stop at the edge of the roof. Should he throw the dagger at the dragon, or leap into him, slashing all the while? The latter would likely get him killed, but there was no guarantee the former wouldn't either. As it turned out, Hydro made the choice for him.

With a puff of the dragon's breath, the human boy fell. He was about to be nothing more than a bloody smear on the cold, stone ground. So much for the *Blood of the Land!* Scotty **surrendered** to his grisly fate and released the dagger. He expected to meet with the ground, but a blood-curdling roar stopped everything.

"What in the holy name of God are you doing?" Hydro raged. One of the dragon's wings caught Scotty and lowered him to the ground. From there, he could see the dagger stabbed securely into a spot of flesh on Hydro's chest, but nothing was happening. No **vortex**, no screams of the damned of the *Black Lava Pits*, nothing! Could the powers of the dagger only be a fairy tale?

The spot of flesh on the dragon's chest transformed into water, and the dagger fell to the ground. Hydro lowered himself to the human boy's level and pushed Scotty over with his long snout.

"It didn't work!" Scotty bellowed, expecting to become dragon feed.

"Of course, it didn't work! The dagger only works on evil people!"

"But you said you serve Seth!"

"If you had been listening, I also said that I serve him for fear of my life! There are many who serve Seth who are not *loyal* to him!"

Hydro backed up, so the boy could stand. When Scotty was up, he said, "You don't have to continue serving him, you know."

"What else is there?"

"You could help us. We could use a dragon on our side."

"Me?"

"Do you see any other dragons around here? Look, I'm sorry I stabbed you, but if you are scared of Seth, don't be. I happen to know God is working. Seth won't hold his throne for much longer. You need to decide whose side you want to be on when that happens. If you oppose God and His plans, you will most certainly suffer. In the *Bible*, when the Pharaoh of Egypt refused to let the people of Israel go, God sent horrible plagues upon him and his servants. I don't know what God will do to free the people of Staranana, but if ever there was a time to switch over to God's side, it is now!"

Hydro hesitated, and then said, "Would you really want me?" His light and his size began to *diminish* to their former state.

"Sure, I mean, I don't have my friends anymore. I could use your help."

"Oh, that! I can take care of that," Hydro chuckled. He turned toward the two frozen bears, covered his left nostril with a single claw from his left front paw, and huffed. A stream of fire shot from the right nostril. The flames licked at the blocks of ice until Spikey and Sparkey sat panting in puddles of bubbling water.

Spikey was disoriented for a second. Then he turned to see Scotty standing next to the dragon. "Scotty, get away!" he screamed, and he and Sparkey jumped to their feet.

Scotty held up a hand to calm them. "It's okay, guys! I'd like to introduce you to my new friend, Hydro."

"Friend? He tried to kill us!" Sparkey screeched.

The dragon spoke, "My apologies, friends. We got off to a bad start. Young Scotty here has shown me a few truths. I would like to help you if I can."

The bears took their places by Scotty, and Spikey asked, "So, do you trust this guy?"

"I don't have to. The dagger didn't hurt him. He's a good guy, right enough."

"The dagger?" Spikey cocked his brow.

"Oh, yeah, I found it. Where did it go?"

"Here you are, young sir," Hydro said. The dagger had fallen a few dozen feet away. The dragon used his long tail to pick it up, and then he dropped it into Scotty's hands.

"So this is really it?" Spikey beamed.

"Yup! I found it in Splash's hand, up on the roof there. Oh, sorry, guys, but I kind of broke his arm off to get the dagger free."

That's okay; his memory will survive. That is if any of us survive. Right now, we have work to do," Spikey said.

"I guess it's onward to the ***aqueducts***," Scotty quipped.

"***Aqueducts?*** Heavens no!" Hydro balked. "Climb on my back, and I'll take you to the edge of the Nana Forest. It will only take a few hours. Then I'll return and make my report to Seth. I'll tell him I froze the bears and that you fell off a building. That at least will be the truth. I'll say your body was too mashed to bring back."

"Do you think he'll believe you?" Scotty asked.

"He will when I show him this." Hydro tapped at Scotty's pack with his snout.

"My pack, but I…"

"Go ahead, Scotty. We can get another one from the cave," Spikey said.

"Well, okay." Scotty **surrendered** his pack.

Hydro hooked it to one of his teeth, and then said, "Okay, everyone climb aboard." They did so, securing themselves between spikes. Hydro spread his massive wings, and they lifted into flight. He blasted a hole in the cavern ceiling with the fire from his snout, and when they cleared the city, he took to the open sky. From their great height, the snow-blanketed land below looked absolutely breathtaking. It wouldn't be long now. Seth was about to have his second and final encounter with the *Blood of the Land*.

Chapter 31

The Fire Cruiser

*"Unidentified vessel, adjust transmission **frequency** to 6789...7..."*
It had been nearly two days since the strange message had been intercepted by the *New Life*. Colonel Speedway had managed to clear it up a great deal, and they had ***altered*** their course to intercept the mysterious ship, but a ***crucial*** part of the message remained ***garbled***.

"How's it going?" asked General Shortstop as he stepped into the ***cockpit***. Speedway had a set of thick headphones on and was flipping and twisting controls. He did not hear the General. Shortstop tapped him on the shoulder and shouted, "I say, how's it going, Colonel!"

"Oh, sorry, sir! I didn't hear you." Speedway slipped off the headphones and continued, "Well, it's going fine, I guess. We're still about an hour away from intercepting the vessel."

"That soon? It was so far away."

"I know, but they've been moving toward us at a far greater rate of speed than we have been moving toward them. They must really want to make contact with us. They sent a transmission ***frequency***. Trouble is a fraction of the code is still scrambled. I can probably run the numbers through the computer and come up with the rest of the code, but I am not sure that will help us. The signal is on an extremely high bandwidth. I'm not sure we could generate such a signal. It was a miracle that we were able to unscramble as much of the message as we did. One thing is **obvious**, though. That is a far more advanced ship coming our way."

"We'll just have to keep trying to make contact. Maybe once the ship arrives it will be easier to talk to them. Here, let me take over for a while."

"Sir?"

"There is someone I think you should talk to."

"Who?"

"Gloria Moonbeam."

Speedway curled his lip in disgust and protested, "General, really!"

"No arguments, Colonel. I don't like the bad blood that's growing between you two. She may be annoying with all her requests to go back, but think how you would feel if you had family members stranded back on Staranana. Wouldn't you be willing to do absolutely anything to save them?"

"Well..."

"My wife, Dorothy, told me that Gloria is becoming a real inspiration among the crew. She's organizing daily prayer meetings and readings of the *Text of Iren*. People are beginning to question whether we did the right thing or not. Many on the ship are turning back to a true faith in God in droves, myself included."

"Just count me out!"

"Don't make me order you, Speedway! Go talk to Gloria. Patch things up. Listen to what's on her heart. It may do you a lot of good. Now go!"

Speedway grumbled as he left the room. Shortstop hoped things would get better between his first officer and his chief medic. They would all need each other in the weeks and months to come. The last thing he needed was two of his most important bears sparring with one another.

~

"Where in the name of Seth is that ship?" Captain Gonish **cursed**. The *Space Shark* had been searching the area for the *New Life* for almost two days. Given his vessel's vastly superior engines, Gonish believed they should have overtaken the smaller vessel by now. However, their sensor screens remained blank.

The goons aboard the *Space Shark* were relaxing, as far as a goon could relax that is. They all had their hoods down and their cloth masks removed, revealing their maddeningly **grotesque** faces. Goons, of course, were immune to the effects of their own faces. So, it was nice to go barefaced for a change.

"I'm sorry, sir," a goon reported. "They must not be using **conventional** fuel. All I have detected are frozen oxygen particles scattered everywhere. If they were using ion thrusters, there would be a definite trail to follow, but right now, we have nothing."

Gonish scowled, as his radio chief reported, "Maybe we don't need a fuel trail, sir. Listen to this."

The goon flipped a switch, and the bridge of the *Space Shark* filled with the words of an incoming transmission, *"Unidentified vessel, adjust transmission **frequency** to 6789...7..."*

Gonish scratched a patch of itchy fungus on his face as he said, "That **frequency** is beyond even our range. I don't think the bears could generate it."

The sensor officer reported again, "I have adjusted the sensors to locate the source of the transmission. I am detecting two vessels. One is definitely the rebel ship. I can't identify the other one, but I don't believe they pose a threat to us."

Gonish barked, "Signal the crew! All hands to battle stations! Helmsman, how long will it take us to get there?"

"Forty-five minutes, sir. Our course is already plotted and laid in!"

"Excellent!" Gonish smiled. "We have some bears to kill."

~

"Gloria?" Speedway said as he entered the tiny medical bay of the *New Life*. Gloria was doing yet another test on the *ice blood* levels in one of the passengers, an old woman. Gloria whispered something to her and then turned to Speedway.

"What do you want, Colonel?"

"Look, well, I guess I haven't exactly been as nice to you as I should have been, and well, I wanted to apologize."

Gloria was stunned, "Really?"

"Yeah, I mean, I can imagine how you feel, having lost your family and all."

"I remember when you lost Lily," Gloria said in understanding.

Speedway wheezed at the memory. Three years past, after his only son was born, his wife, Lily, had been killed in a dragon attack. At the time, they had lived in a small village far from the Palace. Lily was working in the greenhouses when the dragons attacked. She had been burned to death while tending her flowers. Speedway, his son, and the rest of the survivors had fled to Moonville – the headquarters of the rebellion.

The Colonel felt a tear form in his eye as Gloria placed a hand on his shoulder. "It's all right. I understand."

Speedway brushed the tear away and said, "Yeah, I guess I do too. Thanks for reminding me, and I am really sorry for everything I've said to you."

"Don't worry about it."

The Colonel nodded and turned to leave. Before he was out the door, Gloria called after him, "You know, Colonel, we're having a prayer meeting tonight around 6:00. You're welcome to come."

Speedway smiled and said, "Maybe I will."

~

"Any luck?" Speedway asked as he stepped back into the

cockpit.

"A little. I finished the code. It's 6789.5473. But you were right. We can't generate such a signal."

"How long until we meet up with the vessel?"

"About another twenty minutes. I suppose I can wait that long to learn who these people are."

"Yeah, but it will be a long twenty minutes. Maybe we can..." Speedway began, but he was cut off by the wail of the onboard alarm and an explosion that rocked the ship. The control panel in front of Shortstop blew apart, sending shards of metal and wire across the *cockpit* and throwing the General to the floor.

Speedway rushed to his side. "Sir, are you all right?"

Shortstop tried to push himself up. The area near the pilot's chair was in flames, threatening the rest of the *cockpit.* "Put that out!"

Speedway grabbed a fire extinguisher and set to work as Shortstop raced to the auxiliary controls at the copilot's chair. He punched the control for the onboard intercom and called out, "All passengers, return to your seats immediately! All crew to battle stations! We're under attack!"

"Who's doing this?" Speedway asked. The fire was out, but half the *cockpit* was now black.

Before the General could respond, another explosion pelted the ship. He looked up at the status display over his chair. The green dot representing the primary engines transformed into a hellish red. Several other less critical systems also went offline.

"It's a good thing we don't need the real engines anymore. The new explosive-decompression engines completely bypass them," Speedway said.

"Never mind that!" Shortstop snapped. "Look at this!" He pointed to a large red blip on the infrared sensor display. "It's a massive vessel. I don't even want to guess what kind of weapons they are using. Let me see if I can use the exterior cameras to get a better picture of it."

The General adjusted a few controls until an image appeared on the display screen. The enemy vessel's long, almost rectangular *fuselage* extended back several hundred feet ending in what looked like a fish's tail fin. The sides of the great vessel had what looked like flippers with thrusters under them. On the top of the ship was a tall dorsal fin with missile launchers attached. At the very front of the vessel, a strip of glass windows took the place of eyes, and an open mouth of razor-sharp, metal teeth released another barrage of weapons fire.

The fiery explosives ripped into the smaller craft again, tearing a gouge into the hull. "Hull breach on deck two!" Speedway screamed.

"*Evacuate* that section, and seal it off!"

"I've sealed it off, General, but it's too late for an evacuation. The compartment has vented. Twenty bears have been sucked into space!"

Shortstop *cursed* under his breath and then activated the intercom again, "All hands get to the center of the ship. Avoid the outer areas at all costs!" He turned back to Speedway, "We have to do something about this!"

"What about the laser drills?"

"It would barely be a pinprick to that ship, but it's the only chance we have. Here, you man the lasers. I'm going to try and steer us into that asteroid field off our port side. Maybe we can lose them in there."

"Should we send out a distress signal to the mystery vessel?"

"We can't risk it. That shark ship could trace the signal. Now get going! Aim for the viewing glass on the front of the ship!"

"Aye, sir!" Speedway piped, and then he bellowed, "More incoming missiles."

They braced themselves for another round of explosions. The pursuing enemy vessel would see them destroyed within minutes if they didn't escape.

"We lost another section of the hull. No *casualties* this time," Speedway reported.

"I'm taking the thrusters to full!"

~

"Those idiots!" Gonish chuckled as a few more pinpricks of laser light met with the viewing glass of the bridge, causing no damage.

The sensor officer reported, "They're heading into the asteroid field. Our vessel is much too large to safely maneuver in there."

"I thought we took out their engines?" Gonish questioned.

"Apparently, they have completely overhauled their propulsion system. They are using several of their airlocks as thrusters," the officer reported.

"Well, then take us to the edge of the asteroid field, and start blowing up rocks. Once we cripple their ship, we'll take on prisoners. Leave enough of the vessel *intact* to smash into the Palace when we return to Staranana," Gonish commanded.

~

"Do you think we'll really be safe in here, sir?" Speedway asked. Outside the ship, an enormous chunk of jagged rock cast a shadow over the tiny *New Life*. For the moment, the missiles had stopped.

"For now, I hope, but we don't have much of a ship left to defend. How much longer until the mystery ship arrives?" Shortstop asked.

"I think about ten minutes, if they can find us. Even if they can, we may just end up getting them destroyed as well!"

"General!" panted a voice as its owner stumbled into the *cockpit*. It was Jesse Nova, Gloria's assistant. He was bloodied and bruised.

"What is it, Jesse?" Shortstop asked as Speedway helped him to a chair.

"Sir, the crew is suffering. In the first hull breach, we lost several children, some of our best engineers, and even Nick's mother, but the worst is yet to come. Fragments from those missiles are dumping massive levels of radiation into the ship. People are getting sick. The entire medical deck is covered in vomit. Gloria is giving everyone more *ice blood*. She thinks it will help for now. I brought you two each a shot, but the main thing is we need to get off this ship and fast."

"Where would we go?" Speedway asked. "There are no escape pods, and there aren't enough maintenance pods to accommodate everyone."

"Is there an asteroid with an atmosphere anywhere around here?" Nova asked.

"No, and even if there was, we couldn't get to it. I'm afraid there is only one thing we can do. We'll have to send a distress signal to the mystery ship," Shortstop said.

"But, sir, like you said before, that will give away our position," Speedway cautioned.

"We have no choice! Jesse, go back and help Gloria if you can. Colonel, tell the crew to prepare to abandon ship!"

As the two bears set off to their tasks, Shortstop turned to the radio transmitter. He tapped a few controls and said, "This is General Henry Shortstop of the Starananian spacecraft *New Life*. We are under attack by an unidentified vessel. Our crew is dying, and our vessel is nearly destroyed. We require any and all assistance!"

~

"We have them, sir!" the sensor officer reported. "They are behind the asteroid directly ahead."

"Load a full spread of missiles and fire!" Gonish commanded.

Four fully loaded warheads streaked from the mouth of the *Space Shark*, sending trails of burning plasma behind them. One by one, they impacted upon the surface of the jagged space rock, shattering it into thousands of pieces and revealing the treasure it concealed, the *New Life*.

~

"What do we do now, sir?" Speedway asked. The hull had been completely **compromised**. Only the inner sections and the **cockpit** remained airtight. Radiation levels were continuing to grow. It didn't seem there was much left to do, except die.

"If we **surrender**, they'll kill us or turn us into goons. We're not going out like that. I'm setting a collision course. Maybe we can take them out with us."

Speedway didn't argue with the General. He was right. It was better to go out in a blaze of glory, and maybe take the enemy down too, than to die at the hands of Seth's **minions**.

~

"What do they think they're doing? Do they honestly think that will work?" Gonish asked. "Weapons officer, finish them!"

"Aye, sir, I'll..." the officer began, but before he could finish, a blinding light filled the bridge of the *Space Shark*, and Gonish was smashed to the floor. Panels exploded, and goons burned everywhere on the bridge, to say nothing about the rest of the ship. Gonish scrambled back to his command chair.

"What was that?" he barked.

"An atomic charge, sir! There is another vessel out there!" the sensor officer reported.

"Let's see it!" Gonish demanded. A viewscreen near his chair flickered into life. On it, against the black backdrop of space, a pearl-white vessel glimmered. It was the shape of a perfect saucer with two long nacelles extending out either side of the **fuselage**. The hull was dotted with hundreds of round windows, and a central bridge tower sat on top of the saucer. The vessel was at least five times larger than the *Space Shark*, which was four times larger than the *New Life*.

"Where did that come from?" Gonish **cursed**.

"We're being hailed, sir!" the comm officer reported.

"Put them on!"

A voice crackled to life over the communications system, *"Unidentified vessel, break off your attack, and prepare to* **surrender** *your ship. The rebel vessel is under our protection now! Break off your attack, or you will be destroyed!"*

"Who is this?"

"This is Captain William Noble of the Stararockan vessel Fire Cruiser, flagship of the Starananian Liberation Force! I repeat, **surrender** *or be destroyed!"*

Despite the destruction around the bridge, Gonish had not lost his confidence. "Who is he kidding?" he **mocked**. "Weapons officer, take them out!"

The weapons officer moved to **comply**, but he never got the chance. His control panel exploded with the impact of yet another atomic charge, which set his body aflame. A third charge destroyed the sensor panel. Soon its operator was nothing but a charred corpse on the floor. The fourth charge ended it all. Gonish felt the flames lick at his already marred flesh as the *Space Shark* cracked open like an egg. The vacuum of space tugged at him, and it was useless to resist. For a timeless moment, he hung breathless among the stars, and then everything faded to black and became quiet. The next sounds he heard were the cries of the damned as he joined them in the *Black Lava Pits*.

~

In the **cockpit** of the *New Life,* Shortstop and Speedway sat stunned. The *Space Shark* had been blown to bits. Its burning wreckage still lit up the darkness of space. The mystery vessel, or the *Fire Cruiser* as Captain Noble had called it, had saved the day! Unfortunately, the *New Life* was still in bad shape.

"The *Fire Cruiser* is hailing us, General," Speedway reported.

"Quick, put them on!"

The *New Life's* transmitter was half fried, but a commanding voice boomed over the speakers nonetheless, *"This is Captain Noble. Are you all right over there?"*

"This is General Shortstop, Captain. Thank you for coming to our rescue. To answer your question, no, we are not all right. Twenty of our people have been killed, and many of the others are suffering from radiation poisoning. Our vessel is damaged beyond repair. We could still use your help."

"I hear you loud and clear, General. Evacuation shuttles are being dispatched. They'll reach you within minutes. We'll take your passengers and crew aboard our ship and get to know one another."

"I look forward to that, Captain," Shortstop replied. "We'll see you in a few minutes."

Chapter 32

The Nobles and the Secret

General Shortstop ducked through the airlock hatch that led onto the *Fire Cruiser*. It had taken nearly half an hour to **evacuate** all the rebels from the *New Life*, which was now nothing but a hunk of twisted metal drifting in space. The most serious medical cases had been rushed to the *Fire Cruiser's* sickbay. Shortstop's shuttle was the last to dock.

Meandering figures, all mumbling and carrying on conversations, surrounded the General as he stepped onto the deck. *"Get these meds to the doctor on the double. We have to help these people!"* one officer called.

"Ensign Hanick, go to the docking bay and tow their vessel aboard! But be sure to set up radiation dampeners around the docking bay," another commanded.

"Can you believe we're having banana mush again for lunch? This is no way to treat our new guests!" yet another complained.

"General Shortstop, I presume?" The hustle and bustle about the **corridor** prevented Shortstop from noticing the tall, muscular figure trying to get his attention, as well as his stocky companion.

The figure tapped Henry on his shoulder and repeated, "General Shortstop?"

"Oh, I'm sorry. Yes, I'm Henry Shortstop. You must be Captain Noble?" Shortstop was pleased to see a smiling face, to say nothing about the fact that the two figures before him were also bears. Everyone on the *Fire Cruiser* appeared to be. Their fur was a bit redder. Their bellies were a bit more round, and their collective faces bore many more smiles. But, everything else aside, they were bears, which meant they were family.

By that time, Colonel Speedway had joined Shortstop, and Noble replied, "Yes, I'm Captain William Noble, and this is my brother, Commander Josh Noble, my first officer."

The shorter bear extended his hand and shook that of the General and the Colonel. "I'm glad we finally met up with you," he said. "We've been trying to make contact for over a week."

"We received your transmission, but it was on too high of a bandwidth for us to reply," Speedway explained.

"Oh, sorry about that. I guess we were so surprised to see a vessel heading our way from Staranana that we didn't think about that," William said.

"How did you know we weren't one of Seth's patrols?" Shortstop asked.

"We have spent centuries hiding Stararocka from Seth. We know what most of his ships look like. Besides, we detected only bear life signs on your vessel," the captain explained.

Speedway was amazed, "Your sensors are that powerful?"

"Yes, and we…"

"Sorry to interrupt, Captain Noble, but we've all been through quite a bit. I was wondering if I could check on my passengers and crew. Then, maybe we can sit down and have a proper debriefing," Shortstop said.

"Of course. They're in the medical bay about five decks up. Follow me please." They began to walk through winding **corridors** toward one of the elevators. Unlike the *New Life*, this ship was spacious and professionally constructed. Every bulkhead gleamed, every bolt was fastened tight, and even the carpet was of the finest quality fabric and completely stain free. It had taken years to piece the *New Life* together from scraps they had salvaged from Seth's junkyards. Most of the floor didn't have carpet, and it wasn't uncommon to trip over a loose bulkhead every now and again.

Captain Noble beamed with pride, "Our father built this ship. He was the head of our military until he passed away about five years ago. She's the fastest and strongest ship ever built on Stararocka; well, at least until recently. She serves the planet, but she is owned by the Noble family."

"I can see why you're proud of her. This ship is amazing, but what do you mean she was the most advanced until recently?" Shortstop asked.

"I'll explain that after we tend to your crew." The two Stararockans led them aboard an elevator, and they were quickly on their way to the sickbay. When they arrived, they were greeted by a familiar voice.

"General, Colonel, over here!"

Captain Noble led the way across the spacious sickbay. The room had literally dozens of examination tables. The walls were lined with glass cabinets containing every imaginable kind of medicine, and there were at least ten doctors and nurses tending to people. The room also had an overflow of Starananian patients.

"Guys, I'm glad you're here," the female owner of the voice said. Josh Noble felt his heart pound. Even though she was **obviously** a few years older than he was, she was gorgeous. It was all he could do to keep his mouth from spreading into a ridiculously boyish grin.

General Shortstop presented her, "Captain and Commander, allow me to introduce our chief medical officer, Dr. Gloria Moonbeam."

Josh took her hand eagerly and said, "Very glad to know you, Miss Moonbeam."

Gloria returned his smile, but said, "Actually, it's Mrs. Moonbeam. My husband is still on Staranana."

"Oh, sorry," Josh apologized, trying not to let his disappointment show. Though, his slumped shoulders and suddenly absent smile were not accomplishing the task very well.

"Moonbeam? You wouldn't be any relation to Spikey Moonbeam, would you?" Captain Noble asked.

"Yes, actually, he's my husband."

Shortstop was **dumbstruck**. How in the world did this bear know about Spikey? As far as he knew, no Starananian, rebel or otherwise, had had contact with Stararocka in centuries. "Wait a minute! You know about Spikey? How? Gloria, what's this all about?"

Gloria fidgeted and looked at the floor. "Out with it!" Shortstop demanded.

"Oh, well, I promised not to tell, but since I'm never going to see Spikey again, I guess it doesn't matter. General, Spikey is not actually Starananian. He's Stararockan."

"What?"

"It's true. How do you think I got all my great intelligence on Stararocka? Spikey told me where he came from when we got married, but he told me never to tell anyone. I don't think even his adoptive parents knew. I imagine the captain here knew Spikey at one point. By the way, what are your names?"

Captain Noble continued the story, "William and Josh Noble, ma'am, and yes, I did know Spikey. He was pretty much my best friend until he got **banished**."

"Banished?" Speedway questioned.

"It was about twenty-two years ago when Spikey was eight years old. We had been observing the goings on of Seth from a distance for a long time. For the first few centuries, we were mainly concerned with keeping ourselves safe and the location of our planet a secret. In **recent** decades, though, many groups of our citizens have started to speak out for Starananian liberation. None of those were so **charismatic** and persuasive as Charles and Heidi Moonbeam, Spikey's birth parents."

"I'm with you so far, Captain," Shortstop put in.

"Well, anyway, the Moonbeams have always had very mechanical minds. Spikey's parents drew up plans for a long-range, high-powered, energy weapon. It was kind of like a laser, but far more powerful. The weapon was to be built on the surface of Stararocka. It would then be programmed with a specific target on Staranana. Our target of choice was Cosmic Bubble Palace. The Moonbeams were so precise with their alignment of the weapon that it could have hit something the size of a coin, even from that distance, with almost perfect accuracy. We all knew that the weapon probably wouldn't kill Seth. The **prophecies** of Iren made that clear enough, but we still wanted to help if we could."

"So what happened?" Speedway asked.

Captain Noble continued, "An accident really. The weapon was built in a secure location deep inside the Rocka Jungle. The Moonbeams went to the Capital Biosphere to hold a **lecture** on the weapon and its capabilities. One afternoon, after a speaking session, they were walking down one of the exterior corridors in the biosphere. An airlock exploded, and they were blown out onto the **exposed** surface. They were burned to death. A full investigation was conducted, but it revealed that the *accident* really was an accident and not foul play. Many are still **suspicious**, though, but it doesn't make any sense that one of our people would want to hinder the project. Anyway, I digress."

Shortstop got the captain back on track, "I take it that Spikey was not with them at the time since he has led a very full life on Staranana for the past twenty-two years."

"That's right; he was with his grandparents. They were given charge over him after his parents' deaths. It was not long after that, that Spikey ran away. I never figured out how he did it, but he found the secret compound where the weapon was. Even at that age, Spikey was good with machines, and he had learned enough from his parents to know how to operate the weapon. He programmed it for its **designated** target and set the power to full."

"Well, the Palace is still there, so what went wrong?" Speedway asked.

"Something that nobody could have predicted. The weapon

was scheduled to be tested on a few asteroids in the area of our planet, so we could work out the bugs. That never happened. When Spikey used the full force of the weapon, it knocked the beam ever so slightly out of alignment. However, that slight misalignment translated into thousands of kleps once it reached Staranana. The beam struck Staranana's polar ice cap, an act that destabilized the rotation of your planet about its axis."

"The Marsh Season!" Shortstop exclaimed. "For just about the past twenty-two years, for one month every year, all the ice melts, and the planet virtually becomes a swamp. We've learned to live with it, but you're telling us it was Spikey that caused it?"

"Yes, it was. He was just a child, but our laws are very strict. After being oppressed by Seth for millennia, our people established a legal system that would prevent such a thing from happening again. Basically, you share in the suffering of your victim or victims. For example, and this is an extreme case that has never taken place, if you murder someone's child, your child is killed."

Shortstop was horrified, "That's appalling!"

"I know, General. As I said, that has never come up. And if it did, we would likely find an alternative. However, for Spikey, there was no alternative. When our scientists *confirmed* what had happened, Spikey was found guilty. His punishment was to be *banished* from Stararocka and to live out the rest of his days on Staranana. A small, one-person transport ship was programmed to take him to the Nana Forest. The Moonbeam family was very large at the time the first colonists left. Not all of them left Staranana, and the Nana Forest was the most likely place for him to find family who could take care of him."

Gloria continued, "He did. A couple of very distant cousins took him in, and they later adopted him. He told me they thought he was a runaway slave whose parents had been killed. They never learned the truth, even up until the day they were killed ten years ago. Spikey hid his ship, and he later took it apart and started making inventions with it."

Speedway could just see the poor, young cub being cast out into the cold, cruel universe. All he had wanted to do was honor the memory of his parents. That was no reason, no matter what the consequences of his acts, for pretty much sending him to Hell. There was one thing Speedway had to give Spikey credit for, though. If Staranana was Hell, then Spikey sure loved Hell. He was far more patriotic than any native-born bear Speedway had ever known. "Was that really an *appropriate* punishment for a child?" Speedway asked.

"I didn't think so at the time. Spikey was my best friend. But nothing so major has happened since. And the arbiter did place a pardon clause in Spikey's sentencing papers. His exile will be rescinded if the *Blood of the Land* orders it so."

Shortstop sighed, "It's not likely we'll see him anytime soon."

"But…" Josh began.

"How is the crew doing, Gloria?" Shortstop asked, not noticing that he had interrupted the commander.

"Great, all things considered. They have medicines here that I haven't even imagined. I feel like a rookie nurse, not the head of the rebel medical department. Their head doctor promised to bring me up to speed. The crew and passengers are recovering well. They should all be in perfect health by tomorrow. Other than the twenty we lost in the hull breach, there have been no fatalities."

Shortstop felt a pang of sorrow at that. He had intended to get all three hundred bears safely to Stararocka, but that *obviously* hadn't happened. He asked Captain Noble, "Do you have a deck or an empty cargo bay where I might gather the people from my ship and have a memorial service for our dead?"

"Of course, General. Josh can show you the way."

"Good, then we can be on our way to Stararocka. My people are eager to begin their new lives."

Captain Noble hesitated, "Ah, well, if you're planning on going to Stararocka, you may have to wait a while. We're heading in the opposite direction. This is the Starananian Liberation Fleet."

"Fleet? What fleet?" Speedway asked.

"Come with me," the captain said and led the way over to the window. Outside, gasses swirled, and asteroids drifted. They were still a long way from Stararocka, but among the **vast** fields of space rock, four more signs of that world came into view. They were nothing but pinpricks of silver, barely visible to the naked eye, but Shortstop knew what they were. They were ships.

"I feel another long story coming on," Speedway chuckled.

Josh suddenly spoke up, "Yes, but you might not believe it. All four of those ships are built exactly like the *Fire Cruiser*. There is the *Moon Cruiser*, the *Volcano*, the *Dragon's Blood*, and the *North Star*."

"What's the part we wouldn't believe?" Gloria asked.

"Well," Josh hesitated, "an angel told us to build them."

"An angel?" The question came from all three Starananians.

"Yes, five years ago, a being of light appeared in our capital. He had red hair, a red beard, and a flowing white robe. His **countenance** was as bright as the sun, if not brighter. He told us that he was an angel of God, and he said, *'The Blood of the Land is knocking at the door. Prepare for him! Take your father's ship and build it again four times. When you are finished, wait. When I come again, you will launch.'* My brother and I were having lunch in the central square that day. There were many people there, but we were the only ship builders and the only ones whose father owned a spacecraft. We obeyed the angel's command and put teams together to build the other ships. It took nearly two years. We waited another three years, and we were beginning to think the angel had forgotten about us. But then nine days ago, he came back. He told us to launch and head for Staranana. He said we would know what to do once we got there."

William broke in, "Yes, and we can't turn back now. I'll speak to my engineers. It may be possible for them to repair your ship enough for you to continue your journey, but it will take a few days. And by that time, our ship will have taken us all the way to Staranana. You'd have to start your trip over again, which would be pointless, because, in a very short time, your home world could be free."

The three Starananians stared at one another. Could it be true? Was God actually going to keep His promise? It seemed too good to be true. Spikey may have been right all along. For all they knew, it could have been his *Door* that brought the *Blood of the Land* to Staranana. Captain Noble was right. They had to go back. They had to go home.

Shortstop smiled and said, "Well, Gloria, I guess you'll get your wish after all. We're going back!"

Gloria could not contain her enthusiasm, and she embraced the General full force. Had he been human, the General most definitely would have been blushing. Speedway shocked them all when he asked, "Captain, Commander, do you pray?"

"We do," they replied.

Speedway held out his hands and said, "Then let's pray to our Lord." They formed a circle and knelt near the tiny window praying. Speedway led them. After all these years, it had finally happened. He knew where God was. God had come back to Staranana!

Chapter 33

The Last Prophecies

"How long should we let him sleep, Dad?"

"As long as he needs to."

"But it's been eighteen hours already!"

Spikey and Sparkey Moonbeam sat at the old, splintered table in the center of their family cave. Spikey had his copy of the *Text of Iren* open, and he was jotting notes in the margins. Sparkey sat watching his human friend. Scotty was stripped to his undergarments, wrapped in a heavy fur rug, and lying very close to the fire, asleep.

A day before, Hydro had dropped them off at the edge of the Nana Forest. When they returned to the family cave, they found TB and the *Door* in good health. TB reported no unusual activity in the area. Spikey encouraged Scotty to get some sleep. The true task of the *Blood of the Land* was close at hand, and the human boy would need all the rest he could get. Scotty had gotten out of his thermal suit, wrapped up near the fire, and was out like a light. In eighteen hours, he hadn't even stirred.

Four hours later, a pop from the fire finally woke Scotty. He sat up quickly and felt the heat of the fire on his back and the chill of the air on his chest. Sparkey chuckled and walked over to him, "Welcome back, Sleepyhead." Sparkey held Scotty's human clothes in his hands.

Scotty pulled them on and asked, "What's your dad doing?"

"He's reviewing the last **prophecies** of the *Blood of the Land* in the *Text of Iren*. There is not much left before Seth gets what's coming to him."

"Really?"

"Yeah, why don't you come over and check it out. We have a bowl of hot stew waiting. There isn't any fish in it, I promise. There is also a cup of hot, honeysuckle apple cider."

"Sounds great! What time is it, by the way?"

"Just about dawn."

"Have you guys slept at all?"

"We each slept for about eight hours. You've slept for twenty-two, buddy."

"Wow! Well, I feel like I could stay awake for a week now."

Scotty and Sparkey slid into chairs across from Spikey. He barely noticed them. His brow was furrowed, and his eyes were locked on the pages of the *Text of Iren*. Scotty shoveled the stew into his mouth and chugged the cider, though it did burn his tongue a bit. He was soon very satisfied.

"All right, there, that's the last one!" Spikey finally said. In addition to his scribbled notes in the book, Spikey had created a list on a piece of yellow **parchment**. He closed the book and held up the **parchment**. "This is a list of the last **prophecies** which involve the *Blood of the Land* and the defeat of Seth."

"Well, let's hear them!" Scotty exclaimed.

Spikey nodded and began, "First it says, *Rise up you humble and weak! Stand up you sick and sore, and cast off your burdens. Strike down the proud and the strong. I will make you a mighty army.'* The second **prophecy** says only, *'Strike down the faces of light.'* The third is, *'Blessed be the Lord God that heals.'* The fourth says, *'Fire shall rain down from the skies.'* Number five says simply, *'Heaven and Hell shall meet on Staranana.'* Then the last **prophecy** says, *'And evil shall be cast from the throne. The Blood of the Land shall be established upon it even until the coming of the Lord. Whether the Blood of the Land sleeps or lives until that time, no one else shall take his throne until the Lord is*

enthroned *before all.'* There are no other **prophecies**."

"And you're sure these all deal with me...uh, I mean the *Blood of the Land?*" Scotty asked.

"No doubt. The trouble is **interpreting** them. Take, for example, this first one. It talks about the weak becoming a mighty army. But who are they?" Spikey asked.

The word *weak* sprung a song into Scotty's head, *"...They are weak, but He is strong."*

"What?" Sparkey asked.

"Oh, sorry," Scotty apologized. "It's a song kids sing in Sunday school, *Jesus Loves Me.* It talks about how Jesus takes care of the weak. It's all over the *Bible* how God opposes the proud and gives grace to the humble."

"Well, Seth **obviously** fits into the category of proud, but who are the weak?" Sparkey asked.

Spikey rubbed the fur on his face and thought for a moment until it hit him! "Of course, the slaves!"

"The slaves?" Scotty asked.

"Yes, the majority of our **population** has been enslaved. Many live in huts and tents outside the Palace walls. There have to be at least several hundred in that area. If I were going to raise up an army from among the weak, what better place to start than right on Seth's doorstep?"

"Well, assuming you're right, that still leaves five **prophecies** to deal with," Scotty said.

"Yeah, and I don't like what I'm thinking about the **prophecy** that says, *'Strike down the faces of light.'* It sounds almost like a command to the enemy. The best I can figure is that something is going to go wrong before things get better. Light always refers to goodness, so **obviously,** this **prophecy** is describing a slaughter. Many bears will most likely lose their lives. Maybe someone will **betray** us?" Spikey said.

"Do you think it could be Hydro, Scotty?" Sparkey asked.

"I doubt it. If all you say about the dagger is true, if he was evil, he should have been sucked into the *Black Lava Pits* when he got stabbed, but that didn't happen. I think he's really on our side. So, who else does that leave?"

"No one," Spikey said. "Anyway, we should be on our way."

"On our way where?" Scotty asked.

"The slave camps, of course."

"What about the rest of the *prophecies*?" Scotty questioned.

"Their meanings should become clearer as time passes, but right now, we should act on what we know. We'll go to the slave camps and start organizing things there."

"How will we get there?" Sparkey asked.

Spikey smiled, and Scotty shuddered, knowing what he was going to say. "Not the *aqueducts*!" the boy complained.

"Sorry, Scotty, but there are no dragons to come to our rescue this time. Don't worry, we have to take a different passage than the one you did. It should only take about four hours. Now, you guys get ready."

The three spent the next few minutes filling new packs with supplies. Spikey fiddled with a few controls on TB, and then he tucked his list into his pocket. Scotty put his thermal suit back on, and they were ready to once again face the challenges of the *aqueducts*. Scotty whined under his breath, "I'm not getting paid enough for this!"

Chapter 34

The Slave Camps

"Make way for His Majesty, the Great Emperor Seth!" a loud voice bellowed. It was a goon. He and around twenty of his **compatriots** were marching down what had been so appropriately **designated** *Hate Street*. It passed through the slave camps directly to the outer gates of the Palace walls, and it had been the site of more bloodshed than anywhere else on the planet.

The slaves in the area scrambled to get out of the way. They had learned from bitter experience that when a goon gave a command, you listened or you died. Many of the slaves wore nothing but shredded rags, and every one of them bore scars from many encounters with Seth's **horde**. The children wore nothing but their fur, which barely protected them against the cold. The huts and tents throughout the camp were rotting and filled with holes, and no one was well fed.

The troop of goons marched by and entered the Palace gates. Two dragons, waddling along on stubby legs, followed them, and finally, four bears slowly trod down the road. On their shoulders, they carried a heavy, golden throne. A human in a thermal suit (save the mask) sat on the throne, and a plain, golden crown rested on his sandy-blond head. A six goon security squad surrounded the throne.

A tall bear, in a dirty, stained robe with a hood, stood and watched from within the crowd. He had managed to steal his garment from a dead goon that died face down in the mud some years past. He didn't like wearing the clothes of the enemy, but at least they kept him warm.

Another bear approached the first and asked, "So, what is it this time, Mr. Garlan?"

"Bad news I'm afraid, Sam. A dragon returned to the Palace yesterday. Seth was still out searching for the human boy, so the dragon could not give his report. Lizard Face radioed Seth with the dragon's news, and Seth has just now returned."

"The rumors about the boy are true?" Sam asked.

"Yes, from what I heard, but he escaped from the Palace."

"What was the dragon's news?"

"Wait, look at that!" Garlan pointed to the street where a tiny girl had wandered into the path of Seth's throne. One of the throne bearers did not notice the girl, and before he did, he had tripped over her. The other three lost their balance as well, and Seth went flying into the mud.

"You little fool!" Seth screamed. He removed a dagger from his side and lunged to slit the girl's throat. Simultaneously, one the goons placed a rifle at the temple of the bear that had tripped and pulled the trigger. He fell down dead, his blood gushing into the snow.

Before Seth could kill the girl, an old woman threw herself at Seth's feet and began kissing them. "Please, Great Lord, have **mercy** on this child," she begged. "She is not yet old enough to have served you properly. Please, Your Majesty, I beg you!"

A smile curled over Seth's lips and he said, "Very well. I forgive you, young one. Go and play." The girl smiled and hurried away into the crowd as Seth turned to face them all. He declared, "My beloved servants, I offer grace to you this day, for it is a day of joy. I am sure you have heard the rumors of a human boy in our midst. For you *loyal* subjects of my empire, I bring good news. The boy has been slaughtered by one of my dragons.

Do not fear! Your gracious emperor will remain upon his throne forevermore."

The hearts of every bear in the area sank at the Emperor's news. Seth was merely playing the part of the benevolent dictator. The truth was he had no *loyal* subjects in the slave camps and very few in the Palace. But if the human boy had been defeated, it didn't matter who was *loyal* to him. He would always rule.

Seth's smile never faded as he returned to his throne. Another bear was dragged from the crowd, and he joined the other three in carrying Seth's throne. A few minutes later, Seth's entire *entourage* disappeared inside the Palace walls.

"It can't be true, Mr. Garlan, can it?" Sam asked.

Garlan shook his head and said, "I don't know. They don't have a body, and that's a good sign. Besides, the dragon that made the report was Hydro. Seth killed his brothers, and Hydro hasn't killed a single bear. I'd want to find out more, but I don't know where to start."

~

"Ah, Lt. Gakic, come in, come in! You bring good news of the *Sspace Sshark,* I take it." Lizard Face ushered the young goon into his chambers. News of the destruction of a **vast portion** of the shipyard and the deaths of several hundred goons had been a blow. However, when news reached the Palace that the *Space Shark* had launched successfully, Lizard Face's hope in their plans returned.

"I'm sorry, sir. I have bad news. May I use your terminal?" Lizard Face led him over to his personal computer, and the goon slid a data crystal into the side port. An infrared sensor display appeared on the screen. Huge blobs of red covered the display, accompanied by several smaller dots of the same color.

"What is this?" Lizard Face hissed.

"These small dots are metal fragments. The larger blobs are

fields of atomic radiation."

"Ah, **obviously**, the *Sspace Sshark* has destroyed her target. That wasn't exactly the plan, but I am *ssure* Captain Gonish took on prisoners. *Sso*, what is the problem?"

"You don't understand, Master Lizard Face. The *Space Shark* was not equipped with atomic weapons. These pieces of metal are from her hull. Given the radiation levels, I believe the vessel has been destroyed!"

"What!"

"We cannot make contact with them, or pick them up on scanners. We have to believe the worst, but there is some good news."

"And what is that?"

Lt. Gakic tapped a few controls, and the image transformed. The red atomic blurbs vanished, and the red pieces of hull did as well. They were replaced by several smaller green blurbs and over a dozen almost **microscopic** green dots.

Gakic reported, "These are pieces of another ship. The integrity of the metal is very poor. It could only be the rebel ship. These small dots **confirm** this. They are the bodies of bears floating in space."

"*Sso* the *Sspace Sshark* destroyed her target before *sshe* was destroyed?"

"It appears that way. But we have no idea what destroyed our ship. Sensors are picking up nothing. Sir, without the *Space Shark*, your plans to overthrow Seth may not work. The troop ship you ordered to be repaired is nearly ready. We can **evacuate** tomorrow if you like."

Lizard Face calmed him, "Patience, Lieutenant. We don't need to give up *sso* quickly. Do not forget that the majority of the goons are with us. I need only give the word, and they will rise up. And I think the time has come to give the word. Tomorrow night, I will give the order, and *Sseth* will lose his throne."

"What about the human boy?"

"Have you not heard the report? He's dead!"

"Yes, I know. I heard, but do you actually trust Hydro? I mean, he has a zero kill record."

"Until now."

"If his report is true, but I have my doubts. The boy already fulfilled several **prophecies**, and never in history have Iren's **prophecies** failed."

"Maybe *Sseth* finally got the best of his father. But just in case you're right, we'll move *sseveral* hundred goons to the troop *sship*. Take them from all over the planet, and take only the loyalist ones."

"You want me to do it, sir?"

"Yes, Lieutenant. *Sseth* has overlooked your *sskills* for far too long. Don't *sspread* the word amongst the troops who are **loyal** to *Sseth*, but I am promoting you. You will *sskip* the next few ranks and become a full Captain. Take charge of this project, and be ready for launch. Oh, and, Captain, no bear-goons. The bears your people transformed may make good *sslaves*, but I want no *Sstarananian* blood on my *sship*. I will bring whatever troops I can from the Palace if the need arises to **evacuate**. But I am *sstill* holding out for a happy ending."

"How will you get to the ship, sir?"

"We'll take one of the hopper pods on the roof. It *sshould* fit about fifty goons. But I don't plan to *sspend* tomorrow night making a run for our troop *sship*. I plan to *sspend* it *ssleeping* in *Sseth's* bed."

"Excellent, sir!"

~

"You know, if I become emperor, I think I'm going to order every last gator in the **aqueducts** killed!" Scotty **cursed**. Spikey's estimate of a safer, four-hour trip through the **aqueducts** had turned into a five-hour run for dear life, bashing gators all the way.

"Scotty, I've never heard you talk like that!" Sparkey scolded.

"Oh, I know. I'm sorry. But at the very least, I am going to build you guys a better sewage system."

They emerged from the **aqueducts** just beyond the outer border of the slave camps. The Palace was only a few kleps down the road. They hid behind a pile of rotting wood and observed the camp.

It was a pitiful sight. Hundreds of scrawny bears were meandering about. On the opposite side of the only road, there were several piles of timber, stones, and metal. They were supplies for Seth's various desires, **obviously** produced by slave labor. Food seemed to be a rarity in the camp, but there was no shortage of the stench of death. There were dead bodies everywhere. Apparently, the bears had neither the strength nor the desire to properly bury them. Death had become commonplace.

"What are we going to do now, Dad?"

Spikey thought and then replied, "We need to find their leader if they have one. But I don't want to excite them. And I can think of nothing that would excite them more than a human boy strolling through their camp. Seth could be out here and on us within minutes."

Scotty had the mask of his thermal suit on, and he asked, "Won't my mask conceal me?"

"What bear would ever wear a suit like that? Even I only wore it in secret when I...Well, when I needed to when I was a kid, but I soon got used to the cold. Besides, I think Seth has a similar suit without the mask. Any smart bear could put two and two together and figure out there wasn't a bear in there."

"So what choice do we have, Dad?"

"I don't know. Wait, what's that?" Spikey pointed to a long piece of wood lying in the snow. It had about the same width and length as a bed. Next to it was a long piece of brown cloth, stained, wet, and sporting several holes. "Scotty, wait here. Sparkey, come help me," Spikey commanded.

The two bears crept from their hiding place and dug the

board and the cloth from the snow. They then dragged them back behind the pile of wood. They were not noticed. "What are we going to do with those?" Scotty asked.

"Lie down," Spikey commanded.

"What?"

"How do you feel about being dead, my friend?" Spikey asked.

"Dead! Are you crazy? I'm only a kid! Besides, I always hoped I would die on Earth."

"Oh, Scotty, don't be silly! I'm not talking about you really dying. We're just going to pretend. You lie on this, we put the cloth over you, and we pretend we're just two sorry souls looking for a place to bury a friend. Hopefully, by asking around, we can find their leader. Maybe we can do it before our arms get tired."

"All right, let me try this thing on for size." Scotty lay down on the board and pulled the cloth up to his neck.

Before covering his head, Spikey said, "Whatever you do, be very quiet and still. Don't worry; we'll **resurrect** you soon." With that, Spikey covered the boy's head, and he and his son picked up their makeshift stretcher.

~

"Oh, give up hope, boys. No one ever gets buried here. It's forbidden."
"Who are you guys? Are you new?"

The questions came and came as Spikey and Sparkey carried the stretcher through the slave camp. They had asked a few people if there was a leader they could speak to, but no one had been helpful. Many were too sick, and the ones who were strong were working and could not be interrupted. The little children were the most receptive. They were always running up to the bears and touching their clothes, which were in much better condition than anything the slaves wore. However, most of the children could not speak, and those who could knew nothing worthwhile.

"This is getting us nowhere, Dad!" Sparkey complained.

"I know. Come on; let's find a place to hide."

"That hut over there looks abandoned. Let's go there." They made their way to a half-collapsed hut a good hundred feet off the road. They really couldn't understand why it had been abandoned. The rest of the slaves' homes were hardly in better condition. But, at least, it was a place to rest.

Scotty sat up, "All right, I've been dead for over an hour, and it's getting boring."

"Sorry, Scotty, but I don't know what we are going to do," Spikey said. "We can't find their leader. Maybe it's stupid to even think they have one. They are slaves after all. If they had a leader, it would be much easier for them to resist Seth."

"We can't just give up, Dad."

"Over here, Mr. Garlan! I think the strangers went this way," came a voice from outside.

"What was that?" Scotty hissed.

"Time to die again! Quick, cover up, Scotty." Spikey pulled the cloth back over Scotty's head, and he and Sparkey sat quietly. The hut had a single window that allowed a **minimal** amount of light into the structure. Spikey prayed no one would pass by that window.

"Look, the footprints go into this hut," the voice said again.

A shadow eclipsed the light from the window, but Spikey and Sparkey remained quiet as the heavy cloth over the doorway pulled back, and two bears stepped inside.

"Who are you?" one asked. His voice was different than the voice they had heard outside.

Spikey stood and addressed the two bears, "My name is Spikey Moonbeam. This is my son Sparkey. We're rebels from the Nana Forest."

"Who's your friend under the sheet?" the one with the familiar voice asked.

"Not so fast. First, tell me who you are," Spikey said.

"My name is Garlan, and this is my assistant Sam," the one

with the unfamiliar voice said. "I'm the minister here. I run an underground study of the *Text of Iren*. Unfortunately, our group of believers is small. Because of what they have endured, most of the slaves have given up hope in God."

It wasn't really that important, but Sparkey had to ask, "Why can't you bury your dead?"

Sam replied, "If they're killed by one of Seth's **minions**, we aren't allowed to touch their bodies, or we risk the same fate. The goons remember the bears they've killed. They like to keep score with each other. If a body is gone, they kill whoever is closest to where it was, whether they had anything to do with moving the body or not. People who die by other causes have their bodies dragged out of the camp. The snow buries them soon enough. If your friend here was killed by goons, you had better take him back. You're risking other people's lives."

"They don't need to bury me!" Scotty said and sat up quickly.

Garlan and Sam felt their hearts jump in their chests. They had not expected a dead body to suddenly lurch back to life. Scotty's features were still concealed beneath his thermal suit.

"Who's that?" Sam exclaimed.

"Better yet, what's he wearing?" Garlan asked.

"Take it easy, guys," Spikey said. "He's just wearing a thermal suit."

"Why?" Sam asked.

"Because he can't handle the cold. He's the reason we're here, but before I have him take off his mask, I need to ask you a question. Have you heard about the human boy that was discovered in the Palace about a week-and-a-half ago?"

"Yeah, rumors are everywhere," Garlan said. "Seth has been looking for him ever since he escaped from the Palace. But Seth also told us himself that the boy was killed by one of his dragons."

"Don't believe everything you hear," Spikey cautioned. Then he walked over to Scotty, took the top of his mask in his hand, and pulled.

Garlan and Sam fell to their knees as the human boy's face was revealed. Sparkey said, "Allow me to introduce Scotty Fields, the *Blood of the Land*."

Garlan was almost weeping as he crawled on his knees over to Scotty. He then cupped the boy's face in his hands. The fur tickled, and Scotty giggled a bit before Garlan wrapped him in his arms. "It's true! It's true!" the bear wailed and began sobbing uncontrollably. His companion soon joined him. Scotty only smiled politely, and he did his best to keep breathing under the heavy embrace of the bears.

Spikey, Sparkey, and Scotty spent the next half-hour telling their story to Garlan and Sam. Finally, Spikey came to their purpose for that day, "One of the last **prophecies** says that a great army will arise from among the weak to take on Seth's forces, and they will be victorious. We figured the best place to look for the weak would be in the slave camps. Besides, you're the only bears left in the area."

"Weak we are at that, but not so much in our physical ability as in our spiritual lives. As I said, many have lost faith in God's promises because they have been so long in coming. I can't imagine how we could build an army from them," Garlan said.

"All it takes is a single moment of inspiration to change a heart. I have a few ideas of how we can make that happen," Spikey said.

"How?" Garlan asked.

"The first thing you should do in any situation beyond your control is pray. I want you to gather five of your most spiritual bears. Find them a comfortable place, out of sight. We'll take Scotty there. Scotty and those bears will start praying. I'll draw up a list of requests if you can find me a scrap of parchment. Then you, Sam, Sparkey, and I will begin going through the camp telling people that the *Blood of the Land* is here. We'll arrange a gathering where everyone can come and meet him. When would be a good time?"

"We're allowed a break for lunch at midday, but it's only

about ten minutes long. The best time would be after sundown when the workday ends. Most of the people meet in the center of the camp then to share a meal and talk. There are usually no goons. It will be a good time to introduce Scotty," Garlan said.

"Great, then let's get to work. You go find your prayer group and then a place. I think we should carry Scotty there on the stretcher. I don't want to create a stir that might alert the Palace guards. When we tell people the *Blood of the Land* has arrived, we need to tell them to keep their excitement in check. Anyone with a loose tongue should not be told, and everyone we tell should be instructed not to talk about Scotty after we leave. Is that understood?"

Garlan nodded, and Spikey said, "Okay, go find your people. Come back when they're ready." Garlan and Sam hurried out the door. It was all they could do to keep themselves from screaming for joy.

~

An hour later, the prayer group was created, and Scotty joined them. For all his biblical knowledge, Scotty was still a child, and he was often distracted during prayer. It was a failing common among Christians. However, what he experienced with the prayer group was far more potent than any prayer experience he had ever had. They wailed and cried, and a few fell on their faces, thanking God for His **provision**. Scotty felt the presence of God more deeply than he ever had. He felt his sins being convicted, his spirit being energized, and his purpose being clarified. One thing he was sure of, God was definitely listening.

Meanwhile, Spikey, Sparkey, Garlan, and Sam began to move through the camp. They traveled together to give their message more credibility. The faithful students of the *Text of Iren* were overjoyed and went about their chores with a new spring in their step. The **skeptics** expressed their doubts, but most promised to attend the meeting later that night. It took until late afternoon, but eventually word had gotten to the entire camp.

"Thank goodness, we're done!" Spikey said, slumping onto a stump to rest his feet. He and his team had stopped at the very end of *Hate Street* where the camp ended and a winding road led across a snowy plain into the forest.

"Sure, we get to introduce Scotty to them, but how are we going to turn them into an army?" Sparkey asked.

"Don't you worry about that," Garlan said. "Follow me." He led them a short distance down the winding road until it ran parallel with the tree line.

"Exactly how far away from camp are you guys allowed to go?" Spikey asked.

"Not far. Going into the forest is forbidden, and we must be present for roll call every morning. Basically, we can go anywhere on this plain. Of course, a few of us break the rules every now and again."

Garlan looked back toward the Palace. There were no guard towers, but you never knew when the enemy might be watching. Garlan put his hood on and said, "You three walk in front of me. From the Palace, I'll look like a goon. If anyone notices us at all, they'll think I'm taking you into the forest to kill you."

"Why would you do that? Wouldn't a goon just kill us right here?" Spikey asked.

Sam explained, "Goons get a special bonus for killing runaways. Sometimes they drag people into the forest to make them look like runaways, and then they kill them to get the bonus. Seth never does any real checking, and all the goons keep their **compatriots'** secrets."

They walked into the forest, and they had barely crossed the tree line before Garlan stopped them in a small clearing in-between a dozen towering trees. Garlan and Sam knelt in the snow and began to dig. Spikey and Sparkey watched them until they uncovered a small, wooden trapdoor. "Follow us," Garlan said, and the two slaves led the way down.

They climbed down a rope ladder into a dark and musty, dirt

cave. Garlan, apparently knowing his way in the dark, stepped to a wall and found a lantern. Somehow, he lit it, and Spikey's mouth dropped at what he saw.

Piles and piles of swords, rifles, daggers, clubs and ammunition filled the tiny cave. There had to be at least two thousand separate weapons, Spikey thought. The place was a treasure trove for any resistance against Seth. "Where did this all come from?" he asked.

"Lots of places," Garlan said. "Many of the bears who serve inside the Palace have been able to sneak supplies out. Also, anytime the rebels engaged the goons, we managed to sneak a slave to the battlefield. They picked up any weapon that was broken or **deemed** useless to the rebels, who might have otherwise appropriated it. They brought those weapons back here, and we fixed them. We also refine more metal than our quota requires. We keep the excess and forge them into weapons as well. This cave is over two hundred years old."

"And no one thought of using these?" Spikey asked.

"Oh, we thought about it, but there is the little matter of the **prophecies** that make Seth impervious to an attack by bears. Besides that, most of our people are too downcast and depressed to offer much of a resistance against Seth. The incident with Kelcott, fifteen years ago, gave us further reason not to rise up. We basically decided to keep collecting weapons until the *Blood of the Land* arrived, which he did today," Garlan explained.

Spikey giggled, "This is too good to be true! After tonight's meeting, we'll begin passing these out, and we'll have more than a surplus. Let's get back to the camp."

"No can do, Mr. Moonbeam. We can't risk being spotted. If anyone did spot us heading into the forest, they'll think I'm just an off-duty goon enjoying my kill. We must wait until nightfall to return to the camp. That is only about an hour away," Garlan said.

Spikey and Sparkey agreed, and they spent the next hour inventorying the weaponry. They would definitely be able to do some serious damage with the weapons, but the *weak* army attack would be nothing more than a diversion. The real battle would be between Seth and Scotty, alone.

~

"Is he really human?"
"Let us touch him!"

When the sun set, Spikey and his group returned to the camp, and Scotty's prayer session ended. They, along with the slaves, had gathered before a huge bonfire, as had been discussed, but beyond that, nothing had gone according to plan. Spikey, Garlan, Sparkey and Sam had to hold the multitude back as they tried desperately just to touch Scotty. Scotty was a little **anxious** at first, but then something clicked inside of him, and his mouth began speaking like it had in Seth's chamber.

He climbed up onto a crate and shouted, **"You would dare to worship a child, and not the One True God? Get back, all of you! The *Blood of the Land* came to fulfill God's promise, but that fulfillment can wait longer still if you do not obey!"**

In **unison**, the crowd pulled back and dropped to their knees. A few cried out, "Forgive us, Lord God! We are blind to Your glory."

Others called, "Bless the Lord who brought us this deliverer, but all power and honor and glory are God's alone."

The flash of anger inside Scotty faded, and he stepped from the crate. Spikey stepped into the firelight and sounded, "The time of Seth's downfall is at hand! God has brought the *Blood of the Land* to us, and the boy has the *Dagger of Promise*. The next part of the story falls to you."

"What can we do?" someone shouted.

Garlan stepped forward, "The *Text of Iren* promises that an army comprised of weak soldiers will defeat Seth's **horde**. As far as we can tell, that's us. We have enough weapons for all of you."

"What of our children?" a woman asked. "They can't fight!"

"I have an idea about that," Sam said. "This attack has to take place soon, even tonight, so there will be no more roll call. According to Spikey, the rebels of the Nana Forest left behind dozens of empty caves when they left the planet. I am willing to lead the women and children there for safety. That should still leave us with about six hundred bears to create our army."

"Good idea, Sam," Spikey said. Then he continued, "We'll need about twenty of you to come with us and start hauling the weapons back to camp. We must move quickly and quietly. I'm no expert, but I think I can give you all a crash course in how to use the weapons in about an hour. We make our attack at midnight. That's about six-and-a-half hours from now."

"How will we breach the Palace gate?" someone near the front asked.

"We'll go several kleps into the forest, cut down a tree, and create a battering ram. From that distance, no one at the Palace should see or hear the tree fall. Our objective is to storm the Palace and begin taking control of it floor by floor," Garlan explained.

"That only leaves six bears to hold each floor, assuming we all survive that long. That will never work," another complained.

"Don't worry," Spikey said. "The *Text of Iren* promises we'll get some help from Heaven. It also gives some bad news, saying that the *faces of light*, us I assume, will have many of our numbers struck down."

The people sighed, and Spikey continued, "I know it's a hard thing we're asking, but think of the thousands of bears all over the planet who will benefit from your faithfulness to God. We need you to do this."

"You can count on me!" a bear called. Another sounded that he was with them as well, and soon the entire crowd was roaring.

Garlan hushed them and said, "Good, then let's get to work! All the women and children go with Sam. Take nothing burdensome with you. You will not be gone long. You twenty bears here in the front, come with me and Spikey."

As everyone organized, Spikey turned to his son and said, "I guess this is goodbye, Sparkey."

"Dad, I don't want to go with Sam! I can fight!"

"I'm not asking you to go with Sam. Listen, I need you and Scotty to take the *aqueducts* and get back inside the Palace. You need to find a place where you can see what is going on outside and be close to the throne room without getting caught. I believe Scotty will know when the right time comes to confront Seth."

"All right, Dad. I'll do my best. Will you be okay?"

"Yeah, don't worry about me. I hate to put this on you, son, but the real fate of Staranana lies with you and Scotty. Now, get going!"

Sparkey called Scotty over as Spikey joined the group going for the weapons. "What now?" Scotty asked.

"We take the *aqueducts* into the Palace. This is it, my friend. You ready?"

Scotty nodded, "Yeah, I finally am. I have the dagger. Now, let's go give this planet back to the people it truly belongs to."

Sparkey smiled and followed his friend into the night.

Chapter 35

The Faces of Light

"Okay, no one is in here! Let's go!" Scotty pulled himself up through the trapdoor in the cellar, and then he pulled Sparkey up. Their journey through the *aqueducts*, as was typical, had not been easy, but it had at least been easier than the last two times. It was now one hour before midnight.

"What now?" Sparkey asked.

"Well, where is the throne room?"

"I think it's on the sixteenth floor. When we were spreading the word about you earlier today, I noticed a huge set of bay windows on the Palace six floors over the wall. Since we know the wall is ten stories tall, those windows would be on the sixteenth floor. They'd be the perfect place to put a throne room. Seth could look out over the slave camp from the comfort of his throne."

"All right, we'll go there, but how are we going to get there?"

"We could always try the *dumbwaiter* again," Sparkey quipped.

"Yeah, sure, and just pass right by Lizard Face's chambers again. I don't think so."

"Well, what other choice is there?"

"I don't know. Hey, is this a door? I never noticed it before," Scotty said. He walked to the outer wall of the cellar on which was a wooden door with a rusted chain attached where a door handle should have been. Near the top of the door was a small, circular window.

"Boost me up, Sparkey," Scotty said, and the young bear cupped his hands together. When Scotty was high enough, he peered through the window. "I think that's the courtyard out there. I can't see much - just a few bushes, but I can see the outer gates."

"So what? We can't go out there."

"Oh, yes we can!"

"What?"

"Someone we know is out there."

"Who?"

Scotty climbed down and said, "It's Hydro. He's pacing back and forth by the gate. If we can get his attention, maybe he can help us."

"How?" Before Sparkey got an answer, Scotty was out the door. Sparkey *cursed* and followed him. They crept along the wall in the shadows. Besides Hydro, the courtyard was empty. No goons were on duty. Torches illuminated the area, and the environmental regulators were on, keeping the courtyard warm. All the windows on the front of the Palace were dark. No one would likely notice them. Even so, the boys did not dare to move from the shadows.

Scotty stopped at the edge of the shadows, fifty feet from the pacing dragon. "Hydro!" he hissed. The dragon looked agitated, and he barely noticed Scotty's cry. When Scotty cried again, he turned his attention to the shadows. He could not see who was there, so he bared his teeth to kill.

"Hydro, no! It's us!" Scotty wailed as the dragon prepared to pounce.

"Scotty?" Hydro questioned.

"Yes, friend! It's us!"

"What are you doing here?" Hydro growled. "Never mind, say nothing. It's not safe here." The dragon returned to his pacing without another word. Scotty and Sparkey were confused at first, but then they noticed something quite odd.

Though he was still pacing, a narrow stream of water began flowing from the dragon's feet. The water flowed directly toward Sparkey and Scotty. Just when it was about to begin flowing over their feet, it suddenly diverted course and began moving toward the cellar door. A voice spoke directly out of the stream, *"Follow the water!"* Scotty and Sparkey, though thoroughly confused, said nothing. They simply obeyed.

When they were back inside the cellar, the water formed into a puddle and began to glow. The liquid asked, *"Okay, now, what are you doing here?"*

"Hydro?" Sparkey questioned.

"Yes, it's me," the puddle spoke. *"This is one of my more unusual powers. I can extend my consciousness through water. As long as this puddle is connected to my body outside, we can talk together."*

Scotty felt odd speaking to a puddle, but he got to the point, "Hydro, we need your help. Tonight is the night. We've got an army ready to bash down the Palace gate, and I have the dagger. The *Blood of the Land* is taking over!"

The light from the puddle pulsed and Hydro said, *"That's wonderful, and not a moment too soon! They are growing* **suspicious** *of me. Your pack wasn't exactly convincing. I could tell Lizard Face had his doubts. Seth even grilled me this afternoon after he got back. I think I convinced him, but I don't know. What is really weird is that I was assigned guard duty tonight. I am usually assigned dawn patrol or long-range missions like the one to Stony City. I never get guard duty. I think they want to keep me close for some reason."*

"You should get out of here, Hydro! I don't want the army to attack you by mistake," Scotty said. "But we need your help first. Can you get us to the throne room? Or at least close to it?"

"Yes! Yes, I can! Oh, this couldn't have been a more perfect night!"

"What do you mean, Hydro?" Sparkey asked.

"Despite his suspicions, Seth was very excited to hear you had been killed. He canceled all the night shifts except mine, which makes me wonder if they trust me. Since I killed you, I of all people should have been rewarded.

In any case, the goons spent most of the night celebrating and drinking plume-berry juice. By now, they'll all be asleep in their quarters."

"Boy, people sure go to bed early around this joint, especially on a party night," Scotty laughed.

"Anyway, there is a clear path for you to get to the fountain."

"The fountain? Who cares about that? We're trying to get to the throne room!" Scotty complained.

"You don't understand! The fountain can get you to the sixteenth floor."

"How?"

"Am I or am I not a water dragon? I can manipulate all water. You hop into the fountain, and I'll increase the pressure and lift you to the sixteenth story."

"Yeah, and we'll be soaking wet!"

Instead of retorting, the glowing puddle exploded, and a blazing flame rose to the ceiling of the cellar. The puddle reformed under the flame, but it did nothing to **quench** it. Hydro said, *"I'll dry you off if it's that important to you!"*

"Okay, so what if we get caught?" Sparkey asked.

*"Well, since I'm going to be **liberated** in the morning anyway, I guess I don't have to be one of them anymore. I'll bust in and save you if the need arises."*

"Uh, I don't mean to be rude, but we don't have much time. It has to be close to midnight by now. We need to get into place," Scotty said.

"Right, right, shall we go, boys?"

"Can the puddle follow us up the stairs?" Sparkey asked.

"Are you kidding? I'll beat you up there!" The flame vanished, and the puddle became a stream again. It moved to the base of the winding stairs, and then arched and began bouncing up the steps.

"What do you think, Sparkey?"

"I think we should go," Sparkey said, and he followed the stream up the stairs.

~

"No, no, hold it like this. There you go. Now, put your finger right here on the trigger. Okay, do you think you can handle it?" The *elderly* bear nodded at Spikey's question, and Spikey smiled, and then he continued checking on his ragtag army. Over the last several hours, he had done his best to equip the slaves for battle. He was no military tactician, but he had good reason to be proud of what he had accomplished. Every male bear, down to the teenagers, had been given weapons. The slower ones had been given rifles, so they could take on the enemy from a distance. The very brave, young ones were given swords and clubs. And the *foolhardy* ones, who would rush in where angels feared to tread, so to speak, were given daggers. Everyone had the perfect weapon for his abilities. That left only one weapon of war to be *obtained.*

"Have you seen Garlan and the battering ram troop? It's only about twenty minutes until midnight," Spikey asked a passing bear.

"Last I knew, they hadn't come back from the forest yet," the bear said.

Spikey sighed. They had to get back and soon.

~

"The ship is ready, Master Lizard Face," Captain Gakic reported over the transmitter in the lizard's chambers.

"Excellent! *Sseth* thinks the goons are all drunk. Really, they're just waiting in their quarters for my orders," Lizard Face replied.

"Excellent, sir! I hope to be back at the Palace with you soon!"

"*Ssee* you then, Captain."

~

"Thanks, Hydro! See you soon," Scotty whispered as their liquid companion descended from the sixteenth story. Their ascent had gone off without a hitch. There hadn't even been a goon in sight. Hydro used the fountain to lift them up, and then he dried them. None of the residents stirred.

The sixteenth floor was horrific, and Scotty and Sparkey kept their eyes locked on the floor to keep from looking at the walls, but even the floor was disturbing. Dozens and dozens of pictures of dead bears, bears being tortured, and bears being disemboweled lined the walls. All the pictures were painted, but the boys guessed they were based on real events. The halls were also filled with stone bears, perhaps from Stony City, which had been defaced in one way or another. The floor was not covered in carpet, but wall to wall bear fur. The entire level was ***grotesque***, and everything clashed, but that didn't matter. It was the perfect tribute to Seth's evil.

"Where do we go now?" Scotty asked.

Sparkey pointed down the hall, as his stomach churned, "Those bay windows should be in this direction. And let's hurry! I need to get away from this stuff."

The boys began jogging down the hall and soon came to a large set of double doors. They were not ***offensive***, thankfully. They were carved of a wood similar to oak, and they were finely polished. The handles were made of gold, but other than that, the doors had no decorations.

Scotty opened one of the doors a crack, and Sparkey hissed, "Are you crazy? You're going to get us caught!"

"Relax, buddy! It's pretty dark in there, only one torch, but the place is huge. Come on; I think it's safe." Scotty pulled the door open and walked inside.

Despite the low light, the boys were amazed by what they saw. The throne room was every bit dignified. The floor was pure-white marble and spanned out in a thousand-foot by thousand-foot square. To the left of the doors, about five hundred feet away, was the bay window. The window was one solid sheet of glass that spanned the entire length of the outer wall and about twenty feet to the ceiling. In the very center of the room was a fountain identical to the one in the entry chamber. Along the outer walls were huge pillars, carved of diamonds, in the shapes of **phoenixes** and angels. There were also various other decorations like silk tapestries hanging from the ceiling and golden cherubs in various places. Given the heavenly nature of most of the decorations, Scotty assumed the throne room had looked like this when Iren was emperor. Against the far wall, opposite the windows, raised about ten feet to look over the fountain, sat a golden throne.

"Wow!" Sparkey said.

"You can say that again," Scotty returned. "We need to find a place to hide. If I'm right, it's only about ten minutes until the army comes busting in, and you can bet Seth will be in here once that happens."

"What about up there?" Sparkey asked.

"Where?" Scotty followed the bear's pointing finger to the ceiling. Beyond the silk tapestries were several **exposed** beams.

"Looks like Seth is doing some renovating. Maybe he wants a *larger* throne room," Sparkey **mocked**.

"Well, it will work, but how do we get up there?" Scotty asked.

"Leave that to me!" Sparkey piped. He proceeded to open his pack, and then he removed a long rope with a grappling hook attached.

Scotty chuckled, "You never cease to amaze me!"

~

"Oh, thank the Lord! There you are," Spikey said, coming alongside Garlan. The minister and around eighty other bears were carrying an enormous tree on their shoulders. The base of the tree, where they had cut it down, was nearly half the size of the outer gates.

Garlan stopped and said, "Look, if I put this tree down, I'm not picking it up again. So let's get this done now!"

Spikey nodded and quickly began directing, "Okay, everyone who is not with the battering ram troop, get behind the tree." The people moved and ended up nearly one hundred feet away at the end of the gigantic tree. Spikey followed them and said, "Okay, daggers in front, followed by clubs, then swords, and finally, rifles in the very back. Remember your targets. You with the rifles, don't get *foolhardy* and shoot your fellow bears by mistake."

The army lined up in the *appropriate* rows, and then they stood to await the command to attack. Spikey found a crate and stood on it, "If those of you holding the tree will forgive me, there are a few things I need to say. A few weeks ago, it seemed that God had completely forgotten our world. My own family and friends had given up hope, and they left Staranana searching for a new life. I planned to die in a suicide mission to help their effort to escape. But, as He so often does, God proved to have different plans, and I was not killed. Two days later, I met the *Blood of the Land*. He may be just a boy, but in the week-and-a-half that I have known him, it has become evident that God is with him. And God is with us! Seth will not prevail this night, and by dawn, we will all be free! It may cost more than many of you want to give, but God's promises are not empty. We have His glory to make our way, so let's get this done!"

The entire crowd roared with whoops and hollers that were certain to be heard all the way inside the Palace. Spikey waved his own sword in the direction of the outer gates and shouted, "Ram troop, charge!"

~

The sound of an incessant pounding woke Emperor Seth. Someone was beating on his chamber doors. Seth sat up in his bed and screamed, "I swear I will kill whoever is doing that!"

The door swung open, and the light from the hall revealed the *silhouette* of Lizard Face. "Your Majesty, the *sslaves* are trying to break down the outer gates!"

"What?" Seth **cursed**, jumping from bed and racing to the window. In the distance, he could see the flickering lights of dozens of burning torches, and he could just make out the large shape of a tree being smashed against the outer gate. The courtyard was empty.

"Where is that blasted dragon?" Seth demanded.

"He's gone, S*sire!*"

Seth muttered curses as he walked back to his bed and pulled on his robe. He turned to Lizard Face and commanded, "I want that courtyard swarming with goons now! Kill those bears. Send word to the rest of the dragon guard, and get them here as fast as possible. Tell the goons hoods and masks off. I want every last one of those slaves either dead or goonified within the hour. Get a few goons up on the wall to pick off as many as they can before they break through. I'll be in the throne room. Go now!" Lizard Face bowed slightly and exited. He would not be playing the part of the *loyal* second-in-command much longer.

~

"Keep going hard!" Spikey shouted. They had broken a huge gash in the wood of the outer gates, but the gates hadn't given way yet. Garlan and the others continued to heave, and Spikey moved back among the other troops. He continued checking weapons and encouraging people.

He finally came to a rather nervous teen carrying a club, "How are you doing, son?"

"Pretty good, sir. I guess."

"Don't be afraid. Come what may, God will see us through."

"Thanks, I…" The young bear was cut off, and Spikey gasped as blood splattered his shirt. The young bear crumpled to his knees and fell into the snow, blood pouring from his chest. Spikey dove for cover as the air filled with energy bolts.

All but the ram troop scrambled, and Spikey screamed,

"They're firing from the wall! Rifles return fire!" The rifles complied, but had little success, and the bodies of bears began dropping left and right.

~

"This is too easy!" a barefaced goon laughed. "I just wish they were close enough to see my face."

"Maintain your target, Lieutenant," his equally barefaced commander said.

"I know you," came a voice.

The commander turned and had to shut his eyes against a blinding light. When he was finally able to open them, they were met by a holy form. A man, maybe a human, in flowing white, with a red beard and red hair, stood before him. His *countenance* was brighter than the sun. The man said, *"You were there when the rebels were killed by the Ice Sea, and for that you will die!"*

The goon commander was amazed that his face did not affect the glowing figure, but his amazement did not last long. The man drew his sword and beheaded him.

~

When the rain of bolts finally stopped, Spikey called all his troops back into formation. They had lost at least twenty bears, but he had not expected to get through this without any *casualties*. He returned to Garlan.

"How's it going?" Spikey asked.

Sweat was pouring from the minister's furry face, despite the frigid cold. "A few more bashes and we should be through," Garlan wheezed.

Spikey elbowed his way in behind Garlan and helped the troop. With one bash, splinters went flying. With two, they broke a hole large enough to see through. And with one final bash, the gates came toppling down. Spikey turned back to his army as the ram troop dropped the tree and shouted, "Forward!"

~

"All right everyone, you know what to do!" Lizard Face said. "Take out the bears as ordered, hoods and masks off. But when you're done, we're taking over this place!" The goons cheered at that. Lizard Face had gathered them just inside the Palace doors in the fountain chamber. When they heard the bears break through the gate outside, Lizard Face screamed, "Charge!"

~

Bears stormed into the courtyard in hordes. Their goal was the front doors, but they had not even made it halfway across the courtyard before a flood of goons poured from the Palace, faces **exposed**. Spikey could feel his own heart pound, and he shielded his eyes. He would fight his way blind into the Palace if he had to. But then, something miraculous happened.

The face of every last goon began to glow so brightly that all ugliness was concealed. Spikey was struck to the core. They had completely misinterpreted the **prophecy**. It was, in fact, a command to the bears. Spikey waved his sword in the air in jubilation and shouted, "Strike down the faces of light!"

Chapter 36

The Battle

"Keep going!" Spikey screamed. "We have to get inside!" The lit up goons continued to pour from the Palace, but they were having little effect. In the face of another fulfilled **prophecy**, the bears had a new energy, and they were striking down the goons in droves. So far, the **casualties** of the bears had been light. A broken arm, a broken wrist, but no one had been killed since they crossed into the courtyard.

A few of the **foolhardy** teens fought their way straight to the center of the courtyard and tossed a few ropes around the huge statue of Seth. They heaved and tugged, and, at last, the massive sculpture fell and shattered on the ground. The bears cheered, and the battle continued.

Garlan ran over to Spikey, striking down a goon on his way. "We're doing fairly well," Garlan said. "But there must be thousands of goons inside the Palace. They'll keep coming for hours. We may never get inside."

Spikey thrust through another goon as he said, "We need to find a way to cut off their extra troops or at least get some more help."

The words were no sooner out of his mouth than someone shouted, *"Blessed be the Lord God who heals!"*

Spikey was confused for a moment, but then he looked in

horror as dozens of the goons suddenly stopped glowing. Spikey squeezed his eyes shut and was ready to make a suicide run at the goons, but Garlan grabbed his shoulder. "Wait, Spikey, look!"

Spikey opened his eyes and could hardly hold back the surge of joy that came with what he saw. Garbed in the stained robes of the goons were dozens of bears. The robed bears dropped to their knees and began praising God. In the shock of the moment, the battle paused.

"What happened?" Spikey asked.

"Don't you see? It's one of the last **prophecies**. Those bears were goons only a few seconds ago. They were the ones the goons turned into goons with their **hideous** faces. God has healed them!"

"That means we could have hundreds of bears inside. We'll need them when we get there, but I need to talk to these ones now," Spikey said, and he left Garlan. He screamed, "Keep going!" as he ran, and the battle continued.

Bullets once again rained through the air, and blood red replaced the lively green of the grass in the courtyard. Most of it was goon blood, thankfully. Spikey killed five glowing goons before he reached a small group of the healed ones. They were still on their knees praying, and the rest of the bear army had the good sense to try and protect them. Spikey was all for praying, but he needed these bears, now.

He had to nearly yell to be heard over the roar of the battle, "My name is Spikey Moonbeam! We have the *Blood of the Land* with us. You'll see him soon, but we need your help to fight our way inside the Palace."

It was as if lightning surged through the veins of the former goons. The small group near Spikey leaped to their feet, and their **compatriots** all around followed suit. They began yelling and growling and charged into the battle, weapons blazing. Their own goon training was working to their advantage, and the goons began falling faster than they had before.

Spikey had never known goons to be so ineffective in battle. He had engaged them a few times over the years, and more bears had always fallen than goons. Spikey could only assume that the light *emanating* from their faces somehow *inhibited* them as much as it helped the bears. Even so, what they lacked in strength, they made up for in numbers. Hundreds of goons were still pouring from the Palace.

Spikey returned to Garlan. "Those bears should help us a little," he said.

"A little?" Garlan chuckled. "Look at them, they're like avenging angels. Nothing stops them."

"They have a lot to fight for. We all do. Oh, watch out!" Spikey warned as a goon charged Garlan. Garlan whirled, swung his sword, and the goon lost his head. Spikey turned his attention to a group of the ex-goons. One of them looked his way, and Spikey waved a victorious fist in the air until the bear went flat! He and three others were transformed into a mash of bloody goo as they were crushed beneath the massive paw of a dragon.

"Dragons!" someone screamed, and everyone scrambled. There were, in fact, six dragons. The inferno of their mouths began consuming bears left and right. There would be no fighting these monsters, not without more help at least, and Spikey had no idea where that help was going to come from.

"What are we going to do, Spikey?" Garlan shouted over the roar, slicing down another goon in the process.

Spikey thought quickly, "We have to organize. We can't afford to stay out here any longer. We need to get inside. The cellar door is right over there. That'll be the first thing we *conquer.* I'll take a bunch of bears and get in there. You find as many bears as you can with any kind of medical experience and send them in. We'll set up a triage *facility.* Drag the wounded there."

"We have no medicine!"

"No, but at least we can get them out of the battle. I want that cellar defended. No goons. Now go!"

Garlan hurried away. There were only a few bears he knew with any knowledge of first aid. He prayed they were still alive. The dragons had killed at least fifty bears, and it seemed like they were fighting this battle in Hell itself. The entire courtyard was on fire. Many were burned, even killed, simply by falling into the flames. The goons were the most vulnerable, as their robes were highly flammable. Most of them had retreated back inside the Palace.

Garlan sent three bears to the cellar. He hoped they would prove useful. There was only one other he needed to find. The dragons had ceased spewing fire, but they were now crunching bears like bugs. Garlan had been lucky so far and had avoided the dragons, but that luck was about to fade.

"Die, maggot!"

Garlan felt a shadow cover his body, and he looked up to see a black and red, scaly dragon's paw. He closed his eyes and prayed, "Here I come, Lord!"

"NO!" thundered a voice from above, and to Garlan's surprise, death did not come. Instead, the dragon that had been about to crush him found his own head smashed against the ground. A shower of rain, real rain, followed. The water doused the courtyard, leaving behind a field of black grass and burned bushes. Garlan raced to the outer wall for safety, and he looked up to see what had happened.

A huge, blue-green dragon had crushed the head of the other dragon. Garlan was confused at first, but then he remembered Spikey's story of how a dragon had joined their side. This had to be Hydro. Garlan wanted to thank him, but he never got his chance.

The other five dragons pounced on the water dragon, ripping at his flesh. That had little effect since Hydro could change his flesh into water at will, but even he could not withstand the strength of five dragons. Hydro began spewing icy liquid in their faces, and they retorted by blasting fire back at him. Garlan could only watch.

"Garlan! Garlan!" shouted a voice. It was Spikey. He was running from the direction of the cellar. When he arrived, he said, "We've taken the cellar and the kitchen, and triage is underway."

Garlan nodded, and Spikey turned his attention to the fighting dragons. "Is that Hydro?" Spikey asked.

"Yes, I mean, at least, I assume so from what you told me about him. He saved my life," Garlan replied.

With Hydro's help, though it seemed even he would die that day, the bears had regained the advantage. As many as could had entered the Palace through the cellar. The rest had pushed the goons back and were now entering through the front doors. The courtyard was soon *devoid* of bears, except for Spikey and Garlan.

Hydro, on the other hand, was being beaten senseless, and even his water powers were not helping him. In the beginning of the fight, he could have easily turned into water and escaped, but that might have cost the lives of even more bears. At least this way the dragons were distracted. He was now too weak to do anything. When he finally stopped fighting, the dragons got off him.

"No!" Spikey *cursed*.

The largest of the five dragons began to beat his wings and rose into flight. The gust of his flapping wings knocked the bears over, and he was hovering fifty feet over Hydro in seconds. The dragon bore his teeth and lowered his head to make a dive for the kill. A sinister expression crossed his face, and he exploded, though not in a fury of rage. He really exploded! Chunks of his flesh shot away, and the length of his body began to burn in a glowing red flame. The creature wailed in agony, and it was clear, he would never touch the ground again, alive.

"What in the world?" Garlan screamed. The dragon was still burning in the sky, and a stream of fire trailed all the way back to the stars. As the charred flesh of their brother fell to the ground, the other dragons scrambled. They no sooner leaped into flight than the mysterious beam of fire consumed them as well.

"What's going on?" Garlan asked, frantic.

"Another **prophecy!** This has to be the fire from Heaven! But quick, we have to shield Hydro!"

"Why?" Garlan asked.

"God can use ordinary things when it suits Him. I think He's doing that now. Those fire streams look like lasers. Someone in space is trying to help us, but they won't know Hydro is on our side!"

"How will we let them know?"

"I don't know. Maybe if we just get on top of him, they'll be able to tell. It's the only plan I've got!"

Garlan nodded, and he and Spikey ran to Hydro and climbed onto his upturned stomach. The dragon was unconscious, but at least from there, they could tell he was still alive. They began waving their arms, hoping someone would see them.

~

A hundred kleps above, Gloria asked, "Can I see what's going on down there?" The *Fire Cruiser* and the rest of the liberation fleet had arrived minutes before and had detected the battle at the Palace. So far, the tactical officer was the only one who had been watching what was going on, so he could pick off the dragons.

Captain Noble addressed his officer, "Put the battle on the front screen." The officer complied, and Noble watched from his command chair with Gloria and Shortstop next to him.

The courtyard was black from fire. It had nearly been destroyed by the look of things. The officer reported, "There is another dragon down there. Should I take him out?"

"By all means," Captain Noble replied.

"Wait!" Gloria barked. She moved closer to the screen and pointed to the tiny shape of the dragon. It looked like two fleas were jumping on him. "Can you magnify this?"

The officer did so, and the fleas grew into bears. Gloria recognized one immediately. "Spikey!"

"What?" Captain Noble asked.

"That's Spikey down there. I have no idea who the bear is beside him, but there is no doubt that's Spikey! We have to get down there!"

Captain Noble addressed his brother at the helm, "Josh, take us down. Land in the clearing beyond the slave camps. We're joining this battle. Tell the rest of the ships to locate any other strongholds of goons and dragons throughout the planet and eliminate them."

"Yes, sir!" Josh piped and turned back to his controls. A huge grin threatened to consume Gloria's face. At last, she had finally come home.

Chapter 37

Confrontations

Scotty twisted the handle of the *Dagger of Promise* in his hands. His palms were sweating, and he was growing very **anxious**. "Take it easy," Sparkey whispered. He and Scotty were straddled on an **exposed** beam above the throne room. Seth was below them looking out the window at the battle. Though they did not have a clear view, from what they could tell, the battle was going well, and Seth was growing more enraged every moment.

Scotty nodded at Sparkey. His moment would soon come, but it hadn't come yet. In the meantime, he continued to squeeze the dagger.

"Your Majesty!" screamed a voice. It was Lizard Face, and he came bursting into the throne room.

Seth turned to him, "What is it? And it had better be good news. I just saw six of my dragons die!"

"I'm *ssorry, Ssire!* There are bears on every level below us. The goons are having no effect, and all of the bears we turned into goons previously have been healed and have joined the *sslaves*. Our numbers are dwindling quickly!"

Seth slammed his fist into the window, managing to crack it slightly. He hung his head and was silent, but then he perked up, "It doesn't matter! According to the **prophecies**, bears can't kill me, nor take my throne. With the boy dead, I have nothing to worry about!"

"Bears can't take your throne, but the **prophecies** *ssay* nothing about a lizard taking it!"

"What?" Seth **cursed** and turned back toward Lizard Face to find the barrel of a pistol pointing in his face. "What are you doing?"

"Meet the new emperor of *Sstaranana*, *Sseth*. You've had the throne long enough! Most of the goons are with me. You will die tonight, and by dawn, the rebels will know what pain really is!"

"Traitor! I'll kill you!"

"You won't get the chance! Now, *ssit!*" Lizard Face motioned with his pistol that Seth should sit on the floor, and the man reluctantly complied.

~

"Spikey, oh, thank God!" squealed Gloria as she wrapped her arms tightly around her husband. They had landed the *Fire Cruiser* minutes before. The hatch was barely open before Gloria jumped out and raced through the camp to reach her husband. Shortstop, Speedway, and the Nobles followed her, along with over a hundred heavily armed Stararockans.

Spikey was shocked, but he returned her embrace and kissed her. "Gloria, what are you doing here?"

"It's a long story. The *New Life* was pretty much destroyed. These people rescued us." She waved her hand at the crowd, "Spikey, they're Stararockans!"

Captain Noble extended his hand, "It's been a long time, Spikey."

Spikey took his hand and smiled as **recognition** set in. "Will? Will, is that you?"

"Yeah, my friend. I'm glad to see you made a life for yourself here."

Gloria said, "I'm sorry, Spikey, but I told them about you."

Spikey sighed, "It's okay. I guess there is no need for secrets anymore. I should tell you all something else. The *Blood of the Land* is in there right now, with my son."

"What?" Shortstop exclaimed.

"It's true! He arrived the day after you left, through my *Door*. Sparkey brought him through."

"So, Sparkey is okay!" Gloria was so relieved. "But what do you mean he's in there? Isn't that a little - no make that - very dangerous?"

"Listen, honey, Sparkey and Scotty - the *Blood of the Land* - have proven themselves in more ways than you can imagine. They have also become great friends. I could think of no one more **appropriate** to help Scotty right now," Spikey explained.

"A little cub is friends with a great human man? That's a bit strange, isn't it?" Speedway asked.

"No, because Scotty is not a great human man. He is a nine-year-old boy."

Everyone was amazed. It was hard to believe everything was happening just as Iren had said it would. Shortstop was about to apologize for doubting Spikey, but Josh Noble pushed his way to the front of the crowd. "If the *Blood of the Land* is in there, can we go inside and help him? It's cold out here!"

"Oh, yeah, sorry!" Spikey said, for the first time noticing that the Stararockans were shivering. "Gloria, they could sure use your help in the triage center we've set up in the cellar. The door is right over there."

"I'm on it!" she said, clicking into doctor mode. She soon disappeared inside the cellar.

"The rest of you follow me!" Spikey yelled, and he began leading them into the Palace. "Oh, yeah, if any of you know anything about dragons, could you help our friend here? This is Hydro. He's a friend of the *Blood of the Land*." Two of the Stararockan doctors agreed to stay behind, despite the cold, and the rest of them stormed into the Palace.

~

Seth felt like he was going to explode. In five thousand years, no one had dared to **betray** him. Lizard Face had served him for two thousand of those years, and though Seth had had his suspicions, the lizard had always obeyed him. Rumors had been circulating for a while now of an uprising, and Lizard Face was the first person Seth suspected. But, eventually, he decided the rumors were just that, and he continued to trust his second-in-command. What a fool he had been!

Lizard Face lounged in Seth's throne, pistol still in hand. He had moved Seth so that the human sat directly below him. "I can *ssee* why you like this chair, *Sseth*. How do I look?"

"Less than royal!"

"You know, you're right. *Ssomething* is missing." Lizard Face **dismounted** the throne and came up behind Seth. He pulled Seth's crown from his head and placed it on his own. "There, that's better," he said and returned to the throne.

~

Sparkey and Scotty held their breath. They had positioned themselves directly above the throne, and, thankfully, the tapestries concealed them. They had known of Lizard Face's treacherous plot, but they had no idea that his coup would occur in the midst of a bear invasion.

Scotty was still twisting the dagger in his hand. "Knock it off!" Sparkey whispered frantically.

Scotty replied, "You're right. I'll put it away." He fidgeted and tried to put the dagger back in the sheath Spikey had fashioned for it, but he missed, and the dagger fell!

"NO!" Sparkey screamed and lunged for the dagger. He missed as well, and then he lost his hold on the beam and fell.

Sparkey's shout had both Seth and Lizard Face on their feet instantly. The cub slammed into Lizard Face, and the reptile crashed to the floor. His weapon clattered away toward Seth, the crown tumbled from his head, and his breath left him. Sparkey landed squarely on Seth's throne.

Seth picked up the pistol and pointed it at Sparkey. "Well, what do we have here? Thank you, little one. You took care of a problem for me. But what were you doing up there?"

Sparkey said nothing, and Seth turned his attention to the ceiling. Beyond the silk tapestries, Seth made out the form of a human boy, and ***recognition*** instantly set in. "You!" he ***cursed***. He raised his pistol, and a bullet exploded from the barrel.

"AH!" Scotty screamed as the bullet ripped through his shoulder. He lost his hold and fell to the marble floor. Upon impact, he felt the bones in his legs snap, and his head slammed into the floor. He was still conscious, but just barely.

Seth walked over to him and pointed the pistol at his head. "So, you are still alive? Anyway, not for long! I welcome the privilege to kill you myself. But first, there is someone else I must deal with."

Seth returned to Lizard Face, who was struggling to push himself up. The Emperor placed a foot on his back and slammed him back into the floor. He cocked his pistol and put the barrel against the creature's head. "Enjoy the *Black Lava Pits*, traitor!"

"Get off of him now!" a voice raged as Seth began to squeeze the trigger. He looked up to see three goons entering the throne room. Their faces were glowing, and all three had rifles trained on him.

Lizard Face recognized the voice of the one who had spoken. "Gakic?"

"It's me, Master. I came back for you. We have a hopper pod waiting on the roof and a clear path to get there," Gakic said. He then addressed Seth, "Now, get off of him, Your Majesty!"

Seth backed away, and Lizard Face leaped up. He joined his troops and looked at the broken human boy on the floor. He chuckled, looking back at Seth, "Goodbye, Your Highness! We will not meet again." Then he followed Gakic and his men out the door.

Scotty's vision was becoming blurred, and it looked like five *Seths* were approaching him. Despite the pain in his legs, head, and shoulder, another spot of discomfort seemed to draw his attention. He was lying on something, but what? Using his good arm, he fished around under his belly until his hand met with a metal **hilt**. *It was the dagger!*

"At least I can still kill you!" Seth raged. Scotty couldn't speak, but with all the strength he could muster, he pulled out the dagger. He waved it at Seth, and the man recoiled in terror.

"Where did you get that?" Seth demanded, though he already knew. From the fight of the dragons outside, he knew Hydro was a traitor. The water dragon must have let the boy escape with it.

Scotty groaned, still unable to speak. Seth regained his composure and laughed, "Never mind. I know exactly how to deal with this!"

Sparkey had been pretty much ignored since Scotty had fallen. Though he longed to help his friend, killing a small bear would mean nothing to Seth, and Sparkey still believed that God would help Scotty, so he had remained put. He continued to watch Seth, but then something else drew his attention.

"Renounce God, or die!" The voice was not Seth's, but it was deep, and it hissed like a snake. Sparkey could not figure out where it was coming from until he looked up. Winding down a pillar next to the throne was a huge, venom-dripping snake.

Sparkey had heard about snakes from the stories of the fall of Adam and Eve and the satanic conversion of Seth. But if they had ever lived on Staranana, it would have been back when Iren was emperor. The frozen environment of the present age would have killed them easily.

This was no typical snake, however. Its body was coiled all the way up the pillar and across the beam on the ceiling. It reached all the way to the other end of the room. Sparkey wondered where it had come from. It certainly hadn't been up there when he was.

What was most unusual about the creature was that its body

277

was not made up of scaly snake flesh. Instead, the entire length of its reptilian body seemed to be composed of a dirty, swirling wind. It was like a tornado, only instead of being shaped like a funnel, it was shaped like a snake.

Sparkey, still trapped on the throne, felt the wind from the creature churn his fur. When it locked its enormous, red eyes on him, Sparkey froze, and he felt the sting of burning venom, dripping from the creature's fangs, make contact with his hand. However, the snake quickly lost interest. Sparkey was not its target. As it moved on to its real prey, it continued its hissing cry, *"Renounce God, or die!"*

"I'd like to introduce you to someone," Seth said as the snake came alongside him. The creature bared its fangs, and its head spread into a massive hood. It looked exactly like a cobra.

Scotty held fast to the dagger, but he could not move. He managed to utter, "Who?"

"This is my god, human. He is the great and powerful one. The one who opened my eyes to the impotence of the One you call Lord and God. This is Licen. I believe you call him Satan."

Scotty felt his throat constrict, and his breath left him. Of all the unusual things he had seen since he arrived on Staranana, he never expected to come face to face with the Devil himself. Licen began to circle him, continuing his cry. Scotty did not have the ability to refuse or agree with the creature's demonic request either way. If it came down to it, though, he would certainly die for God.

Seth laughed, "Let's see how effective your little dagger will be against what we have in store for you next." Seth raised his arms over his head, and to Scotty's confusion, Licen ate the older human. He hadn't imagined Seth was that insane, but then the man's intentions became clear. The snake swelled until it was three times larger. Its eyes burned with a blinding, red light, and when it spoke, it was with a mixture of Seth's voice and Licen's.

"Now you die!" the demonic-human hybrid hissed.

"Away!" commanded a voice. It was neither loud, nor

emotional, but the instant it spoke, the snake's mouth snapped shut, and it backed away. And then it was as if time froze. Nothing moved, and as Scotty tried to turn his head to locate the speaker, the room vanished in a flood of light.

"How are you, young one?"

Scotty sat up. The wound in his shoulder was gone, and his two broken legs worked perfectly. His head also felt better. He stood and recognized the angelic being that had spoken. "Joshua?"

"Yes, young one, it's me."

Scotty looked around. He saw nothing but beautiful light. He also thought he heard faint singing in the distance. He asked, "Joshua, am I dead?"

The angel laughed. Scotty had not heard him do that before. *"No, young one. This is the fulfillment of the last prophecy. Heaven and Hell have met on Staranana."*

"Where are we?" Scotty asked.

"The throne room of Cosmic Bubble Palace. The light of God has simply obscured it for now. The Lord has healed your wounds. You know your task."

Scotty hung his head and continued to fidget with the dagger. "Joshua, I don't think I can do this. I'm scared, and I've never killed a man before."

"It is time for him to face God, and only you can send him there. You are God's instrument to deliver him to judgment. You are the Blood of the Land."

"Still, I..."

Joshua knelt before Scotty and took the boy's hands in his. *"Young one, do what you always do when you are fearful. Pray to the Lord your God. He hears you. Better yet, use the words of a famous king of long ago. Repeat these words after me, and lift them to Heaven as your prayer."*

Scotty repeated the words as Joshua quoted from Psalm 27:

"'The Lord is my light and my salvation -

Whom shall I fear?
The Lord is the stronghold of my life -
Of whom shall I be afraid?
When evil men advance against me
To devour my flesh,
When my enemies and my foes attack me,
They will stumble and fall.
Though an army besiege me,
My heart will not fear;
Though war break out against me,
Even then will I be confident.

~

For in the day of trouble
He will keep me safe in his dwelling;
He will hide me in the shelter of his tabernacle
And set me high upon a rock.'"

By the time he had finished praying, Scotty was crying. He opened his eyes, expecting to see the angel. He was gone, and Scotty was once again lying on the floor of the throne room.

The cobra creature spoke as though nothing had happened, *"God fails here, fool!"*

Scotty pushed himself up off the floor, and Seth/Licen **cursed,** *"What is this?"*

Scotty preached, "Nothing God does depends on me! He had the victory two thousand years ago when Jesus died on the cross. You, Satan, are out of your league. As ancient as you are, you should have learned by now that you don't mess with God." Scotty wasted no more time with words. With the dagger in hand, and a prayer in his heart, he lunged at the creature in a fire of holy rage.

He jumped into the windy reptile, and it felt like he passed through into Hell itself. There was no turning back now. He was in the ring with the Devil. He could feel evil itself tugging at his flesh, like a million ants creeping over his skin, as he floated in the swirl of dirty wind. He could see nothing beyond the innards of the wind snake, but Seth was directly in front of him.

"Fool, do you honestly think you can stop me?"

"I'm not the fool here! ***Surrender***, and I'll send you to the *Black Lava Pits* as painlessly as possible."

Seth laughed and ***seized*** Scotty by the wrist holding the dagger, "If I'm going to Hell, you will not be the one to send me there!"

Seth's grip was powerful and try as he might, Scotty could not break it. It was not very sportsmanlike, but Scotty had long ago decided that, if faced with a life and death situation, he would not hesitate to fight dirty. This would be as dirty as it got! With all the rage and strength he had, he thrust his knee directly into Seth's groin!

Seth released his grip and wailed in pain. Scotty should have known better, as a fellow male, but that was a lesson the nine-year-old had yet to learn. The moment had finally come. Scotty spun in the cyclone, bore his teeth, and with the terror on Seth's face reflecting in his eyes, he plunged the *Dagger of Promise* into Seth's chest!

The wind snake vanished instantly, and Scotty and Seth fell to the throne room floor. The dagger was still in Seth's heart, his eyes were wide, and blood was pouring from his mouth. He tried to speak, saying, "It wasn't...it wasn't...", but he never finished his sentence. His eyes rolled back in his head, and he died.

Sparkey rushed to Scotty's side. "Scotty, what happened?"

Scotty's hands were trembling, and he backed away from Seth's body. Sparkey put his arm around the boy, and Scotty said, "Joshua, the angel, came, and God healed me!"

"I didn't see an angel," Sparkey said. "One minute you were broken and bleeding on the floor. The next you jumped into the snake."

Scotty stared at Seth's body and said, "I thought he was supposed to..." But he never finished his thought. The area around Seth's body began to shimmer with heat. A small cyclone formed and began to circle the body. There was a flash of blinding light, and Seth's body was gone. The *Dagger of Promise* clattered to the floor.

Sparkey sighed and asked, "What now?"

"It's over, my friend," Scotty replied. "It's over."

Chapter 38

The Crowning

Garlan reported, "We have bears on every floor, except number sixteen, which you told us to stay away from. With the added troops of the *Fire Cruiser,* we've managed to hold our own. There are still a few pockets of goon resistance throughout the Palace, but they will be eliminated soon."

Spikey nodded. The battle had been hard and bloody. Counting those who had been killed before they breached the outer gate, nearly one hundred-fifty bears had lost their lives. Many of those had been teenagers. Their families would cry themselves to sleep that night, no matter what other great things happened that day.

Spikey and Garlan now stood in the kitchen, which had been set up as a command center for the attacking bears. Spikey asked, "How's Gloria doing?"

"Last I heard, great. But she's moved back to the *Fire Cruiser,* and the wounded are being treated in their sickbay. Everyone who didn't die is expected to make a full recovery."

"That's good, but we still took heavy losses. How's Hydro doing by the way?" Spikey asked.

"Well, the doctors who tried to help him really didn't know anything about dragon anatomy, so they couldn't treat him. But I guess he's doing fine because he started walking around about an hour ago. He's still outside."

"An hour? What time is it, Garlan?"

"Almost dawn."

"It is not!"

"Yes, it is, sir. It's 6:10 a.m."

Spikey shook his head. Where had the time gone? Had the battle been so involved, so intense, that six hours slipped by almost unnoticed? Were he to guess, he would have said it was no later than 2:00 a.m. He never got a chance to argue further, because a voice broke out over the Palace intercom.

"Attention, this is General Henry Shortstop. I am speaking to you now from the royal bedchamber of Emperor Seth himself, and I am pleased to report that the bears now have full control of Cosmic Bubble Palace!"

The sound of whoops and cheers and **hysterical** laughter echoed through the **vast** halls of the Palace. It could be heard from the top floor to the bottom. Spikey and Garlan threw their arms around each other and started jumping up and down hysterically. Then they caught themselves. Spikey backed away and muttered, "Good job, Garlan."

Garlan returned, "You too, Mr. Moonbeam." But they couldn't help it. They started smiling stupidly at each other and started laughing, and then they went wild again.

When the jubilation finally paused, Shortstop continued, *"There has still been no word on how the Blood of the Land is doing with Seth, but we leave that to God. The Fire Cruiser has scanned the Palace and has **confirmed** that it is one hundred percent goon free. We're doing a room by room check just to be sure. I would like to request that all bears not currently involved with the search begin evacuating the Palace and start massing in the courtyard. We should all be ready to greet the Blood of the Land, or should I say, our new emperor!"* And the cries of joy continued.

~

"Are you all right?" Sparkey asked.

Scotty was still shaking, but he nodded. It had been a long

night. They were now walking down the hall of floor sixteen, ripping down the **grotesque** pictures. The bear fur carpet would take a little more work to get rid of. When they finally reached the lift tubes at the end of the hall, Sparkey paused.

"Things are going to be very different now. Staranana belongs to you."

"You know, it seems like you guys get nothing but grief from your emperors. It sounds like even Iren had his **shortcomings**. Have your people ever thought of governing themselves?"

"I don't know. I think that too many people were looking forward to the *Blood of the Land* ruling us. Besides, Staranana only exists because God created it to honor the humans. Without humans, there is no us. Don't worry. You'll make a great emperor."

"I hope so," Scotty sighed. Then he said, "All right, let's go."

"Go where?"

"Into the tube of course!"

"What? Are you crazy? We'll fall to our deaths!"

"Don't worry. I know how these things work," Scotty said.

"No thanks! I think I'll take the stairs."

"Ugh! No you don't!" Scotty said, and he grabbed Sparkey by the arms. "Now, let's go!" he insisted and pushed the little bear into the tube.

~

"What should we do?" Gloria asked.

"I don't know," Spikey **surrendered**. "Garlan, you have any ideas?"

The minister shook his head, and General Shortstop said, "Imagine this whole thing being derailed because of a technicality."

"Awful isn't it?" Speedway consoled.

~

"Can we...oh, WOW!" Scotty exclaimed as he stepped from the main entry of the Palace out into the courtyard. The place was packed with one dragon and over a thousand bears. Many did not even look Starananian. However, Sparkey recognized one very well.

"Mama!" he shouted and ran into her arms.

"Oh, Sparkey!" she screeched and began to cry as she embraced him. "I don't know whether to scold you or congratulate you," she said, and Sparkey laughed at that.

"Let's hear it for the *Blood of the Land!*" someone shouted, and the courtyard erupted in a thunderous applause. Scotty was more than a little embarrassed, and he found his instinct to be shy taking over. But then, just as suddenly as it began, the applause stopped, and the bears started looking awkwardly at their feet.

Scotty walked down the front steps of the Palace until he reached Spikey. "What's wrong?"

Spikey rubbed the back of his neck. "We've run into a bit of a problem. You see, in order to become the emperor, you have to be crowned, and you can only be crowned by someone who is royal. As you can probably tell, none of us fits that bill. Even Splash wasn't officially the emperor when he ruled. So, we have no idea who is going to crown you."

Scotty had no suggestion to offer, but then someone said, ***"I'll do it."***

Scotty did not even have time to see who had spoken before the entire assembly of bears fell to their knees, knowing a representative of God was near. Scotty turned to see the familiar, glowing ***countenance*** of Joshua. He held Seth's crown in his hands.

Joshua knelt before Scotty and said, ***"God gives you this gift, young one. Cherish it. You are now His representative in this world, for angels will come to Staranana no more. God's work is on Earth, and soon, yours will be too. The time of His return is near, but there is still much work to be*** *done. Remember, your greatest adventures are meant for that world, not this one. Enjoy this place while you can, for one day, it will fade like a dream. And at the coming of the Lord Christ – the true and Hidden King of Staranana - it will become something far different. Until that time, it is yours. I hereby crown you Emperor of Staranana."*

Joshua placed the crown on Scotty's head, and then he turned to face the crowd. *"I hereby present to you the Blood of the Land, Emperor Scotty Fields."* The crowd erupted into applause once more, and as a few hints of the morning sun tickled the crown, the angel vanished.

Scotty stood before the assembly and said, "I wish I had some great speech prepared about how glad I am to become your emperor, but I don't. All I can say is that this is because of God, not me. And if there were one piece of advice I could give to you, it would be to learn all you can about Him. I understand that the *Text of Iren* has been brought to a completion, but there are so many other places you can learn about God. When I come next, I'll bring *Bibles*. I want you all to study and learn. This will be God's world again. I know the planet is kind of a wreck right now, but I promise we'll fix that. Until we can begin rebuilding your homes, every bear in the area is invited to stay in the Palace. I ask that you work to help rebuild your world, but for your work, you will be greatly rewarded. Slavery is finished. Those that will be my servants will be paid and treated well, and they will serve me only so long as they wish. We will restore Staranana to what it once was. God bless you all!" And the crowd erupted again.

~

The next two days were spent burying the dead of both the goons and the bears. Scotty made a decree that all people, no matter who they were, must have a proper burial. They also spent the time repairing the Palace and moving in.

The sixteenth floor was ripped up and was being remodeled.

Scotty found a bedchamber, half the size of Seth's, on the 100th floor. Everything Seth had stolen from the people, except lives, was returned to them.

After they had helped get the reconstruction process underway, the Stararockan ships headed for home. However, Captain Noble left behind transmitters, so the Stararockans could remain in constant contact with their Starananian cousins.

Lizard Face had escaped, and he was still a threat. But by that time, he was long into deep space, so they would have to deal with him another day.

Spikey moved his family into a large apartment on the twentieth floor of the Palace. In the apartment was a room with a huge bay window (though it was nothing like the one in the throne room). Spikey set the room up as the workshop he had always dreamed of. Gloria was also given permission to set up her own clinic on the twelfth floor. Scotty and Sparkey continued growing closer and were becoming the best of friends, but then, late the third night after Scotty had taken the throne, the time finally came.

"Spikey, I want to go home," Scotty said. He was sitting with his favorite bear family in their apartment, the lights low, a fire burning in the hearth, sipping honeysuckle apple cider.

Spikey nodded and smiled, "I figured the time would come pretty soon. The *Door* is ready and waiting. Before you go though, thank you again so much for what you have done."

Scotty nodded, and they all went into the workshop, and Spikey fired up the *Door*. As the passage formed, Scotty pulled off the duplicating necklace and handed it to Spikey.

Sparkey asked, "Will you be back?"

"You can count on it!"

After

Scotty stepped through the *Door* and arrived in his tiny bedroom in Prineville, Oregon. It was still dark outside, but the hour was nearing morning. The covers on his bed were **ruffled**, and he found a pair of blue shorts under them. ***Obviously***, the duplicate had been sleeping. He had also been a bit of a slob from the look of things. Smelly socks and dirty shirts, along with dozens of toys were everywhere. Scotty chuckled. It figured he was now the emperor of an entire planet, but he would still have to clean his bedroom.

He checked the calendar he had always marked the days off on and learned he had been gone for exactly two weeks. Apparently, Spikey's *temporal differential* hadn't happened. He'd have to ask him about that. Nevertheless, it was Saturday again, and for that he was thankful. He could sleep, but there was something he had to do first.

~

"Noah has a track meet this afternoon. You going, honey?" Mrs. Fields asked her husband as she stirred a batch of pancake batter.

"Yeah, I'll be there," he said.

"Mom! Dad!" a voice bellowed from down the hall. Scotty ran into the room and threw his arms around both his parents.

Mrs. Fields laughed, "Well, good morning! You'd think you

hadn't seen us in ages."

"You have no idea, Mom. You have no idea!" he said and hugged them once more. He was glad to be home, but of one thing he was sure. He had not seen the last of Staranana!

Do you know Jesus Christ?

The best thing in this life is coming to personally know our Lord and Savior Jesus Christ. As the Gospel of John explains, God made the world through Him and without Him nothing was made that has been made (John 1:3). However, there is a problem. Long ago, the ancestors of all mankind, Adam and Eve, disobeyed God and fell into sin (Genesis 3). Sin literally means missing the mark of God's perfection. Since the time of Adam and Eve, their sinful nature has been passed down through all the successive generations of humanity.

"Why is this a problem?" you may ask. Because God's standard is absolute perfection, and it is His nature to punish all sin. This punishment is eternal separation from Him in a place of sorrow and misery called Hell. Fortunately, God is also a God of Love, and He willingly went to the greatest possible length to redeem us from the power of sin.

As John 3:16-17 explains, *"For God so loved the world that He gave His one and only Son, that whoever believes in Him shall not perish but have eternal life. For God did not send His Son into the world to condemn the world, but to save the world through Him"* (NIV). Jesus Christ is God's Son. God sent Him to be born as a human (John 1:14), and He is the only human that has ever lived without sin (2 Corinthians 5:21). Even so, God punished Christ for all of our sins by having Him crucified on a Roman cross (Hebrews 12:2).

Three days later, God raised Him back to life, conquering sin and death (John 20) and granting eternal life to any who repent of their sins and believe in what Christ has done and who He is

(Acts 2:38). As the author of Staranana, it is my sincere hope that you will see Jesus for who He is and accept Him as your Savior. It is the best decision you will ever make.

Even so, the *Bible* is clear in Philippians 2:9-11 that God has "…exalted [Jesus] to the highest place…" and given Him "…the name that is above every name…" so that "…at the name of Jesus every knee should bow…" and "…every tongue confess that Jesus Christ is Lord to the glory of God the Father" (NIV). One day everyone will submit to Christ, but only those who do it in this life will have any joy on that day. I encourage you to make that decision while there is still time. It is one decision you will never regret.

About the Author

David "Scott" Fields II was raised in the farming community of Prineville, Oregon. It was here, during long summer walks along the endless pastures of the surrounding farms, that Scott first discovered his love of storytelling. He would spend these walks making up countless stories that he would then share with his friends and family. The very first of these was *Green Elephant*, which Scott wrote at the tender age of 8. Inspired by an outstanding third-grade teacher and his mom's collection of glass elephants, the young Scott put pencil, pen, and crayon to paper and quickly had his first masterpiece. "I knew even then that this was only the beginning," says Scott, and he was quite right. It wouldn't be long before inspiration would strike for his crowning literary achievement - his *Chronicles of the Imagination* series.

Scott describes the beginning of the series saying, "It all began one day on the fourth-grade playground at Ochoco Elementary School under what I called the *Elephant Tree*. Bored that day and with no friends around, I created the character Sparkey Moonbeam, a young, personified bear cub from the icy planet Staranana. From there, the idea exploded and Staranana took on a life of its own. Recesses from that point on would often take my friends and me to Staranana for great adventures. For me, it was non-stop fun and imagination. Eventually, I became too old for make-believe, but the idea of Staranana never died. I knew it was time for my beloved ice-planet to exist in another form, and so I wrote my first novel, *Chronicles of the Imagination: Staranana.*"

In homage to those early make-believe games, *Staranana* and the novels to follow include all the original characters Scott created in the fourth grade - Sparkey Moonbeam, Lizard Face, etc. - and a version of Scott himself is also featured, called Isaiah Scott Fields in the novels with the nickname *Scotty*. Says Scott, "I could have changed the names of all the characters, and including myself as a main character was something I thought long and hard about, but in the end, it just didn't seem right to change anything. I wanted to preserve Staranana as it was, and I am glad I did."

Scott's first novel, *Staranana*, was published in 2008 by *Thrive Christian Press*, followed thereafter by the novels *Lizard Face*, *Nana-Old Testament*, and *Nana-New Testament*. His collection of novellas includes *The Betrayal of Kelcott* and the *Parallel Encounters* series. Regarding all of these works, as a *Bible*-believing, born-again Christian, Scott has insisted that all of his books are written to the glory of God, and every book in his collection has a Gospel-centered theme. In fact, in two of the novels, Scott takes the characters from *Staranana* back in time to experience the events of the *Bible* firsthand.

When asked about his future as a writer and the end of the *Chronicles of the Imagination* series, Scott said, "As C.S. Lewis told a young fan of *The Chronicles of Narnia* once, when this story stops telling itself to me inside my head, that's when I'll end it, but I haven't foreseen that day yet. As for the rest of my writing career, when I get to be 99, I'll think about stopping...maybe."

Classroom Extras

Study & Discussion Questions

Before & Chapter 1: The Moonbeams

Journal Prompt:

- Every story begins with what is called an *exposition*. It is also often called a *hook*. The purpose of the *exposition/hook* is to catch the attention of the readers and to get them so interested in your story that they will keep reading. After reading *Before*, how successful was this author in capturing your attention? What predictions do you have about what will happen in the rest of the novel? Who do you believe the villagers were, and why were they killed? Answers these questions in a minimum five-sentence journal.

Study & Discussion Questions:

1. Who do you think the person watching the attack in *Before* was?
2. Personification is when non-human things are given human characteristics. What animal has been given human characteristics in this first chapter?
3. Spikey Moonbeam is in disagreement with his family in this chapter. Describe a time when you got into an argument with someone you loved over what you believed in. What was the result of the argument?
4. What decision do you think Spikey will make?
5. What are your first impressions on the Moonbeam family?

Words to Know:

Countenance   Feign   Horde   Prophecy   Tinker

Chapter 2: The Meeting

Journal Prompt:

- After the *exposition* of a story comes the rising action. Here the author generally introduces the main protagonists (heroes) and antagonists (villains) as well as the chief conflicts of the story. We will discuss protagonists and antagonists a bit more later. For now, what do you think the chief conflicts of this novel will be? Remember that a conflict can be internal (happening inside a character's thoughts and feelings) or external (happening between characters or between a character and his environment). In a five-sentence journal, make predictions about the internal and external conflicts the Starananians will face in this novel.

Study & Discussion Questions:

1. Do you think the Starananians are justified in wanting to run away? Why/Why not?
2. Using specific references from the *Bible*, explain why God sometimes takes a long time to fulfill His promises.
3. Do you agree with Spikey's decision to sacrifice his life for his friends? Why/Why not?
4. Can you think of a way that Spikey could still help his friends without sacrificing his life?

Words to Know:

Evacuate   Facility   Inexhaustible   Representation   Wince

Chapter 3: Farewells

Journal Prompt:

- A key component of any novel is the setting. Generally, we think of the setting as the time and place where a story occurs, but a good author must be much more detailed than that. They must include all the sights, sounds, smells, tastes, tactile sensations, and emotions associated with the story. After reading Chapter 3. Take a moment to review what you know about the setting of Staranana so far. In a minimum five-sentence, journal describe the setting using as many sensory details from the novel as possible.

Study & Discussion Questions:

1. A protagonist is a hero in a story. However, a hero cannot be too perfect or we won't be able to relate to them. They must have what is called a *fatal flaw* – or a problem in their personality or abilities. Select a few of the protagonists you have met in the novel so far and list some of their fatal flaws.
2. Describe a time when you had to say goodbye to someone you loved. Was it forever?
3. At the end of the chapter, Sparkey Moonbeam makes a promise saying, *"I'll save you, Dad. No matter what happens, or what it takes, I'll save you."* However, Sparkey is only 7 years old. Do you think he is capable of keeping such a promise? What does the *Bible* say about the abilities of young people?
4. What do you imagine Sparkey Moonbeam might be planning in order to rescue his father?

Words to Know:

Circulate   Hysterical   Intent   Interact   Neutralize

Chapter 4: The Courtyard

Study & Discussion Questions:

1. How is General Shortstop's team able to get inside the Palace undetected?
2. What emotions might Spikey be feeling as he heads out into the courtyard?
3. While in the courtyard, Spikey encountered a statue of Emperor Seth. Based on the description of the statue and other things described in the courtyard, what predictions do you have about this character who will be the chief antagonist of the novel?
4. The *Bible* says, *"Greater love has no one than this: to lay down one's life for one's friends"* (John 15:13 NIV). Spikey was certainly willing to do this for his friends. What biblical characters were willing to sacrifice their lives for Christ? Has anyone in your own life sacrificed themselves for their friends, family, or the Lord?
5. Dialogue is what characters say, and it usually appears in quotation marks. Dialect is how characters speak. For example, many people in the Southern United States speak with an accent that is different from those in the North. What character introduced in *Chapter 4*, has a dialect different from other characters we have encountered so far? Describe the difference.
6. Predict what will happen to Spikey after he is captured. Do you think Lizard Face will kill him or spare him?

Words to Know:

Aqueduct   Devoid   Ego   Exaggerate   Hideous

Chapter 5: The Kitchen

Journal Prompt:

- In this chapter, we are introduced to Chef Berry, the chief cook of Cosmic Bubble Palace. Throughout this novel, we will be introduced to several foods native to Staranana. A good author will describe the food in his novel so well that it will make his reader's mouths water with hunger. In a minimum five-sentence journal, describe your favorite food with as much detail as possible. Then share your journal with your classmates. Afterward, ask them if they are now hungry for your special delicacy.

Study & Discussion Questions:

1. Imagine what life must be like as a slave in the Palace. Do you think it was enjoyable? Consider Chef Berry's description.
2. **Outside Research:** Though we don't often think of it, slavery still exists in our world today. As a class, research some parts of the modern world where slavery of any kind is still in practice. Discuss with your classmates what you can all do to fight back against slavery in the 21st century.
3. Describe a time when your faith helped you get through a hard time. What was the situation and what was the result?
4. Do you believe Berry can be trusted? Should the bears trust anyone they meet in the Palace? Why or why not?

Words to Know:

Betray   Deny   Reinforcement   Relic   Subside

Chapter 6: Flames of Royalty

Journal Prompt:

- As General Shortstop and his team journey through the Palace, they are forced to take refuge in a fountain when Seth unleashes a firestorm against them. Part of the design of this fountain included a huge jade elephant. This elephant is a subtle reference to a jade elephant owned by the author's mother and to the very first story Mr. Fields ever wrote called *Green Elephant*. Without that elephant, the inspiration for this novel might never have come. In your life and in the things you love to do, what inspires you – whether things, places, or people. Respond in a minimum five sentence journal.

Study & Discussion Questions:

1. What events do you think led Seth into his evil life?
2. Just as a protagonist must have a *fatal flaw*, an antagonist (or villain) must have a *redeemable characteristic* – or something about their character that is good or that we can feel compassion for. From the little bit you have read so far about Seth, can you see any redeemable characteristics in him? What are they?
3. A theme is an idea or message an author is trying to share with his readers. This novel has several themes, and one of them is *betrayal*. Think first of the *Bible*. What Apostle betrayed Jesus and for what price? Then, describe how Seth is like that person? As you continue to read and learn more about this character, add more to the discussion.
4. **Personal Reflection:** Have you ever hurt one of your friends for personal gain? What was the result? How should you have responded in that situation?

Words to Know:

Intolerable   Mesmerized   Minion   Pachyderm   Phoenix

Chapter 7: The Clock

Journal Prompt:

- A *genre* is a type of literature, usually broken into the major categories fiction (not real) and non-fiction (based on real life). This novel is fictional and falls under the genre Christian-fantasy. Christian fiction typically seeks to share the message of Jesus Christ through a made-up story. Fantasy writing includes elements that cannot or do not exist in real life. In a five-sentence journal, describe how *Staranana* fits into the genre of Christian-fantasy. Use examples from the text to support your analysis.

Study & Discussion Questions:

1. As the bears near the clock, Cak wants to impress the others. Reflect on a time when you wanted to impress the people in your life. Was it for a good or bad reason?
2. Seth dishonored his father by dishonoring his clock. In what ways do people dishonor their loved ones with or without meaning to? What are some good ways that we can honor the people who are important to us?
3. What was the combination to the secret passageway inside the clock? How did the bears enter the combination?
4. As the bears neared their goal, what thoughts do you think might have been going through their minds?
5. Summarize what you know about Starananian culture thus far. Include things like their history, food, goals, etc.

Words to Know:

Liberate
Pendulum
Precarious
Synchronized
Unison

Chapter 8: The Roof

Journal Prompt:

- In Chapter 8, one character unexpectedly loses his life. Life is a precious gift from the Lord, but, unfortunately, we lose people from this world all the time. Thankfully, for those who know Christ, we will see our loved ones again one day. It is important that we tell the people in our lives that we love and appreciate them as often as we can. For this journal, write a short note to someone in your life letting them know you appreciate them.

Study & Discussion Questions:

1. What items did the bears have to get from the roof before they could parachute to safety?
2. For what reason does General Shortstop decide to descend the secret staircase again?
3. When Shortstop is about to escape the Palace, he sees several guards leading Spikey away. He chooses not to rescue him. Do you believe he was justified in making this decision? Why/Why not?
4. In what way was Nick Grass like Jesus Christ?
5. Do you think the bears will make it off of Staranana? What further obstacles might stand in their way?

Words to Know:

Ambush
Corridor
Hunch
Perimeter
Stealth

Chapter 9: The Escape

Journal Prompt:

- A *symbol* is anything in a story that stands for something else. For example, an author might use a bird as a symbol for freedom. There are many symbols in this novel and one example is the spacecraft of the Rebellion – the *New Life*. In what ways might the *New Life* be a symbol for the Christian life? What obstacles does the ship face while leaving the planet, and how might these be symbols for what a Christian believer faces? Address these questions in a minimum five-sentence journal, and be sure to include specific examples from the text.

Study & Discussion Questions:

1. General Shortstop neglected to tell Gloria that Spikey had not been killed until it was too late to do anything about it. Has someone ever done something similar to you? How did you respond?
2. Why do you think Sparkey believes he can rescue his father by himself? Would you be willing to risk your life for someone you love?
3. In order to get off the ship, Sparkey had to lie to a guard and steal his keys. Do you feel he was justified in doing these things? Is there ever an acceptable time for a Christian to lie or steal? If your answer is *no,* how else might Sparkey have escaped from the ship?
4. **Outside Research**: In this chapter, we are introduced to our first dragon characters, including Captain Perdi Torinth. What other books have you read with dragons in them? What do they look like and what are their abilities? In those stories, are dragons typically good or evil?

Words to Know:

Adrenaline   Circumstance   Lavatory   Restrain   Suspicious

Chapter 10: The Door

Journal Prompt:

- **Outside Research:** In this chapter, Sparkey encounters his father's invention the *Door*. He also meets the *Door's* operating system, an artificial intelligence nicknamed TB. For homework, do some research on the work science is currently doing with artificial intelligence. What is the purpose of these technologies, and how do they serve society? Your teacher can set the length requirement, but strive for at least two paragraphs (10 sentences) of facts.

Study & Discussion Questions:

1. How has the setting of Sparkey's family cave changed when returns there? Have you ever returned to a home you have moved out of? How did you feel, and how were things different?
2. Sparkey finds an unexpected friend in TB. Describe a time when you were able to be a friend to someone who might not have expected it or a time when someone became a friend to you that you did not expect.
3. If Sparkey goes to Earth, how might things change on Staranana when he returns? If his parents knew about his plans to go to Earth, how might each of them respond? Use what you know of their personalities so far to help you answer these questions.
4. What fears would you have traveling to a different planet for the first time? Would you ultimately be willing to take on the adventure?

Words to Know:

Artificial   Cautious   Compromise   Extremist   Instill

Chapter 11: Scotty

Journal Prompt:

• A *prophecy* is a prediction about an event that might occur in the future. Or, in God's case, it is a *promise* about something that *will* happen in the future. The *Bible* is filled with many prophecies, and most of them have to do with Christ in some way shape or form. For homework, research some of these biblical prophecies about Christ. Which prophecies give you the most comfort or encouragement? Use the Internet to help with the search if needed, but always check with your parents or teacher before logging on. Try to record and analyze at least three prophecies.

Study & Discussion Questions:

1. Why do you think God will not allow most humans to see Starananians?
2. In what ways is the setting of Loan Oak Elementary School and Scotty's home dramatically different from Staranana?
3. After reading about how Seth became evil, do you have any compassion for him? Do you think he deserved for Iren to turn his back on him?
4. If you were tortured like Seth, do you believe you would have turned on God? Why/Why not?
5. Do you believe Scotty is the *Blood of the Land*? If so why would God have chosen a child and not a full-grown man?
6. If the *Blood of Land* were a symbol for one character in the *Bible* whom do you think he would be? (Hint: The *Blood of the Land* is not a symbol for Jesus Christ).

Words to Know:

Bizarre   Deem   Dire   Surrender   Vortex

Chapter 12: Breakfast and New Worlds

Journal Prompt:

- This series is called *Chronicles of the Imagination* because originally all the characters were part of an imaginary play world the author had when he was a little boy. Playing *make-believe* can be wonderfully adventurous, and most children have fun doing it. Think back to when you were little. Did you ever have an imaginary friend? What was their name, what did they look like, and what did you do together? Do you ever still think about them? Respond in a minimum five sentence journal.

Study & Discussion Questions:

1. What sensory details does the author use to describe the setting of Bobby Thomson's house?
2. Bobby seems utterly clueless about Sparkey. He thinks he is only an imaginary friend. Do you think Bobby will ever figure out the truth? Why/Why not?
3. How do you think Scotty's life will change once he leaves Earth?
4. **Predict:** Will Mrs. Thompson discover Scotty is missing before he returns?
5. Sparkey thanks Scotty before they return to Staranana. Describe a time when someone did something nice for you. How did you show your gratitude?

Words to Know:

Disuse   Garbled   Grimace   Microscopic   Savory

Chapter 13: Return to Staranana

Journal Prompt:

- Remember that this is a *Christian-fantasy* novel, and the point of *Christian-fantasy* is still to share the message of Jesus Christ. In this chapter, Scotty shares what it means to be a Christian. The *Bible* also says, *"If you declare with your mouth, 'Jesus is Lord,' and believe in your heart that God raised him from the dead, you will be saved"* (Romans 10:9). If you are a Christian, write a minimum five-sentence journal about how you came to know the Lord. If you are not a Christian, what questions or concerns do you have about Christ or Christianity? Discuss these with your teacher and classmates.

Study & Discussion Questions:

1. What is Scotty's very first reaction to Staranana? Do you think this will cause trouble for him throughout the rest of the novel?
2. TB says that Scotty will have to kill Seth, which Scotty won't accept. Why do you think that is?
3. **Discuss:** Do believe it is ever acceptable for a Christian to kill, even in a war?
4. What does Sparkey say they should do first, before worrying about taking on Seth?
5. What weapons do they leave the cave with?

Words to Know:

Component
Conquer
Cursed
Delicacy
Resurrect

Chapter 14: Aqueducts: The Gators

Journal Prompt:

- In this chapter, Sparkey and Scotty must head deep underground in order to sneak into the Palace. However, along the way, they will face many dangers in the aqueducts. Facing anything scary or uncertain requires a great deal of bravery. In a five-sentence journal, describe a time when you faced a scary situation and had to be brave. What was the ultimate result? If you cannot think of one for yourself, share one about a person close to you.

Study & Discussion Questions:

1. **Activity:** Scotty is amazed by what he sees in the forest. Draw a picture of the Nana Forest including as many visual details as possible.
2. Scotty uses a lesson he learned in school to help them find a boat. Describe a time when something you learned in school was important for your success outside of school.
3. Using a much detail from the text as possible, describe a *gator*.
4. How are Sparkey and Scotty able to use the gators to help them?
5. **Predict:** What will happen to Sparkey and Scotty as they head deeper into the aqueducts?

Words to Know:

Altered
Ancestor
Conceived
Consistent
Eternal

Chapter 15: Everybody Else

Journal Prompt:

- *Dynamic characters* are those characters that change over time. For example, they might learn something that will help them respond differently to the same situation at a later time. Select two characters from *this* chapter, and explain how they have changed over the course of the first 15 chapters of the book. Write your response in a minimum five-sentence journal.

Study & Discussion Questions:

1. What plan does Lizard Face suggest to chase down the *New Life?*
2. After hearing this suggestion, Seth mentions the *only* failure of his 5,000-year reign. Describe this failure.
3. Why do you think it is important that we learn the history of the characters in a book? Why isn't simply dealing with the current events of the plot enough?
4. A flat character is one that we know very little about. What flat character is mentioned in Seth's story? Do you think he will come into the novel again?
5. Why do you think Lizard Face wants to betray Seth?
6. How do you think Gloria learned all of her secrets about Stararocka?
7. **Outside Research:** Spikey refuses to give up his friends even after being tortured. Describe a Christian who was willing to do the same thing for the cause of Christ.

Words to Know:

Interrogate
Linger
Miserable
Resourceful
Vast

Chapter 16: Aqueducts: Bats and Crystals

Journal Prompt:

- *Chapter 16* ends saying, *"...there was nothing left of them but the echo of their last dying cries."* This statement implies that the two main characters of the novel have just been killed. We are then left to wonder about their fate for at least another chapter. This literary device is called a *cliffhanger*, where a story suddenly ends at a moment of great intensity. The story then continues at a later time or even in a later book. Think of books you've read or movies or television programs you have watched. In a five-sentence journal, share the most intense cliffhanger you have ever experienced.

Study & Discussion Questions:

1. Scotty was almost killed when he tried to touch a viola crystal. Describe a time when you or someone you know touched something they weren't supposed to, and it led to significant trouble.
2. The Starananians have a book they reference when studying their own history and prophecies. What is the name of this book?
3. Scotty describes his parents to Sparkey. He truly admires them. Describe someone you truly admire and why.
4. What creatures do Sparkey and Scotty encounter in Black Eye Canyon?
5. Do you think Scotty and Sparkey are really dead at the end of the chapter? What direction might the story go if they are?

Words to Know:

Abyss   Banshee   Encompass   Ominous   Pinnacle

Chapter 17: More with Everybody Else

Journal Prompt:

- **Outside Research:** In *Chapter 17*, Spikey Moonbeam languishes in a dungeon cell waiting to be executed. Spikey is only a fictional character, but there are many people all over the real world who have been imprisoned for their faith in Jesus Christ. Conduct some research and learn the names and locations of some of these people. If possible, as a class, consider writing letters of encouragement to these prisoners for Christ. Also, remember to pray for them every day.

Study & Discussion Questions:

1. Describe Spikey's prison cell.
2. If you knew you were going to die tomorrow like Spikey did, what would you want to do with your last day?
3. Gloria Moonbeam has invented a new type of medicine to help the Starananians adapt on Stararocka. What is the name of this medicine and why is it necessary?
4. Gloria seems willing to do anything to save her family. What would you be willing to do to protect the people you love?
5. What are your impressions of General Shortstop so far? Have you seen any changes in him from the start of the novel?

Words to Know:

Forsake
Provision
Pursuit
Relentless
Squander

Chapter 18: Aqueducts: Escape from Black Eye Canyon

Journal Prompt:

- One of the things that is so great about a good book is that we often lose ourselves within its pages. We find ourselves connecting with the characters, predicting what will happen next, and even making plans of how we would react in a similar situation. In *Chapter 18*, Scotty and Sparkey ride a giant recklor bat. Pretend you are one of these characters, and, with as much vivid detail as possible, describe this experience. Shoot for a minimum of five sentences.

Study & Discussion Questions:

1. What had actually happened to Sparkey and Scotty at the end of *Chapter 16*?
2. Why does the giant recklor attack them? How do they escape?
3. Sparkey insists that Scotty trust him when they are about to be eaten by the giant recklor, which he does. How important is it for you to be able to trust your friends and for them to be able to trust you?
4. What does Sparkey say will happen to the human that defeats Seth? How does Scotty respond to this?
5. How do Sparkey and Scotty plan to get rid of the giant recklor?
6. Do you think Scotty and Sparkey have been through the easy or the hard part of their adventure? Explain.

Words to Know:

Adjacent   Comply   Detour   Foreboding   Impenetrable

Chapter 19: The Goons

Journal Prompt:

- In this chapter, we learn that Sparkey is a pretty great shot (later we will see this is with a slingshot). Skills like this will help him throughout the novel. If you were a character in this novel, what special skills do you have that you feel might be a benefit to the adventure. Describe your skill(s) in a minimum five-sentence journal.

Study & Discussion Questions:

1. After escaping from the recklor, Sparkey and Scotty pause to have a brief meal. What food does Scotty reluctantly eat, and what is his reaction to it?
2. Sparkey says the goons were a very proud race before Seth cursed them. What does the *Bible* have to say about pride?
3. What was the curse of the goons?
4. What had Sparkey hidden and then forgotten about that ends up helping the boys in this chapter?
5. Scotty states clearly that Jesus Christ is the only Savior. Have you ever been tempted to trust in someone other than Christ in a time of trouble? Explain.
6. Scotty uses Scripture to help him and Sparkey defeat the goons. Have you ever used Scripture to help you when you were in trouble? Describe the situation.

Words to Know:

Ditch
Hoist
Persuade
Portion
Savior

Chapter 20: Back to the Kitchen

Journal Prompt:

- In *Chapter 20*, Sparkey and Scotty finally make it inside Cosmic Bubble Palace. This had to be very encouraging for them after everything they had been through, but they still have a great deal of danger to face. In a brief journal, give the boys advice about how they can best be prepared for potential dangers they might face. Write your journal in the form of a letter to one or both of the boys. Include details about what you know about Staranana and the characters in this book that might influence future events in the story.

Study & Discussion Questions:

1. What is the first thing Scotty does when he enters the kitchen?
2. What does Sparkey see when he looks out of the kitchen into the main chamber?
3. Sparkey uses a Starananian curse word in this chapter. How can using curse words negatively affect our Christian witness?
4. Why do you think the bears use both primitive and advanced technology?
5. What do Sparkey and Scotty decide to use to help them get to the 10th story?
6. This chapter ends with the phrase, "This was too easy!" Do you agree or disagree? Why?

Words to Know:

Appropriate
Dumbwaiter
Equivalent
Incentive
Threshold

Chapter 21: Lizard Secrets

Journal Prompt:

- In this chapter, Lizard Face has a secret. He is plotting the downfall of Emperor Seth. Even though his secret was an evil and deceptive one, not all secrets have to be evil. Do some research and in a brief journal describe what the *Bible* has to say about keeping secrets? Are there some secrets it is all right to keep? What is your opinion about keeping secrets?

Study & Discussion Questions:

1. Whose chambers do Scotty and Sparkey stop the dumbwaiter right outside of?
2. Lizard Face wants to work against the prophecies of God and take the Emperor's throne for himself. Why do you think people like Lizard Face and Satan believe they can overcome God?
3. How do the boys get caught? How does Scotty start behaving when this happens?
4. Since God has gotten the boys so far already, Scotty has faith that He will get them the rest of the way – but then they get captured. Do you think Scotty was wrong to have faith in God? What might the Lord have in mind by allowing them to get captured?
5. What truth does Sparkey reassure himself with as the chapter ends?

Words to Know:

Chaos
Deliver
Loyal
Mock
Population

Chapter 22: Reunion

Journal Prompt:

- Sadly, many kids these days are separated from people they love for a long time. Some might be part of military families, and since they move often, they have to leave their friends behind. They might also have a parent who must leave them to serve overseas. Other kids might also be separated from someone they love due to a divorce or death in the family. Saying goodbye is very hard for everyone involved, but reuniting can be amazing! In a five-sentence journal, describe a time when you were reunited with someone whom you love who had been gone for a long time.

Study & Discussion Questions:

1. What additional details do we learn about the setting of Spikey's dungeon cell?
2. Describe Spikey's first reaction to seeing Scotty.
3. Sparkey describes Scotty as a "goof." Do you think God will be able to work through Scotty despite his shortcomings? List some characters in the *Bible* that He was able to work through despite their shortcomings.
4. Spikey quotes a passage from the *Text of Iren* to encourage the boys when they are imprisoned. What passages from the *Bible* are the most encouraging to you when you are discouraged?

Words to Know:

Distinct
Qualification
Recognition
Silhouette
Whimper

Chapter 23: The Humans

Journal Prompt:

- In this chapter, Scotty meets his true enemy in this novel for the very first time. Though Seth is a murderer and a tyrant that must be stopped, most of us won't have enemies like that, and Christ was very specific on how we are to respond to our enemies. Do some research in the Gospels – *Matthew*, *Mark*, *Luke*, and *John*. How does Jesus say to treat our enemies? Do you think this is hard or easy to do? Why or why not?

Study & Discussion Questions:

1. Lizard Face asks, "...how can a *ssimple* boy defeat the most powerful man on the planet?" In your view, does he have a point? How could a nine-year-old boy defeat a 5,000-year-old emperor?
2. What is Seth's plan to cause the people to lose faith in the promises of God and the *Blood of the Land*?
3. What does Scotty believe is the light that will lead them to freedom? What actually happens to that light?
4. Make a list of the ways in which Scotty and Seth are different. (Shoot for five.) Discuss why you think they turned out so differently.
5. Scotty knows Seth wants to kill him. How would you feel being in the same room with someone who wanted to kill you?
6. Who do you think was speaking through Scotty? Explain.

Words to Know:

Blemish
Hearth
Hilt
Jeopardy
Lecture

Chapter 24: The Light

Journal Prompt:

- The phrase *Deus Ex Machina* literally means "God from the machine." In ancient Greek plays among others, an actor playing a Greek god would enter the stage through the use of a crane or other device at some critical point in the plot, so the god could save the day. These days, the phrase relates to something extraordinary suddenly changing the direction of the plot. In this chapter, Scotty meets an angel of God Himself, and we will soon see the plot of this story take a dramatic turn. In a brief journal or class discussion, how else do you imagine God might directly intervene in the plot of this narrative?

Study & Discussion Questions:

1. What did Scotty see in the sky when he returned to the dungeon cell?
2. Describe the Angel Joshua in detail. Who was really the Light that would bring them to freedom?
3. How does Joshua describe the *Blood of the Land*? For what reason is Scotty chosen for the role?
4. Why did God create Staranana, and why does Joshua say it is currently suffering?
5. The angel Joshua says that Jesus only died for humans. Why might this be? What verse in the *Bible* states clearly that God does not forgive fallen angels?
6. Joshua says that any Christian could have rescued Staranana. What are some other amazing things you have heard of that Christians have done throughout history?
7. Do you believe Scotty will become prideful like Seth if he becomes the emperor? Explain.

Words to Know:

Diminish   Petrified   Pierce   Tentative   Wield

Chapter 25:
Escape from Cosmic Bubble Palace

Journal Prompt:

- At the end of *Chapter 25*, Lizard Face blames and kills the goons who were with him, even though it was his fault Scotty and the bears escaped. Though we hopefully won't ever go to this extreme, blaming other people for our mistakes can be very tempting. In your life, have you ever blamed someone else for a mistake you have made? What do you think Christ would have preferred you do? Why is this so difficult? Respond in a minimum five sentence journal.

Study & Discussion Questions:

1. What is Spikey's reaction when Scotty tells him about Joshua?
2. Later, what signals Spikey that it is time to wake up?
3. What day of the week does Scotty realize it is? Why is this significant?
4. What *Bible* verse does Scotty share to encourage his friends?
5. Describe in detail how Scotty and the bears escape.
6. Why do you think Joshua gave Spikey back his bomb?

Words to Know:

Inmate
Loathed
Mercy
Mutilate
Tousled

Chapter 26:
Return to the Moonbeam Cave

Journal Prompt:

- In this chapter, Spikey expresses his pent up anger with the crew of the *New Life*. You will answer a question about this incident below, but for now, think about times you have been angry in your own life. Research and find out what the *Bible* has to say about anger. Is there ever a time when it is appropriate for a Christian to be angry? Respond in a five-sentence journal.

Study & Discussion Questions:

1. After returning to the Moonbeam cave, why does Spikey say they have to go to the ruins of Stony City?
2. Where do you think Spikey got the Stararockan book?
3. How had TB fooled everyone on Earth into thinking that Scotty was not missing? What new invention does Spikey give Scotty to keep up the subterfuge?
4. What must they cross to reach Stony City? Why is Sparkey excited about this?
5. Why do you think Spikey is suddenly angry with the people who left on the *New Life*? Is his anger justified?

Words to Know:

Concentration
Intact
Nutrients
Precaution
Transmit

Chapter 27:
The Transmission

Journal Prompt:

- Throughout the novel, Gloria Moonbeam has several tense encounters with Colonel Speedway. The colonel does not believe that the promises of God are worth trusting. In your opinion, what is the best way to respond to a person who doesn't believe or trust in God? Should we just *live and let live*, so to speak, or should we do something else to help them understand and appreciate the Lord more? Explain your point of view in a five-sentence journal.

Study & Discussion Questions:

1. What does the *New Life* detect?
2. Describe Colonel Speedway. What are your impressions of him? Why does he seem to dislike Gloria so much?
3. What had Gloria started on the ship? How does Speedway react to this news? How does Gloria respond to him?
4. Who do you think sent the mysterious transmission?
5. Gloria quotes a passage from the *Text of Iren* that describes God's deliverance. Read Revelation 21 and 22 in the *Bible*. What does the *Bible* say about God's ultimate plan for the future of the human race?

Words to Know:

Binge
Cockpit
Disembark
Frustrate
Recitation

Chapter 28: The White Desert

Journal Prompt:

- In this chapter, Scotty has the chance to make a big decision, which we will discuss momentarily. In your own life, have your parents ever let you make a big decision? Describe it. How did it make you feel? What was the result? Respond in a minimum five-sentence journal.

Study & Discussion Questions:

1. How far did Scotty, Sparkey, and Spikey have to walk each day to reach the White Desert?
2. Spikey gives Scotty his first command decision as the future emperor. What two choices did he have to choose from, and what choice does he make?
3. Who is the goon in charge of the shipyard? What news does Lizard Face give to this goon, and what becomes their plan?
4. How does Spikey decide to use the bomb? How did he get the bomb into position?
5. What horrible mistake is made in this chapter, and what ends up happening as a result?
6. Scotty's decision ended up being wrong. What do you think the consequences will be?

Words to Know:

Expendable
Fuselage
Lunatic
Portal
Tattered

Chapter 29: Stony City

Journal Prompt:

- Stony City was the location of one of the greatest battles and greatest defeats in all the history of Staranana. On Earth, we preserve the locations of many old battles and other historical sites. Do you believe there is value in this? Why do societies insist on preserving relics of their past? Respond in a minimum five-sentence journal.

Study & Discussion Questions:

1. How did Spikey know they were nearing Stony City?
2. Describe a honeysuckle apple. What is so unique about this fruit?
3. Describe the *Dagger of Promise*. Why does Spikey believe it will be able to defeat Seth?
4. Scotty takes off his duplicating necklace because he is homesick. If you were in his situation, would you be homesick? Do you think Scotty will end up staying on Staranana permanently?
5. How do you think the bears feel walking through hundreds of their people who have been turned into stone?
6. What do Scotty and the bears encounter as they step outside into the sunken city?
7. When Sparkey and Spikey are frozen, predict what Scotty might have to do to stop Seth on his own.

Words to Know:

Ebony
Endow
Intimidation
Resilient
Spew

Chapter 30: The Dragon and the Dagger

Journal Prompt:

- An unexpected turn in a story is called a *twist*. It usually involves a drastic change that the reader does not see coming. This chapter includes something of a twist in relation to the dragon Hydro, however, authors and movie makers have been using twists for a very long time. Think of your favorite book or movie that included a twist. In a brief journal, outline the basic plot and the twist of the work in question. Did you see the twist coming?

Study & Discussion Questions:

1. Where does Scotty find the *Dagger of Promise?* What does he have to do to get it?
2. The *Dagger of Promise* can destroy anything that is evil. What weapon has God given us on Earth to overcome Satan's evil?
3. After Hydro gets stabbed by the *Dagger of Promise*, what happens?
4. Hydro serves Seth out of fear. What advice would you give to him? What advice does Scotty give him?
5. After what happened, do you think Sparkey and Spikey will ever truly trust Hydro? Why/Why not?

Words to Know:

Appreciate
Debris
Hatchling
Immense
Imprison

Chapter 31: The Fire Cruiser

Journal Prompt:

- In this chapter, Speedway apologizes to Gloria for his behavior even though it is difficult. Describe a time when you had to do the same thing to someone you cared about, or they apologized to you. How did you feel afterward? Was if difficult? How does the *Bible* say we should react to people who have wronged us? Answer in a brief journal.

Study & Discussion Questions:

1. When Speedway apologizes to Gloria, his wife is mentioned. What had happened to her?
2. Captain Gonish was overconfident that he could destroy the *New Life*. Research the life of the Pharaoh in Exodus. In what ways was he overconfident? How did God humble him?
3. The *Fire Cruiser* comes to the rescue of the *New Life*. Has anyone ever come to your rescue when you were in great need? Describe it.
4. In what way might the *Fire Cruiser's* rescue of the *New Life* be an example of *Deus Ex Machina*?
5. Predict what is going to happen when the Starananians finally meet the Stararockans.

Words to Know:

Conventional
Crucial
Frequency
Grotesque
Inspire

Chapter 32: The Nobles and the Secret

Journal Prompt:

- In this chapter, Gloria finally confesses how she knew so much about Stararocka and where Spikey actually came from. While this secret was not sinful, the *Bible* does speak of the power of confessing our sins to each other saying in James 5:16, "Therefore confess your sins to each other and pray for each other so that you may be healed. The prayer of a righteous person is powerful and effective" (NIV). Why do you think confession has such a power to heal?

Study & Discussion Questions:

1. Describe the *Fire Cruiser* in detail.
2. What are the names of the *Fire Cruiser's* captain and first officer? How do they know Spikey?
3. Why do you think Spikey kept the fact that he was a Stararockan a secret?
4. Stararockan law is rather harsh. Come up with three laws you feel would allow their society to remain safe, but also not require harsh punishments like Spikey endured.
5. Who commanded the Nobles to build the liberation fleet? What is the purpose of the fleet?
6. Predict what is going to happen when the *Fire Cruiser* reaches Staranana.

Words to Know:

Banish
Charismatic
Detect
Dumbstruck
Recent

Chapter 33: The Last Prophecies

Journal Prompt:

- As mentioned in a previous journal prompt, a *theme* is a central message an author wants to convey through their writing. Another theme of this novel is *faith*. Spikey perhaps of all the characters has demonstrated the most faith. However, faith does not come easily for most people. One thing in the *Bible* we are asked to have faith in is that Jesus Christ will one day return. Even so, He has already waited over 2,000 years to fulfill this promise. Do you believe He will ultimately fulfill this promise? Explain why or why not in a brief journal.

Study & Discussion Questions:

1. Upon returning to the Moonbeam cave, how long did Scotty sleep for?
2. How many prophecies did Spikey discover were left for the *Blood of the Land* to fulfill?
3. What are some of the prophecies the *Bible* says will come to pass before Jesus returns to set up His kingdom?
4. What do you believe is meant by, "Strike down the faces of light!"?
5. Do you believe we have to understand the *Bible* perfectly in order for God to work in our lives? Why/Why not?
6. Why does Spikey want to go to the slave camps immediately?

Words to Know:

Enthrone
Interpret
Jot
Obvious
Parchment

Chapter 34: The Slave Camps

Journal Prompt:

- An *idol* is anything that takes the place of the true God in your heart. In ancient times an idol was a statue that represented a false god. In this book, the Starananians begin to treat Scotty as an idol when they begin to worship him. He becomes angry and rebukes them for this (seemingly it was God speaking through him). What types of idols exist in our world today? How can we work to keep idolatry out of our own lives? Answer in a brief journal.

Study & Discussion Questions:

1. What was the name of the street that ran through the slave camps?
2. For what reason did Seth spare the little girl that had caused him to fall into the mud.
3. What were Sparkey and Spikey warned about when they were seen carrying a *dead* body through the camps?
4. What was the name of the camp minister and his assistant?
5. What had the slaves been hiding in a dirt cave in the forest? How does Spikey react to this revelation?

Words to Know:

Credible
Designate
Entourage
Minimal
Skeptics

Chapter 35: The Faces of Light

Journal Prompt:

- Chapters 35, 36, and 37 are essentially the *climax* of this novel. A climax is the moment of greatest intensity in a story, and we will see the ultimate climax occur in Chapter 37 when Scotty finally confronts Seth. In the meantime, take a moment to review the major internal and external conflicts that you have encountered in the rising action of the novel. Also, what protagonists have you encountered, and what are their fatal flaws? What antagonists have you met and what redeemable qualities do they have? Who are dynamic, round, static, and flat characters in this novel. Describe and analyze each in a brief essay.

Study & Discussion Questions:

1. How are Scotty and Sparkey able to get up to the 16th floor?
2. Hydro turned from evil to good, and he ended up helping Sparkey and Scotty a great deal. Can you think of anyone from the *Bible* who became a devout servant of God after living an evil life?
3. Because of his faith, God made Spikey into a great leader. What types of things has God done in your life that you would not have been able to accomplish without faith in Him?
4. Where do Scotty and Sparkey hide in the throne room?
5. What is the real interpretation of the *faces of light* prophecy?

Words to Know:

Elderly   Foolhardy   Obtain   Offensive   Quench

Chapter 36: The Battle

Journal Prompt:

- An *allusion* is a casual reference in a story to something in another piece of literature, art, or history. For example, when a person says, "My cup runneth over" implying that they are greatly blessed, they are alluding to Psalm 23:5. In this chapter, when a group of teens pulls down Seth's statue, this is an allusion to a common practice when dictators are overthrown on Earth. Do some outside research and describe three dictators in world history that this has happened to? Why did people rebel against them, and how were they ultimately overthrown. Respond in a brief essay.

Study & Discussion Questions:

1. God heals the bear-goons in the battle. How did people in the *Bible* respond to God after they had been healed?
2. How do the former bear-goons respond when Spikey asks for their help?
3. Where does the slave army set up a triage facility, and what is a triage facility?
4. Hydro has to turn against the other dragons in order to help his new friends. Would you be willing to stand against the desires of your friends and family if it were necessary to serve God? Explain.
5. There are two examples of *Deus Ex Machina* in this chapter. What are they? There was also an example in the previous chapter. What was it?

Words to Know:

Casualty   Compatriot   Emanating   Inhibit   Stronghold

Chapter 37: Confrontations

Journal Prompt:

- This chapter is the final and ultimate climax of this novel. In a brief journal, explain what you believe is the moment of greatest intensity? How did other events in the novel help build to this point? Did the story turn out the way you expected? Share your thoughts in a minimum five-sentence journal.

Study & Discussion Questions:

1. What reasons might Lizard Face have to steal the throne from Seth? Do you think he would make a better emperor than Seth? Can evil ever rule anything successfully?
2. How is Lizard Face's plot to kill Seth foiled? Who shows up to rescue Lizard Face and where do they go?
3. How does Seth respond when he sees Scotty hiding in the rafters?
4. How do Heaven and Hell meet on Staranana?
5. When Joshua comes to help Scotty what passage of scripture does he use to strengthen him?
6. Scotty kills Seth. Do you think he was right to do so? Why/Why not? What would you have done in his place?

Words to Know:

Anxious
Dismount
Exposed
Seize
Tabernacle

Chapter 38: The Crowning & After

Journal Prompt:

- Following the climax of a story comes the *falling action*. Here, the characters must deal with the consequences of climax. Finally, a story ends with the *resolution* when the conflicts of the novel are brought to a final conclusion. In these chapters, how do the characters deal with Seth's death, and how is the plot brought to its ultimate resolution? Answer in a brief journal.

Study & Discussion Questions:

1. The bears cannot crown Scotty because they are not royal. What does the *Bible* say about the royalty of believers in Christ?
2. Joshua says Scotty's real adventures will be on Earth. What type of adventures does the *Bible* say are ahead for believers?
3. What do you think Scotty's next adventure on Staranana might involve?
4. Do you have any questions about the events or message of the novel? Discuss these with your teacher and classmates.

Words to Know:

Assembly
Confirm
Eliminate
Ruffle
Shortcoming

Staranana Test

Chronicles of the Imagination: Staranana Test

Please circle the correct answer for each of the following questions.

1. What is Spikey Moonbeam's occupation?
    A. Doctor
    B. Teacher
    C. Inventor
    D. Chef

2. In what type of house do the Moonbeams live?
    A. Cave
    B. Log cabin
    C. Brick house
    D. Apartment

3. How many bears were to go on the mission to Cosmic Bubble Palace?
    A. 6
    B. 3
    C. 8
    D. 9

4. In order to reach the Palace, General Shortstop and the others had to travel through the
    _____.
    A. Ice Sea
    B. Aqueducts
    C. Stony City
    D. White Desert

5. **What story was the secret staircase in the Palace located on?**
   A. 5th
   B. 6th
   C. 10th
   D. 99th

6. **Spikey believed the _____ would come and free Staranana from Seth.**
   A. *Blood of the Land*
   B. *Prince of Power*
   C. *Son of Light*
   D. *King of Peace*

7. **What happened to Spikey when he tried to plant the bomb in the Palace courtyard?**
   A. He broke his leg.
   B. He was captured by Lizard Face.
   C. He set it off early.
   D. None of the Above.

8. **_____ helped the bears reach the secret staircase in the Palace.**
   A. Seth
   B. Lizard Face
   C. Kelcott
   D. Chef Berry

9. **While blasting off from Staranana, the *New Life* was attacked by _____.**
   A. Goons
   B. Seth
   C. Recklor Bats
   D. Dragons

10. **When Gloria learned Spikey was still alive, she wanted to _____.**
    A. Return to rescue him
    B. Leave as quickly as possible
    C. Write a letter requesting his release
    D. None of the above

11. **_____ sneaked off the *New Life* to try and rescue Spikey?**
    A. Gloria
    B. Toby
    C. Sparkey
    D. Cak

12. **Sparkey used his father's *Door* to travel to _____ to find the _____.**
    A. Earth; *Blood of the Land*
    B. Mars; *King of Peace*
    C. Jupiter; *Son of Light*
    D. Venus; *Prince of Power*

13. **Scotty lived where?**
    A. New York City
    B. Beaufort, North Carolina
    C. Anchorage, Alaska
    D. Prineville, Oregon

14. **When Scotty and Sparkey return to Staranana, Scotty is _____.**
    A. Surprised at how warm it is
    B. Overwhelmed by the cold
    C. Invited to the Palace by Seth
    D. Taken to a secret meeting in the forest

15. **What obstacles do Scotty and Sparkey face in the aqueducts?**
    A. Cave elephants, recklor bats, poison crystals
    B. Gators, snakes, cave wolves
    C. Gators, recklor bats, poison crystals
    D. Molten lava, acid lakes, poison crystals

16. **When they reach the Palace, Scotty and Sparkey are captured by _____.**
    A. Lizard Face
    B. Seth
    C. Kelcott
    D. Hydro the Water Dragon

17. **Scotty, Sparkey, and Spikey are set free by _____.**
    A. Seth
    B. Joshua
    C. Kelcott
    D. Hydro the Water Dragon

18. **In order to defeat Seth, Scotty and the bears must find the _____.**
    A. *Sword of Destruction*
    B. *Bow of Conviction*
    C. *Dagger of Promise*
    D. *Bat of Power*

19. **Who do Scotty and the bears meet in Stony City?**
    A. Lt. Gakic
    B. Captain Gonish
    C. Captain Noble
    D. Hydro the Water Dragon

20. _____ is the minister of the slaves who helps Spikey build an army from them.
   A. Sam
   B. Garlan
   C. Chef Berry
   D. Nick

21. Which *prophecies* come true when the slaves invade the Palace?
   A. Rivers become fire, the Palace walls fall, bear-goons are healed.
   B. The faces of light, fire rains from the sky, bear-goons are healed.
   C. Rivers become fire, the moon falls from the sky, Lizard Face melts.
   D. The faces of light, rivers become fire, time stops.

22. When the bears are attacked by dragons, who comes to their aid?
   A. Hydro the Water Dragon
   B. Kelcott
   C. The Goons
   D. The Ice Sea rebels

23. Gloria, Shortstop, and the others return on the_____ to help free Staranana.
   A. *New Life*
   B. *Fire Cruiser*
   C. *Dragon's Blood*
   D. *Space Shark*

24. What evil creature comes to help Seth defeat Scotty?
A. Licen/Satan
B. The Dark Phoenix
C. The Dragon of Death
D. The Gator of Destruction

25. What happens to Scotty at the end of the story?
A. Seth defeats him.
B. He gives up and returns to Earth.
C. He defeats Seth and is made the emperor of Staranana.
D. He is forced to retreat, but he vows to return and defeat Seth one day.

Creative Writing Activity

Creating a World
Creative Writing Activity

In *Chronicles of the Imagination: Staranana* readers are introduced to an entirely new planet with a unique culture, customs, and history all its own. Even so, the characters of the novel are quick to point out that the same God that created our world created theirs. We don't know yet if there is really intelligent life on other planets, but if and when we do get the answer to that question, you can be guaranteed that God created them as well. The *Bible* indicates as much in Psalm 19:1 saying, *"The heavens declare the glory of God; the skies proclaim the work of His hands"* (NIV).

One of the great things about writing is that it gives us the opportunity to imitate our Creator by using our imaginations. During this project, you will use your imagination to create a world of your very own. Use the Guidelines below to create your world. Your teacher will decide on how many points the project is worth, but a suggested number of points is listed for each step.

1. _____ **(5 points)** - Please type and double space your paper.
2. _____ **(10 points)** - Keep your project free of grammatical error
3. _____ **(5 points)** - Your world should have a unique name.
4. _____ **(10 points)** - Write a one-paragraph introduction of your world. You must list where it is located (in our universe or another), and tell us what is unique about it.

5. _____ **(10 points)** - Write a one-paragraph description of your world's budget. Your budget should list essential expenses, including schools, law enforcement, maintenance, utilities, and anything else you feel may be relevant.

6. _____ **(10 points)** - Write a one-paragraph description of the people living on your planet. Are they humans like on Earth, animals like on Staranana, or something else?

7. _____ **(10 points)** - Write a one-paragraph description of the leadership of your world? Do they have a king, president, emperor, dictator, etc.?

8. _____ **(5 points)** - List three unique laws that have been established on your planet. These should be realistic for the world you have created.

9. _____ **(10 points)** - Create a detailed map of your world. You must include a compass rose, at least three countries, rivers, mountains, oceans, and cities.

10. _____ **(15 points)** - To conclude your project you will write the creation story of your world. Describe how your world came into existence and then take us through a day in the life of one character. This story should be at least three paragraphs long.

11. _____ **(10 points)** You will present your world to your classmates.

Total: _____/100

Words to Know Activities

Words to Know Activity #1
Before, Chapters 1 & 2

Place the appropriate word from the word bank in the correct blank below.

Countenance	Inexhaustible
Evacuate	Prophecy
Facility	Representations
Feign	Tinker
Hordes	Wince

1. All children are trained from an early age to _____ their school when they hear the fire alarm sound.

2. It was hard to get my son not to _____ when I had to use a needle to remove a splinter from his finger.

3. Her _____ fell when I told her that her dog had died and she began to weep.

4. The crosses that hang in many churches are merely _____ of the cross that Christ died on.

5. The life and power of God are completely _____.

6. Please do not_____ ignorance when I ask you where your homework is.

7. Those with mechanical abilities often love to _____ with new gadgets.

8. The new sports _____ can accommodate 10 different athletic competitions at the same time.

9. The _____ that the messiah would be born in Bethlehem can be found in Micah 5:2.

10. No matter how great the _____ of Satan, the power of Christ will always prove greater.

Words to Know Activity #2
Chapters 3 & 4

Place the appropriate word from the word bank in the correct blank below.

Aqueduct	Hideous
Circulate	Hysterical
Devoid	Intent
Ego	Interact
Exaggerate	Neutralize

1. The village's new _____ system allowed them to easily pump clean water into every hut.

2. Sparkey Moonbeam described the faces of the goons as so _____ that if you looked at one you would be driven insane.

3. In past Jews and Gentiles did not _____ well together, but now they can all be part of the same body of Christ.

4. Men who have excessive pride are said to have an inflated _____.

5. Please do not _____ about the accident; give me the facts exactly as they happened.

6. The Devil is _____ of any virtue.

7. A rumor can seem to _____ at the speed of light.

8. _____ laughter is not ever lacking during our family game night.

9. Radiation therapy is one technique doctor's use to _____ cancer.

10. What is the _____ of your visit today?

Place the appropriate word from the word bank in the correct blank below.

Betray	Pachyderm
Deny	Phoenix
Intolerable	Reinforcement
Mesmerize	Relic
Minion	Subside

1. *Wolf* is to *Canine* as *Elephant* is to _____.

2. *Ashes* are to a _____ as *Christ* is to the *Tomb*.

3. *Lackey* is to _____ as *Subject* is to *Peasant*.

4. *Build* is to *Destroy* as *Confirm* is to _____.

5. *Hypnotize* is to _____ as *Scream* is to *Yell*.

6. *Judas* is to _____ as *Cain* is to *Kill*.

7. _____ is to *Artifact* as *Student* is to *Pupil*.

8. *Backup* is to _____ as *Projectile* is to *Bullet*.

9. *Bearable* is to _____ as *Likeable* to *Despised*.

10. *Intensify* is to _____ as *Fill* is to *Drain*.

Place the appropriate word from the word bank in the correct blank below. Match each word with its synonym.

Ambush	Perimeter
Corridor	Precarious
Hunch	Stealth
Liberate	Synchronized
Pendulum	Unison

1. Counterweight _____

2. Hall _____

3. Border _____

4. Uncertain _____

5. Harmonized _____

6. Free _____

7. Attack _____

8. Secret _____

9. Agreement _____

10. Intuition _____

Place the appropriate word from the word bank in the correct blank below.

Adrenaline	Extremist
Artificial	Instilled
Cautious	Lavatory
Circumstances	Restrain
Compromise	Suspicious

I could feel the _____ (1) begin to pump through my blood as I waited in eager anticipation. It was proving impossible to _____ (2) my enthusiasm, but my coach had _____ (3) patience and focus in me, and I was not about to _____ (4) the trust he had in me. I knew I had to be _____ (5). When it came to boxing my opponent was nothing short of an _____ (6); he was always willing to try the most violent moves. I had trained hard, and I believed I could win, but when my opponent was ten minutes late to the match I began to grow _____ (7). Had he chickened out? Was all the publicity he had received merely an _____ (8) creation, and not a true reflection of his real skills? Suddenly an announcement bellowed over the speakers, "Attention Please — Our champion has grown sick and has gone to the _____ (9). Under the _____ (10) the match has been cancelled." I suppose victory will have to wait for another day.

Words to Know Activity #6
Chapters 11 & 12

Place the appropriate word from the word bank in the correct blank below.

Bizarre	Grimace
Deem	Microscopic
Dire	Savory
Disuse	Surrender
Garbled	Vortex

1. The _____ flavor of a tender stake makes my mouth water.
2. Towns filled with buildings that have fallen into _____ are often referred to as ghost towns.
3. Her behavior has been very _____ for the last several weeks; I cannot determine what is wrong with her.
4. No situation is so _____ that Christ does not have things completely under control.
5. The HIV virus is one example of a _____ lifeform that can cause a great deal of damage.
6. Do you _____ it appropriate to add more debt to your credit report, or should you begin paying your bills?
7. The radio broadcast was fairly _____, but we still managed to enjoy listening to the ball game.
8. Choosing to _____ to Christ is the only way to know freedom from sin.
9. The _____ on my son's face made it very plain that he did not care too much for what I had made for dinner.
10. Some scientists believe that a _____ in space can serve as a shortcut to a distant location in the universe.

Words to Know Activity #7
Chapters 13 & 14

Place the appropriate word from the word bank in the correct blank below. Match each word with its antonym.

Altered	Consistent
Ancestor	Cursed
Component	Delicacy
Conceived	Eternal
Conquer	Resurrect

1. Descendant _____

2. Blessed _____

3. Temporary _____

4. Surrender _____

5. Whole _____

6. Kill _____

7. Misunderstand _____

8. Sustained _____

9. Chaotic _____

10. Gruel _____

Words to Know Activity #8
Chapters 15 & 16

Place the appropriate word from the word bank in the correct blank below.

Abyss	Miserable
Banshees	Ominous
Encompass	Pinnacle
Interrogated	Resourceful
Linger	Vast

The realm of the accursed dead is sometimes referred to as an _____ (1). The *Bible* makes it clear that a _____ (2) number of people (all those who reject Christ) will end up there. Every soul condemned there will endure eternity in _____ (3) conditions. Sorrow will _____ (4) every day, and joy will not _____ (5) even for a single moment. This pit will be _____ (6) and dark, and I can almost hear the screams of the _____ (7). No matter how _____ (8) a person might be, they will never escape that place. After Christ has _____ (9) those destined to go there, He will say, "Depart from me, for I never knew you!" That moment would be the very _____ (10) of sorrow in a person's existence. Thankfully, we can avoid it by accepting Jesus Christ as our Savior.

Place the appropriate word from the word bank in the correct blank below.

Adjacent	Impenetrable
Comply	Provisions
Detour	Pursuit
Foreboding	Relentless
Forsake	Squander

1. He was absolutely _____ in his determination to be the best runner at his high school.
2. Fort Knox is considered to be _____.
3. In order to save us from our sins, God the Father had to _____ Jesus Christ for a short time.
4. You must _____ with my orders or you will face disciplinary action.
5. Please don't _____ your entire allowance on candy.
6. I have packed _____ for a three day trip.
7. No matter how hard we tried, we could not _____ her from her decision.
8. Despite the fact that the cave was incredibly _____, I decided to go ahead with my spelunking plans anyway.
9. A tiger's _____ of its prey can be both fascinating and terrifying.
10. His house is _____ to mine on 5th Avenue.

Determine whether each word from the word bank is used correctly (Yes) or incorrectly (No) in the sentences below.

Appropriate	Incentive
Ditch	Persuade
Dumbwaiter	Portion
Equivalent	Savior
Hoist	Threshold

1. **Yes or No** – At dinner last night we had such a _**dumbwaiter**_.
2. **Yes or No** – Since he was able to _**persuade**_ me, I completely rejected his plan.
3. **Yes or No** – What _**portion**_ of the land would you like as your inheritance.
4. **Yes or No** – Harsh prison sentences tend to be enough _**incentive**_ to avoid committing crimes.
5. **Yes or No** – Jesus Christ is the **Savior** of the world.
6. **Yes or No** – God is the _**equivalent**_ of Satan.
7. **Yes or No** – Please help me _**hoist**_ this box up onto the shelf.
8. **Yes or No** – It is never acceptable to wear _**appropriate**_ clothing to church.
9. **Yes or No** – Please fill the _**ditch**_ with water.
10. **Yes or No** – I carried my wife over the _**threshold**_ when we purchased our new home.

Place the appropriate word from the word bank in the correct blank below.

Chaos	Population
Deliver	Qualifications
Distinct	Recognition
Loyal	Silhouette
Mock	Whimper

1. Your _____ for this job are excellent! We are very eager to hire you.
2. My father has such a distinct _____ that when I saw his shadow I was not afraid.
3. Today I will _____ a speech to my 5th period civics class.
4. People often feel it is appropriate to _____ their leaders and disrespect them. However, if they were in the position of those leaders they might feel differently.
5. Christ is always _____ to his servants.
6. When my son skinned his knee, he started to _____, but he was too proud to cry.
7. The teeth of the T-Rex are much too _____ to confuse them with those of any other dinosaur.
8. When King David conducted a census against the will of the Lord, the _____ of Israel decreased drastically due to a plague.
9. Trying to hold a birthday party for 25 five-year-olds turned into complete _____. It will take me weeks to get my house cleaned up.
10. The award was given in _____ of his bravery during the house fire, in which he saved four lives.

Place the appropriate word from the word bank in the correct blank below. Match each word with its correct analogy.

Blemish	Lecture
Diminish	Petrified
Hearth	Pierce
Hilt	Tentative
Jeopardy	Wield

1. *Hot* is to *Cold* as *Perfection* is to _____.

2. *Trigger* is to *Gun Barrel* as *Blade* is to _____.

3. *Peace* is to *Security* as *Danger* is to _____.

4. *Car* is to *Steering Wheel* as *Home* is to _____.

5. *Office* is to *Meeting* as *School* is to _____.

6. *Gun* is to *Shoot* as *Sword* is to _____.

7. *Angry* is to *Violent* as *Fear* is to _____.

8. *Accelerate* is to *Slow* as *Increase* is to _____.

9. *Pummel* is to *Punch* as *Puncture* is to _____.

10. *Stone* is to *Rock* as *Uncertain* is to _____.

Words to Know Activity #13
Chapters 25 & 26

Place the appropriate word from the word bank in the correct blank below.

Concentration	Mutilated
Inmates	Nutrients
Intact	Precautions
Loathed	Tousled
Mercy	Transmit

During World War II the Nazi _____ (1) Camps were notorious for their cruelty. Many of the _____ (2) were _____ (3) or killed in cruel experiments. Most did not receive the proper _____ (4) to remain healthy and strong. Few of the Nazi soldiers offered _____ (5) to their prisoners. Rarely did a family that entered a camp together leave still _____ (6). In short, everyone _____ (7) these camps and took great _____ (8) to avoid being captured by the Nazis and sent there. The Jewish culture more than any other was _____ (9) like leaves in the wind by the Nazis, as many were forced to flee their homes to avoid this persecution. When news makers were finally able to _____ (10) via radio that the final camp had been liberated, it was a day of great rejoicing.

Place the appropriate word from the word bank in the correct blank below.

Binge	Fuselage
Cockpit	Lunatic
Disembark	Portal
Expendable	Recitation
Frustrated	Tattered

1. It was rather embarrassing when my brother showed up to my wedding in a _____ tuxedo.
2. A significant hail storm caused such damage to the _____ of our aircraft that our flight was cancelled.
3. My son absolutely loved it when the pilot of our airline invited him to sit in the _____.
4. Please _____ the ship in an orderly fashion.
5. I was very _____ when my son was two hours late for his curfew.
6. Sparkey Moonbeam used a _____ to travel from Staranana to Earth.
7. It is unwise to put your fate into the hands of a _____.
8. Her _____ of Psalm 119 was flawless.
9. When you choose to _____ on sweets, your overall health is sure to be affected.
10. No person's life should ever be considered _____.

Place the appropriate word from the word bank in the correct blank below. Match each word with its synonym.

Appreciate	Immense
Debris	Imprison
Ebony	Intimidation
Endow	Resilient
Hatchling	Spew

1. Vomit   _____

2. Confine   _____

3. Value   _____

4. Black   _____

5. Chick   _____

6. Great   _____

7. Wreckage   _____

8. Bestow   _____

9. Threat   _____

10. Tough   _____

Words to Know Activity #16
Chapters 31 & 32

Place the appropriate word from the word bank in the correct blank below.

Banish	Dumbstruck
Charismatic	Frequency
Conventional	Grotesque
Crucial	Inspired
Detect	Recent

1. After Guinevere betrayed him, King Arthur chose to _____ her from Camelot rather than execute her.

2. Scientist are constantly trying to _____ life on other planets.

3. What _____ you to become a musician.

4. After my _____ illness, I chose to take a sabbatical from my lecture tour.

5. He was such a _____ speaker that people would come from hundreds of miles around to hear him.

6. Please tune your radio to the _____ 88.5 FM to hear great Christian music.

7. Is sea salt _____ to that recipe or will regular salt work?

8. I consider surgery of any kind too _____ to watch.

9. I was _____ when my best friend told me his deepest, darkest secret.

10. Removing your hat when entering a building is a _____ practice in the United States.

Place the appropriate word from the word bank in the correct blank below. Match each word with its antonym.

Credible	Jot
Designate	Minimal
Enthrone	Obvious
Entourage	Parchment
Interpret	Skeptic

1. Essay _____

2. Believer _____

3. Usurp _____

4. Excessive _____

5. Confuse _____

6. Leader _____

7. Obscure _____

8. Stone Tablet _____

9. Dismiss _____

10. Deceptive _____

Place the appropriate word from the word bank in the correct blank below. Match each word with the correct analogy.

Casualty	Inhibit
Compatriot	Obtain
Elderly	Offensive
Emanate	Quench
Foolhardy	Stronghold

1. *Murder* is to *Victim* as *War* is to _____.

2. *Wet* is to *Dry* as *Cautious* is to _____.

3. *Encourage* is to *Inspire* as *Stop* is to _____.

4. *Desert* is to *Parch* as *Oasis* is to _____.

5. *Puppy* is to *Dog* as *Young* is to _____.

6. *Water* is to *Flood* as *Light* is to _____.

7. *Tall* is to *Tower* as *Impregnable* is to _____.

8. *Get* is to *Give* as *Lose* is to _____.

9. *Coworker* is to *Colleague* as *Citizen* is to _____.

10. *Despise* is to *Hate* as *Disgusting* is to _____.

Place the appropriate word from the word bank in the correct blank below.

Anxious	Exposed
Assembly	Ruffle
Confirmed	Seize
Dismount	Shortcomings
Eliminate	Tabernacle

I can only imagine how _____ (1) the _____ (2) of Israel must have felt when the _____ (3) in the desert was finally completed. The Lord had _____ (4) that they were his people by delivering them from the power of Egypt. It is true that they had many _____ (5), but God would never abandon his people no matter what their problems were. In the centuries to come, many enemies would try to _____ (6) the descendants of Abraham, and even more would try to _____ (7) control of their land. One could say without exaggeration that the Israelites have been _____ (8) to every kind of evil this world has to offer. Even so, this small nation has proven impossible to _____ (9) like so many feathers on a bird, and one day Christ will return, _____ (10) His heavenly warhorse, and take His place as their King forever.

Glossary

~A~

- **Abyss** – A noun meaning a bottomless pit.
- **Adjacent** – An adjective meaning close to but not necessarily touching.
- **Adrenaline** – A noun meaning a catecholamine secreted by the adrenal medulla in response to stress.
- **Altered** – An adjective meaning changed in form or character without becoming something else.
- **Ambush** - A noun meaning the act of concealing yourself and lying in wait to attack by surprise.
- **Ancestor** - A noun meaning someone from whom you are descended.
- **Anxious** - An adjective meaning eagerly desirous.
- **Appreciate** - A verb meaning to highly value.
- **Appropriate** - An adjective meaning suitable for a particular person or place or condition etc.
- **Aqueduct** - A noun meaning a conduit that resembles a bridge but carries water over a valley. In this novel, it is an underground water and sewage system.
- **Artificial** - An adjective meaning manmade.
- **Assembly** – A noun meaning a gathering of people or things.

~B~

- **Banish** - A verb meaning to drive away from a place, especially one's home region.
- **Banshee** - A noun meaning a female spirit who wails to warn of impending death.
- **Betray** - A verb meaning to turn against one's previous allies.
- **Binge** – A verb meaning to overindulge.
- **Bizarre** - An adjective meaning very unusual.
- **Blemish** - A noun meaning a mark or flaw that spoils the appearance of something.

- **Casualty** - A noun meaning a decrease of military personnel or equipment.
- **Cautious** - An adjective meaning very careful in one's actions.
- **Chaos** - A noun meaning the state of being completely without order.
- **Charismatic** - An adjective meaning possessing an extraordinary ability to attract.
- **Circulate** - A verb meaning to cause to become widely known.
- **Circumstances** - A noun meaning information that should be kept in mind when making a decision.
- **Clinch** - A noun meaning the act of one boxer holding onto the other to avoid being hit and to rest momentarily.
- **Cockpit** - A noun meaning a compartment where the pilot sits while flying the aircraft or spacecraft.
- **Compatriot** - A noun meaning a person from your own country.
- **Comply** - A verb meaning to act in accordance with someone's rules, commands, or wishes.
- **Component** – A noun meaning a part of a greater whole.
- **Compromise** - A noun meaning a middle way between two extremes.
- **Conceived** - An adjective meaning formed in the mind.
- **Concentration** - A noun meaning to devote intense attention to something; or a dense gathering in one place.
- **Confirm** - A verb meaning to make more firm.
- **Conquer** - A verb meaning to overcome by conquest.
- **Consistent** - An adjective meaning in agreement with previously disclosed data; orderly.
- **Conventional** - An adjective meaning following accepted customs and proprieties.
- **Corridor** - A noun meaning an enclosed passageway.
- **Countenance** - A noun meaning the appearance conveyed by a person's face.

- **Credible** - An adjective meaning appearing to merit belief or acceptance.
- **Crucial** - An adjective meaning of extreme importance.
- **Cursed** - An adjective meaning deserving condemnation.

~D~

- **Debris** – A noun mean remains of something that has been destroyed; wreckage.
- **Deem** - A verb meaning to keep in mind or convey as a conviction or view.
- **Delicacy** - A noun meaning a rare and highly favored food.
- **Deliver** - A verb meaning to convey either an object or a speech.
- **Deny** - A verb meaning to declare untrue.
- **Designate** - A verb meaning to assign a name or title to.
- **Detect** – A verb meaning to discover.
- **Detour** - A verb meaning to reroute from an originally planned path.
- **Devoid** - An adjective meaning completely lacking.
- **Diminish** - A verb meaning to lessen something.
- **Dire** - An adjective meaning causing fear or dread or terror.
- **Disembark** - A verb meaning to get out of a vehicle, often a ship to go ashore.
- **Dismount** - A noun meaning the act of getting off of an animal or vehicle used for transport.
- **Distinct** - An adjective meaning easily recognizable.
- **Disuse** - A noun meaning the state of something that has been unused and neglected.
- **Ditch** - A noun meaning a long narrow excavation in the earth.
- **Dominate** - A verb meaning to have the power to defeat.
- **Dumbstruck** - An adjective meaning as if struck silent with astonishment and surprise.
- **Dumbwaiter** - A noun meaning a small elevator used to convey food (or other goods) from one floor of a building to another.

- **Ebony** - An adjective meaning of a very dark black.
- **Ego** - A noun meaning the conscious mind.
- **Elderly** - An adjective meaning advanced in years.
- **Eliminate** - A verb meaning to kill or destroy in large numbers.
- **Emanate** – A verb meaning to issue from.
- **Encompass** - A verb meaning to include as part of something broader.
- **Endow** - A verb meaning to furnish with a gift or fund.
- **Enthrone** - A verb meaning to put a monarch on the throne.
- **Entourage** - A noun meaning the group following and attending to some important person.
- **Equivalent** - An adjective meaning being essentially equal to something.
- **Eternal** - An adjective meaning unending.
- **Evacuate** - A verb meaning to leave a location often due to some real or perceived threat.
- **Exaggerate** - A verb meaning to enlarge beyond the truth.
- **Expendable** - An adjective meaning able to be dispensed with without major consequences.
- **Exposed** - An adjective meaning not covered or hidden.
- **Extremist** – A noun meaning a person will to go beyond reasonable boundaries to achieve their goals.

~F~

- **Facility** - A noun meaning a building or location used for a specific purpose.
- **Feign** - A verb meaning to make-believe with the intent to deceive.
- **Foolhardy** - An adjective meaning marked by defiant disregard for danger or consequences.
- **Foreboding** - An adjective meaning ominous and dangerous.
- **Forsake** - A verb meaning to abandon someone who needs or counts on you.

- **Frequency** - A noun meaning the number of times a vibration repeats itself – specifically vibrations used to transmit signals/messages.
- **Frustrate** – A verb meaning to defeat or thwart; aggravate.
- **Fuselage** - A noun meaning the central body of an aircraft or spacecraft that is designed to accommodate the crew and passengers.

~G~

- **Garbled** - An adjective meaning broken in pattern.
- **Grimace** - A noun meaning a contorted facial expression.
- **Grotesque** - An adjective meaning distorted and unnatural in shape or size; hideous.

~H~

- **Hatchling** - A noun meaning any recently hatched animal from an egg.
- **Hearth -** A noun meaning the floor of a fireplace usually extending a short way into the room.
- **Hideous** - An adjective meaning so extremely ugly as to be terrifying.
- **Hilt** - A noun meaning the handle of a sword or dagger.
- **Hoist** - A verb meaning to lift to a higher position or elevation.
- **Horde** - A noun meaning a vast multitude.
- **Hunch** - A noun meaning a gut instinct or decision based on intuition.
- **Hysterical** - An adjective meaning marked by excessive or uncontrollable emotion.

~I~

- **Immense** - An adjective meaning unusually great in size or scope.
- **Impenetrable** - An adjective meaning impossible to break through.
- **Imprison** - A verb meaning to lock up or confine.

- **Incentive** - A noun meaning a positive motivational influence.
- **Inexhaustible** - An adjective meaning incapable of being entirely consumed or used up.
- **Inhibit** - A verb meaning to hinder from progress.
- **Inmate** - A noun meaning a resident of a prison.
- **Inspire** - A verb meaning to supply the inspiration for.
- **Instill** – A verb meaning to infuse slowly.
- **Intact** - An adjective meaning undamaged in any way.
- **Intent** - An adjective meaning giving or marked by complete attention to.
- **Interact** - A verb meaning to act together or toward others.
- **Interpret** - A verb meaning to make sense of.
- **Interrogate** - A verb meaning to pose a series of questions.
- **Intimidation** - A noun meaning the feeling of being made to feel afraid or timid.
- **Intolerable** - An adjective meaning incapable of being put up with.

~J~

- **Jeopardy** - A noun meaning a source of danger.
- **Jot** - A noun meaning a brief (and hurriedly handwritten) note.

~L~

- **Lavatory** - A noun meaning a small closet with a toilet.
- **Lecture** - A noun meaning teaching by giving a discourse on some subject.
- **Liberate** - A verb meaning to grant freedom to.
- **Linger** - A verb meaning to take one's time.
- **Loathe** – A verb meaning to utterly despise.
- **Loyal** - An adjective meaning steadfast in allegiance or duty.
- **Lunatic** – A noun meaning a person who is insane.

~M~

- **Mercy** - A noun meaning great kindness shown toward the distressed or undeserving.
- **Mesmerize** - A verb meaning to draw one's complete attention as though by a spell.
- **Microscopic** - An adjective meaning too small to be seen except under a microscope.
- **Minimal** – An adjective meaning barely adequate.
- **Minion** - A noun meaning a servant often of someone evil.
- **Miserable** - An adjective meaning characterized by physical agony.
- **Mock** – A verb meaning to imitate in a disrespectful manner.
- **Mutilate** - A verb meaning to destroy or injure severely.

~N~

- **Neutralize** - A verb meaning to make without power.
- **Nutrient** – A noun meaning nourishment; something consumed to provide strength.

~O~

- **Obtain** - A verb meaning to come into possession of.
- **Obvious** - An adjective meaning easily perceived by the senses.
- **Offensive** - An adjective meaning unpleasant or disgusting especially to the senses.
- **Ominous** - An adjective meaning indicating coming ill fortune.

~P~

- **Pachyderm** - A noun meaning any of various hoofed mammals having very thick skin, such as elephants, rhinoceroses, and hippopotamuses.
- **Parchment** - A noun meaning skin of a sheep or goat prepared for writing on.
- **Pendulum** - A noun meaning an apparatus consisting of an object mounted so that it swings freely under the influence of gravity.

379

- **Perimeter** - A noun meaning a border enclosing an area.
- **Persuade** - A verb meaning to cause somebody to adopt a certain position.
- **Petrified** - An adjective meaning so frightened as to be unable to move.
- **Phoenix** - A noun meaning a legendary firebird that would burst into flames upon its death and then be resurrected from its own ashes.
- **Pierce** - A verb meaning to puncture.
- **Pinnacle** - A noun meaning the highest point whether literally or in terms of achievement.
- **Population** - A noun meaning the people who live in a place.
- **Portal** - A noun meaning a passage from one place to another place at a far greater distance, generated by means of advanced technology (in other lore by use of magic).
- **Portion** - A noun meaning the allotment of some amount by dividing something.
- **Precarious** - An adjective meaning affording no ease or reassurance.
- **Precaution** - A noun meaning an action taken to ward off impending danger.
- **Prophecy** – A noun meaning a prediction about a future event.
- **Provisions** - A noun meaning necessary supplies.
- **Pursuit** - A noun meaning the act of chasing in an effort to capture.

~Q~
- **Qualification** - A noun meaning an accomplishment that gives a person the right to perform a certified task.
- **Quench** - A verb meaning to satisfy (often in regard to thirst).

~R~
- **Ration** - A noun meaning the food allowance for one day.

- **Recent** - An adjective meaning near to or not long before the present.
- **Recitation** - A noun meaning a public instance of reciting or repeating something prepared in advance.
- **Recognition** - A noun meaning the determination that something has been previously seen or known.
- **Reinforcement** - A noun meaning extra support, often provided in a military campaign.
- **Relentless** - An adjective meaning never-ceasing.
- **Relic** - A noun meaning an antiquity that has survived from the distant past.
- **Representation** - A noun meaning something that stands for or in the place of something else.
- **Resilient** - An adjective meaning recovering readily from adversity, depression, or the like.
- **Resourceful** - An adjective meaning having inner resources; imaginative.
- **Restrain** A verb meaning to hold back.
- **Resurrect** - A verb meaning to cause to become alive again after death.
- **Ridiculous** - An adjective meaning completely unbelievable to the point of being absurd.
- **Ruffle** - A verb meaning to move into a state of disarray.

~S~

- **Savior** - A noun meaning a person who rescues you from harm or danger.
- **Savory** - An adjective meaning pleasant in taste and/or aroma.
- **Seize** - A verb meaning to capture or take control of.
- **Shortcoming** - A noun meaning a failing or deficiency.
- **Silhouette** - A noun meaning the outline of an object, filled in with some uniform color.
- **Skeptic** – A noun meaning a person who has strong doubts about something.
- **Snob** - A noun meaning a person regarded as arrogant and annoying.

- **Spew** - A verb meaning to eject or send out in large quantities, also metaphorical.
- **Squander** - A verb meaning to spend extravagantly.
- **Stealth** - A noun meaning avoiding detection by moving carefully.
- **Stronghold** - A noun meaning a strongly fortified defensive structure.
- **Subside** - A verb meaning to decrease or die down.
- **Surrender** - A noun meaning the delivery of one's power or possession into the lawful custody of another.
- **Suspicious** - An adjective meaning to be in doubt about something.
- **Synchronized** - An adjective meaning operating in unison.

~T~

- **Tabernacle** - A noun meaning a portable sanctuary like a tent used for worship, most notably in which the Jews of ancient Earth carried the Ark of the Covenant on their exodus.
- **Tattered** - An adjective meaning worn to shreds; or wearing torn or ragged clothing.
- **Tentative** - An adjective meaning under terms not final or fully worked out; uncertain.
- **Threshold** - A noun meaning the border between two locations, most commonly used in reference to a door.
- **Tinker** - A verb meaning to work on (often without much foreknowledge) some mechanical device.
- **Tousled** - An adjective meaning in disarray; extremely disorderly.
- **Transmit** - A verb meaning to send from one person or place to another often by means of electronic communication.

~U~

- **Unison** - A noun meaning a perfect agreement; to be in harmony.

~V~

- **Vast** - An adjective meaning unusually great in size.
- **Vortex** - A noun meaning a powerful circular phenomenon consisting of a funnel, an eye, and an event horizon. Vortexes can appear in many forms and locations (i.e. water, space, and air).

~W~

- **Whimper** - A noun meaning a complaint uttered in a plaintive whining way.
- **Wield** - A verb meaning to handle effectively.
- **Wince** – A verb meaning to cringe, often in pain.

~X, Y, Z~
- **No associated words.**

Answer Keys

Staranana Test - Answer Key

Note: Remove answer keys from the text before distributing to students.

1. C – Inventor
2. A – Cave
3. A – 6
4. B – Aqueducts
5. C - 10th
6. A - *Blood of the Land*
7. B - He was captured by Lizard Face
8. D - Chef Berry
9. D – Dragons
10. A - Return to rescue him
11. C – Sparkey
12. A - Earth; *Blood of the Land*
13. D - Prineville, Oregon
14. B - Overwhelmed by the cold
15. C - Gators, recklor bats, poison crystals
16. A - Lizard Face
17. B – Joshua
18. C - *Dagger of Promise*
19. D - Hydro the Water Dragon
20. B – Garlan
21. B - The faces of light, fire rains from the sky, bear-goons are healed.
22. A - Hydro the Water Dragon
23. B - *Fire Cruiser*
24. A - Licen/Satan
25. C - He defeats Seth and is made Emperor of Staranana

Study & Discussion Questions - Answer Key

Note: Remove answer keys before distributing to students. Most questions are meant to prompt discussion, so answers will vary. Answers are not provided for the journal prompts.

Before & Chapter 1
1. Answers will vary, but it was an angel.
2. Bears
3. Answers will vary.
4. Answers will vary.
5. Answers will vary.

Chapter 2
1. Answers will vary.
2. Answers will vary, but many might cite 2 Peter 3:9, "The Lord is not slow in keeping his promise, as some understand slowness. Instead, he is patient with you, not wanting anyone to perish, but everyone to come to repentance" (NIV).
3. Answers will vary.
4. Answers will vary.

Chapter 3
1. Answers will vary, but Spikey is stubborn, Gloria is angry, Shortstop is doubtful, and Sparkey can be rude.
2. Answers will vary.
3. Answers will vary, but some students might cite 1 Timothy 4:12, "Don't let anyone look down on you because you are young, but set an example for the believers in speech, in conduct, in love, in faith and in purity" (NIV).
4. Answers will vary.

Chapter 4
1. They approach the Palace through the underground aqueducts and then enter through a trapdoor beneath the cellar. Shortstop learned about this passage from his ancestors.
2. Answers will vary, but possibilities include fear, anxiety, determination, hope, passion, love, etc.
3. Answers will vary, but most will agree that Seth will be a very proud, powerful, and cruel dictator.
4. Answers will vary. Examples of Biblical characters include Stephen, Peter, James, Paul, John, etc.
5. Lizard Face is this character, and he speaks with an extra *s* at the beginning or end of his words. This is likely because he is a lizard and makes a hissing noise when he speaks.
6. Answers will vary.

Chapter 5
1. Answers will vary.
2. Answers will vary.

3. Answers will vary.
4. Answers will vary.

Chapter 6
1. Answers will vary.
2. Answers will vary, but they might include that Seth is intelligent and a capable leader since he has been able to maintain control of Staranana for over 5,000 years.
3. Judas betrayed Christ for 30 pieces of silver. Students will ultimately learn that Seth betrayed and murdered his father.
4. Answers will vary.

Chapter 7
1. Answers will vary.
2. Answers will vary.
3. The combination was entered using the hands on the clock. The combination was 12-2-7. Then the clock had to be returned to the correct time. Students might also mention the number of times Shortstop had to pass each number before landing on it, but do not require this much detail unless you feel it is important.
4. Answers will vary.
5. Answers will vary, but students will likely mention that the Staranians are a bear-like race that has been oppressed by a cruel dictator for over 5,000 years. Those who are "free" live in caves in the forest, but many are enslaved. Two specific types of food we have been introduced to are honeysuckle apples and oboca rabbit meat. Currently, the goals of the rebellion include escaping from Staranana and going to Stararocka.

Chapter 8
1. Fuel and power cells.
2. By disrupting the time on the clock, he could kill the power throughout the Palace. This would give the bears the chance to get the supplies they needed and escape undetected.
3. Answers will vary.
4. Answers will vary, but most students will cite that Nick Grass gave his life to help his friends. In the end, he died so that they could escape the planet.
5. Answers will vary.

Chapter 9
1. Answers will vary.
2. Answers will vary.
3. Answers will vary. Those who be believe lying and stealing are not justified might cite the 10 Commandments. Those who think they can be justified in some instances might cite the story of Rahab (Joshua 2). Allow students to debate this, but do not contradict God's command that we are to be people of truth.
4. Answers will vary.

Chapter 10
1. The cave is now devoid of the sounds, smells, belongings, and warmth that made it once feel like a home. It is now simply cold and dark with only a

few discarded belongings left behind. Answers will vary to the last part of the question.

2. Answers will vary.
3. Answers will vary, but most will believe if Sparkey can find the *Blood of the Land* the Starananian people will finally have hope for freedom. Some will say that Gloria will be very upset with Sparkey for going to Earth, and yet Spikey would probably be proud of him since it was his plan in the first place.
4. Answers will vary.

Chapter 11
1. Answers will vary, but some students might say that God does not want humans interacting with aliens from other planets.
2. Prineville is a warm and sunny country town filled with laughter and learning. Staranana, on the other hand, is dark and cold, and the people always had to keep quiet out of fear for their lives.
3. Answers will vary.
4. Answers will vary.
5. Answers will vary.
6. Answers will vary, but some might say he is like King David since he will rule Staranana. Others might say he is like John the Baptist since he will prepare the way for Christ on Staranana. It is important that students realize that the *Blood of the Land* is NOT a Christ-figure. Christ came to Earth to pay the price for our sins, and that is not the purpose of this character. Throughout this series, you will see Jesus Christ lauded as the only true Savior.

Chapter 12
1. It is comfortable and warm, even though Scotty and Sparkey slept on the floor. There is the sound and the smell of bacon and eggs frying. Scotty also imagines what they will taste like. There is also a large cat that waddles through the house, and there is laundry to be cleaned, implying the smell of soap suds.
2. Answers will vary, but point out to students that in most stories there are what are called flat characters and round characters. We only learn a little about flat characters, and they are usually not in the story very long. Bobby is one of these characters. Round characters, on the other hand, are in the novel quite a bit and we learn a great deal about them.
3. Answers will vary, but many students might say he will be forced to be much more heroic and outgoing.
4. Answers will vary.
5. Answers will vary.

Chapter 13
1. He begins to freeze because the temperature is 20 degrees below zero Celsius. Answers will vary.
2. Answers will vary.
3. Answers will vary.

4. Sparkey says they should first try to rescue his dad.
5. They leave the cave with clubs.

Chapter 14
1. See student work.
2. Answers will vary.
3. Gators are similar to alligators. They have gnarled and twisted bodies with green and black scales. Their gums are usually bloodied and their teeth are razor-sharp. It can be implied that since the aqueducts are sewers, and the gators float in the water, they must smell horrible. They can be easily angered and will attack anyone that taunts them. Smashing a gator's eye will send them into a wild rage. Generally, they eat fish, but they will eat Starananians. In this case, they paralyze their victims without killing them. They then consume the bear slowly over weeks while they are still alive.
4. They bait a rope with fish and then tie it to their stone vessel. They then taunt the gators into chasing them. When the gators find the fish they begin to eat, but the fish had hooks in it which Scotty and Sparkey use to force the gators to drag their boat into the water.
5. Answers will vary.

Chapter 15
1. He suggests that they repair one of their damaged spacecraft in the White Desert to chase after them.
2. 500 years earlier, Seth attempted to attack the worlds of Lord Nimbus. However, his ship was destroyed and he crashed on a jungle planet where he was stranded for 50 years.
3. Answers will vary, but by knowing each characters' backstory we can understand their motivations better. It also makes them seem more like real people because real people have backstories as well.
4. Lord Nimbus. Answers will vary.
5. Answers will vary, but Lizard Face is power hungry, and he may resent Seth for ruling so long. Both characters are equally cruel.
6. Answers will vary, but some students might guess she has somehow been there before.
7. Answers will vary.

Chapter 16
1. Answers will vary.
2. The Text of Iren
3. Answers will vary.
4. The recklor bats.
5. Answers will vary.

Chapter 17
1. It has a single window that allows him to see the sky and the sun. He had a pile of wet and moldy hay to sleep on.
2. Answers will vary.

3. The medicine is call *ice blood*. The Starananians have to take it because the climate on Stararocka will be much too hot for them. The *ice blood* will help them adapt.
4. Answers will vary.
5. Answers will vary. Some students might mention that Shortstop now encourages Gloria to trust the prophecies. Earlier in the book, he seemed less than willing to do this himself.

Chapter 18
1. They had fallen down the canyon, but a series of ledges had broken their falls, and they had survived.
2. Scotty and Sparkey use candles to help them see as they climb back up the canyon. The giant recklor is attracted to the light. Using a series of maneuvers, Sparkey and Scotty manage to get onto the creature's back. Sparkey then uses a makeshift torch to cause the bat to fly in the direction they want to go.
3. Answers will vary.
4. Sparkey says the human that defeats Seth will be made the emperor in his place. Scotty insists that won't be possible for him because he is a kid. Plus, his parents might believe he has been killed if he never returns to Earth.
5. Sparkey plans to toss his torch back down the canyon so the bat will chase after it.
6. Answers will vary.

Chapter 19
1. Scotty eats a fish raw. Fish are his most hated food, and as he eats it, he thinks the taste is disgusting, and he can feel the bile rising in his throat. From his perspective, it took an eternity to get the whole thing down.
2. Answers will vary, but one key passage, Proverbs 16:18 says, *"Pride goes before destruction, a haughty spirit before a fall."*
3. The goons were cursed to become so grotesque that anyone who looked on them would be driven insane and then become a goon themselves.
4. Answers will vary.
5. Answers will vary.

Chapter 20
1. He finds what he calls *real* food and immediately begins eating a honeysuckle apple.
2. The remains of some bears that had been executed and two goons gloating over them.
3. Answers will vary, but the *Bible* says in James 3:10, "Out of the same mouth come praise and cursing. My brothers and sisters, this should not be" (NIV).
4. Answers will vary.
5. They use a dumbwaiter to get to the 10th story.
6. Answers will vary.

Chapter 21
1. They stop outside of Lizard Face's chambers.

2. Answers will vary. You might read, Isaiah 14 which describes Lucifer's pride and desire to usurp the throne of God, and then his failure to do so.

3. Scotty sneezes, and then he begins to speak and act very foolishly, to which Lizard Face has nothing but contempt.

4. Answers will vary, but you might point students to the story of Joseph. Specifically address Genesis 50:20 which says, *"You intended to harm me, but God intended it for good to accomplish what is now being done, the Saving of many lives"* (NIV).

5. Sparkey assures himself that he will be seeing his father again really soon.

Chapter 22

1. We learn that the cell has a very heavy wooden door that creaks. It is also implied that there is very little light.

2. He is stunned and asks, "Who? What? How?" To which Scotty replies, "You forgot – where, when, and why…"

3. Answers will vary. Suggest *Bible* characters like Noah, Abraham, Lot, Job, Peter, Paul, etc. if students need help thinking of any.

4. Answers will vary.

Chapter 23

1. Answers will vary.

2. He planned to kill the boy and then cart his body around the planet. When the bears saw that the *Blood of the Land* was dead, they would stop believing in the prophecies, and if they stopped believing, God would have no reason to honor them.

3. Scotty believes the glowing chunk of viola crystal is the light, but the crystal goes dark even as he suggests it.

4. Answers will vary.

5. Answers will vary.

6. Answers will vary, but it was God.

Chapter 24

1. He saw a flaming cross.

2. He is a powerful angel with a flowing white robe, banded at the chest in gold. He has red hair and a neatly trimmed red beard. His countenance is as bright as the sun if not brighter. His skin is flawless and his teeth are pearly white.

3. The *Blood of Land* refers both to all Christians in general, and one Christian specifically. Any Christian was capable of fulfilling the promises God made to the bears, but Scotty was chosen because he was the very least of them. God usually prefers to work through people like that.

4. God created Staranana to honor the human imagination, and it is now suffering because humanity has fallen into sin.

5. Answers will vary, but point out that only humans are created in the image of God. 2 Peter 2:4 says, *"…God did not spare angels when they sinned, but sent them to Hell, putting them in chains of darkness to be held for judgment…"* (NIV).

6. Answers will vary.

7. Answers will vary.

Chapter 25

1. Spikey believes every word of Scotty's story about Joshua. He also explains that angels were once quite common on Staranana. Spikey also remembers his own encounter with the angel 15 years earlier, but he does not mention it to the boys.
2. Spikey is awakened by the cries of snow phoenixes that sing every morning just before the dawn.
3. It is Sunday, which is when Scotty would normally be going to church.
4. He shares Joshua 1:9.
5. A goon alerts Lizard Face that an angel is attacking the Palace, just as Lizard Face was about to take Scotty and the others to be executed. He shuts the cell door and leaves, but he forgets to lock it. When Scotty, Spikey, and Sparkey discover this, they open the door and leave. They find a bridge to the Palace wall where climbing equipment and Spikey's bomb have been left for them (presumably by Joshua). They descend the wall and head back into the forest.
6. Answers will vary.

Chapter 26

1. Stony City was the last known location of the *Dagger of Promise*, the weapon destined to defeat Seth when used by the *Blood of the Land*.
2. Answers will vary.
3. He tapped into the phone systems in Prineville and made a series of calls to fool everyone. Spikey gives Scotty a particle duplicator which will make a copy of him to send back to Earth while he is on Staranana.
4. They must cross the White Desert. Sparkey is excited because he knows that is where Seth is repairing a ship to chase after the *New Life*. He wants to stop it.
5. Answers will vary, though he might resent the fact that he was not rescued by Shortstop's group and had to suffer for days under Lizard Face's torture.

Chapter 27

1. They detect a transmission on an extremely high frequency.
2. Speedway is General Shortstop's attaché. He is a stern military bear who has very little time for or trust in God. He dislikes Gloria because she is beginning to emulate her husband's faith.
3. Gloria has started a study of the *Text of Iren* on the ship. Speedway gets upset with her over this and flat out rejects any promise that God will help them. Gloria quotes a passage about the Staranananians abandoning God which describes the passengers of the *New Life* perfectly.
4. Answers will vary.
5. God will ultimately redeem the human race, and those that love Christ will live forever on a perfected New Earth.

Chapter 28

1. They had to walk 30 miles a day through horrible, frozen conditions.

2. Scotty has to choose between going to the White Desert to stop the goon ship from leaving or going directly to Stony City. He chose to go to the White Desert.

3. Captain Gonish is in charge. Lizard Face delivers the news that he will not be able to go with the ship because Seth is beginning to suspect treachery on his part. Lizard Face orders him to crew the *Space Shark* with only 150 goons, even though it needs 300. The 150 left behind will begin repairing another ship that Lizard Face and his followers can use to leave the planet if the need should arise.

4. He will put it into the frozen lake right under the ship the goons are repairing. He gets it into place using the ship's sewage system.

5. The ship they blow up was only the goons' quartering ship. It was not the *Space Shark*. Later in the chapter, the *Space Shark* launches.

6. Answers will vary, but the most obvious consequence will be that the *Space Shark* will attack and destroy the *New Life*.

Chapter 29

1. They were in the middle of a honeysuckle apple tree forest. Before it was destroyed, Stony City was a leading producer of honeysuckle apples.

2. They grow from some of the most resilient trees on Staranana. They are large and silver, and they can restore a person's strength and stave off sleep for several hours. As the name implies, the apples taste like honey.

3. The dagger is made of a substance called brillium amber. This amber is imbued with power from God and whenever it cuts someone who is evil, they are sent directly to the Black Lava Pits – the Starananian version of Hell. Unfortunately, when it comes to Seth, it will only work if wielded by a human. This is why Spikey believes Scotty will be able to use it to defeat Seth.

4. Answers will vary.

5. Answers will vary.

6. A sleeping blue-green dragon with razor-sharp claws and a long goatee.

7. Answers will vary.

Chapter 30

1. He finds it in the hands of Splash Moonbeam, Spikey and Sparkey's ancestor who had been turned to stone. He is forced to break Splash's stone arm in order to get the dagger free.

2. God has given us His Word, the *Bible,* as the best weapon against Satan's evil. In this way, the *Dagger of Promise* is a symbol for the Word of God.

3. Nothing.

4. Answers will vary. Scotty asks Hydro to turn against Seth and join the rebellion, which he does.

5. Answers will vary.

Chapter 31

1. His wife's name was Lily and she had been killed in a dragon attack several years earlier.

2. Answers will vary, but the Pharaoh of Exodus stubbornly refused to release the people of Israel from slavery. As a result, God sent 10 plagues that completely devastated Egypt.

3. Answers will vary.

4. The rescue of the *New Life* by the *Fire Cruiser* was unexpected and the ship was vastly superior to the *Space Shark*. The goons did not stand a chance.

5. Answers will vary.

Chapter 32

1. The *Fire Cruiser* is a massive and professionally built spacecraft. It is shaped like a saucer with nacelles along the sides. Its weapons are capable of obliterating an enemy vessel in only a few shots. The interior of the ship is sharply designed and well maintained with incredibly advanced technologies. The ship is large enough to hold the *New Life* in its shuttle bay.

2. William and Josh Noble. They knew Spikey when he was a child on Stararocka.

3. Answers will vary, but he left Stararocka in shame, so he might not have wanted the Starananians to know where he came from since he was responsible for the Marsh Season.

4. Answers will vary.

5. An angel commanded them to build the liberation fleet. It is heavily implied that the angel was Joshua. The purpose of the fleet is to liberate Staranana.

6. Answers will vary.

Chapter 33

1. Scotty had been asleep for over 22 hours.

2. There were five prophecies left for him to fulfill.

3. Answers will vary, but Matthew 24 outlines most of them.

4. Answers will vary.

5. Answers will vary.

6. The best place to create an army of the weak would be in the slave camps.

Chapter 34

1. It was named Hate Street.

2. Seth had received news that Scotty had been killed by Hydro, so he was trying to be good spirited and benevolent when he told the slaves, even though it was the worst possible news the slaves could hear.

3. They were warned that it was illegal for the slaves to bury their dead.

4. The minister's name was Garlan, and his assistant's name was Sam.

5. They had been hiding weapons, and Spikey realizes this is exactly what he needs to build his army.

Chapter 35

1. Hydro uses his power over water to boost them up using the jade elephant fountain.

2. Answers will vary, but Paul will be a popular answer. Other examples include Mary Magdalene, Levi the tax collector, Zacchaeus the tax collector, the King and people of Nineveh, King Nebuchadnezzar, etc.

3. Answers will vary.

4. They hid on some exposed beams in the ceiling of the throne room.
5. When the goons began their attack at the end of the chapter, they had their hoods off. This would have driven anyone who saw their faces insane and turned them into a goon. However, God made all of their faces glow intensely preventing anyone from seeing their faces.

Chapter 36
1. Answers will vary. Most were grateful, and many people disobeyed Christ's command not to tell anyone how they were healed.
2. They immediately jumped into the battle. Garlan describes them like avenging angels.
3. They set up their triage facility in the cellar of the Palace. A triage facility is where wounded are taken during a battle to receive the most immediate medical care (often just first aid) that they need.
4. Answers will vary.
5. First, Hydro attacks his fellow dragons to protect the Starananians. Second, the *Fire Cruiser* kills the dragon that was about to kill Hydro. In the previous chapter, the angel Joshua beheaded some goons that were shooting at the army from the Palace wall. It is indicated that these were the same goons that killed the villagers in the *Before*.

Chapter 37
1. Answers will vary.
2. Sparkey falls on top of him from the rafters while he is sitting on Seth's throne. Before Seth can kill Lizard Face, Captain Gakic shows up with armed goons, and they escort Lizard Face out with Seth at gunpoint. Lizard Face and his goons then leave the planet.
3. He shoots Scotty and the boy falls from the rafters, and when he hits the floor, he is basically crippled.
4. Licen (Satan) shows up in the form of a serpent made of wind. He merges with Seth. Joshua shows up and heals Scotty and encourages him with scripture before Scotty and Seth have their final confrontation.
5. Joshua uses Psalm 27 to strengthen Scotty.
6. Answers will vary.

Chapter 38 & After
1. 1 Peter 2:9 says, "But you are a chosen people, a royal priesthood, a holy nation, God's special possession, that you may declare the praises of him who called you out of darkness into his wonderful light" (NIV).
2. Answers will vary, but true believers will face persecution and some will face death for their beliefs. The world will hate followers of Christ, but ultimately Christ will return and redeem his people and bring them into a kingdom where there will be no more sorrow, pain, or death.
3. Answers will vary.
4. Answers will vary.

Words to Know - Answer Keys

Note: Remove answer keys from the text before distributing to students.

Words to Know Activity #1
1. Evacuate
2. Wince
3. Countenance
4. Representations
5. Inexhaustible
6. Feign
7. Tinker
8. Facility
9. Prophecy
10. Hordes

Words to Know Activity #2
1. Aqueduct
2. Hideous
3. Interact
4. Ego
5. Exaggerate
6. Devoid
7. Circulate
8. Hysterical
9. Neutralize
10. Intent

Words to Know Activity #3
1. Pachyderm
2. Phoenix
3. Minion
4. Deny
5. Mesmerize
6. Betray
7. Relic
8. Reinforcement
9. Intolerable
10. Subside

Words to Know Activity #4
1. Pendulum
2. Corridor
3. Perimeter
4. Precarious
5. Synchronized/Unison
6. Liberate

7. Ambush
8. Stealth
9. Unison/Synchronized
10. Hunch

Words to Know Activity #5
1. Adrenaline
2. Restrain
3. Instilled
4. Compromise
5. Cautious
6. Extremist
7. Suspicious
8. Artificial
9. Lavatory
10. Circumstances

Words to Know Activity #6
1. Savory
2. Disuse
3. Bizarre
4. Dire
5. Microscopic
6. Deem
7. Garbled
8. Surrender
9. Grimace
10. Vortex

Words to Know Activity #7
1. Ancestor
2. Cursed
3. Eternal
4. Conquer
5. Component
6. Resurrect
7. Conceived
8. Altered
9. Consistent
10. Delicacy

Words to Know Activity #8
1. Abyss
2. Vast
3. Miserable
4. Encompass
5. Linger
6. Ominous
7. Banshees

8. Resourceful
9. Interrogated
10. Pinnacle

Words to Know Activity #9
1. Relentless
2. Impenetrable
3. Forsake
4. Comply
5. Squander
6. Provisions
7. Detour
8. Foreboding
9. Pursuit
10. Adjacent

Words to Know Activity #10
1. No
2. No
3. Yes
4. Yes
5. Yes
6. No
7. Yes
8. No
9. Yes
10. Yes

Words to Know Activity #11
1. Qualifications
2. Silhouette
3. Deliver
4. Mock
5. Loyal
6. Whimper
7. Distinct
8. Population
9. Chaos
10. Recognition

Words to Know Activity #12
1. Blemish
2. Hilt
3. Jeopardy
4. Hearth
5. Lecture
6. Wield
7. Petrified
8. Diminish

9. Pierce
10. Tentative

Words to Know Activity #13
1. Concentration
2. Inmates
3. Mutilated
4. Nutrients
5. Mercy
6. Intact
7. Loathed
8. Precautions
9. Tousled
10. Transmit

Words to Know Activity #14
1. Tattered
2. Fuselage
3. Cockpit
4. Disembark
5. Frustrated
6. Portal
7. Lunatic
8. Recitation
9. Binge
10. Expendable

Words to Know Activity #15
1. Spew
2. Imprison
3. Appreciate
4. Ebony
5. Hatchling
6. Immense
7. Debris
8. Endow
9. Intimidation
10. Resilient

Words to Know Activity #16
1. Banish
2. Detect
3. Inspired
4. Recent
5. Charismatic
6. Frequency
7. Crucial
8. Grotesque
9. Dumbstruck

10. Conventional

Words to Know Activity #17
1. Jot
2. Skeptic
3. Enthrone
4. Minimal
5. Interpret
6. Entourage
7. Obvious
8. Parchment
9. Designate
10. Credible

Words to Know Activity #18
1. Casualty
2. Foolhardy
3. Inhibit
4. Quench
5. Elderly
6. Emanate
7. Stronghold
8. Obtain
9. Compatriot
10. Offensive

Words to Know Activity #19
1. Anxious
2. Assembly
3. Tabernacle
4. Confirmed
5. Shortcomings
6. Eliminate
7. Seize
8. Exposed
9. Ruffle
10. Dismount

Other exciting titles from *Thrive Christian Press* **include:**

Chronicles of the Imagination: Staranana (Standard Edition)
ISBN 978-0692553503

After enduring centuries under a vicious tyrant, the people of the icy planet Staranana must decide whether to abandon their faith or continue to trust in the promises of God. The results of that decision will spark an adventure beyond the imagination!

Chronicles of the Imagination: Lizard Face
ISBN 978-0-9800600-3-4

A time of peace has dawned, but on the eve of the first Christmas on Staranana, an ancient enemy returns. Faith, friendship, and family will all be tested, and a single wrong decision could very well spell the doom of Staranana!

Chronicles of the Imagination: Nana-Old Testament
ISBN 978-0-9800600-6-5

The Starananians find themselves stranded in Earth's biblical past, and if they are to find their way home, they'll have to enlist the help of some of the greatest characters from throughout the *Old Testament*.

Chronicles of the Imagination: Nana-New Testament
ISBN 978-0-9800600-7-2

Having been trapped in the biblical past for months, hope is fading from the hearts of the Starananians. If they are to make it home, they must seek out the source of hope Himself, but this adventure won't end until the blood of one of them has been shed.

Find them today at www.amazon.com in paperback as well as on *Amazon Kindle* and *Barnes & Noble Nook.*

Enjoy these *Classroom Classics* from *Thrive Christian Press*:

Rudyard Kipling's The *Jungle Book* – *Enhanced Classroom Edition*
ISBN – 978-0-615-70585-9

From Mowgli's relentless battle against the man-eating tiger Shere Khan to Rikki-Tikki-Tavi's great war against the sinister cobras Nag and Nagaina, Rudyard Kipling's classic *The Jungle Book* has been filling our lives with excitement for more than a century now. No personal library is complete without this timeless novel, and this edition enhanced for use in the classroom is a must have for any teacher about to embark on this literary adventure.

Steven Crane's *The Red Badge of Courage* - *Enhanced Classroom Edition*
ISBN – 978-0-615-80812-3

How does a coward become a hero? Henry Fleming is about to face that very question. Though he had, "...dreamed of battles all his life...", he soon finds that a soldier's life is more than he bargained for, and a single wrong decision runs the risk of branding him a coward for what little of his life he thinks he has left. Will he ultimately find the hero within, earning, if necessary, his own red badge of courage, or will he die a coward?

Sir Arthur Conan Doyle's *The Hound of the Baskervilles* –
Enhanced Classroom Edition
ISBN – 978-0-615-83170-1

There is a realm in which the most experienced of detectives is helpless – The Supernatural, and master detective Sherlock Holmes is about to plunge headfirst into that realm in this stunning adventure. *The Hound of the Baskervilles* takes Holmes and Dr. Watson to the Baskerville Estate where a mysterious hound of Hell has caused the deaths of many members of the Baskerville family. Will Holmes be able to crack this case before the latest heir to the Baskerville fortune meets his demise?

Mark Twain's The Adventures of Tom Sawyer – Enhanced Classroom Edition
ISBN – 978-0-692-02147-7

Tom Sawyer returns! In this latest edition of Mark Twain's classic *The Adventures of Tom Sawyer*, we are once again reunited with one of the most beloved literary characters of all time. Together with his best pal, Huckleberry Finn, Tom will play pirate, search for treasure in a haunted house, witness a grisly murder, come back from the dead, and ultimately face the wrath of the nefarious Injun Joe. This enhanced edition includes journal prompts, study and discussion questions, and vocabulary activities great for use in the classroom.

Mark Twain's The Prince and the Pauper – Enhanced Classroom Edition
ISBN – 978-0692389096

Edward Tudor, the Prince of Wales, was born destined to be the king of all England. Tom Canty was born in squalor and destined for a life of misery in the slums of the London streets. However, a chance encounter between these two doppelgängers will send destiny into a tailspin as Edward and Tom suddenly and unexpectedly trade places. Now the race is on for each one to be restored to his proper place before England's crown is passed to the wrong person. This enhanced edition includes journal prompts, study and discussion questions, and vocabulary activities great for use in the classroom.

Also available...

To Kill a King
ISBN 978-0-9800600-8-9
By Anna and Claire Trujillo

Linna, a fighter in training in the futuristic city-state of Domina, has been marked for death by her own father. Her only hope of survival is to assassinate an enemy king, but is she brutal enough to carry out the deed?

Book 1 – Parallel Encounters: The Prism's Echo
ISBN 978-0-692-32996-2
By David Scott Fields II

To the naked eye, *The Prism's Echo* is just an old, dusty book, but to a reader with the right question, it can open the door to infinite possible realities. Unfortunately, the wrong question, opens the door to a future where the Nazis have conquered humanity…and this time there may be no stopping them.

Book 2 – Parallel Encounters: Salvage
ISBN 978-0-692-35235-9
By David Scott Fields II

Four tense years have passed since the rebels captured the Nazi Space Port, and Captain Brooks wonders when the inevitable retaliation will come. As the station's supplies dwindle, hope comes in the form of a mysterious alien spacecraft floating dead in space. Now it will require a literal space race to capture the ship before the Nazis can.

Book 3 – Parallel Encounters: Allegiance
ISBN 978-0-692-37545-7
By David Scott Fields II

Hell hath no fury like a woman scorned. The crew of the *RSS Intruder* is about to learn that lesson firsthand. Once a member of the rebellion, Captain Jess A. Bell is now one of its deadliest enemies. In order to protect her crew, Captain Brooks will have to strand them deep within Jupiter's atmosphere, and their only hope of escape will rest in finding a friend in a very unexpected place.

Thrive Christian Press is eager to see the Gospel of Jesus Christ spread throughout the world. If you would like 70% of the royalties from your most recent purchase donated to a Christian missionary or ministry of your choice, please complete the form below and mail to:

Missionary Donation Request
Thrive Christian Press
1120 Huffman Rd. Ste. 24-447
Anchorage, AK 99515

Missionary Name _____

Christian Ministry _____

Ministry Address _____

_____

Ministry Website _____

     Can we donate via this website? *Yes*   *No*

Ministry Email _____

Title Purchased _____

Retailer Amazon.com CreateSpace.com BarnesandNoble.com

Please include a copy of your receipt. Visit www.thrivechristianpress.com to submit your request via email. Click on the *Missions Support* tab.

*All donations are subject to verification of the Christian ministry in question and purchase. Not all Thrive Christian Press titles qualify. Donations will be made in electronic form on ministry websites. Payment will be made within 60 days of the request. This form is for paperback titles only. Please visit www.thrivechristianpress.com to request a donation for a Nook or Kindle title.

Donations by Title & Retailer

The Betrayal of Kelcott

Amazon	CreateSpace	B&N	Kindle	Nook
$1.00	$1.85	$0.17	$1.46	$1.36

Chronicles of the Imagination: Staranana

Amazon	CreateSpace	B&N	Kindle	Nook
$1.47	$3.16	N/A	$1.95	$1.81

Chronicles of the Imagination: Lizard Face

Amazon	CreateSpace	B&N	Kindle	Nook
$1.37	$3.05	N/A	$1.95	$1.81

Chronicles of the Imagination: Nana-Old Testament

Amazon	CreateSpace	B&N	Kindle	Nook
$0.83	$2.93	N/A	$2.44	$2.27

Chronicles of the Imagination: Nana-New Testament

Amazon	CreateSpace	B&N	Kindle	Nook
$1.00	$3.00	N/A	$2.44	$2.27

Green Elephant

Amazon	CreateSpace	B&N	Kindle	Nook
$1.67	$3.00	$0.24	N/A	N/A

The Hound of the Baskervilles

Amazon	CreateSpace	B&N	Kindle	Nook
$1.50	$2.90	$0.09	$1.96	$1.68

Parallel Encounters

Amazon	CreateSpace	B&N	Kindle	Nook
$1.00	$1.85	$0.17	N/A	N/A